Praise for
POWERS OF ATTORNEY

D0802077

POWERS OF ATTORNEY

MIMI LAVENDA LATT

POCKET STAR BOOKS

New York London Toronto Sydney Tokyo Singapore

This book is a work of fiction. Names, characters, places and incidents are products of the author's imagination or are used fictitiously. Any resemblance to actual events or locales or persons, living or dead, is entirely coincidental.

A Pocket Star Book published by
POCKET BOOKS, a division of Simon & Schuster Inc.
1230 Avenue of the Americas, New York, NY 10020

ISBN: 0-671-86916-7

First Pocket Books printing December 1994

10 9 8 7 6 5 4 3 2 1

POCKET STAR BOOKS and colophon are registered
trademarks of Simon & Schuster Inc.

Cover art by John Stevens

Printed in the U.S.A.

Acknowledgments

When I told my husband, Arron, that I wanted to devote more time to writing and less time to being a lawyer, he told me to go for it. It was his love, support, and faith in me that made this book possible. Without my daughters, Carrie and Andrea, I never could have maintained my perspective—their love and unfailing humor provided strength for the inevitable ups and downs of a writer's life. My beloved parents, Sylvia and Isidor Lavenda, believed I could do anything and be anyone I chose to be. Those thoughts kept me going against all odds. And a special mention to the late Sandra Bloom for her love and encouragement.

I am indebted to the following people: My colleagues from law school and our yearly reunions, which inspired parts of this book. Marjorie Miller, who taught me so much and provided a safe and creative environment for my writing to flourish in. The talented members of my writing group, who gave caring support and constructive criticism. Lisa Rojany, an accomplished writer and editor, was always there for me. Her skillful editing of the early manuscript

Acknowledgments

helped me to the finish line. My dear friend, Prosecutor Loretta Murphy Begen, lent me an insider's view of the district attorney's office. Even as she was being wheeled into the delivery room, she was still offering invaluable technical assistance. No one could have been more generous with her time and expertise.

Also sharing their immeasurable knowledge and professional experience: Prosecutors Myra Radel and Harvey Giss; probate attorney Vicki Fisher Magasinn; attorney/writer Lisa Siegel; authors Judith Balaban Quine and Ellen Jones; and psychologists Dr. Enid Zaslow and Dr. Sharon Bloom. Joyce Rudnick and Ellie and Ron Simon patiently read the first draft; to those friends and all the others who gave so liberally of their skills and time, who helped and advised me, I owe credit for much of what is accurate in these fictional pages. Any mistakes are mine.

To my agent, Anne Sibbald, at Janklow & Nesbit, heartfelt thanks for believing in me and my book. For her understanding, guidance, and support while introducing me to the wonderfully mysterious world of publishing, I am forever grateful. And thanks must go to Cullen Stanley for her faith in my work and her contagious confidence while doing such a great job of introducing this book to publishers worldwide.

To the people at Simon & Schuster, thank you for the brass ring. I couldn't have asked for better editors than Michael Korda and Chuck Adams, who provided great enthusiasm, firm editorial guidance, and remarkable insight, taking the time and energy to nurture me along in this first endeavor. For all their efforts I shall always be thankful.

IN MEMORY OF
SYLVIA AND ISIDOR LAVENDA,
TO CARRIE AND ANDREA,
AND TO ARRON, FOR EVERYTHING

POWERS OF ATTORNEY

1

Kate Alexander heard the murmur of voices and the peals of self-conscious laughter as she approached the lavish ballroom that sprawled at the rear of the stately Bel Air mansion. Poised on the threshold, she surveyed the carved oak walls and the shimmering crystal chandelier blazing from the high ceiling while the aroma of fresh-cut flowers and sumptuous food wafted over her. Formally clad waiters passed through the throng carrying large silver trays arrayed with beautifully tempting hors d'oeuvres, and the strains of music played by a live band drifted in through the French doors that opened onto the patio.

She caught her breath in anticipation, her gaze sweeping over the men in black tie and the women in long, glittering gowns, her eyes seeking out that someone in particular. Not seeing him, she sighed, squared her shoulders, and plunged with resolve into the crowd where tonight the elite of the Democratic party mingled with the cream of Los Angeles society.

"Kate!"

There he was. Charles Rieman, his silver-laced black hair framing a handsome face, approached her in purposeful strides. As he made his way through the packed room, he nodded to several people, flashing his usual confident smile.

"You look gorgeous!" he exclaimed, his black eyes lighting up with admiration. Gently touching the bare flesh of her upper arm, he leaned forward and brushed his lips against her ear.

"Charles . . . ," she cautioned, coloring slightly. She glanced around quickly, then looked back at him, puzzled.

One corner of his mouth turned up in amusement. "If you're looking for Ann, she's not here." Then, his tone eager, he added, "Come, I want you to meet someone."

"Who?"

"Our host, James D'Arcy."

"Give me a moment," Kate said, grasping his arm, restraining him. "I'm nervous. A lot is riding on tonight." She raised her hand to her chest.

"He'll love you." He tucked a firm hand under her elbow and propelled her forward.

She prayed she would remember all the information she had crammed into her head until the wee hours of the morning.

As they neared a group of people, she recognized the distinguished-looking man surrounded by several important legislators. James D'Arcy was the scion of the famed D'Arcy family, which had made its billions in everything from oil to California real estate. He was a tall man, solidly built, whose thinning brown hair made him look older than his forty-seven years. There is definitely an aura of power about this man, Kate thought.

"James, I want you to meet Kate Alexander," said Charles. "She heads Manning & Anderson's criminal defense department."

James D'Arcy reached for Kate's hand while his unwavering brown eyes scrutinized her. "Charles has been raving about you," he said in a deep, vibrant voice. "He thinks you could go all the way to the governor's mansion."

Kate smiled, aware she was shaking the hand of one of the most important men in the Democratic party. "I'll try not to disappoint either of you, Mr. D'Arcy."

"Call me James." He made a slight bow, then spoke to the men standing with him. "Kate wants to be our next district attorney," he told them, "and from what I hear, she'd be dynamite."

She was pleased. According to Charles, D'Arcy's backing was critical to her political success. If he didn't like her, her career could be over before it started. "I'd certainly give it my best," she assured him.

"Kate was a prosecutor for four years before Charles snatched her away to his law firm high atop Century City," said James.

"You make it sound like a kidnapping," joked Charles.

"But this time," Kate interrupted, laughing, "the captors paid the victim the ransom."

James threw his head back and roared. "I like a woman with a sense of humor." He whisked out his handkerchief and wiped his forehead. He was sweating profusely. "So, how do you like being on the defense side?"

"Well, it's quite different, of course. I miss the excitement of the D.A.'s office," she admitted, "but the change has given me a chance to see both sides."

James told the others, "Our D.A.'s office is the largest prosecuting agency in the world." His next words were directed at Kate. "How would *you* improve it?"

"I'd start by making it more cost-effective and responsive to the taxpayers without sacrificing quality," she answered quickly.

"That's where it's at," agreed James, obviously satisfied with her reply. "If you public officials"—he wagged his finger at the men standing around him—"don't make us happy, we'll stop writing those checks that get you elected."

"Well, don't stop yet," protested Charles, his eyes twinkling. "We need some rather large ones for the next election."

James laughed. "I won't. You know, Charles, you were right. Kate's a natural. I'm going to steal her away for a short time. There are a few people I'd like to introduce her to." He looked at Charles, his eyebrows raised in mock seriousness. "To get those large checks, of course."

3

"Of course," echoed Charles as James led Kate away.

Charles Rieman was delighted at the way James and Kate had hit it off; he prided himself on spotting talent. The first time he saw the beautiful young prosecutor in action, he had been duly impressed.

He could still remember the thrill he had felt as he listened to the way she articulated her arguments, her eyes flashing with emotion. And what eyes, big and almond-shaped with odd green lights. He had also watched her willowy figure and long legs as she paced back and forth in front of the jury. Her short, ebony hair, the black, uptilted brows, and luminous ivory skin lent Kate's oval face a hint of the exotic. He had known then he had to have her for his firm. And for himself.

Charles smiled at the host of a popular TV game show. He was pleased with the mix of celebrities and socialites that had come tonight. He got a kick out of the fact that he, a kid whose parents came to this country as poor immigrants to run a mom-and-pop grocery store, was now a partner in one of the best law firms in the city. In political circles he had become a power to be reckoned with. People often said, "If you want something done, call Charlie Rieman." He liked being able to bestow favors. It made life fun.

He especially loved the excitement of fostering someone's political career. And with Kate, it was a double pleasure, since she was not only bright and motivated but also a dynamic fighter for the causes she believed in. She had a bright future. He was sure of it.

Kate, with James at her side, was busy shaking hands and fielding questions.

"So, what do you think?" James asked, guiding her off to the side of the room for a moment's rest.

"It's quite an experience." Her face filled with enthusiasm. "Your friends ask very pointed questions."

"Aren't you glad you did your homework?"

"You noticed."

"I never miss a thing. People want a candidate to know what he or she is talking about, and on a variety of subjects."

"I have Charles to thank," she admitted. "He's taught me so much."

"From what I can see, you were a good student. Charles says you're ready now to begin the big race."

She smiled at his words as her intent gaze met his. "I'm grateful for all your help tonight. I didn't expect people to be willing to pledge funds so soon. The primary is almost a year away."

"You've got to start early. Besides, they don't dare refuse me."

"I can see that." She studied him while he made some quick notes in his little black book. As Manning & Anderson's largest client, he was extremely important to the firm. Certainly he seemed charming, yet she sensed a certain ruthlessness beneath the polished surface.

He waved his book at her. "I always write it down. I make sure they see me do it too. That way, later, they can't renege." He peered knowingly at her as he put the book back into his breast pocket. "Come, let's say hello to the governor."

A robust Governor Brandon vigorously shook Kate's hand and slapped James on the back.

"Kate's got some ideas on how to improve our justice system," said James. "Given the chance, I think she'd light some fires under some rather stodgy behinds, if you know what I mean." He rolled his eyes.

The governor looked at Kate with interest. "I'd like to hear them. Let's talk later?"

She smiled eagerly. "I'd like that."

"Good, good," said the governor. His attention appeared to focus behind them. "There's Senator Hardin," he said. "I must excuse myself."

"Go ahead," said James. He seemed distracted for a moment as he glanced at his watch. "Kate, would you excuse me for a few minutes? I need to find out what's keeping my wife."

"Of course." She watched him as he made his way to the marble foyer, then lumbered up the curved staircase. She noticed as his smile was replaced by a scowl.

"Don't forget what this man's capable of . . . he's got more power than God," said Sandra D'Arcy, huddled in front of the gilt mirror on her priceless Louis XIV dressing table. She could hear the noise from the party downstairs but she didn't feel like joining James. Society people. Politics. Yuck. Her husband's friends were so boring. The cigarette she held in her free hand burned brightly in the dimly lighted room elaborately decorated in shades of seafoam green and dusty pink.

As she spoke into the telephone, her tone was hushed and urgent, her young face dreamy. "This isn't a fucking fairy tale. He gets away with—"

Her bedroom door flew open and her husband strode in, slamming it shut behind him, rattling the expensive perfume bottles on the vanity. "What the hell's taking you so long?" he bellowed. "The governor's downstairs already along with Senator Hardin and half the goddamn state legislators. *My* wife's expected to be by *my* side."

When he saw the telephone in her hand, his face turned ugly. "Who's that?"

"No one." She quickly hung up without saying goodbye.

"Why haven't you come down?"

"I told you, I don't feel well." She gave him a bored glance and flicked her cigarette. The ash fell onto the polished surface of the dressing table.

He stomped over and seized the cigarette out of her hand, crushing it in the Waterford ashtray. Grabbing a fistful of her pale blond hair, he twisted it, forcing her to turn toward him. Sandra cried out in pain. "You're hurting me!"

"You'll do as I say," he warned. "I expect you downstairs in two minutes. Now get dressed! And do something with your hair."

He let her go so abruptly that she fell back against the table. Bottles of perfume crashed to the floor.

She stared up at him, her light blue eyes glittering with

hate. "Charles and the governor should see their best friend now."

"Bitch," he spat out. "Don't try my patience. Be downstairs in two minutes flat, dressed and by my side. Or you'll live to regret it." A menacing look accompanied his command before he left the room, slamming the door a second time.

"You fucking bastard," Sandra muttered under her breath as the sickeningly sweet odor of mingling scents assaulted her nostrils. "I wish you were dead."

Charles took two flutes of champagne off the silver tray and handed one to Kate. "You made quite an impression on James."

She felt her face flush with excitement. "Did he say something?"

"He doesn't have to. I could tell. You're on your way, Kate." He lifted his glass in a toast.

"Sounds good! I've dreamed of helping people, of making a difference in the world since I was twelve years old."

"I know." He winked at her, then gave her a thoughtful look.

She lowered her voice. "I really appreciate all you've done for me."

"They don't call me a kingmaker for nothing."

The sound of raucous laughter made Kate look across the room, where she caught sight of a woman in a magnificent black creation, surrounded by several men. "My competition seems to be having a good time," said Kate, gesturing toward the stunning redhead.

"She may be bright but she's way too pushy for my taste," Charles responded.

Kate watched as Lauren Cunningham threw her head back and laughed again, while three men, hanging on her every word, jockeyed for a better position next to her. As if sensing she was being looked at, Lauren caught Kate's eye and waved her over.

"Ah," said Charles, "the spider beckons the fly."

"And I'm the fly?" Kate asked, amused.

"You could be if you're not careful," he warned. "For the next several months you can't let down on your billing hours one iota. Our little southern belle will stand on her head to outshine you. And she's used to getting what she wants."

"Well," Kate said, with a smile, "this time she's not going to." She inclined her head in Lauren's direction. "Are you coming?"

"Go ahead, I'll join you in a minute."

Kate sensed Charles's eyes on her as she crossed the room.

"Kate! What a nice white taffeta dress," gushed Lauren in her soft southern drawl as Kate neared the group. Lauren gestured toward herself with bright red fingernails. "How do ya like my little outfit?"

"It's beautiful," Kate said. She recognized it as a Dior —it must have cost thousands of dollars. Kate wondered what it would feel like to own a designer original. The black of the dress against Lauren's perpetually tanned skin made her bluish-green eyes stand out even more than usual, and they were highlighted by the outrageous diamonds at her ears and throat.

Although they both made good money as associates at Manning & Anderson, Kate knew that it wasn't Lauren's salary that allowed her to buy designer clothes and jewels. Her father was one of the wealthiest men in Texas and he loved to shower his only child with things she wanted.

"I've heard some people bandying your name about as a possible candidate," oozed Lauren sweetly.

"I'm testing the waters." Kate kept her voice even, non-committal.

Lauren wrinkled her small, upturned nose as her eyes widened. "How very exciting."

"Yes, it is," Kate responded coolly, ignoring the sarcasm in Lauren's voice, refusing to let her colleague spoil her night.

Kate and Lauren had met in law school. They had become friends, but from the start there had been an element of rivalry in their relationship. At first, the competition had been for grades and class standing, the kinds of things that went on your résumé. The rivalry had abated after graduation while Kate was at the D.A.'s office, but it resurfaced when Kate was asked to join Manning & Anderson, where Lauren was already a fourth-year associate. Kate knew that Lauren thought only someone with her family background and connections was entitled to work at such a prestigious firm. Kate had been a scholarship student and had worked her way through school. The conflict had worsened lately since they were both up for the same partnership within the firm.

As Charles joined them, Lauren turned her entire attention on him. Leaning forward so that her dress fell open provocatively, she asked in a pointedly breathless voice, "Where's Ann?"

"She's away."

"Oh," she murmured. "Well, please give her my best when you see her. But in the meantime, since you're alone and I'm alone, I'd really love to dance, Charles." Lauren tossed her red hair and batted her eyelashes.

Charles tried to hide his annoyance. "Excuse us, please," he said lightly to Kate. "This must be Lauren's song." He led Lauren toward the marquee, where the band was playing "The Lady Is a Tramp."

Kate smiled to herself at Charles's sly dig, but she was not overly amused at Lauren's blatant move on him. She couldn't let her jealousy show, however. It definitely wouldn't do either of their careers any good to have people know about Charles and her. Not yet, at least.

Returning from freshening up in the powder room, Kate saw James D'Arcy pulled aside by an intense man with a sculptured face and long hair the color of burnished copper. Although the two men were standing under the landing of the stairway and couldn't see her, Kate could hear what they were saying.

"Why have you been avoiding me, James? I've been trying to reach you for days."

"I've been busy. What's it this time, Theo?"

9

"I have a new proposal for the D'Arcy Foundation."

There was a harsh laugh. "Another one of your hare-brained notions?"

"Don't dismiss it so lightly. I've got several experts who support it as a way to help struggling young artists—"

"My dear brother," interrupted James, "I'm sure it's as poorly thought out as the rest of your ideas. As for artists," he snickered, "who gives a fuck?"

Theo stiffened. "By rights I should get a say in how *our* family's funds are spent."

"Says who?"

"Father left—"

"Don't tell me about Father. He put me in charge of everything. He obviously didn't trust you."

"He never meant for you to totally shut me out."

"Stop bothering me. Now get lost!"

"You'll regret this, James," threatened Theo.

Kate saw the younger man emerge, beet-red. He shot a startled glance at her as he hurried away. She tried to recall what Charles had told her about the two D'Arcy brothers. James had the business head and therefore ran the D'Arcy family enterprises. Theo was more artistic and ran a chic Beverly Hills gallery. And then there was the D'Arcy Foundation, which was said to rival the philanthropic endeavors of the Rockefeller and Ford foundations. Why had James treated his brother so despicably? Certainly he didn't sound like the same man who had been so gracious to her just a little while ago. She looked up as she heard a light clicking on the stairway. A young woman was descending the stairs, her skin pale as porcelain, translucent, with a faint, rosy hue that extended to the nape of her neck where her blond hair was pulled back into a knot. She was wearing an elaborate and obviously expensive red gown, a trifle too flashy for this gathering, thought Kate.

James, seemingly unruffled by the nasty exchange with his brother, went over to the young woman, kissed her on the forehead, and with her arm tucked possessively underneath his, led her off toward his guests.

The woman is at least twenty-five years younger than

James, thought Kate. Suddenly, she felt a finger run down her bare back. She shivered and turned. "Charles. I was just about to look for you."

He inclined his head toward the departing couple. "That was Sandra D'Arcy."

"So I figured," said Kate. "She's very pretty."

"Yes," he agreed, "in a showy sort of way. But she'll learn. It's a long way from Bakersfield to the D'Arcy riches. You know," he continued, "the President offered James a cabinet post, but he refused. Said he didn't want to uproot his wife and child. Personally, I think he was worried about taking someone as young and unsophisticated as Sandra to Washington."

"Hmm, perhaps, but she must be clever." Kate's manner suddenly became confidential. "Wasn't it rumored she got him to marry her because she was pregnant?"

"You heard right," he said, smiling. "Their kid is the first and only heir to the D'Arcy fortune."

"Aha." Kate nodded, wondering if Sandra, having snared one of the richest men in the country, ever regretted her decision. Her eyes flicked to Charles. "How was your dance with Lauren?"

He laughed. "She wanted to know what I was doing after the party."

"She did?" Kate couldn't conceal her surprise. "What did you say?"

"That I already had a date with you."

She shook her head and gave him a mischievous smile. "What did you really say?"

"That I was a happily married man."

After all the guests had left and the house was silent, a nervous Sandra tiptoed into her husband's room. Good, he was snoring.

She moved quietly to the nursery to check on Jimmy. Her heart fluttered as it always did when she looked at her sleeping child. He was the most wonderful thing that had ever happened to her. Don't worry, Jimmy, she silently promised. I'll always take care of you, no matter what.

11

The young boy was lying on his side, and as she bent over to kiss his warm, soft skin, she smelled the talcum and baby oil mixed with his sweet breath. She brushed her lips against his hair.

Still moving quietly, she made her way down the stairs. The house was dark except for a lamp James always left on in the library. The caterers had cleaned up and departed. Everything was back in place. Were it not for the profusion of flowers still filling the rooms with their scent, and the marquee, ghostly white over the patio, it would have been impossible to tell that a gala event with hundreds of people had taken place here that night.

In the room off the kitchen, Sandra deactivated the alarm. Then she opened the door and noiselessly slipped out. Walking swiftly now, with her coat pulled tightly around her body, she made her way down the driveway. It was so cold everything around her felt damp. She shivered and quickened her pace.

"Please, please let him be here," she whispered.

At the bottom of the hill, she took out her remote control and clicked it. The gate opened silently in the black night. She slipped through and turned to the left. Her heart leapt. There was his car parked away from the streetlight. She hurried toward it.

Her pulse raced as the car door opened and she caught sight of his lanky frame and brooding face. He ran to meet her.

"Oh Tommy, you came," she murmured as she fell into his welcoming arms.

He kissed her quickly and then eagerly brought her back to the darkened car. Once inside, he grabbed her and buried his head in the smooth silk of her hair, kissing her cool neck and tiny ears.

Sandra made little mewing sounds as she felt his strong arms around her and his young body, hardened with arousal, pressing against her.

He pulled back and gazed at her. His adoring expression changed to one of shock. "Your eye!" he cried. "What happened?" She looked away, her hand moving quickly to her face. "Nothing."

He moved her hand down and gently traced his fingers over the swollen skin above the delicate cheekbone. "Did he do this?"

She shrugged and turned her head away. She didn't want to talk about it.

Tommy became enraged. "God damn him! Leave him. I love you. I'll take care of you, I promise."

"I can't."

"Why? The damn money?"

"No, it's not that. It's Jimmy."

"You're his mother. Any judge would give you custody."

"Not when the great man helped get him elected."

"There must be someone he couldn't get to."

"He knows every judge."

"This is a free country."

She shook her head stubbornly. "His money makes it different. If I divorce him, he'll take my baby away from me."

"I could kill that fucking bastard!" Tommy exclaimed, lowering his head into his trembling hands.

2

The streetlights came on just as Kate turned her car into Century City, a modern office complex of steel-and-glass skyscrapers standing where Twentieth Century–Fox once had its back movie lot. In the underground garage of the Park Towers, she left her car with the attendant and dashed for the elevator. Her briefcase in one hand and her purse over her shoulder, she managed to squeeze her way through the elevator doors a split second before they closed.

As she smoothed the silk blouse she was wearing under her black pin-striped suit, she caught a whiff of familiar cologne. Charles? Glancing around expectantly, her eyes met those of a tall blond man who stood in the back of the elevator. She stared boldly into the stranger's eyes, her confident gaze implying, Look all you want, I'm taken.

On the twenty-sixth floor, she exited into the immense two-story reception area of Manning & Anderson. Bleached-wood floors and walls of glass contrasted starkly with Oriental rugs, leather furniture, and splashes of contemporary art. She took a deep breath, once again experiencing a flush of excitement at belonging to this high-powered firm.

She stopped to look at the sparkling lights of the skyscrapers in the revitalized area of downtown Los Angeles. Our skyline's beginning to look like New York's, she thought. During the day the panoramic view from the office encompassed the lush greenery of West Los Angeles all the way to the beach, and if it was a clear day, Catalina Island beyond. At night the blinking lights of distant airplanes lighted up the sky over Los Angeles International Airport. Glancing farther north, she could see the rolling lawns of the Los Angeles Country Club and the Hollywood Hills.

"Charles still here?" she asked the night receptionist.

"Yes, Miss Alexander," said the girl as Kate hurried through the side door.

Passing the secretarial bays, which were mostly empty now, Kate almost collided with a thin woman whose hawklike face was partially concealed behind tortoiseshell glasses. Rita's staying after hours again making sure no one has left an untidy desk, Kate thought, smiling to herself. The office manager's end-of-the-day ritual never failed to amuse her. At the same time, it reminded Kate of her tedious stint as a legal secretary which had helped to pay her way through law school.

"Good evening, Miss Alexander."

"Hi, Rita," Kate responded, wishing she could convince this woman, at least sixty to Kate's thirty-two, to call her by her first name. "How's your mother?"

"Better, thanks to you." Rita's eyes fluttered slightly when she smiled. "Thanks for straightening out that problem with Social Security."

"Glad to help." Kate smiled warmly as she continued down the hall to see if Charles had had any feedback from last night's party. She stuck her head into his sumptuous corner suite and although he was on the telephone, he motioned for her to come in, pushing a button that automatically closed the door behind her.

He's talking politics for a change, Kate thought wryly, overhearing snatches of the conversation. As she glanced around his office, her eyes focused on the pictures on the wall behind his sofa: Charles standing head-to-head with Teddy Kennedy; Charles in between the President of the United States and the First Lady; Charles flanked by California's Governor Ned Brandon and Senator Pat Hardin; and, her favorite, Charles and a smiling Sally Field, arm in arm, posing for the press.

Against her will, her eyes were drawn to the photograph of a much younger Charles with his family, placed on the credenza behind his desk. Even though his son and daughter were now grown up and away in college, she felt a momentary pang of guilt.

Charles, as if reading her mind, put his hand over the receiver. "It's not your fault," he whispered. "It was never a happy marriage."

Kate smiled, marveling at his quick intuitiveness. As he resumed his conversation, she watched his strong hand scribble on a pad, remembering how that same hand had felt on her body last night. The memory caused a shiver of pleasure to travel down her spine.

She forced herself to concentrate on her surroundings. His office reminded her that there was a definite pecking order for lawyers at Manning & Anderson. At the top were the partners like Charles. They were the more senior and experienced attorneys who were responsible for making all the management decisions, who shared the profits and risks of the firm. As a partner, Charles was entitled to this corner suite as well as a million-dollar income.

Below the partners came the associates. These were usually the younger lawyers like herself, employed by the firm at a large annual salary, all of whom dreamed of being tapped for future partnership. It was common knowledge that one partnership slot, and only one, would be opening up this year and both she and Lauren Cunningham wanted it.

"I've got great news," said Charles, finishing his call. "The governor's decided to go along with James and back you for D.A. in the primary."

"Oh, Charles, that's great!"

"I thought you'd be pleased." He smiled. "Also, on top of his own financial support, James has promised to raise the remaining funds for your campaign from his friends."

"I can't believe it," she said ecstatically, her mind reeling from the good news. "It's *finally* happening!"

A grin spread over Charles's tanned face, surprisingly youthful for forty-five. "You deserve it. You've worked long and hard." He crossed over to her and pulled her to him tightly. "I'm glad you're happy." Then he gently released her. "Someone might come in," he said, more to himself than to her, cautious as usual.

She nodded, a wave of irritation making her shiver. How did she ever get into this position? The Other Woman. She had resisted Charles's advances in the beginning in spite of the strong attraction between them. In the end, however, it had been impossible to ignore what they felt for one another.

She knew that for him, too, becoming involved with her had not been a smart move. He had to be careful that Franklin Manning, the senior partner of the firm as well as his father-in-law, didn't find out. "Did James and the governor say when they would announce their support?" she asked, forcing the guilty thoughts from her head.

"Right after you're made a partner in the firm."

"You know I'd make a great partner," she said, a hint of challenge in her voice.

Charles laughed, his eyes telling her he adored her. "I have more good news." He beamed.

"More?"

"Yes." He tilted his head. "We had a partnership meeting a short time ago and Franklin announced his retirement."

Her breath caught in her throat. "You're kidding. How soon?"

"Immediately. Right after the partners vote on who takes Franklin's place, Dickson or myself."

Kate sighed.

"Don't worry. I know it'll be me. Then I'll see that you become a partner too."

"But Dickson is Franklin's son and you're only his son-in-law. A lot of the associates think that Franklin will feel compelled to pick his own flesh and blood." What she didn't say was that everyone knew Charles and his brother-in-law, Dickson Manning, didn't like each other. Although the two men had met in college and become friends, they were now competing against each other for control of the law firm.

"Franklin trusts me. He knows if Dickson becomes the senior partner, it's only a matter of time before he arranges a merger with a large New York firm. Franklin and I are both against that."

She gave an involuntary shiver. "I hope you're right, because Dickson doesn't like me. If he becomes head of the firm, my days here are numbered." Kate thought she knew why he didn't like her, but she couldn't tell Charles.

"It's not personal. Dickson probably doesn't like you because I brought you into this firm."

"You think that's it?"

"Yep. He hates everything I do. He's just jealous. Don't let him get to you." He smiled. "Let's be positive. I think I have the support of the other major partners as well as the clients who matter, such as James D'Arcy. It's going to be fine. You'll see."

"I hope so, Charles."

"I promised you, didn't I?" He gazed at her tenderly, his jaw set in that determined way she loved so much. "Now, tell me," he said in his best business voice, "how'd court go today?"

Kate was filling Charles in on the day's events when his private line rang.

He pressed the speaker switch. "Hello."

"Help me . . . it's James . . . there's blood . . . it's everywhere . . . the car . . ."

"Sandra?" he shouted, turning pale. "What's happened?"

Kate heard panic in the woman's voice as her sobs increased, overwhelming the coherence of her words.

"Did you call the police?" demanded Charles, jumping to his feet.

"Uh huh," came the mumbled reply.

"I'm on my way." He hung up the phone.

"Need help?" asked Kate.

He peered at her. "Yes. You better come with me."

She got up quickly to join him.

On the lower floor of the Manning & Anderson firm, where most of the associates had their offices, Lauren Cunningham rushed back into her office and slammed the door. She had just heard the news about Franklin's retirement and she had to talk to her father . . . now! She looked at her watch. Her father was probably back in Texas already. Now that he had his new jet, he traveled much faster.

She dialed his office number, her mind racing. If Charles Rieman became the senior partner, her own chance at the next partnership slot was dead. With Charles in place, she knew, the job would go to Kate. Lauren wished her father would understand how important it was to her to become a partner. But then, he had been against her becoming a lawyer in the first place, wanting instead for her to stay in Texas, marry, and become a society matron like her mother. He was so predictable. Well, Lauren had no intention of following in her mother's footsteps. She might marry someday, but the man had to promise some excitement and for sure he had to respect her for her mind. What she didn't understand was why she had to work so hard to get respect when Kate seemed to get it automatically.

With a toss of her red hair, she forced a smile to her face.

It would take all of her southern charm to get her father to help her. "Daddy, hi, it's me."

"Hi, sugar," said Miles Cunningham, in his thick Texas accent. "What's up?"

"Franklin Manning announced his retirement, effective as soon as the new senior partner is picked."

"That sly ole fox," said Miles, chuckling. "He didn't say a word the other day when I saw him."

"Daddy, I need you to talk to him. If Charles Rieman takes over, I'm finished. I just know he'll pick Kate as the next partner over me." She crossed her legs. "I won't be able to hold up my head ever again."

"Now calm down, sweetheart."

"I am calm, Daddy. But you've got to help me. My boss, Arnold, hates me just because you helped me get this job. You've got to use your friendship with Franklin. It's the only way."

"Lauren baby—"

She interrupted him. "I wouldn't ask you to do this for me if it wasn't *really, really* important to me." A big sigh escaped her parted lips. "Please?"

"All right, sugar. I have a few things to take care of. I'll fly there tomorrow."

"Could be too late. Call Franklin now, Daddy, please!"

"Lauren . . ."

"I really need you, Daddy. Promise me you'll do it."

There was a momentary silence on the line. Then Miles coughed. "You know I can't refuse my little gal anything," he said. "I'll do it, I promise."

Lauren hung up the phone, pleased with herself. If anyone could help her get the partnership, her daddy could.

As Charles turned into the cul-de-sac where James and Sandra lived in Bel Air, Kate saw the street was lined with police cars. She shuddered.

"There's James's car." Charles pointed to a gray Mercedes, its doors ajar, sitting in front of the open gates to the curving driveway. It was surrounded by police. "Must have been an accident."

Before they could turn into the wide driveway, one of the officers stopped them. Charles rolled down his window. "I'm Charles Rieman, the D'Arcys' lawyer, and this is my associate, Kate Alexander. Mrs. D'Arcy called me."

"Any ID?"

"Certainly." Charles handed over his wallet. "Can you tell me what's happened?"

"They'll tell you up there," said the officer, handing back the wallet. He took Kate's license from her and looked at it. "O.K. Drive on up."

"Thank you, Officer," said Charles.

Kate stared ahead as the glare of the headlights flashed on the huge Mediterranean-style mansion perched at the top of the hill.

At the door, Charles rang the bell but then rushed in without waiting for someone to answer. Kate followed him through the marble foyer and into a small sitting room where two men stood talking. Her heart skipped a beat as she recognized a homicide detective she had known during her days as a prosecutor. Next to the two men, in a stiff-backed chair, sat Sandra D'Arcy. Her pale blond hair was disheveled and her blue eyes looked wild.

Taking immediate control, Charles said. "I'm Charles Rieman, the D'Arcy family lawyer, and this is my associate, Kate Alexander. What's going on?"

Sandra gazed up, a look of relief on her face at the sight of Charles.

One of the men, middle-aged and overweight, stepped forward to introduce himself as Detective Bower and his partner as Detective Donaldson. "Mr. D'Arcy has been shot."

"How badly is he hurt?" asked Charles.

"Well . . . he's dead."

Charles turned white. "Oh God," he said as his hand came up to his mouth.

Kate felt her stomach drop. James D'Arcy was dead? It couldn't be. She had just met him last night. Her eyes focused on the young widow. How dreadful.

Detective Bower went on. "In the car we found a bag with champagne and a cash receipt. Looks like he stopped at a liquor store and someone followed him home." He glanced from Kate to Charles, his words choppy and without any hint of emotion. "Been a lot of follow-home robberies around here."

The doorbell rang. Kate saw Dickson Manning ushered in by Donaldson.

With his shock of blond hair, pale blue eyes, and weak cleft chin, Dickson reminded her of the late duke of Windsor, Edward VIII. Next to Dickson was the man she had seen arguing with James D'Arcy at the party the night before, Theo D'Arcy.

At the sight of Charles, Dickson seemed to stiffen. Ignoring his brother-in-law, Dickson introduced himself to the police. Then he introduced James D'Arcy's brother. "What's going on?"

Bower briefly filled them in.

"He's dead?" choked Theo D'Arcy, his face twisted in shock.

For a moment Kate thought he was going to faint. Bower apparently realized this too, because he motioned for the man to sit down.

When Theo regained his composure, he gazed around. "Where's Jimmy?"

At the sound of her son's name, Sandra looked up. "Sleeping. I'll . . . go . . . check on him." Her words were barely audible as she left the room.

Dickson turned to Charles, his voice cold. "Thanks for telling me."

"There wasn't time," protested Charles.

Dickson ignored him, eyeing Kate for the first time. "What are you doing here?" His tone was caustic.

"I asked her to come with me," retorted Charles, rushing to Kate's defense.

Kate suddenly wished she had not come. She didn't want conflict with Dickson. True, he was arrogant and condescending, but because he was Franklin's son, he wielded a lot of influence.

Dickson had been rude to her since she had arrived at Manning & Anderson but this was his first show of open hostility. Maybe Charles was right that Dickson didn't like her merely because Charles had hired her. Whatever the reason, it was apparent that while Dickson and Charles struggled for control of the firm, she, unfortunately, was caught right in the middle.

Bower turned to Theo. "You up to answering some questions?"

Dickson answered for him. "Certainly. Let's sit down." Dickson sank into the overstuffed couch and motioned for his friend and client to settle next to him.

Theo collapsed, holding his head in his hands. Suddenly, his body heaved with sobs.

Feeling that she was intruding on this family's tragedy, Kate stepped back to a vantage point near the window. In spite of the hostility she had witnessed last night between James D'Arcy and his brother, Theo, the man seemed genuinely upset.

Dickson spoke up, assuming a tone of authority. "What can we do to help you?"

"I'd like somebody to go downtown and ID the body," explained Bower.

Kate saw Theo tremble at the mention of the body.

Dickson patted his friend's back. "I'll do that, Officer," he said calmly.

"I'll come too," said Charles.

"Fine," said Bower.

Kate caught the angry glare Dickson directed at Charles and she could tell that Bower had seen it too.

The detective pulled out a notebook and turned to Theo. "You ready?"

Theo took the tissue Charles handed him and wiped his eyes. "Has anybody notified my mother or sister?" he asked.

"Maybe," answered Detective Bower. "Mrs. D'Arcy made some calls, but I dunno who to."

"Let's find out as soon as she comes back," said Charles.

Theo turned toward Bower. "Go ahead," he said faintly.

"Your brother usually wear jewelry?" asked the detective.

"Yes. A gold Rolex and a diamond ring."

Theo's voice was very low and Bower had to lean forward to hear it. "How about cash? He carry a lot?"

"Probably two, three thousand dollars."

Bower glanced at his partner. "He keep his money and credit cards on him?"

"I think he kept his money in his front pocket in a gold nugget money clip." Theo nervously fingered the tissue. "His wallet and credit cards he usually kept in his back pocket."

As the detective scribbled on his pad, Dickson frowned. "Were any of those items missing?" he asked.

"Didn't find any cash or other valuables on him," confirmed Bower. "Just a empty wallet."

Kate saw the brother wince again. What a shock to have your brother die so suddenly and so violently.

"So what do you think happened?" asked Dickson.

"Right now? Looks like robbery."

"I see," said Dickson. "Where was he shot?"

"Backa the head," responded Bower.

Kate's heart skipped a beat as Theo and Dickson exchanged glances. This didn't sound like a robbery to her. Robbers usually faced their victims. They didn't usually shoot them in the back of the head. What was going on?

Sandra came back into the room and Theo spoke to her. "Did you call Abigail or Victoria?"

She frowned and paused as if in a daze. "No . . ."

"Coupla more questions," said Bower to Theo and Sandra, "and that's it for tonight."

A darling little towheaded boy wearing yellow pajamas bounded into the room carrying a toy truck tucked under his arm. There was no mistaking the child's resemblance to his mother. A chubby Hispanic woman ran after him. At the sight of all the people, the little boy stopped and looked around, confused.

Kate saw him gaze over at his mother, who was facing the other way, talking to the detectives. The child looked like he was about to cry as the woman with him tried to pull him away. He stubbornly stood his ground. Kate went over and knelt in front of him. "Hi. My name's Kate. What's yours?"

"Jimmy."

"Hi, Jimmy. I like your red truck. Do you have other trucks in your room?"

The child nodded.

"Can you show me?"

He again gazed toward his mother. A look of resignation settled on his face as he realized she wasn't going to pay him any attention.

"Come. Show the nice lady your toys," said the maid.

The little boy put his warm hand into Kate's and led her away.

Bower closed his pad and stood up. "O.K. That's about it for now."

"Please keep us apprised." Dickson saw them to the door. After the two policemen were gone, Charles shook his head. "Poor James, I hope he never knew what hit him." He glanced at his watch. "It's only nine o'clock—I better go tell Abigail what happened before she hears it on the news."

"That's Theo's job," Dickson said pointedly. "He's now the eldest son."

"James always wanted me to take care of his mother," insisted Charles.

"No, Dickson's right," Theo said, turning to his friend for support. "I should tell her."

"Abigail is Theo's responsibility now that James is dead." The anger showed in Dickson's face as his fair complexion turned pink and his right eye started to twitch.

"Look," said Charles, his tone conciliatory. "I've been the family lawyer for years. It's my place to be there too. How about if we go together?"

"No. I'll go as the representative of the firm," insisted Dickson.

Charles peered at Theo. "Is that what you want?"

"Yes."

"I see. Fine, whatever you want," Charles responded, one hand tightly clenching the other.

* * *

Outside, Bower gestured toward the house and said to Donaldson, ''Body's not even cold and they're already at it.''

''What makes you say that?'' asked his partner.

''Years of working homicides. Never fails. Lotsa uptight people in there.'' He waved his arm. ''Just between us? The man was murdered, all right, and not for some fancy watch.''

Donaldson looked up, interested. ''How so?''

''The way he was shot.'' Bower nodded. ''Those people in there? Something else. All that goddamned money. Corrupts 'em. Time'll tell. Let's go see what else the boys came up with.''

3

''**I**t was an execution,'' Kate said confidently.

''What?'' demanded Charles, visibly upset as they got into the car after viewing the body.

''D'Arcy was executed. He was shot in the back of the head by someone who knew what he was doing,'' said Kate.

''Don't be ridiculous. Who'd want to kill him?''

''I don't know, but armed robbers don't usually shoot from behind.''

Charles shook his head, frowning. ''But it doesn't make sense, it just doesn't make sense.''

Kate reached across the seat and put a comforting hand on his shoulder. She had never seen him this shaken before.

''God, I could barely look at James's body,'' he said

sadly. "I couldn't believe it. My best friend laid out on a slab."

"It's a hard thing to do. I've done it many times, although fortunately not for friends, and it still gets to me."

Charles stared at her incredulously. "And you want to go back to prosecuting criminals?"

"Yes. It's gory at times," she agreed. "But I miss it."

He shook his head. "I'll stick to mergers and acquisitions."

As they drove in silence, Kate studied the man next to her, how the lights from the street flickered across his face. Sometimes she felt she knew him so well; other times, she felt she didn't know him at all.

She broke the silence. "Why did James use you as his lawyer while Theo seems to rely on Dickson?"

He peered at her with a half-smile. "You don't miss a thing, do you?"

"I try not to. Besides, it's my training."

"James and Theo didn't get along," he said matter-of-factly. "I suppose Theo felt I took his brother's side."

"Why didn't they get along?"

"Who knows. James didn't like the things Theo was interested in. Theo's very artistic."

"And James thought business was more important . . . ?" She let her question hang in the air.

"Yes."

"Any other brothers or sisters?"

"One sister, Victoria. But she and James got along O.K. The problem seemed to be between James and Theo. James was very cruel to Theo at times."

"Mmm," she said, wondering who had been the real James D'Arcy—the charming man she had met last night or the one she had seen harass his brother? Suddenly, she remembered the conversation she had overheard. Theo had threatened James, but she had not taken it seriously. But now she wondered, had Theo hated James enough to kill him?

And what of the young widow? She hadn't looked particularly happy last night either. Had she decided to rid herself of an older, and very, very rich husband?

* * *

Dickson pressed the speed dialer, glad when Theo answered on the first ring. "How are you feeling today?"

"Shaky," Theo confessed, his voice weak.

"It'll take time," Dickson assured him. He paused, then cleared his throat. "We have to find that document James mentioned."

Theo sighed. "Can't it wait a few days?"

"Absolutely not. It's extremely important."

"I can't just barge in on Sandra or my mother and search their homes."

"No. You must be subtle," cautioned Dickson. "Explain to Sandra you've got to find certain papers before the funeral. If you mention that it will help her receive some money, she'll like that." He snickered. "As for Abigail, your mother never leaves her upstairs rooms. She won't know what you're doing."

"I've gone over it again and again in my mind," said Theo. "It definitely sounded to me like James had already prepared the damn thing. Are you sure Charles doesn't have it?"

"I don't want to ask him directly, yet. If he doesn't know about it, I don't want him to even suspect it exists until I know where it is. So far, the firm's computer shows nothing."

"Shit."

"Right. That's why you've got to look," retorted Dickson. "There's a lot more at stake than money. It's the actual running of the D'Arcy Foundation, the grants to the arts, the charities, all the things you love, Theo. Do you want Charles heading it instead of you?"

"You know I don't."

"Good. Keep in mind how hard it was to get James to even consider it." Dickson lowered his voice. "Unless we find the document, it could all have been for nothing." He paused. "By the way, on a somewhat related matter, my father announced today he's postponing his retirement."

"Why?"

"Because of James's death."

"I'm sorry," said Theo. "I know you're anxious to have the issue of the new senior partner settled."

"Yes. Well, Father claims it's only for a few weeks, until things calm down. And the postponement does give me more time to lock up my support."

"Uh huh."

"Listen, Theo, I want you to search immediately for that document. If we can't find it, well . . . uh . . . what I may have to do to fix the situation could take some time."

"O.K.," sighed Theo.

Detective Bower stifled a yawn as he rang the bell at the D'Arcy home. He was tired. He glanced at Donaldson, realizing his partner also looked tired. Just then the maid opened the door.

"Mrs. D'Arcy in?" asked Bower.

"Señora D'Arcy sleeping."

"Sorry . . . hmm, *lo siento pero* . . ." Bower fumbled, decided against trying and simply flashed his badge.

The woman motioned for him to wait and scurried away.

A few moments later she reappeared. "Mrs. D'Arcy say she coming, please to wait."

"Thanks," mumbled Donaldson.

After waiting almost fifteen minutes Bower was surprised to see Sandra enter the room dressed in a pink sweatsuit outfit and high-top running shoes. Her makeup was carefully applied and her pale blond hair was pulled back into a ponytail. Only her eyes revealed that something out of the ordinary had happened. They were bloodshot.

"Yes?" she said irritably.

"Sorry to bother you, ma'am"—Bower tried to be as gentle as possible with the recently widowed young woman —"but we need to ask a few questions."

"Why can't you guys just leave me alone?"

He tried to hide his shock. The bereaved usually responded with tears, not anger. "Wish we could, but it's a homicide. Last night you were obviously under a lot of stress. We wanted to give you some time."

"I'm thrilled by your kindness," she snapped.

He ignored her sarcasm. "Ma'am, we need to know more about your husband's habits."

"Like what?"

"He usually stop on the way home?"

"No."

"Any idea why he bought champagne last night?"

"No."

"Special occasion?"

"No." She tapped her foot impatiently.

"Ma'am," said Bower, his voice firm, "you have a wine cellar or a bar where your husband kept champagne?"

"Yes."

Bower glanced at Donaldson. He was getting tired of her one-syllable answers. "Can we see it?"

"I guess. Follow me." Sandra led them down a long hallway. Stopping in front of a door, she took a key off a hook and opened it. Then she flipped on a light switch and stepped back. "Be my guest." She did not move to join them.

"Thanks." Bower made his way down the stairway with his partner close behind. At the bottom, he gazed around and whistled quietly. There were bottles lined up in dark wooden racks all along the walls, wines and champagnes.

Back in the small sitting room again, Bower turned to Sandra. "Know someone who drives a white or light-colored, newer-model Mustang?"

"No. I'm afraid not."

"Take your time," the detective urged. He was sure he'd seen a flicker of recognition on the woman's pretty face. "Last night your neighbor saw a car like that drive away in a hurry right after he heard a noise. Said it sounded like a backfire or a shot."

Sandra rubbed her forehead. "The answer's still no."

"O.K. Well, can you tell us why your son's bike was outside the gates last night?"

"Was it?"

"Yeah. Lyin' in the driveway in front of the gates. You know, that area near the street."

"So?"

"Your son always ride his bike out there?"

"It was a tricycle and I'd have to ask Maria." She gazed at her index finger as she chipped at her pink nail polish with her thumb, but otherwise showed no sign of movement.

Bower felt his usually calm temper begin to rise. "Would ya please ask her?"

"Maria," she called. When the maid came into the room, Sandra spoke to her in broken Spanish. The housekeeper shrugged her shoulders. "She doesn't seem to know."

"Ask why she didn't bring the trike back to the house."

Again Sandra spoke in Spanish and the maid responded rapidly. "She says my son fell, scraped his knee, and she had to carry him back to the house. He was crying and his knee was bleeding." Sandra put her hand on her hip. "She must have forgotten about the trike."

"I see," answered Bower, exhaling deeply. "If you or her remember anythin' else, call me. Number's on the card."

"Is that all?"

"Yep. For now. Sorry to bother you, ma'am."

Sandra slammed the door behind them.

"How's your Spanish?" Bower asked his partner as soon as they were standing in the driveway.

Donaldson's sky-blue eyes were somber. "Not too good."

"Mine neither," admitted Bower. "But I coulda sworn the maid didn't say half of what Mrs. D'Arcy said."

"Yeah," agreed Bower.

Kate found Charles in his office. "How are you?" she asked.

"Well as can be expected." His face was grave and his dark eyes puffy as if he had not slept well. He was looking down at what appeared to be a college graduation picture. "You know, James and I, along with Dickson, all went to school together."

"Wasn't James older than you?"

"I skipped a couple of years." He handed her the picture.

She gazed at a young Charles. Except for the gray at his temples and the few lines on his more mature face, he looked the same. "This has to be hard on all of you," she said.

He nodded. "The phone hasn't stopped ringing. In fact, I just hung up with the President. He wanted me to know how much he appreciated James's support over the years." He took the picture back. "The President was at school there too, but he was two years ahead of us."

He placed his briefcase on the desk and started to stuff it with papers. "Abigail D'Arcy's expecting me so we can go over the details of the funeral."

Kate had often heard the D'Arcy matriarch referred to as the power behind the throne. "How's she taking it?"

"She's devastated, but stoic," he stated. "She's been issuing orders about the funeral all day. I often think Abigail's the closest thing we have to royalty in this country." He glanced at Kate with one eyebrow raised. "I'm sure she'll manage to arrange her own funeral from the grave."

Kate couldn't help but smile. "And how's Sandra doing?"

"Supposedly Sandra had a big fracas with her sister-in-law, Victoria, you know, James's sister, and ordered her out of her house."

"I take it they don't like each other?"

He shook his head and grimaced. "The D'Arcy family didn't exactly welcome Sandra into their circle with open arms. In fact, after divorcing his wife of twenty years to marry the pregnant Sandra, James rather shoved his young bride down their throats. Abigail, being the lady she is, tolerates Sandra. But Victoria"—he hesitated—"well, let's just say she's hard for anyone to get along with under the best of circumstances." He paused. "By the way, in light of James's death and my extra load because of it, Franklin's postponing his retirement."

Kate's face fell as she caught her breath.

"Don't worry," he hastened to say, as if understanding how desperate she felt. "It's just for a few weeks."

She quickly regained her composure. "I'm sorry. I shouldn't complain when you've just lost your best friend." With a quick hug, she left him. In the hallway, she stopped for a moment, troubled. Only yesterday, both her personal and political futures had looked fabulous. Now, everything looked bleak.

The day of the funeral was gloomy and overcast. Kate dreaded funerals and this one was going to be worse than most. Charles's wife, Ann, would be there with him. Over the years she had heard gossip that Ann was a difficult woman. Charles himself said little, except that they weren't compatible and that if it hadn't been for his son and daughter and his respect for Franklin, he'd have left her years ago. But now, even armed with the knowledge he planned to divorce Ann after he was named the new senior partner, Kate didn't find the waiting any easier. Especially since Franklin's retirement had been postponed.

When Lauren asked to ride to the funeral with her, Kate eagerly agreed, grateful today for the company.

"I thought you'd be going with your father," said Kate as Lauren gingerly slid into Kate's car, the simple black Escada suit contrasting smartly with her red hair and golden skin.

"Some kind of emergency came up." Lauren's southern drawl was noticeable as usual. She crossed her legs and fastened her seat belt. "I'm absolutely exhausted. Can you believe the tension in the office the last two days?"

"Everyone's upset over James's death. So many things to decide so quickly." As Kate made a right turn onto Santa Monica Boulevard, she silently wondered again what James's death was going to mean for her own political future. Then she quickly chastised herself for having such selfish thoughts when the man lay dead in his coffin.

"It's not just his death," said Lauren pointedly, "but how it affects the firm now that Franklin's postponed his retirement."

"He only put it off for a short time." Kate changed lanes. "Just until the D'Arcy things get squared away."

"Don't be so naive, Kate," drawled Lauren. "In case you hadn't noticed, our firm's divided into two armed camps lately over the question of who's going to succeed Franklin: Dickson or Charles? James's death has just prolonged the agony." She paused before continuing. "But something else is going on too."

"What's that?"

From beneath her thick lashes, Lauren peered at Kate. "I was hoping you could tell me."

Kate shrugged. "I'm afraid I don't know of anything."

Lauren was quiet for a moment before continuing. "Dickson and Arnold have been holed up since the tragedy happened. Theo D'Arcy's been with them too. Something's up."

"Why don't you ask Arnold?"

"He'd rather die than tell me anything."

Kate noticed the bitterness in Lauren's voice. She was obviously unhappy working under Arnold Mindell. The fact that Kate had been brought to Manning & Anderson to head her own department while Lauren still had to answer to a partner was a sore point in their relationship.

"At any rate," Lauren continued, "I wouldn't be surprised if the firm dissolves over the choice of Franklin's successor."

"I hope not!" exclaimed Kate. "It's true Charles and Dickson don't always see eye-to-eye, but I'm sure they both want what's best for Manning & Anderson."

"Ha!" scoffed Lauren.

All of Kate's senses were immediately alerted. "What are you getting at?"

Lauren leaned toward her, her tone conspiratorial. "I hear that if Dickson becomes senior partner, we'll merge with a New York firm that wants to gobble us up."

Kate knew Charles was dead set against a merger. She was too. "I hope you're wrong. Large firms are too impersonal. I've no desire to be in a firm of over seven hundred lawyers."

"Afraid of being a small fish in a large pond?" taunted Lauren.

Kate bit back the barbed response that was on the tip of her tongue. It was getting more and more difficult for her to talk to Lauren as a friend since each wanted to become a partner.

It wasn't that Kate craved the prestige of the position, which she was sure was Lauren's reason. No, she needed the financial security that becoming a partner would give her. Lauren didn't have to worry about mundane things like money, but *she* did, and she knew that despite Charles's fund-raising efforts on her behalf, running for political office would be a personal financial drain. With a partnership, Kate would still be able to receive profits through a blind trust.

She turned left on Rodeo Drive in the heart of Beverly Hills, went through the shopping district and into the residential area. As they neared the Church of God's Shepherd, she could see limousines parked up and down both sides of the street. "Looks like quite a crowd," she said, thankful that she could turn her own car over to one of the parking attendants.

The police were holding back the crowd of gawkers who had lined up outside trying to catch a glimpse of the celebrities. There were even television crews there to tape the event.

At the door, as people scrambled to squeeze in, fire marshals counted heads and monitors consulted guest lists.

Kate watched Lauren greet many of the dignitaries. Although she hated to admit it, she was a little envious of the way Lauren had been born with such easy access to power while she had had to struggle up each rung of the ladder.

The church, with its Spanish architecture, graceful arches and covered walkways, was filled to capacity. She was grateful to find that another associate at the firm had saved some seats, as she and Lauren slipped into the last row of benches.

Kate glanced quickly at the well-dressed gathering, glad she had run to the cleaners to pick up her black crepe suit. The pungent smell that emanated from the white gardenias, tuberoses, and pink gladioli nearly overwhelmed her. She shivered. Despite the huge crowd, it was chilly and quiet in the church.

"Remind me to tell you about the gorgeous defense lawyer I'm dating," whispered Lauren. She began to give Kate a rundown on his most salient features.

Kate held her finger to her lips as the organ began to play a mournful melody. She gazed at the expensive bronze coffin draped with flowers and then at the backs of the immediate family sitting in the front. Even from where she sat, it was impossible not to notice the way the D'Arcy family shunned Sandra.

Sandra D'Arcy sat numbly, slightly apart from the others. She still couldn't believe James was dead. She watched his eighty-year-old invalid mother, Abigail, being wheeled in by her chauffeur. She shuddered at the sight of the old woman in her fancy black mink coat and matching hat with veil and black gloves. Abigail has never forgiven me for marrying her precious James, thought Sandra. She hates me.

Her thoughts flew to Jimmy. She was worried. Abigail's driver had picked up her poor child that morning and taken him to Abigail's estate. A nanny had been hired to care for him during the funeral. Why couldn't he have stayed with Maria, whom he knew and loved? But Abigail wouldn't hear of it. Everything always had to be done her way.

Oh God, Sandra thought, now that James was dead, was it possible his family was going to try to take her son away from her? It was something she hadn't considered until that moment.

She shifted her position on the hard bench, causing James's sister, Victoria D'Arcy Mandeville, to give her a dirty look. Sandra felt so alone, totally surrounded by people who disliked her. Why couldn't Tommy be here to help her face them?

The heady aroma of the flowers, mixed with the sweet smell of Victoria's perfume, began to make Sandra feel sick. Her stomach lurched with anxiety. Trying to focus elsewhere, she turned to gaze at the mourners filing into the church. What could have happened to Tommy? she wondered. He hadn't returned her calls the last two days. Because of all that had happened, she'd been afraid to drive over to his place to check on him. Some of the questions the police were asking made her worry that they might know about him.

Her eyes shifted to Victoria's husband, Raymond Mandeville. She was repelled by his beefy face and his red nose lined with veins. He was whispering to Victoria, pointing out the important people who were in attendance—the Vice President of the United States and his wife, the former president and first lady. Several senators. To hear him boast, it could be a coronation rather than a funeral.

And what's wrong with Theo? she wondered. He was the only one in the family who had ever been nice to her, but even he hadn't been around since the night of James's death. Does he even feel bad his brother's dead, she wondered, or is part of him glad too? She glanced up as Dickson sat down behind Theo and whispered into his ear. The two of them were up to something, she was sure.

Charles leaned over and put his hand on Sandra's shoulder, interrupting her thoughts. "How are you feeling?"

"All right," she whispered, wondering what kind of pill the doctor had given her earlier that morning. It was making her mouth dry. She hadn't wanted to take it, but Victoria had insisted. "When's it going to start?" she asked.

Victoria stiffened. "Shush! As soon as everyone is here, Sandra!" Her voice was shrill and scolding.

"Come on, Victoria," chided Charles. "This is all a little scary for Sandra." He turned to Sandra. "We're waiting for the governor. Won't be long now."

"Thanks," Sandra mumbled. She wished she were anywhere but here. She hated Victoria and her disgustingly superior attitude even more now for trying to humiliate her in front of Charles.

From her place at the back of the church, Kate watched as Charles consoled D'Arcy's widow. Then a hush fell over the crowd as the Reverend John Martin stood to say a prayer for the departed soul of James D'Arcy.

Governor Brandon ascended to the lectern, pausing for a moment, patiently waiting for the full attention of the audience. Then he began to speak. Kate listened intently to the man's powerful yet beautifully soothing voice as he eulogized his childhood friend. By the time he finished, many were openly crying.

Every few minutes throughout the service, Kate caught herself staring at the back of Charles's head and at Ann, sitting next to him. She saw Ann's blond head turn toward Charles as she whispered something into his ear. Don't, Kate thought with a stab of jealousy. He's mine.

Detective Bower sat with Donaldson near the back of the church. During the service their trained eyes scanned the room, looking for anything unusual. At the moment, the motive for James D'Arcy's death appeared to be robbery; however, there were many things that made Bower doubt that motive. After all, Bower had been on the police force for eighteen years, ten of which were spent in homicide. His instincts were good, and he had a certain objectivity—a trait that had helped him survive the stress of police work without getting burned out or turning to drink.

"Tell me," he had asked Donaldson over and over, "whaddya think the chances are of a kid's trike blocking the gates to his house?" It just didn't fit to him, not in Bel Air. "And look at the way Mrs. D'Arcy lied. She was worried enough about where that trike was to make up an answer for that Latino woman. Add to that piece of the equation the idea that on this particular night some perp was cruising around looking for a mark wearing some fancy jewelry, carrying lotsa cash, who'd hafta get outta his car in front of his gates to his house."

It just didn't add up, Bower thought as he scanned the faces of the assembled mourners. Even Donaldson's argument that statistically most follow-home robberies were random didn't wash. "But if the guy didn't know where D'Arcy lived," Bower had countered, "how did he find time to drive ahead of D'Arcy to the house, park his car, and hide in the shrubs where we found a footprint?

And thinka the way D'Arcy was shot in the back of the head. Point-blank range. Execution style. Who else but a deliberate murderer or hired hit man is gonna shoot like that?''

No, this whole thing just doesn't make sense, Bower thought. Already he had decided to run a check on all of D'Arcy's dealings, as well as his family and acquaintances.

Forgetting for a moment where he was, Bower turned to Donaldson and said, "What I really wanna know is why a guy with lotsa bottles of Dom Perignon 1986 in his own private wine cellar goes to a liquor store and buys the same exact thing."

4

Kate scanned the patio of Abigail D'Arcy's palatial home, looking for Lauren. She wanted to leave. From the moment Kate had walked in the front door, Ann Rieman had fixed her unrelenting blue eyes on her, even following her from the house out onto the patio—always at a discreet distance, of course. That, added to the pressure at work and the uncertainty brought on by James D'Arcy's death, was taking its toll on her nerves.

When she found Lauren, she whispered in her ear, "I've got to get out of here."

"Soon," responded Lauren. Ignoring Kate, she turned blithely to speak to someone else.

Kate angrily headed for the bar. Even though it was the middle of the day, she suddenly needed fortification. I'll probably be good and sorry, she told herself, knowing how woozy even one drink could make her in the afternoon.

As she sipped her wine, Kate's eyes traveled over the rolling green lawns of D'Arcy Oaks and back again to the English-style mansion looming behind her. She was surprised to find the D'Arcy family receiving condolences at Abigail's estate. Why not Sandra's home? she had wondered out loud as she and Lauren drove to Holmby Hills. Lauren was sure it was because the D'Arcy family had never accepted Sandra.

Lauren had also told Kate what she knew about the D'Arcy matriarch. Abigail was confined to a wheelchair due to a fall down a flight of stairs. Before her husband William's death ten years ago, Abigail's parties had been legendary for bringing together world leaders with the chieftains of business and industry. To give the affairs color and diversity, Abigail always included a smattering of famous musicians, artists, writers, and academicians, even the occasional actor.

When Kate first walked into the drawing room, furnished in priceless English antiques, she had been overwhelmed by the art hanging on the walls. The D'Arcy collection was one of the world's finest privately owned collections. Rumor had it that it was promised to New York's Metropolitan Museum upon Abigail's death. Kate had reluctantly forced herself to look away from the paintings to search for the D'Arcy family so she could pay her respects.

On a small love seat next to Abigail's wheelchair sat Theo and his sister, Victoria. The three of them were positioned so that people could come to them, say a few words, and then move on. To Kate's astonishment, Sandra was not included.

Holding her drink, Kate strolled back into the house. The family was seated in the same place. Abigail's beautiful face, surprisingly unwrinkled for her age, was somber and framed by perfectly coiffed silver waves. Kate could readily understand why Charles had referred to the matriarch as royalty. Her bearing was aristocratic and her demeanor elegant, all the way down to her simple black dress. At her ears and throat were the famous D'Arcy diamonds, their brilliance flashing in the light. Kate had the distinct impression that the woman's piercing black eyes missed nothing.

Next to Abigail sat Victoria. She had her mother's dark eyes, and fair skin that appeared to have been stretched taut across her prominent cheekbones. She was too thin—almost anorexic-looking—to be called pretty, thought Kate, and her behavior appeared not so grand as it did haughty.

On Victoria's left sat Theo. He was the one who intrigued Kate the most. His aesthetic face had today been a kaleidoscope of emotions. She had seen him shed tears at the burial. But here with his mother and sister he seemed numb, like a puppet being put through the motions of grieving. His long copper hair and loose, casual clothing contrasted glaringly with the formality of Abigail's domain.

Kate turned her gaze from this trio and sought out Sandra, who had been left to fend for herself. Kate's feelings were mixed as she watched the young widow flit about the room, her pretty face a mask of stone. On principle, Kate didn't have much respect for someone who hadn't worked for what she had—or worse, who married for money. Yet seeing the pathetic way Sandra roamed from group to group, fitting in nowhere, her lush figure stuffed into a black suit cut too low to be proper, Kate felt a rush of sympathy. She knew what it was like to be an outsider.

Kate's father had walked out on her mother when Kate was only five. Kate had seen him only sporadically after that. When she was eight, John Alexander died suddenly, a traumatic event from which Kate had never fully recovered. Although Carole Alexander remarried and had two more children, Kate's stepfather barely made enough to pay the rent. The family was always moving in the middle of the night to avoid the newest landlord's wrath. By the time she was sixteen, Kate had lived in fifteen different places and gone to as many schools.

To make matters worse, she had fought with her stepfather all the time. Nothing she did was right. He didn't like the way she dressed or her choice of friends. He especially didn't approve of Kate's plans to go to college and become a lawyer. "College is stupid for a girl," he claimed.

Feeling she had no choice, Kate left home the day after she

graduated from high school at the age of seventeen. It was a terrifying time. Trying to put together the deposit for first and last months' rent on an apartment had taken six months of hard work and sleeping on the floor of a friend's bedroom. During that time Kate held down two jobs and went to college. When she finally managed to get a place of her own, she was forced to ask three other girls to share it to meet the rent. All she remembered about those days was the lack of privacy and sleep.

Kate's glance fell on Charles. His face was animated as he spoke effortlessly to the Vice President of the United States. Charles had not been born into this crowd either. In both college and after, it had been James D'Arcy and Dickson Manning who had helped him enter their privileged world of old money and political clout. Even though Charles seemed at home in this milieu, Kate knew he too remembered how it felt not to belong.

As she searched again for Lauren, Kate passed a number of tall, clean-cut men standing aimlessly, their eyes in constant motion. Must be Secret Service men guarding the Vice President, she guessed. She spotted Lauren's red hair, golden in the afternoon sunlight. "I'm leaving," she whispered. "If you don't want to go, get a ride with someone else."

"I'll meet you outside in a few minutes." Lauren waved her hand as if in dismissal.

She can damn well find her own way home, thought Kate, determinedly heading toward a marble foyer the size of her living room. Charles was suddenly at her side. "Leaving?"

"Yes." She felt a nervous twitter in her stomach from his closeness, knowing Ann could not be far away observing the two of them.

"Doesn't look as if I'll be back to the office today. Would you see if there's anything Nancy can't handle?"

Although his words were about business, she felt him caressing her with his dark eyes.

"Of course."

41

He smiled, showing his even, white teeth. "Did you meet the Veep?"

"No."

"Come." With his hand on her shoulder, Charles guided Kate over to where the man was standing. "Mr. Vice President, I'd like you to meet Kate Alexander, an associate with our firm and, many of us hope, a future governor of California."

The Vice President grasped Kate's hand. It was plain from the way his eyes unabashedly undressed her that what she had heard about him was true. He was definitely a womanizer. "I'm pleased to meet you," he exclaimed with a wide grin.

"The honor's mine, Mr. Vice President." Kate tried to keep her dislike from showing. This was the part of politics she hated.

"And this is Lawrence Wasserstein, chairman of the National Democratic Committee." Charles indicated a short, stout man with a shock of white hair standing next to the Vice President.

"How do you do, Mr. Wasserstein?" Kate shook the man's outstretched hand. Charles had described him as a walking calculator. He looked more like a kindly professor than a cold mathematician in charge of the party's money.

"When Kate becomes district attorney and has proven she's a fabulous vote-getter, we'll be looking to the national committee for support," said Charles.

"James mentioned Kate to me the night . . ." Wasserstein caught himself, then added, "He thought highly of you, Ms. Alexander."

Kate smiled, wondering again about her future. Charles and she had hoped James would act as the linchpin, attracting other political bigwigs to support her. Now that he was dead, would she be able to convince major players like Governor Brandon and Lawrence Wasserstein to back her candidacy?

Lauren chose that moment to show up. She confidently greeted Wasserstein, but not the Vice President, forcing Charles to introduce her.

Inwardly, Kate had her only genuine smile of the day as she observed Lauren appraise the Vice President as surely and as thoroughly as he had done to Kate. Good for you, Lauren, she silently cheered. A few minutes of small talk ensued; then the Vice President excused himself, taking Wasserstein with him.

"I'll be right back," cooed Lauren. With a devilish grin at Charles, she added, "Nature calls."

"She's something else," chortled Charles as soon as Lauren was out of earshot.

Kate nodded.

"There you are, darling," said Ann Rieman, joining Charles and Kate. Her voice was sugary while her vivid blue eyes mercilessly searched Kate's.

"You know Kate Alexander, don't you, Ann?" said Charles.

"Why, of course. How are you?" Ann's mouth curved upward in a smile of feigned delight.

"Very well thank you, Mrs. Rieman." Kate couldn't help but notice that when Ann spoke, she narrowed her eyes to nearly a squint.

"Oh, call me Ann. Mrs. Rieman makes me sound so . . ." Ann shrugged her shoulders, and put her arm through Charles's. She looked up at him with adoration. "So . . . what would you say, darling?"

"So—like the boss's wife," he quipped.

Kate caught his wry glance meant for her.

At that moment, Lawrence Wasserstein reappeared. "Sorry," he interrupted, "I must steal Charles for a moment."

From the expression on Charles's face, Kate could tell he wasn't pleased at the prospect of leaving her alone with Ann.

After the men had gone, Ann turned to Kate. "All my life I've been introduced as either the senior partner's daughter or my brother Dickson's little sister. Then I married Charles and Father took him into the firm. Now I'm a partner's wife." She laughed, a hard, brittle laugh, as she put her hand over her heart. "I guess it's a small price for

43

having such important men in my life," she said grandly.

Kate smiled politely while her stomach performed elaborate flip-flops. Usually quick to respond, she could think of nothing to say to this woman. Ann Rieman was certainly a beautiful woman. She was in her early forties and had small, delicate features. Her face was perfectly made up, and her flaxen blond hair was pulled back into a becoming chignon. Her petite but nicely proportioned body was adorned in a dark blue suit.

"And you, Kate?" She gave a small sigh. "Are you anyone's wife?"

Kate felt the color rise in her cheeks. "I was married once, briefly."

"Oh, what a shame it ended." Ann's harsh tone contradicted the innocent smile on her face.

"Not really," said Kate. "It was a mistake."

"Do you make many of those?" Ann asked pointedly, a malicious glint in her eye.

"I try not to." Kate's heart sank. She had hoped Ann had not guessed about her and Charles, but from the way Ann acted, Kate was positive she knew.

"Hello, Mrs. Rieman," sang Lauren. "I'm ready to go," she said to Kate.

Kate felt enormous relief at the sight of Lauren. Her earlier pique at her rival evaporated as they made their excuses.

"That was the coldest, most formal gathering I've ever been to," said Kate as she waited with Lauren on the front steps for the parking attendant to bring her car.

"I've been to worse. It's the bizarre way James died. No one knew what to say." Lauren leaned forward, her tone hushed. "Some people don't think it was a robbery but a deliberate murder."

"And the suspects?" Kate said, not expecting an answer.

"His brother, Theo, for one. He hated James. Supposedly, Theo wanted to run the D'Arcy Foundation, but James shut him out. And then," continued Lauren, her bluish-green eyes dancing, "there *is* that cheap woman James married. Could you believe her? Her boobs were pushed up like a want ad for her next rich husband. Why James *ever* married that slut's a mystery to me.''

''They do have a child.''

''Oh bull. He didn't have to marry her for that.''

''Maybe he thought it important for his son to have the D'Arcy name. Not to mention how nice it is for a child to have both of his parents.''

''Spare me.'' Lauren's face twisted in mock agony.

Kate laughed in spite of herself.

''Well, back to the salt mine for us,'' said Lauren, as the attendant brought the car and Kate slid into the driver's seat.

Charles had been worried ever since Kate left that Ann had said something to upset her. Pleading that he had to make arrangements for the reading of James's will, he sent Ann home before him.

As he wound his way out of the lush greenery of Holmby Hills, Charles pushed a button on his cellular phone's memory pad. The sound of ringing reverberated in the car.

''Hello,'' Kate's husky voice answered.

''Hi, it's me.''

''Charles,'' she said, surprised. ''I didn't expect to hear from you tonight.''

''I know it's late. You in bed?''

''Not yet.''

''This has been one of the worst days of my life,'' he sighed.

''It can't have been easy.''

He heard the immediate concern in her voice. ''Can I come over?''

''Of course. How far away are you?''

''I'm turning down Sunset. I'll be there in fifteen minutes.''

''See you then.''

Following Charles's car out of Holmby Hills, Dickson tried to keep a safe distance behind him. He didn't want his brother-in-law to know he was there. He had overheard Charles sending Ann home with some lame excuse about attending to the will. No sooner had Ann gone than Charles ordered his car and left too.

Where's he going? he wondered. When Charles reached Sunset and turned right instead of left in the direction of his home, Dickson knew he had guessed correctly. His brother-in-law was definitely up to something.

Dickson wished he didn't have his wife, Alana, with him. He wanted to follow Charles, but knowing Alana, she'd ask too many questions. If Charles was doing something he didn't want known, it might be wiser for Dickson to find out about it on his own. One could never tell how useful something like that could be. No sense giving Alana the chance to screw it up for him.

Kate hung up, frowning as she surveyed the clutter. She was sitting on her white, overstuffed sofa with folders, case files, and papers strewn about. Open lawbooks were scattered across the coffee table and couch. In two days she had to argue an important motion and she needed the quiet time at home to read all the complicated documents in the case.

She stood up and caught a glimpse of herself in the mirror. What a mess I am, she thought, gazing at her five-foot-eight, 120-pound frame hidden underneath her beloved baggy sweats. With Charles on his way over, she'd have to straighten up. Somehow he always managed to look immaculately dressed, even after a three-hour tennis game.

Yanking off her sweats she changed into wool slacks and a sweater. She hurriedly brushed her short black hair, allowing the wisps to fall back across her forehead. Then she added a touch of mascara to her already dark, full eyelashes. That's all, she told herself, nodding approvingly at her image. She peered closer at her figure. She wasn't getting enough exercise. Running every morning was getting harder and harder to do.

As she gathered up all the documents, she wondered when she was going to finish. Darn, she thought, I have so much work to do. Why didn't I say no? But she knew the answer to that. It was hard for her to say no. With a sigh, she stuffed the papers into her briefcase.

After rearranging the room, she glanced around, satisfied. Her dream had always been to own a place of her own, but her first four years as a prosecutor had been lean. Government employees were not paid well, especially in comparison to the private sector. However, after she moved to Manning & Anderson, her salary had immediately tripled. And from there it had steadily climbed upward.

Three years later she had bought this trilevel condominium on the beach in Santa Monica. It was her first home and she adored it. She had lovingly chosen each stick of furniture, most of it contemporary but with a few antiques and some Oriental pieces to soften the modern look.

The doorbell broke Kate's reverie. "Did you just leave Abigail's?" she asked as she closed the door behind Charles.

"Yes. However"—he raised his eyebrows—"I wish I'd left sooner."

"Oh," she said, noting how tired he looked. "What happened?"

"Let me have a drink first, then I'll tell you."

She opened the armoire she had turned into a bar and poured him a scotch. He took a few sips. Then he dropped down onto the sofa, his large frame falling back against the cushions. "Come sit by me," he pleaded, patting the space next to him.

Kate sat down, tucking one foot underneath her.

"You won't believe what a moronic ass my brother-in-law is."

"What did Dickson do now?" she asked, a half-amused smile on her face.

"He had the nerve to ask the governor if James had spoken to him about his will lately. Can you imagine that?" Not waiting for her response, he continued. "Where the fuck is that man's sense of propriety? We just buried our friend today."

Kate could see Charles was agitated.

"We need to make sure James's death doesn't harm the D'Arcy Company or Foundation in any way. The damned will can wait."

A concerned look flooded her eyes. "According to the paper, the D'Arcy Company's sales are down."

His handsome face was somber as he nodded. "The rumor that someone wanted James murdered isn't helping any." He held his glass to his lips. Then, putting it down, he reached for her hand. "What did Ann say to you when I left?"

She shrugged. "Mostly small talk."

He took her face in his hands. "I saw the color rush into your cheeks. She upset you."

"She's just . . ." Kate sighed and hesitated.

"A bitch," he finished for her. "Please, Kate, tell me what she said."

"That it was too bad I wasn't married."

Charles groaned. "I'm sorry. Unfortunately, Ann often has the tongue of a wasp."

"She's difficult," she admitted. "But don't worry. I'm fine."

"Good." He smiled, the corners of his deep-set dark eyes crinkling. "You have no idea how impossible living with her has become."

"She knows about us," she said softly—a statement, not a question.

"No." He shook his head. "Believe me, if she knew about us, she'd cause trouble."

"My intuition tells me she does," she repeated firmly.

He sighed. "Let's not talk about her. Right now all I want to do is bury my head between those soft breasts of yours and forget this nightmare." He pulled her to him, then bent his face to hers, seeking her mouth.

The kiss was long and tantalizing. He reached back, stroking her spine. Kate in turn massaged the back of his neck. She sensed his wish to be cared for tonight. "Come into the other room, where you can relax," she urged.

"Mmm," he murmured, a smile on his face as he gazed at her.

She stood and held out her hand. Then she led him to her bedroom, where she took out a bulky terry-cloth robe she kept for him. He grabbed it and disappeared into the bathroom. She heard the shower running. A few minutes later he was back, wrapped in the robe, his thick black hair glistening and wet.

Kate had slipped into a beige silk robe. She glanced at him, recognizing the desire in his eyes. It warmed her. Her pulse quickened as Charles pulled her down onto the bed and she buried her head against his chest. Feeling his ardor, she trembled. His lips came down, crushing hers.

"I needed to be with you so badly," he whispered.

Kate's response was to let her mouth and tongue journey lazily down his body, past the hard line of his ribs to his lean waist. Experiencing his arousal pressed hard against her through the nub of his robe, she quickly undid the knot and caressed him.

He groaned, then leaned back and stared deeply into her eyes. He touched her cheek with his finger, moving it across her brow, her eyelids, her nose, and then her mouth. "You're so lovely," he said hoarsely, pulling her against him, sliding her body so they were face-to-face. Slowly he traced the outline of her lips and parted them. Then he kissed her again.

As Charles pushed open her robe, his hands eagerly reaching for her, Kate felt her nipples harden. For a moment she let the shivers of pleasure wash over her. Then she whispered, "Lie back."

He sank down into the pillows. Her lips and tongue flicked at his stomach, her hands curled into the thick hair on his chest. She moved her lips down. She felt him shudder and sensed the tension leaving him.

She loved his deeply tanned body, his broad back and massive shoulders. The tip of her tongue traced the outline of his inner thigh where the bronzed skin turned white, then traveled beyond.

His passion excited her. "Oh, please," he moaned. He tried to raise himself but she pushed him back, her mouth still around him. She could feel his body pulsating as she raised her head, then ever so slowly lowered it. His breath quickened. She kissed him lightly one second and harder the next. The moistness of her mouth gripped him. His hands clutched at her shoulders as his body twisted in pleasure. He called out several times, but she didn't let up.

"Oh my God," he cried out finally, holding her head still against him.

She loved him this way, vulnerable, unable to stop his orgasm, forced to trust her. Turned on by the intensity of his release, Kate stroked him lightly, planting kisses in his hair.

After a few minutes, the shaking of his body subsided.

She stood up and opened the blinds so they could gaze out at the darkness and at the moon hanging low in the star-filled sky. The ocean beyond shimmered like black glass.

"Incredible," he said, his voice barely audible.

Kate smiled. She put some soft music on the stereo, lighted the fireplace and went to freshen his drink. Handing it to him, she sat beside him, listening to the music while he sipped.

He offered her the glass, but she shook her head. He took several swallows, placed the drink on the table, and slid his hand up her spine, bringing her forward, his lips searching for hers, his tongue thrusting into her parted mouth. Kate returned his kiss. His mouth traveled down her as he kissed her neck, her shoulders. She threw her head back, enjoying the feel of his damp skin on hers.

He slipped off her robe. She shivered and he warmed her by pressing his naked body against her, nuzzling her breasts and nipples, the beginnings of his beard scratching her lightly, causing her back to arch. He stroked her languorously in slow motion, his hand on her long legs and then on her breasts, taut now under his touch.

His hand running up the inside of her thigh engulfed Kate in a rush of exquisite warmth. She began to undulate under his expert fingers. She sighed and murmured his name, over and over again. His mouth claimed hers and she answered his demand ravenously, guiding him inside her.

She grasped his shoulders, moaning at each deep thrust, then wrapped her legs around his back, trembling with ecstasy. "I love you," she gasped.

With his mouth against her throat, he whispered. "I love *you*, Kate."

As she moved with him, delighting in the heat, his rhythm grew faster. The urgency of Kate's passion spiraled into total abandonment, and she was on a dizzy climb, rising higher and higher with him, out of control as they became one. A final plunge by Charles, and Kate shuddered, crying out as waves of rapture washed over her.

When she finally opened her eyes, she hugged him with all her might.

He brushed a strand of hair away from her eyes. "I can't wait until we can be together. Always."

5

The next morning Kate flicked on the television while sipping her coffee and punched through the channels until she came to her favorite news program.

"On the local scene, wealthy real estate magnate James D'Arcy, who was gunned down in front of his plush Bel Air estate a few nights ago in what police have been calling an armed robbery, was buried yesterday. It was the largest funeral Los Angeles has seen in years. Hundreds of prominent guests filled the Church of God's Shepherd in Beverly Hills to hear Governor Brandon eulogize his friend."

She peered closely at the film clips, searching for a glimpse of herself or anyone else she knew. The Vice President was shown, as were a few other important dignitaries.

"New developments in the case point to the possibility that it may not have been a robbery as first suspected. We'll keep you posted as more is learned."

Using the remote, she turned the TV off. It was getting late. She had to get to work.

Lauren rushed into her office and slammed the door. She had just overheard one of the firm's law clerks saying that Charles was soliciting an important backer for Kate's primary campaign. She was angry. Kate hadn't even had the decency to admit to her she was running for office. But she was also afraid. What if Kate's candidacy gave her more credibility in the eyes of the firm's management? It could virtually assure Kate of the partnership. Lauren knew that political office usually enhanced a partner's ability to generate new business once he or she returned to the firm.

It isn't fair, I was here first, thought Lauren. The partnership belongs to me. How can I keep Kate from encroaching further on my hard-won territory? She fiddled with her pen as her mind raced over different scenarios, different angles of attack. Finally, she came up with a possible solution. Twirling her chair around to face the window, she placed a call.

"District attorney's office," answered the person on the other end.

"Madeline Gould, please," Lauren said. She knew that her and Kate's best friend from law school would be interested in her news.

The line rang one time and then a strong voice answered, "Madeline Gould here."

"Hi, Madeline. It's me. Lauren."

Madeline chuckled. "Is it your turn to remind me about our monthly luncheon?"

Lauren laughed. "That's Rachel's job. I'm calling because I've got some news for you that may not come up at our lunch."

"And what's that?" asked Madeline.

"First, you must promise not to say where you heard it," drawled Lauren.

"Of course."

Lauren's voice dropped. "Our friend Kate is planning to run for D.A."

There was a pause. Then Madeline sighed. "Well, damn, if Kate runs, what chance do I have?"

Lauren knew her news had hit Madeline hard. "You're just as bright," she argued. "Kate became valedictorian by only a small margin."

"It's not that," said Madeline. "Kate was a prosecutor, too."

"But she was only downtown for four years. You've been a deputy D.A. for seven years."

"Yeah, but on top of that, Kate has the backing of a big firm." Madeline sighed again. "Some of your partners over there at Manning & Anderson are well connected politically. They'll be able to line up Democratic party power brokers to back Kate. And that equates directly with money. I won't be able to compete."

Lauren realized it was time to play her trump card. She hoped Madeline knew how lucky she was about to become.

"Maybe I could do something to even up the odds." She paused to let her words sink in. "Let me talk to Daddy. Perhaps we can help."

"What kind of help are we talking about?" asked Madeline.

"Enough money and big backers to scare Kate away. Or at least to make it much more difficult. Let me work on it. But don't say anything to Kate."

"O.K."

"Good. Well, I've got to go now. I'll see you tomorrow." Lauren hung up and played with the paperweight on her desk. She'd have to convince her daddy that supporting Madeline could be beneficial to him. That shouldn't be too difficult. Since he had so much business in California, the state's politics usually interested him. Politics is fun, she thought as a feeling of power washed over her. With a start, she realized she was doing exactly what she'd seen her father do over the years.

She decided to call him and see what he had done about helping her with the partnership. "Daddy, you talk to Franklin about me yet?"

"For heaven's sake, darlin', James D'Arcy just died. It wouldn't have been right."

"He's been dead three days already."

"My impatient Lauren," he chortled. "Trust me, sugar. I know best how to approach these things. Tell me, how was the funeral?"

"O.K." She stuck her lower lip out. She hated when he acted like he was the only one who knew what was best. Why did he have to be so difficult? And why didn't he understand how important the partnership was?

"Who was there?" he asked.

"Everyone. Even the Vice President came. They all asked about you, Daddy, and I made your apologies."

"Thank you, sweetheart. I feel just terrible that I missed it. It couldn't be helped." He coughed. "You hear anything more about Franklin postponing his retirement?"

"According to Kate, he's only putting it off a few weeks."

"And just how does that little gal know that?"

"Charles Rieman told her. He's counsel for the D'Arcy Company and the D'Arcy Foundation. And that's part of the problem. Charles claims he's swamped with the extra work James's death has caused."

"Hmm, I wonder if that means that Franklin is going to support his son-in-law to take his place over his own son." He paused. "What else you hear?"

"Most of the attorneys in the firm seem to think it'll be a tie between Charles and Dickson. Then Franklin will be forced to cast the deciding vote."

Miles Cunningham was quiet for a moment. "Franklin's behaving like a coward. A man should stand up for his son. Tell you what, sugar. I'll try to get out there in a few days and see what I can uncover."

"Thanks, Daddy. You always come through for me. And Daddy?"

"Yes."

"I'm going to need your help on something else. I'll explain it to you when I see you." She wrapped a lock of her reddish-golden hair around her finger.

"What's that, sugar?"

"I want you to back a friend of mine for D.A. in the next election."

"Why, Lauren," he chuckled. "When did you become interested in politics?"

"Since Kate decided to run."

Detective Bower rang the bell of the elegant home up the street from the D'Arcy mansion in Bel Air. A maid in a starched white uniform opened the door. "Mr. Winter." Bower flashed his badge. "He's expecting me."

"Right this way, please." She ushered him into a dark study furnished with bottle-green leather chairs and couches.

Mr. Winter was reading in a large armchair by the leaded-glass window. When he saw Bower, he stood up. "I appreciate your coming to see me at my home, Detective. I'm afraid the events of a few nights ago have left me jittery, and going to the station would have been a trifle much for me right now."

"I bet," said Detective Bower, without thinking. Then he reminded himself to be more sympathetic. Sometimes, after almost twenty years of police work, a cop got callous. "No picnic to find a body like you did."

Mr. Winter nodded. "I was simply out walking my dog and suddenly . . ." He paused. "I believe I told you everything I could think of the other night."

"Yeah, well." Bower looked at Mr. Winter; he was small and wiry. Winter had said he was retired, that he had been the C.E.O. of a large international company. The guy had also said he had a heart condition. "Sometimes people think of something later. I just wanna go over the details of your story again."

"Fine." Mr. Winter gestured to one of the couches.

As Bower sat down, he noticed how tight his pants were getting. Tomorrow, he promised himself, I'm going on a diet. "Now, the car you saw there. You sure it was white, not gray, or maybe beige?"

Winter nodded. "It passed under a streetlight and it certainly looked white. From the partial license plate I gave you, were you able to trace the car?"

Bower shook his head. "Not yet. Unlike what people think, it can take the D.M.V. weeks to find a car with only a partial tag. You said it looked like a late-model Mustang? We got thousands of white, late-model Mustangs in L.A.''

"Oh," said Mr. Winter, surprised. "That's too bad."

"It's O.K. We'll get it eventually." Bower wished he could remove his belt. It felt like it was cutting him in half. "You still think the driver was a male Caucasian?"

"Yes."

"And you didn't see anybody else in the car?"

"That's right."

Bower glanced at his notebook. "You said after you found the body lying there by the car, you ran up the hill to the D'Arcy house. Right?"

"Yes. I was too afraid to touch him to see if he was dead. There was blood around his head and he wasn't moving. His car was still idling in the driveway."

"How did you open the gate?"

"The remote control was lying on the ground. I moved the trike and opened the gate."

"You brought Mrs. D'Arcy back with you?"

"Yes."

"What did she do when she saw her husband lying there?"

"She started to cry, 'Oh no, oh no.' And she just kept her hand over her mouth like she couldn't believe it."

"Did she check to see if he was breathing or not?"

The man paused for a moment. "No, I don't think she did."

"And then," said Bower, "she just got into his car and called nine-one-one?"

"Well, not exactly. I think it was I who said we should call the police. I told her to reach into the car, from the other side of course—the body was right there by his door—and call them."

"What did she say, exactly? On the phone, I mean."

The man shook his head. "Something like 'Come quick, my husband's been shot.' "

Bower's eyebrows raised. "Did you use the word 'shot' to tell her about her husband?"

"I honestly don't remember. I thought the sound I had heard was a firecracker or a car backfiring. But when I saw the body lying there that way, the thought of a shot entered my mind. I may have said to her that her husband was shot." He shook his head again as if trying to remember. "I'm sorry, I don't recall the exact words."

Bower made some notes in his little book. "O.K. Mr. Winter, you said after she called nine-one-one, she ran back to the house?"

"Yes."

"She say why she had to go back to the house?"

"I think she mentioned not wanting her son to wake up and be frightened."

Bower fingered his chin. "Don't they have live-in help?"

"Oh yes. I'm quite sure they do." Mr. Winter smiled apologetically. "I'm afraid everyone around here has help. These homes are quite large and the grounds and all . . ." He stopped as if realizing he was rambling. "I've seen a Hispanic lady with the little D'Arcy boy. The rest of the people that work for them seem to be day help. You know, cleaning crews, a cook, gardeners, that sort of thing."

Bower was thoughtful for a moment. He had seen the Hispanic woman run after the child the night of the murder. "Knowing someone was up there, why do you think she ran away?"

The man seemed puzzled. "I'm not sure. I remember feeling upset that I was left alone with the body. But at the time, I was too rattled to think straight."

"And now that you had time to think about it, you have any thoughts on why she did that?"

The man shook his head. "I'm afraid I don't."

Bower stood up. "O.K. That's it for now. Thanks."

When Bower met Donaldson back at their car, they briefed each other on what they'd learned on their respective interviews. "So this cook who works two houses up the street has seen a white car parked outside the house several times? Recently?" asked Bower.

"Yeah," said Donaldson. "Usually in the afternoon and once very late at night."

"What kinda car? She know?"

Donaldson looked at his notes. "She said it coulda been a small Ford or Chevrolet. Said she'd recognize a picture."

Bower gazed at his young partner. With his hair bleached blond from the sun and his blue eyes, he looked more like a model for a suntan ad than a cop. "She see who was driving it?"

Donaldson shook his head. "So, what next?"

Bower smoothed back his graying hair. "I want to do that check on all the family members. Forensics says we're looking for a .22. Let's see who might have one."

"Will do."

Sandra walked into the other room to answer the phone. She needed to get away from Victoria, if only for a few minutes. What made James's sister think she could come to Sandra's house and tell her what to do? It was making her nervous.

Was James's family going to try to take her kid away from her now? She had worried about that happening when James was alive. It was something he had threatened to do. But now that he was dead, did she still have to worry?

She picked up the phone. She gasped when she heard the voice. It was Tommy, finally. "Tommy, where have you been? I've been going crazy!"

"I was really sick."

"Sandra? Where are you?" Victoria pushed open the door to Sandra's bedroom. When she spied Sandra on the phone, her eyes glinted with suspicion. "Who are you talking to?"

"Just a friend."

"Well, get off. Some of my friends are here to see you."

"I've got to go now. I'll call you later, O.K.?"

"Tell that bitch to mind her own business."

" 'Bye, Lucy. Thanks for calling."

Lauren watched as Andrew Stewart ordered their dinner from the extensive menu at L'Escoffier, located on the top floor of the Beverly Hilton Hotel. She liked a man who took charge of things, just like her daddy had always done. This

58

was also her favorite table because the windows on this side of the room overlooked both the lights of the city and the ones twinkling outside on the garden terrace.

"I may go to Hawaii in a few weeks," he said, after the waiter left.

She sipped her Chardonnay, hoping he would ask her to accompany him. She was amazed at how infatuated she had become with this man in such a short time; they had only been seeing each other for a few weeks.

Andrew was an up-and-coming criminal defense attorney in Los Angeles and one of the best-looking men Lauren had ever met. He had wavy blond hair, dimples, and the most startling blue eyes. She also liked his strong, muscular body and was enjoying imagining what he would look like with his clothes off. As an exercise fanatic herself, she appreciated a man who took care of himself.

"What's going on in Hawaii?" she asked.

"A criminal justice seminar. I thought I mentioned it."

"You might have." She paused. "Something to do with speeding up the trial process?"

For a few minutes he told her how the criminal courts in Los Angeles were overloaded and unable to handle the growing crime rate and violence.

She gave him a bewitching smile across the candlelit table while she listened to both him and the trio softly playing dance music in the corner of the room. "Hawaii sounds like a great idea, Andrew. I could sure use a rest."

He motioned for the waiter to pour more wine and Lauren began to mentally walk through her closet, picking and choosing from her expensive wardrobe the right clothes for a trip to a tropical climate. I'll just need a new bathing suit and some sandals and I'll be ready, she thought. When the waiter left, she glanced at Andrew expectantly. "So?"

"The governor is supposed to be there and a lot of other politicians," he explained.

"Governor Brandon?" Her voice, with its soft southern drawl, rose slightly in pitch, reflecting her suddenly heightened interest.

"Yes. Bringing criminals to trial quicker is going to be a major issue in the next campaign."

"And he needs you at this conference?" She joked coyly, teasing him, knowing full well she looked magnificent, from her golden-red hair, swept up into a mass of curls, to her dress, a black clingy little number that hugged her body and showed off her spectacular figure.

"Not exactly." Andrew laughed, his eyes focusing momentarily on her cleavage. "I just thought I should go. It's good to be seen at these things. Helps the other lawyers remember you when they have a referral."

"Sounds political to me." Her voice was barely a whisper.

He nodded. "Ned Brandon's a shrewd man. He knows if he wants to have a chance at the presidency in the next election, he's going to have to get tougher on this issue. People are screaming. They want to get the criminals off the streets faster and keep them away longer. There are also several victims' groups that are up in arms, complaining about how long they have to wait for justice."

"Mmm," she murmured. "Aren't you defense lawyers the ones that usually ask for most of the postponements?"

"Sure. We don't really want to see things change." He grinned. "In fact, if legislation like they're talking about passes, most of us will see a drop in income."

"That's 'cause you all count on the delays," she drawled. "If judges don't grant continuances, you won't be able to take as many cases and juggle them around the way you do now."

He smiled. "Right on. That's why the governor's got to find some middle ground to make everyone happy and why I want to be there to protect my interests."

Lauren only half listened to Andrew's explanation. Her mind was busy plotting. The thought of a week in Hawaii with Andrew was very appealing. She wasn't sure how she would arrange for the time off, but she'd work it out. Perhaps her old standby: a bad flu. She never worried about being caught in a lie. If it was convenient at the time and helped her out, that's all that mattered. Of course, she'd have to make up the billables on her clients or pad her time sheets. Now, just how to convince Andrew to take her with him was the next order of business. "I might be able to get away for a week," she said huskily.

He laughed as though embarrassed at her forwardness. "Lauren, I'm not even sure I'm going. I have a trial scheduled."

"Another continuance? So much for a speedy trial system."

He gave her a sheepish grin.

Forget the criminals, she thought. I need to speed up *his* process.

"You want another drink?" Andrew asked, his glance fixed on the front of her dress.

She recognized the desire in his eyes. "You having one?"

He reached across the table for her hand. "I wouldn't mind a nightcap at your place."

"Perhaps," she said, pulling her hand back, "but I feel like some more wine now." She impatiently beckoned the waiter.

When it was poured, she drank slowly. Looking through thick lashes, she smiled at him seductively, one hand toying with her glass.

"I'd really like to make love to you," Andrew said brazenly, his eyes challenging her.

"You would, would you," she teased.

"Very much," he responded softly.

"Well, I'd like to dance now." Lauren suddenly stood up, giving Andrew little choice but to follow her out to the dance floor. As they swayed, she moved her body skillfully against him, pleased when his breath became irregular.

"You don't really want to go away without me, do you?" she whispered into his ear, biting the tip.

His voice was ragged. "Let me see what I can do."

That's better, she thought, but still not good enough.

6

Kate strolled into the massive lobby of the Century Plaza Hotel and headed for the Water's Edge. "I looked for you," she said to Lauren, who was already seated at the table, a hint of reproach in her voice as she gave her a peck on the cheek. "I thought we'd walk over together."

"Had an errand to run," said Lauren, kissing the air in return.

Kate circled the table to hug the plump body of Rachel Shulman, whose brassy red hair stuck out in disarray around a plain, freckled face. Kate adored Rachel, who was the one responsible for organizing these luncheons. Married and the mother of two children, Rachel lived in the San Fernando Valley and had a flourishing private law practice nearby.

This monthly luncheon was a commitment Kate and her friends had made in law school, where they had forged a strong bond based on friendship and three years of shared suffering. In their first years in practice, they had been quite faithful about meeting regularly. Lately, however, their plans frequently got changed, canceled, and rescheduled. In fact, their secretaries were becoming friendly with one another as they called back and forth, juggling the crowded appointment books of the women they worked for.

"Where's Madeline?" Kate asked as she sat down next to the window and glanced around quickly. She loved this restaurant, its greenhouse ambience, the crisp whites, the pale salmon accents.

"She left a message saying she'd be late and to order the crab cakes for her." Lauren handed the note to Kate, who gazed at it briefly, then ordered a seafood salad.

"So," said Rachel, "anything new in your love lives?"

Kate shook her head as she fiddled with the napkin on her

"The partners were fighting long before D'Arcy died," confided Lauren. "His death just gave them something else to fight about."

Kate couldn't believe her ears. In a firm with such high-profile clients, it was vital to be closemouthed about their clients' affairs. She managed to mumble a diplomatic, "You're just being dramatic, Lauren. Let's drop it, O.K.?"

Lauren shrugged and with a smirk turned away from Kate.

Rachel directed her question to Madeline. "Won't your office be looking into his death?"

"Perhaps," said Madeline, with a slight smile. "So maybe we better not discuss it."

Kate sighed with relief while Rachel gestured toward Lauren. "Tell us more about this new man of yours."

Lauren smiled and sat back. "His name's Andrew Stewart and he's a well-known defense attorney."

"I've been up against him quite a few times," said Madeline. "He's good, not to mention gorgeous."

"Isn't he," sighed Lauren. "That wavy blond hair and those beautiful blue eyes. For him I'd give up being single."

Kate was surprised to hear Lauren mention marrying Stewart. They couldn't have been dating that long. Only two weeks earlier Lauren had been dating someone else. In fact, if she remembered correctly, Lauren had first mentioned Andrew the day of the funeral. "So is this serious?" she asked.

"Not yet," Lauren responded, "but I think I could persuade him . . . ."

"Marriage, hell, I've tried that," said Madeline. "By the way, next weekend Sam's got the kids. Anyone want to go to MOCA?"

"My daddy's coming in and I'm hoping to see Andrew," murmured Lauren.

"Kids and hubby," Rachel conceded apologetically. "We're having a barbecue."

"I might be away," explained Kate.

"Where ya going, honey?" Rachel asked eagerly.

"Maybe Palm Springs with a girlfriend," lied Kate. She prayed her voice wouldn't betray her.

Rachel looked at her watch. "Got to go. I've got a client coming in at two." She put cash on the table to cover her share of the lunch tab and said goodbye.

"I'll walk out with you." Madeline left her money and hurried out with Rachel.

The attendant brought Madeline's car first. A racy red Toyota, it was her statement of independence from the life she had shared with Sam. During their marriage he had driven the Corvettes, the Porsches, the BMWs.

Madeline had ignored Sam's mother's dire warning: "A good wife never competes directly with her husband," and gone to law school anyway. When she became the second lawyer in their family, Sam's fragile ego couldn't handle it. He'd made their life miserable until Madeline asked for a divorce.

Her mind wandered back to the old frustrations of life with Sam as she pulled into traffic and headed for the freeway and the twenty-minute drive downtown to the D.A.'s office. She was late. At times like today, she had a moment of doubt about having chosen to be a prosecutor. Kate and Lauren both spent their days in luxurious surroundings. She didn't see them checking their watches or worrying about getting back to the office.

She reflected on the possibility of Kate's running for D.A., not thrilled at the prospect of having to compete against her. It would take a lot of money. She wondered if Lauren's offer of help was serious. Lauren was not the type to do anything for anyone without wanting something in return.

After these luncheons, Madeline invariably wondered too whether she hadn't made a mistake sticking with the job as a deputy D.A. She knew what awaited her back at the office—a stack of case files, witnesses to call and interview, police to talk to, investigations to supervise, and no time to prepare any case properly before she found herself in court. Sometimes she was overwhelmed with how notoriously overworked and underpaid prosecutors were. Nonetheless, even though she often griped about the burdens, in her heart she loved her work and the sense of satisfaction it gave her. And someday, she thought, I want the top job.

As Lauren and Kate left the restaurant and walked into the main lobby of the hotel, Lauren glanced at her reflection in one of the mirrored pillars, pleased by what she saw. Catching sight of a group of men standing beyond the pillar, she was surprised to see that one of them was Andrew. He saw her at almost the same time, excused himself, and came toward her.

"Hi." He smiled. Although Andrew's words were directed at Lauren, his blue eyes fastened on Kate, something Lauren noticed immediately. How dare he stare at Kate that way! Reluctantly she introduced them.

"Andrew, this is Kate Alexander. We work together. Kate, Andrew Stewart."

"How do you do." Andrew flashed his smile again and held out his hand to shake Kate's.

"Pleased to meet you," answered Kate.

Lauren watched as Andrew not only held on to Kate's hand longer than necessary but gave it an extra squeeze before Kate pulled it away.

"We've just had lunch and are heading back to the office," said Lauren quickly, trying to grab Andrew's attention for herself. She wasn't going to allow Kate to muscle in on her latest man. "What are you doing here?"

"A late lunch meeting. We're just waiting for one more person." Andrew turned back to Kate and asked, "What area of the law do you specialize in?"

Before Kate could respond, Lauren answered for her. "Kate's in litigation. We've got to go." She gave Kate a nudge in the opposite direction. "We on for Saturday night?" she called out to Andrew.

Andrew nodded absently, still gazing at Kate.

"Great," said Lauren. "Call me later."

"He's gorgeous," said Kate when they were out of hearing. "But why did you tell him I was in litigation?"

Lauren shrugged. "Litigation. Criminal defense. It's all the same thing. Do you want a ride?"

"You brought the car for two blocks?"

"I have another errand."

Kate hesitated. "No. I think I'll walk. It's such a beautiful day." She waved to Lauren.

As Kate made her way to the office, she wondered why Andrew looked so familiar to her. Then she remembered. She had seen him in the elevator the other day.

Back at the office, she ran into Charles in the hallway. "You look lovely today," he said, eyeing Kate's white outfit appreciatively.

"Thanks." She smiled.

"Come into my office for a minute." As the door closed, he asked, "Where were you? I've been buzzing you for two hours."

She laughed. "Today was my monthly luncheon from law school. We always lose track of time."

"You ladies are still meeting?"

"Yes."

He hesitated. "Our . . . relationship doesn't come up?"

"Of course not." Her green eyes flashed angrily at him.

"I'm sorry," he sighed. "I just want to make sure Ann finds out about us from me. Not from some gossip like Lauren Cunningham."

"O.K.," she said, aware more than ever that their relationship was getting to be very difficult for her. "By the way, I think the D.A.'s office is in on the investigation of James's death."

"What makes you think that?"

She shrugged. "It wasn't anything Madeline Gould said. It was more her reluctance to talk about it."

"Isn't that being cautious about a matter she might eventually be handling?"

Kate nodded. "Still . . ." She didn't finish. "We'll see. What did you want to see me about?"

"Good news," he said cheerily. "We can go to Catalina next weekend."

"That's wonderful."

"Of course, I'm going to have to bring work along."

"Me too," she said, smiling. She wasn't worried. They would still have plenty of time to talk once they were there.

Homicide Detective Donaldson sat in front of his computer doing his homework. He was accessing CLETS, short for California Law Enforcement Telecommunication System, a computerized network of information used by law enforcement.

One by one, he entered the names of those people closest to James D'Arcy; in addition, he was waiting to access gun registration information on these people, fed into the computer earlier from different sources. One of those sources was DROS, or Dealer Registration of Sale. All dealers were required to send information on the sale of handguns into the Department of Justice, where it was entered into a computer. When the gun registration information came through, he immediately spotted another angle of investigation.

An hour later Bower and Donaldson parked their car on Hollywood Boulevard in front of Kimbell's Sporting Goods & Guns.

"We need to see the owner," Bower told a freckle-faced employee as he flashed his badge.

After a few moments, a man identifying himself as Jeffrey Kimbell came over to them. He was about five eleven with a ruddy complexion, the kind of guy who obviously spent a lot of time outdoors.

"Looking for me?"

"Yes." Bower showed him his badge. "We want you to check your records for a .22 Ruger semiautomatic purchased here on January seventh of this year."

"I'll give a look," said Kimbell.

He was back in a few minutes. "I sold a .22 caliber Ruger semiautomatic pistol on that date to a Sandra D'Arcy, 2413 Rock Canyon Drive, Bel Air, California."

Bower nodded. "That's the one. Remember anything about the lady?"

"Yeah, she was a real looker." Kimbell rolled his eyes and raised his eyebrows for emphasis.

Bower showed him a picture of Sandra D'Arcy. "This her?"

"Yep."

"You ever see her before that day?"

"Nope." The man looked around his store and Bower got the impression he was anxious to be rid of them.

"We need to know what happened when she came in here."

"She asked for a gun she could keep by her bed at night."

Bower waited for him to volunteer more information. When he didn't, Bower asked, "She tell you why?"

The gun store owner chewed on his lower lip for a moment. "I don't remember. She might have. I just don't remember."

This guy's going to make me pull everything out of him, thought Bower. "She didn't take the gun with her, did she?"

"Nope. She filled out the registration form all legal like." The owner looked at the records in his hands. "It says she picked up the gun on January twenty-first."

Bower calculated that Sandra had waited exactly the two weeks prescribed by law. "She buy any ammo?"

Kimbell looked again at the form. "Yep. She purchased a box of .22 cartridge shells."

"Anything else?" Bower was beginning to get exasperated.

"She asked me to show her how to work it."

"Did you?"

"I like to oblige a pretty lady, but I told her to take it to a target range and practice. I gave her the name of the place I send my customers."

"Where's that?"

"Beverly Hills Gun Club."

Bower made a few notes and looked up. "Thanks. We'll be in touch if we need more."

Back in the car, Bower scratched his chin. "So, the wife owns a gun. We need to pay her another visit."

Donaldson just nodded, a pensive expression on his face.

7

Charles and Ann Rieman arrived at the Bel Air estate of his in-laws for a birthday dinner in his honor. While his wife went to talk to her mother, Charles made his way to Franklin Manning's study.

Dickson stopped him in the hallway. "Father's napping. I don't think you should disturb him."

"Of course not." Charles peered at his brother-in-law. "Heard some interesting news about you today."

"Oh?"

"Richard Weatherspoon called." Charles paused to see Dickson's reaction.

Dickson merely smiled. "How is Richie boy?"

"Fine. He said you've been in touch with a number of New York firms."

"I speak on a regular basis with partners at several New York firms," said Dickson with a shrug of his shoulders. "So what? One needs to keep informed."

"That's not what Richard heard. He says you made a direct overture to Livingstone & Kenter to merge our two firms."

"He heard wrong." Dickson winked. "I doubt I'd be that foolish, my man, don't you?"

Charles found Dickson's attitude maddening. He had counted on the element of surprise to flush out the truth, but Dickson hadn't risen to the bait.

"Nonetheless, you ought to rethink your position," said Dickson. "A merger would give us a major presence across the country as well as enable us to handle clients with global business."

"Practicing law isn't wholesale merchandising," commented Charles wryly. "Big isn't always better where service is concerned."

"As a smaller firm, we don't have expertise in all areas," cautioned Dickson. "More and more clients want one firm to handle everything."

"That may be true, but there are still those who don't want that. Besides"—Charles gestured with his hand—"huge firms are a nightmare to administrate. And you can forget camaraderie between lawyers—most of them don't even know each other."

"Who cares about the social scene as long as we're making more money," retorted Dickson.

"I don't think Franklin would agree with you."

"Ah, my father. But then he's getting rather old, don't you think? Can't count on his being around forever."

"You know, Dickson"—Charles's voice rose despite his vow not to lose his temper—"you're a real asshole."

"And you, my esteemed brother-in-law," snapped Dickson, "are a prick."

"Dickson, Charles," a voice called, interrupting them.

"Looks like we woke him after all," said Charles. He entered Franklin's study and glanced quickly around the walnut-paneled room he loved so much.

As a young man, Charles had been quite impressed by Franklin. Franklin Manning came from old money and was to Charles the epitome of the gentleman lawyer. A number of Franklin's relatives had been in politics over the years, public service constituting a proper way to use one's money and talents. In fact, Franklin's father had been a United States senator, as had Franklin. On the walls hung the many pictures and mementos from those days.

The next logical step for Franklin, once it became apparent that higher political office was not in his future, was to use the position and recognition he had gained to establish a major firm. It would also guarantee a future for his son, who had shown little drive or ambition in school and who was wont to expend his energy instead on petty intrigues.

Franklin had formed a partnership with Stanton Anderson, another lawyer with good connections from a prominent family. Stanton had also been an aficionado of the film industry and brought to the firm many of Hollywood's finest. Even though Stanton was now dead, most of his clients had stayed with the firm. Currently the entertainment division encompassed the movie, television, and recording industries.

As he crossed the room, Charles gazed at the man sitting in front of a blazing fireplace. He was struck by how thin Franklin was. Since his heart attack the year before, Franklin had become almost withered, so unlike his former robust and powerful self.

"We thought you were resting," said Charles as he grasped Franklin's shoulder.

Franklin rewarded Charles with an appreciative smile.

"Hello, Dad." Dickson cleared his throat. "How you feeling?"

"How should I be feeling, having to nap every day like a two-year-old?" Franklin's voice rose, unintentionally. Why did his son always annoy him so?

"It has to be hard on you," Charles murmured.

"It is." Franklin nodded at the handsome man who had become more than a son to him.

Others always mistakenly assumed that Charles was Franklin's son instead of Dickson. For years Franklin had desperately tried to find some area in which his son might excel over Charles, but he had never succeeded.

The two men had met in college when Charles had been hired as Dickson's tutor. After a real friendship developed between them, Franklin had cautioned his son to restrict his friends to his own circle, but Dickson had persisted in bringing Charles home with him regularly. The relationship continued beyond college and into law school. Franklin was sure the whole thing had begun more as part of Dickson's ongoing effort to annoy him than anything else.

At the end of their first year of law school, however, when Charles placed at the head of the class and Dickson was somewhere near the bottom, Franklin grudgingly began to admire his son's friend. After a while, he started to toss the two students hypothetical questions when they were home.

At first, Dickson appeared thrilled as Charles continually

met the challenges set by the elder Manning. Slowly, however, Dickson's feelings of elation deteriorated into jealousy.

When Ann fell in love with Charles, Dickson balked, appalled at the prospect of Charles becoming a member of the family. Surprisingly, it was Franklin who had sided with Ann, for by that time, he too loved Charles. He still did.

"What're you two fighting about?" Franklin inquired gruffly.

"We're not fighting," Charles assured him. "Dickson and I were just having a friendly disagreement."

"That's right," said Dickson.

Franklin doubted either one was telling him the truth. So much was kept from him since his heart attack. Lately everyone treated him like an invalid.

While the men talked business downstairs, Ann Manning Rieman was upstairs in her old bedroom. She glanced in the mirror, fluffed her flaxen hair, and repaired the makeup around her beautiful eyes. Not bad for forty-two, she reflected, turning sideways to admire her trim figure in the mirror. Men still flirt with me, she assured herself.

She gazed around the large room decorated in chintz with the four-poster bed in the middle. It's sweet the way Mother keeps my room, she thought, although certainly it was never this neat. Mother was so understanding for her day. When I think of what I put her through . . . , she mused, recalling how her mother had been against her choice of Charles.

Although Dickson had considered her a bratty younger sister and Charles had ignored her, Ann had adored them both. As she grew older, she found the boys her mother considered "proper" to be boring, at least when compared to Charles. He was different, exciting. The knowledge that he had grown up in a little house with just his mother and father, who both worked, intrigued her. It was so different from her own life, surrounded by wealth, a large family, and a constant parade of important and interesting visitors.

Well, at least I respected Mother's wishes about no sex under this roof. She remembered the first time, the night when she had seduced Charles. It had happened in his car. Her parents had gone away for the weekend. Ann gave the housekeeper the night off after telling the woman her mother had given Ann permission to spend the night at a friend's. Then, from the friend's house, Ann had called home, knowing Charles would answer because she had previously arranged for him to be alone by sending Dickson on a wild goose chase.

When she sweetly asked Charles to come pick her up and take her home, he had, of course, agreed. He was shocked at her insistence he drive her to Lookout Point atop Mulholland Drive, a favorite necking place. "Just do it," she pleaded. "I've got a problem. I want to go where we won't be disturbed." Poor Charles. He had agreed. Once there, she coyly informed him that he was her problem. He had resisted at first, but in the end, she had won. And she intended to keep on winning.

Perhaps it's time to break that rule about no sex under my mother's roof, she thought, smiling to herself. The idea titillated her. Although Ann had engaged in a few discreet affairs, twenty years and two children hadn't changed how much Charles still excited her. Especially when she thought she might be losing him.

Ann was not happy about the looks she'd seen exchanged between Charles and Kate Alexander at James D'Arcy's funeral. Her woman's intuition told her something was going on between them. Kate, beautiful, unmarried, politically ambitious, was a challenge for Charles—the type of woman he might very well leave Ann for. Whatever their relationship, she had to end it. She lifted the intercom. "May I speak to Charles?"

"One moment, madame," the butler replied. Ann heard voices in the background; then her husband answered.

"Yes?"

"I need your help for a moment," Ann murmured sweetly. "I'm upstairs in my old room."

"I'll be right there." Charles excused himself from the family, then climbed the stairs wondering what his wife wanted. As he entered the room, he smelled the exotic perfume she always wore.

He heard the door close behind him but before he could turn, he felt Ann's arms reach around his waist.

"Hi." Ann's voice was breathless as her hands moved to his groin. "Thought I'd give you your birthday present here."

Charles was mildly surprised to feel the warmth of her firm body pressed against his. Although they had once enjoyed an active sex life, the last few years she had seemed too busy. That was fine with him, since recently he had fallen in love with Kate.

Taking her hands in his own, he turned around to face her. "In your parents' house?" he chided, an amused grin on his face.

"Why not?"

He shrugged. "It seems so . . ."

"So what?" She stopped his words with a deep, passionate kiss. Her arms went around his neck, imprisoning him in her softness, her fragrance, her need.

After a moment, he drew back, hoping to discourage her. "Ann . . ."

"Come to the window." She pulled at him, refusing to let him speak. "I want to show you what I bought you."

He let himself be dragged toward the open drapes. Below he saw the terraced gardens rolling down to the Olympic-sized pool and tennis courts beyond. The grounds were lighted and a robin's-egg-blue Corniche convertible, a huge white bow on its hood, was parked in front of the net on the court. Seeing the Rolls Royce below, he exhaled loudly. He looked into her eyes for the catch. All he saw was desire. "It's beautiful, I . . ."

"Good. Now, I'll tell you how you can please me . . ." She gave him a determined look. "Lock the door."

Charles wavered. There was no question he wanted his new toy. It had to have cost over two hundred thousand dollars. Yet he and Kate had become so close lately. She expected fidelity and he had given her the impression that he and Ann didn't have sex anymore.

Gazing at his elegant and sophisticated wife, he recognized the raw lust burning in her eyes. Even after all these years, the fact that she was a *Manning* still acted as an aphrodisiac. Kate will never know, he assured himself. He strode to the door to lock it. When he turned, Ann was taking off her clothes.

He admired his wife's body as she stood there in her expensive satin undergarments and spiked heels. She sat down on the bed and lifted one leg high in the air, trying to unbuckle her ankle strap.

"Let me help you." Crossing the room, he put his hand on her shoe, feeling the silk underneath his fingers, but she shook him off, reminding him that she liked to be the one in control, at least at the beginning.

He let go, watching while she slowly peeled her stocking from one leg and kicked off her shoe. Then she started on the other leg in its gossamer covering. He felt himself beginning to stir.

Charles wasn't quite sure whether it was the new car outside or the thought of her jealous brother downstairs that caused him to harden. Good old Dickson, he mused. He never believed I was good enough to marry a Manning. Those reflections added to the anticipation and tension mounting within him. By the time Ann had her stockings off, all thoughts of Kate were submerged.

Ann reached out to unbutton Charles's shirt, her skillful hands stroking his hairy chest, tangling, pulling, teasing. She undid his belt, peeled down his trousers, which dropped to the floor, then took his swollen member into her mouth. "I don't think your parents would approve," he whispered.

Cupping his balls with her hands, Ann scooted off the bed and dropped to her haunches. "Shush, come down here," she ordered, her voice husky.

He fell to his knees and reached for her breasts, still encased in a flimsy satin bra. Unhooking it, he put one nipple into his mouth, biting the tip hard.

"Oh," she moaned, ripping off her panties.

An involuntary groan escaped his lips as she maneuvered herself expertly onto him, moving her hips slowly, suggestively at first. He ran his hands roughly up her spine while she kissed his neck, his chest, then his lips.

In one quick movement he rolled her over so he was on top.

"Fuck me," she whispered fiercely, opening her legs wide, her hands tangled in his thick hair. He slammed himself into her as hard as he could.

"Fuck me, fuck me hard with your big cock," she cried. "Ram it in, all the way in."

The crudeness of her words in sharp contrast to her lady-like appearance never failed to arouse him. It was so different from the tenderness he experienced with Kate. Ann's raw sexuality brought out the animal in him. He pummeled her with his body, thrusting into her again and again.

Ann groaned under him, fine beads of sweat breaking out on her forehead as she writhed back and forth, impaled by him. Finally, he felt her body arch. "Oh, yes, yes . . . ," she whispered. After a few moments, her frenzied movements stopped.

He heard her try to catch her breath. Only then did he allow himself to plunge into her with utter abandon, finally exploding, the intensity and depth of his own orgasm taking him by surprise.

Dickson peered at his wife, seated next to him. Meek and mousy Alana, with her drab brown hair and gray eyes. He wondered how he had ever been even remotely attracted to her.

He glanced at his mother, Irene Manning, sitting at one end of the table with his father opposite her. Her pale blond hair, touched heavily with gray now, was pulled back in a severe chignon. Her skin was covered in fine lines, and her neck had folds of crepelike skin. Dickson wondered if Ann, who looked so much like their mother, would age the same way.

His thoughts were interrupted as Charles and Ann hurried into the room, looking a bit disheveled.

"Sorry, Ann wanted to show me my present," said Charles.

Dickson looked at his sister, questioning, but she refused to meet his gaze. Charles, on the other hand, flashed him a smug smile. Immediately Dickson knew what had happened, and glanced quickly at the others to see if they had caught on.

The patrician face of his mother, smiling indulgently at his blushing sister and brother-in-law, together with the beaming approval he saw cross his father's face, angered Dickson. It's always Charles and Ann, he thought angrily. He reached for his glass of wine, drinking much of it in one gulp.

While the butler poured the ice water and more wine, Franklin spoke. "What did you think of Banning & Banning's merger last week with Spencer, Dyer & Fremont?"

"Smart move," said Dickson. "Big firms are the future. Smaller firms like ours won't be able to compete."

"If you get too big, you lose contact with your clients," said Charles. "I'd rather farm out the work to other law firms when it's not our specialty."

"That's old-fashioned," asserted Dickson. "Firms that think like that will be gone."

Franklin held up his hand. "Now just a moment there, Dickson. Charles just voiced my sentiments exactly. And I don't consider myself old-fashioned."

"Out of step with the times would be more like it," countered Dickson. "Why farm out work when you can make the money and keep all the loyalty too?" He smiled to hide his chagrin because his father always seemed to side with Charles.

"Dickson is so convinced we need to merge," Charles disclosed, "that he has gone ahead and made overtures on our behalf to the New York firm of Livingstone & Kenter."

"What?" Franklin scowled at his son.

Dickson hadn't expected Charles to be so direct. Now he had to defuse the situation. "*I* haven't made the overtures, Father. But I've been contacted by Paul Kenter of that firm. We met at a seminar last year. He's very interested in a merger with us."

Franklin shook his head. "I don't respect the attorneys

79

there. They steal clients from other firms. Their kind give the whole profession a bad name.''

"It's not 'stealing,' " protested Dickson. "We're in a new age of marketing. A firm that can't keep its own clients deserves to lose them.''

"Lawyering used to be a gentlemanly profession," said Franklin. "We respected each other. Our word to another attorney was written in stone. I don't like what's happening today.'' He sipped his water. "What do you think, Charles?''

"I agree. I like it better when we have more personal contact with our clients.'' Charles smiled. "Besides, when firms merge, they recapitalize and the partners end up with huge personal debts.'' He gestured with his hand. "Do you know what they call five hundred lawyers at the bottom of the sea?''

"No," said Franklin.

"A beginning.''

Franklin laughed heartily, then wiped his eyes.

Dickson was less than amused.

"Father, I'd at least think you'd agree to a meeting. We've nothing to lose by hearing what they have to say.''

"I'm not interested," countered Franklin. "My mind is made up. I don't want you to go any further with this.''

Dickson fumed but tried not to show it. He would just have to work to change his father's mind, and if not, well, he'd get his merger another way.

"Soon," said Franklin, "we'll be making our new partner selection, and we have four good candidates.''

Charles nodded. "Too bad we only have one opening.''

"Who do you think it should be?" asked Franklin.

"Kate Alexander.'' Charles spoke without a moment's hesitation.

"No way," Dickson interjected. "Kate's too aggressive. Our first female partner should be more ladylike.''

"You wouldn't call a man too aggressive," insisted Charles. "Kate's a damn good lawyer.''

Franklin turned to Dickson. "Who do you want?''

"Owen Forrest. The man's extremely capable.''

"If we don't pick a woman partner this time," warned Charles, "the firm's image will suffer."

"I doubt it." Dickson leaned back. "Owen's got three kids and a wife to support. Kate and Lauren aren't even married."

"That shouldn't be a consideration," argued Charles.

"I agree," said Franklin.

The two of them are shutting me out again, thought Dickson. He gazed at Ann, hoping she would support him. His normally outspoken sister had not uttered a word. Ann's face was rigid. He wondered what was wrong.

"Let's leave the firm's politics until after dinner," the older man suggested. "After all, it's Charles's birthday." He ate a mouthful of poached salmon, then dabbed at his mouth with his linen napkin. "I hope you're all planning to come to Palm Springs next weekend?"

"Of course," his son replied quickly.

Charles shook his head. "I'm sorry, Franklin, I can't. I've got problems with Suni Industries' takeover. The government has brought an antitrust suit."

Franklin frowned lightly at him. "The problems will all be there when you return. Besides, lately it seems that you're always working."

"You warned me from the beginning that being a lawyer was not an eight-to-five job."

Ass-kisser, Dickson thought. Didn't Charles ever turn it off?

Driving home at the wheel of the new Rolls, Charles knew he should be feeling happy at the way Franklin had squashed Dickson's merger plans. Instead, he was apprehensive. His wife had been unusually silent all evening. He wondered if she had registered the car to him, but he doubted it. Ann balked at putting things in his name. "Thanks for the car, Ann."

"You're welcome."

He felt the coldness below the surface of her words. A quick glance at her profile told him she was angry. "Something wrong?"

"Perhaps."

"Want to talk about it?"

"Not really." Then, apparently changing her mind, she blurted out, "Charles, you can't fool me. You're seeing Kate Alexander. I won't have it. If you don't stop, it'll be the end of our marriage."

He was stunned by his wife's words, glad that the car was dark so that she couldn't see his face. So Kate had been right: Ann did know. Or was she merely guessing? Part of him felt relieved it was finally out in the open, but at a deeper level a warning bell sounded. A momentary fear ate at his gut. "Ann, where did you get such a crazy idea?"

"Don't lie to me!" She turned in her seat to glare at him. "I mean it, Charles. I've put up with your little indiscretions over the years. I knew they were meaningless. But this time it's different. I refuse to let that woman's ambition ruin my life."

Charles knew she was right. This time it was different; this time he was in love. "Ann, you're being ridiculous." He tried to soothe her, but she was beyond reason, encased in an icy, unapproachable fury. His mind raced. Who had told her?

"If you persist, you'll end up with nothing."

"Ann, be reasonable." Then, in a kidding tone, he added, "Did I act like a wandering husband back at your parents'?"

"What's your answer?"

Damn! He had no intention of being forced into a divorce before he was ready. He reached out to pat her hand. "I'm only interested in Kate as a good lawyer with political and partnership potential. You're getting upset about nothing." He stopped the car and tried to take his wife in his arms.

She stiffened, then pulled back from his grasp, wrapping her fur coat firmly around her. "I'm going to go to Palm Springs. I'll come back with my parents after next weekend. I'll expect your decision when I return."

8

At the Parker Center police headquarters in downtown Los Angeles, Detective Bower wrote down the message as fast as he could. It was at least the fiftieth he had taken since the D'Arcy murder. But years on the force had taught him how to pick out the real anonymous tips from the quacks. Something about this call alerted him. This sounded real. Holding his hand over the mouthpiece, he called to another detective.

"Larry, sst!" He got the cop's attention, pointed to the phone, miming the words "Trace it," then went back to writing. Somehow he needed to keep the caller on the phone. "Excuse me," he said as politely as possible, "my pencil broke. Can you repeat that last sentence?"

The caller shouted, "Fuck!" into the phone and hung up.

Bower jerked from the pain in his ear. "Fuck *you!*" he cursed into the dead receiver.

Larry ran up to him. "No luck, caller hung up too fast."

"Tell me about it." Bower rubbed his ear. "But thanks anyway." He picked up some papers and went in search of Donaldson. He was pissed. The chances of finding out who the caller was were nil. "Hey, Ed, want you to check something out."

The younger officer rocked back in his metal chair as if daring it to fall, a white Styrofoam coffee cup in one hand. "Have a doughnut," Donaldson offered.

"Thanks." Bower picked at several before choosing a large jelly one. "So much for my diet today," he said as he stuffed it into his mouth. Shit, he thought, even good guys need a vice.

"What's up?" asked his partner.

Bower finished the doughnut in one gulp and licked his fingers. "Just got an anonymous call on D'Arcy. Could put a whole new twist on the case."

Donaldson looked up at Bower with interest. "What they say?"

Bower hitched up his pants and refastened his belt around his spreading middle, knowing he had to do something about the weight he was gaining. He read from his notes: " 'Check out Tommy Bartholomew on Sawyer Street in Northridge. He and Sandra D'Arcy were fucking around. He's your killer.' "

Donaldson's intense blue eyes flashed with excitement. "We should have a chat with this character."

"Let's check him out first. Run a D.M.V. on him. With a name and address it oughta be a cinch."

The butler opened the door at Abigail's house. Theo moved inside and said as casually as he could manage, "I need some papers from the library for Charles Rieman." As soon as the words were out of his mouth, he wondered why he felt he had to defend his actions.

"Of course." The butler nodded. "Should I tell your mother you're here?"

"No . . . not yet Arthur."

Inside the massive room, Theo allowed himself the luxury of sitting in his father's deep leather chair. As he remembered his inability to communicate with his father, a feeling of sadness welled over him.

His hands trembling, he took the key he had removed from James's desk and fitted it into the lock. Theo had never been given his own key to their father's desk. He had looked everywhere else, and he couldn't find what he was looking for. This was his last chance.

Theo felt like an intruder. At any moment someone was sure to stop him. The self-confidence he had set out with a few hours earlier was quickly waning. He touched his father's ornate jade letter opener and a spare pair of reading glasses in a brown alligator case. How well he remembered these things.

In the back of the drawer he was surprised to find a picture of him and James as young children, their hands held by Abigail and his father. "You never loved me," he said bitterly to the smiling man in the black-and-white photograph.

As his eyes fell on his brother, the bile rose in Theo's throat. James had delighted in belittling and insulting the younger Theo, from the time they were children right up to the night of the gala party and the next day when he refused Theo's calls.

His palms were sweaty as he methodically started to go through the papers in the desk. "Damn, where the hell could James have put it?" he mumbled out loud.

After the desk, he searched the entire room, book by book, drawer by drawer.

An hour later, frustrated and upset, Theo told the butler he wanted to see his mother.

As he was being ushered into Abigail's rooms, his stomach clenched in anticipation. Why did he always feel this way? Like a small child about to be criticized. Would it ever change? The two most important people in the world to her, his father and his brother, were now dead. No, that's not true, he reminded himself, there's her grandson. Jimmy will get whatever love Abigail has left.

He went over to the bed, where she lifted her face for his dutiful kiss. "Hello, Mother." He brushed his lips against her dry cheek. "How are you feeling?"

"Fine," she said, her head held at a haughty angle.

"Mother, I know this is a hard time for you . . . for all of us, but I need to ask you something." He hesitated, aware that he was trembling. "Did James leave any papers with you before his death?" he blurted out.

"What kind of papers?" Her dark eyes were questioning.

"James talked about making a new will and revoking his prenuptial."

"My God, why would he do that?"

"Because of Jimmy. Said it was time to treat Sandra like a real wife. Anyway, I've looked everywhere. And according to Dickson, there's no record of it at his office . . ."

"Well, I do not have it." She paused. "Do you think he gave it to Sandra?" She looked worried for the first time.

He shook his head. "She would have said something by now."

"Theo," she said sternly, in the manner she had often used to admonish him, "if you find any such documents, you are to bring them to me. Immediately. Do you understand?"

He flinched at the tone of voice she used toward him. "Of course, Mother."

"I mean it, Theo," she warned. "I want nothing changed with regard to Sandra. As for a new will, James would not have done that without consulting me first."

"Consulting you?"

"Of course," she said, her manner dismissing the relevancy of his question.

A few minutes later Theo dialed Dickson from his car. "I can't find it anywhere."

"Shit!" said Dickson.

Immediately after Theo left, Abigail called Charles. "Do you know anything about James drafting a new will or revoking his prenuptial agreement?"

"Where did you get that idea?" he asked, sounding surprised.

"Theo claims James told him he was preparing a new will and revoking his contract with Sandra."

"Did Theo have any documents?"

"No."

"Then I wouldn't worry about it, Abigail. Theo always hoped James would change his mind about letting him run the Foundation, but James never discussed it with me. As for revoking his prenuptial agreement, I can't imagine James would be so foolish."

Abigail sighed. "Thank God. Charles, if you find any such papers, I want your promise you will bring them to me first. I want no one else to see them."

He hesitated.

"Charles," she said firmly, "I must have your word."

"Of course," he replied at last.

* * *

When Bower and Donaldson arrived for yet another visit with Sandra D'Arcy, she looked less than overjoyed to see them. Her fair blond hair fell loosely around her face and Bower noted again that despite her lousy personality, she was quite a looker. "May we come in, ma'am?" he asked.

"If I say no, I don't suppose you'll go away."

"I'm afraid you're right." Bower tried to make it sound like a joke as he smiled at her, but she didn't respond other than to step aside, allowing them to enter. She pointed to the big, comfortable den down the hall and followed them in. The two policemen took chairs facing the couch on which she perched.

"What is it this time?" she asked.

"We were wondering if you by any chance had a gun," Bower inquired. He saw Sandra's face immediately register surprise.

"Why do you want to know?"

"Customary procedure."

Her eyes became wary. "I have one."

"Can we see it?"

"If you want."

"Please," said Bower. He stood up to indicate the sooner the better.

She took the hint and led the way. "What's this all about?"

"We need to check it out," he said. "You ever take it anywhere with you?"

"No," she snapped. "It's never left this house since the day I bought it."

The two officers followed Sandra up the curving staircase to the landing and then through a pair of massive double oak doors. The plush carpet sank under Bower's feet as they entered a large, pastel-colored bedroom suite. He gazed around quickly at the ornate furnishings and fancy bedspread. Probably cost more than I make in a year, he thought.

"It's over here." Sandra impatiently opened a drawer in an antique armoire, shoving her hand into the folds of garments. A look of panic spread across her face as she felt around more quickly, then began dumping the garments onto the floor. "It's gone!" she exclaimed, sitting down on the bed, her mouth open.

"Gone?" said Bower, one eyebrow raised as he and Donaldson exchanged glances.

"I don't understand, I always kept it here." She seemed stunned. Her voice was soft, almost childlike as her cocky manner suddenly dissolved.

"Who else knew about the gun?" Bower asked.

"Just my husband and me."

"When did you get it?"

"Sometime in January."

"This the only gun you owned?"

"Yes. My husband wanted me to get one after we had a break-in."

"When was that?"

"Sometime around July of last year. We came home late one day and the back door was open. Some video equipment, cameras, and a TV were gone. They had messed up the bedroom, but nothing much else was touched."

"You report the break-in?"

"Of course." She rose from the bed and seemed to re-assert herself. "The police sent an officer out to make a report, but so far I haven't heard if any of the things have been found."

"Did they question your housekeeper?"

"Yes. She was sure she locked the door and put on the alarm."

"I see."

"My husband was afraid someone might break in while Jimmy and I were home alone. That's why he wanted me to get a gun and learn how to use it."

"Let's see," said Bower. "The break-in happens sometime in July of last year and your husband tells you to buy a gun. That right so far?"

"Yes."

"But you wait to buy the gun until January of this year, right?"

"That's what I said."

Bower counted on his fingers. "You wait a full six months *after* the break-in to buy the gun?" He couldn't keep the skepticism out of his voice.

For a moment she seemed flustered. "I guess so. Yeah."

"Ma'am, why did you wait so long to buy the gun?"

"I . . . I don't remember. I just didn't get around to it before that. That's all."

Bower looked at Donaldson and then back to Sandra. Her hands were on her hips and he could see she was once again in control. "He go with you to buy it?"

"No, but he wrote down the kind of gun he wanted me to buy and where I should get it."

"You remember where that was?"

"Campbell's or Kimberley's, something like that, a sporting goods store somewhere in Hollywood."

"Your husband own any other guns?"

"Maybe, but he didn't keep any here. You'd have to ask over at his office. Could be one there."

Bower made a mental note to check that out. It hadn't shown up on the gun registration records. "Could any of your help have taken the gun?"

"Maria's the only one I let come in my bedroom. She wouldn't touch my things."

"Ask her anyway, please."

Acting as if they were imposing on her, Sandra turned abruptly and headed downstairs toward the kitchen, where once again speaking in Spanish, she questioned Maria. The maid shook her head.

"Let's go back into the den," suggested Bower. When they were seated, he cleared his throat. "You said your husband wanted you to learn how to use the gun?"

"Yes."

"Did you?"

"The man at the gun shop showed me some things and said I should go to a target range."

"You do that?"

"No."

"Your husband know you didn't go to the target range?"

Sandra seemed to bristle at Bower's intimation that she

had not followed instructions. "He was angry about it, but I just didn't want to. So what?"

Bower wrote some notes in his little black book. "Mrs. D'Arcy, we're still looking for a late model white Mustang with license number NKB something. The neighbor's cook saw a white Mustang parked in your driveway a few days before your husband's death."

"So?"

Bower had had just about enough of this young woman's attitude. She carried on as if she didn't give a damn. "Mrs. D'Arcy, I suggest you search your memory to the best of your ability. We're talking about a car that coulda been driven by the person who killed your husband."

"I don't know what kind of car everyone drives."

Bower almost shouted at her: "This is a serious matter, young lady, and if you don't want to answer our questions, we can arrange a trip to headquarters."

She gave him a long, calculating look. "A friend from exercise class drove me home one day. I know the car was white, but I'm not sure what year or make. It could have been a Mustang, I guess." She shrugged.

"The friend's name?" asked Bower, taking out his notepad.

"I don't . . ." She caught the angry look on Bower's face. "Oh, what the hell. His name's Tommy, but I don't know why he'd drive up here late at night. Besides, there must be thousands of white cars in Los Angeles."

"I'm sure there are," said Donaldson. "What's this Tommy's last name?"

"I'm not sure."

"Get your coat," said Bower. "We're taking you in."

"I think it's Bartholomew," she answered sullenly, her eyes challenging Bower.

"You know where he lives?" asked Bower.

"No."

Bower glared at her, wondering if she was lying and if he should come down hard on her again. He decided against it for the moment. "I'd like the name and phone number of your exercise place."

"I'll go get it."

As soon as Sandra left the room, Bower spoke. "Snippy little bitch, isn't she?" he whispered.

Donaldson shook his blond head. "I think she's just young and scared."

"You young cops all think with your cocks," replied Bower, looking grim.

The minute the cops were out the door, Sandra called Tommy. She got the damn machine again. "Call me," she said, and hung up. Where the hell was he now?

Desperate to hear from him, she had finally called her exercise teacher this morning because she didn't know what else to do. "Tommy hasn't been here in days," he had said. Shit.

9

"**I**'ll have these contracts ready by tomorrow afternoon," said Lauren Cunningham confidently.

Arnold Mindell, the partner at Manning & Anderson in charge of real estate, and Lauren's boss, sat back in his leather chair, a look of dissatisfaction on his face. "Too late. I need them in the morning."

Lauren gazed at him. Despite a few unnecessary pounds, he wasn't a fat man. The extra weight merely added fullness to his handsome features, giving his eyes a slight puffy look many thought sexy. She forced herself to be pleasant. "You've just given them to me."

"Can't be helped." He shrugged. "Guess you'll have to burn some midnight oil."

Lauren felt a white-hot flash of anger, but her lovely face remained impassive as she thrust out her chest. In a pink cashmere dress, she was the essence of femininity. She had often been told that she bore a striking resemblance to a young Rita Hayworth, and usually her sultry looks could ensnare any man she chose. This man, however, was totally impervious to her charms.

Christ, this will be the fourth time in two weeks he's forced me to work late. He's ruining my love life, she thought. She hated him. Once Lauren had overheard Arnold telling another partner that she was unwilling to put in more than an eight-to-five day. And why should she? However, with her chance for partnership coming up soon, she had no choice but to do as he asked.

"You'll have them." Her voice was satin smooth. Only the loss of color in her face betrayed her anger.

"Knew I could count on you," he smirked.

You bastard, she thought. You have me right where you want me. Someday I'll even the score. Holding her head high, she left his fancy corner office with its priceless antiques. She passed the plush offices of the other partners and turned down a long, carpeted hallway.

"Lauren, come on in," called Kate.

"For a second."

"How's it going?"

"Oh, busy as usual. I'm working on the most *interesting* case." She'd be damned if she would give Kate any reason to feel superior.

Kate's phone rang. "I'll only be a minute," she whispered, holding her hand over the mouthpiece.

Lauren nodded. Glancing around Kate's office, she saw the same basic furniture as in her own but in another color scheme. The only real differences were in the accessories, plants, and pictures each lawyer added trying to make the office assume more of his or her own personality. Kate had decorated hers in white, black, and mauve and placed a multitude of beautiful plants, all sizes and shapes, around the room. On her desk was a bouquet of fresh-cut flowers.

It wasn't until associates made partner—if they ever did,

that is, thought Lauren, that their offices became clearly distinguishable from one another. Then, with a healthy budget allocated for decorating, each office began to reflect more clearly the individuality and taste of its occupant.

Because Kate was the only associate at Manning & Anderson who headed her own department, her office was on the floor with the other partners', a situation Lauren did not like at all. With Charles Rieman's backing for the partnership, Kate was in an enviable position, especially if Rieman got the nod from Franklin Manning when he retired.

No, Lauren's only real hope was that Dickson had enough support to prevail when the time came to select a successor. Dickson hated Charles, and Kate had once confided to Lauren that Dickson seemed to dislike her. Lauren thought for a moment. Perhaps she could somehow convince Dickson that she was the perfect choice to become Manning & Anderson's next partner. Couldn't hurt to try.

"Sorry." Kate put the phone down. "I'm getting so many calls about James D'Arcy. You getting a lot too?"

"Oh, yes." Lauren was not about to admit that clients rarely called her. Keeping her isolated and subservient was part of Arnold's perverse punishment for her father's influence in procuring her job for her. "I suppose the rumors that are circulating about James's death have Charles freaked out?"

"He's upset."

Lauren saw the wary look in Kate's eye. Boy, does she ever protect her mentor, she thought. "James was also worth a lot of money in fees to this firm!"

"I'm sure the D'Arcy family will continue to use us."

"One never knows," said Lauren, pleased when she saw Kate frown. "I better get back to my office—I have another rush job for Arnold. I'll see you."

Leaving Kate's office, Lauren continued along the corridor to the end, where an imposing Lucite and brass stairway took her to the lower level. Then, striding hurriedly down another interminable hallway, she finally reached her own office. She hated where they had put her. She felt like a stepchild.

She slammed the door behind her, at last able to vent her pent-up fury. "I could fucking kill Arnold and Kate both," she swore under her breath as she threw the case files down on her sofa. "Bitch, fucking bastard," she muttered.

"I appreciate your support," said Dickson, dabbing at the sides of his thinning blond hair as if to make sure he hadn't lost any more since the last time he looked.

"You can count on me," replied Arnold Mindell. He stood up to leave.

After Mindell left his office, Dickson felt good for the first time in days. He had explained his position fully and was pleased to see that Arnold agreed with him that they should seriously consider a merger with a New York firm. Arnold also said he favored him in the senior partnership selection. Having someone of Arnold's stature on his side would convince other partners to support him too.

Dickson was aware that some of Manning & Anderson's partners deferred to him merely because they believed that in the long run, family blood would prove to be the deciding factor for Franklin Manning in selecting his successor. Thank heavens his father had never relinquished the majority partnership shares in the law firm. Dickson was going to need every advantage he could get in order to outwit and outmaneuver that damnable brother-in-law of his.

If Charles didn't watch out, he would find himself muscled out of the law firm. A self-satisfied smile played around Dickson's mouth. He intended to show Charles just who he was messing with.

Dickson swiveled around in his chair as he planned his strategy. What he really needed was to find some way to lower his father's opinion of Charles. He'd have to keep a closer watch on Charles. Something was bound to surface.

"What's up?" asked Bower as Donaldson rushed up to him.

"The D.M.V. check on Tommy Bartholomew shows an address in Northridge. I also ran him through the computer. He has one prior. Obtaining property under false pretenses."

"Oh?"

"Yeah. Seems he cheated some lady out of her money."

Bower's eyes lighted up. "Very interesting."

"That's not all," said Donaldson, a smirk on his face.

"What else have you got?"

"Tommy Bartholomew's license plate has an NKB in it and he drives a white, late-model Mustang."

Bower jolted forward so fast he spilled some coffee on his pants. "You gotta be kidding?"

"Nope." Donaldson raised his eyebrows at his partner. "I suppose it's time to go have a nice little talk with this guy, don'tcha think?"

"Let's go," said Bower, already halfway out the door.

Thirty minutes later Bower rang the bell at Tommy Bartholomew's address. He had to ring several times before it was finally answered.

"Who's there?"

"Police, open up."

The door was unlocked and then opened to disclose a good-looking man in his early twenties. He had light-colored hair that some might describe as dirty blond, falling forward onto his forehead. The kid's eyes were brown and deep-set and there was a mournful, almost brooding look to him. "You Tommy Bartholomew?" Bower asked.

"Yep."

Donaldson flashed his badge. "Can we come in?"

"Suit yourself." Tommy stood back and with one hand swung open the screen door of his seedy apartment. In his other hand was a lighted cigarette.

Inside, Bower saw that the room was barely furnished. He asked to see Tommy's driver's license. Tommy went over to the table in the corner, got his wallet, and came back. He handed his license to them.

Donaldson wrote down the information while Bower continued to ask questions. "What kinda car you drive?"

"Mustang."

"License number?"

"Four five three NKB." Tommy scratched his chin nervously. "Hey. What's this about?"

"We have a report of a car similar to yours being involved in a traffic incident on Monday night."

"I wasn't in any accident."

"Where were you on Monday evening between six P.M. and midnight?" asked Bower, ignoring his statement.

"Home. I'd gone to a bar up the street where I sometimes hang out. Got there about four. Had a few beers and got sick. Someone brought me home and I was here all the rest of the time."

An unlikely story, thought Bower. "Got anybody to vouch for you?"

"What for?"

"Just answer the question," said Donaldson.

"Didn't see anyone I knew except the bartender."

"What's the name of the place?" asked Bower.

Tommy told him the name of the bar and its location.

"Who brought you home?"

"Let's see . . . his name coulda been Vincent. Never saw him before. I fell asleep and when I woke up, I was sick as a dog with a lousy headache. Kept throwing up, so I knew it was the flu. Been sleeping on and off ever since."

"Can we look around?"

"Well, uh, I'm not sure." Tommy seemed to hesitate as he crushed out his cigarette. "What're you looking for anyway? I don't do drugs."

"Just want to see the condition of the place," explained Bower. "Verify your story."

Tommy shook his head. "Hey, I don't think so."

"Fine," said Bower, deciding to get tough. He gave Donaldson a signal.

"We'll be back with a search warrant," promised Donaldson, puffing out his chest. "And don't blame us if we make a mess."

"A search warrant?" repeated Tommy, a look of fear suddenly in his eyes.

"Up to you," said Donaldson. "Why don't you make it

easy on yourself and sign this.'' He handed him a consent waiver to a search.

Kid's going to give, Bower thought as Tommy glanced at it. Most of them did. Sure enough, after gauging the seriousness on their faces, Tommy signed his name and then opened the door to the bedroom.

Bower went in with Donaldson and reeled from the stench. The room smelled of vomit. The bed was a mess and there were dirty clothes lying all over the floor.

Bower walked over to the pile of garments by the window. A pair of boots lay next to them. He lifted them up and noticed the mud at the bottom. ''When did you last wear these?''

''Monday evening.''

''Looks like mud. Where were you?''

''It's like I told you. I had a few beers and that's the last I remember.''

Casually, so as not to seem too eager, Bower asked, ''Can we take these? Like to run some tests.''

Tommy hesitated and Bower gave Donaldson a look that said, Show him how tough you are.

Donaldson straightened up to his full height and flexed his muscles.

''Suit yourself,'' said Tommy.

Bower couldn't believe his good luck. This kid could've easily said no and he wouldn't have been able to do a thing. By the time he could return with the warrant, the boots could be cleaned up. He began to look through some papers on the chipped wood desk. He saw a receipt from a 7-Eleven, a gas receipt from Union Oil, and some loose change along with two crushed one-dollar bills. Next to these was a folded piece of paper with some writing scribbled on it.

''Give that to me,'' said Tommy as Bower's fingers approached the paper.

Ignoring Tommy, Bower opened it: *Here is the money to take care of the problem, Love Sandra.*

Jackpot, Bower thought, immediately alert. ''What's this?''

"A note. From a friend."

"You know a woman by the name of Sandra D'Arcy?"
Bower watched the kid's face as it became wary.

"Why you wanna know?"

Donaldson reached over and gave Tommy a shove. "We
ask the questions, you do the answering."

Bower stepped in. He only wanted Donaldson to intimidate the kid a little. He didn't need trouble. "Look, this
could be serious. Be better for you if you cooperate.
But"—he spread out his hands—"if you don't want to,
then we'll take you down to headquarters and you can answer questions there."

Tommy glared at Donaldson, then he looked at Bower.
He seemed to be weighing his options. Finally, he shrugged
his shoulders. "What do you wanna know?"

Bower was relieved. The good cop, bad cop routine
worked more often than not. "You know a Sandra
D'Arcy?" he repeated.

"Yeah."

"Where'd you meet her?"

"Exercise class."

"Where? When?" Bower fired his questions rapidly.

"Class meets three times a week. Mondays, Wednes-
days, and Fridays. Two to three in the afternoon." Tommy
gave the name and location of the studio.

"You see the lady outside of class?"

"Maybe a few times."

"You two more than friends?"

Tommy's brown eyes narrowed into slits. "What's that
supposed to mean?"

Bower gave the kid a friendly smile. "You know. Were
the two of you having a thing?"

"We . . . we were friends." Tommy grabbed a pack of
cigarettes from the desk and quickly knocked one out. Then
he lighted it and inhaled deeply.

Bower did not drop his gaze. "You sleeping with her?"

Tommy hesitated and Bower gave Donaldson the look.

"The truth here and now or later downtown—which is it
going to be?" said Donaldson.

Holding his cigarette in his mouth, Tommy shoved his hands into the pockets of his torn Levi's. A strand of hair fell forward. "Yeah," he said. "So what?"

Bower ignored the kid's question. "What's the note mean?"

"She loaned me some money. For my rent."

"How much?"

"Two thousand bucks."

Bower peered skeptically around the shabby place. "And just how much is your rent here?"

"Two thousand."

Bower watched as Donaldson gave Tommy a look of disgust and said, "You better not be bullshitting us. What's the manager's apartment number?"

Tommy scowled. "So it's a little less."

"How much?" asked Bower, stepping in again.

"Around five hundred bucks. She wanted me to pay some bills too."

"Nice of her." Bower shifted his weight. "So what do you do?"

"Trying to be an actor. It's not easy, you know."

"Where you from?"

"Kansas."

"Family?"

"Yeah. A mother and sister in Kansas City. But I haven't seen them in a while."

"You go to high school there?"

"Yeah. Then I joined the army."

"Honorable discharge?" asked Bower.

Tommy shook his head. "Naw. Dishonorable. But it was a bum rap."

"And what rap was that?" said Bower, looking sympathetic.

"Booking bets and running a crap game. But I wasn't running it. I only told the guys where the game was. The army was looking for someone to blame."

"Rough," said Bower. "Ever been arrested?"

"Yeah."

99

"What for?"

"Some broad said I took her money."

"What happened?"

"It was a big mistake. All I did was try to help this broad invest her money. She gave it to me. Told me to do it. Then her friend shows up at my apartment, comes on to me, you know. I knew I shouldn't have boffed her. When the broad found out, she got mad. Yelled thief."

"You serve time?"

"Suspended sentence and probation."

"You still on probation?"

"Nope."

"You work?"

"Yeah. For a contractor. Study acting at night."

Bower reached into his coat pocket. "Listen, Bartholomew, it'd be better for you not to leave L.A. without checking with us."

Tommy looked at the card Bower handed him. "Sure."

The phone rang and Sandra D'Arcy ran to get it. "Tommy!" she blurted out when she recognized the voice on the other end. "I've been calling you for days."

"Why'd you tell the police about me?"

"I didn't. It seemed they already knew somehow."

"Then who told them?"

"I don't know. But they had your name. Were they there?"

"Yeah. They just left."

"What did you tell them?" she asked, feeling frightened.

"I went to a bar, had a few drinks, got sick, and some guy brought me home."

"Oh."

Tommy flipped on the news again as he dialed another number. The phone was picked up on the second ring. "This is Bartholomew. You've gotta give me more time to get the money. . . . I know. I know. But that woman I told you about has some shit going on. The cops are crawling all over the place. . . . Never mind. I swear I'll get it by the end of the week. . . . Yeah, she said she'd help me." He flushed. "Look, I'm not an idiot. I know I have to get the money to you. I just need some more time."

10

Sandra sat miserably in the back seat while the chauffeur, separated from his passengers by a windowed partition, drove the custom Rolls Royce limousine toward Abigail D'Arcy's mansion.

"You're drunk again," Victoria D'Arcy Mandeville said accusingly to the man seated next to her. Her red lips curled back over capped white teeth as she peered critically at her husband. "What's Mother going to think?"

Raymond glared at his wife with bloodshot eyes. He removed a silver flask from his inside pocket and took a swallow. "I don't give a fuck what your mother thinks," he said, wiping his mouth with his hand.

Sandra sat across from her sister-in-law and brother-in-law, her back to the driver. She hated to hear the two of them fight. Why couldn't she drive by herself? Victoria was so mistrustful of her. Did she suspect anything? She remembered what Victoria had shouted to James the first time they met: "You married the slut!" She couldn't afford to have Victoria find out about Tommy. Who knew what she'd do? A shiver ran up Sandra's spine.

God, she was dying for a cigarette, but she knew better than to smoke in their cars or their houses. Too bad there weren't the same restrictions on alcohol. The fumes from Raymond's breath were making her sick.

She knew that after the reading of James's will today,

she'd have some money of her own at last. Then she'd be able to do what she wanted for a change.

In another car, a white Mercedes 560 SEC, Dickson Manning drove while Theo D'Arcy sat in the passenger seat. Dickson was dressed in an impeccably tailored navy-blue suit. His manicured hands rested lightly on the wheel as he guided the car with ease through the many turns in the road. "Don't worry," he advised.

"I'm trying not to." Theo was glad Dickson had picked him up; he needed all the support he could get right now. His finely chiseled face was set in a grim expression. The contents of his brother's will hadn't been out of his thoughts since James's death. His brother *had* to have changed it. He'd promised.

In the spacious second floor suite of rooms she occupied, Abigail D'Arcy sat in front of her dressing table in her wheelchair. Since the death of her husband she rarely left her suite, although she had been confined to a wheelchair for years before his death. James's funeral was one of the few occasions for which Abigail had ventured out of her house in the last ten years.

She gave a final check to her makeup and patted a wave of her flawlessly groomed silver hair. I cannot believe James is gone, she thought as she touched her earrings to make sure they were safely secured. She felt so lonely. The diamonds at her ears and throat glittered in sharp contrast to the severe black of her elegantly simple wool dress.

One son left now. There was no question that she loved Theo, but he was not James. The only one who made this entire situation bearable was her grandson. From the look of things, he would be the only grandchild she would have. Theo did not show any signs of getting married. And since Victoria and Raymond had been married for over twenty years, she had given up hoping for children from them as well.

Abigail rang for the butler to take her down in the elevator. She would do a better job with her grandson.

*   *   *

Kate followed the butler through the immense entry with its gleaming chandelier, mesmerized again by the priceless paintings hanging on every wall. Ushered into the D'Arcy dining room, she saw that everyone was gathered around a huge marble table over which hung an exquisite Tiffany fixture.

Her glance swept the faces. All of them seemed to be looking right through her as if she didn't exist, except for Charles, who sat at the head of the table. He smiled in welcome as Kate gratefully sank into the remaining chair.

She sensed the hostility in the room. Although it was obviously not directed at her, it made the hairs at the back of her neck prickle. Kate knew that lawyers seldom did formal will readings anymore. The more common practice was to hand out copies of the will for people to read themselves, and then they could ask questions of the lawyer. However, Charles had told her that Abigail wanted to observe tradition.

"Now that Miss Alexander is here, we can get started." Charles cleared his throat and began to speak. Everyone, including Kate, gave him their immediate attention.

"Let me first convey my deepest sympathies from all the lawyers and staff at Manning & Anderson. Franklin Manning is unfortunately at home ill today, but he has also asked me to express his heartfelt sorrow over this tragedy."

Kate watched Charles closely, aware of how quickly he could take command of a room and receive the respect of those in it. In fact, she often thought the man possessed an amazing ability to win people over.

"We're all grieved by the passing of James," continued Charles. "He was my closest friend as well as my client and I'm going to miss him terribly."

"Thank you, Charles." Abigail's voice was firm. "On behalf of my family"—she gestured toward Victoria and then Theo—"we appreciate what everyone at Manning & Anderson has done to help us through this difficult time."

"You're very welcome," said Dickson, jumping in to accept the thanks before Charles could acknowledge it.

"No need to thank us," Charles murmured. He took a crystal glass from the tray next to him. After a few sips, he opened a manila folder in front of him, from which he removed a long white envelope. Tearing its large flap, he withdrew a sheaf of papers and began to read solemnly.

As Charles's voice droned on through the important clauses, Kate watched the faces of the others.

Abigail sat very still, her dark eyes fastened on Charles, her hands folded together in her lap. Victoria watched her husband with an expression Kate could swear was filled with loathing. Raymond, on the other hand, cracked his knuckles and fidgeted like a child unable to sit still. Dickson also appeared nervous. His right eye twitched as Kate had seen it do before when he was upset. Theo was white-lipped and looked tense.

Charles stopped to clear his throat again, flipped the page, then went on, his voice resounding with its usual confidence.

Kate listened as the prenuptial agreement between James and Sandra was referenced and Sandra was left five million dollars in trust. The income was payable right away and the capital in two years. While five million was quite a fortune, it was small compared to the value of the D'Arcy holdings. Charles had indicated that James had been worth well over a billion dollars.

" 'In addition to this,' " read Charles, " 'she is to have the full use and benefit of the real property and residence.' "

While Charles read the legal description, Sandra played with her fingernails. Every now and then she dabbed at her eyes with a handful of tissues.

Watching the young widow, Kate couldn't help but wonder if her tears were genuine. Something made her doubt that the beautiful girl had truly loved her husband. In any case, her husband's death had certainly made her a very rich young widow.

As Charles continued, Kate became aware of the looks now being exchanged between Dickson and Theo. A darkening cloud seemed to mar Theo's thin face as he began to squirm restlessly in his chair. Dickson's eye twitched even more.

The palpable tension in the room increased as she listened to Charles, appointed to act as executor and then trustee over James's estate, including his shares of stock, until his child, James D'Arcy, Jr., turned twenty-five. Kate knew that the shares represented the majority interest in the D'Arcy Company. It was clear that Theo was furious over the designation of Charles as trustee. But Charles had told her that James had also made him trustee in all his previous wills. For that reason alone, it certainly shouldn't have been a total surprise to anyone here today.

The next section of the will indicated that it was James's wish that Charles, as executor and then trustee of his estate, head the D'Arcy Company and Foundation. Kate saw Theo blanch. Only in the event of Charles's death or inability to serve was Theo D'Arcy to succeed him.

Charles finally came to the end of the document. "This will is signed James D'Arcy, dated and witnessed by three people at the law firm of Manning & Anderson, on the thirty-first day of January of last year."

Theo stood, his anger apparent, and abruptly bolted from the room.

Abigail stiffened. "I think you had better see what's the matter, Charles," she suggested in a calm voice.

"I'll go too," offered Dickson.

Charles, along with Dickson, followed Theo into the library. "What's wrong?" he asked after he had closed the door behind them.

"He told me he changed it!" Theo's brown eyes filled with pain.

"What do you mean?"

"James was supposed to change his will to name Theo trustee of his estate so that Theo could be head of the Foundation," said Dickson, answering for Theo.

Charles glanced at Theo. "Can you remember *when* he discussed this with you?"

"We talked a few times," responded Theo, his voice so low Charles had to lean closer to hear it.

"Can you be more specific? What exactly did he say?"

"That if something happened to him, I should be the one to take over—"

Dickson interrupted. "Didn't James also tell you, Theo, that it was taken care of?"

"Is that true?" Charles asked Theo.

"Yes. A few days before his death, he said he had taken care of it."

Charles shook his head. "He never said a word to me." From Dickson's expression, Charles could clearly see that Dickson didn't believe him, but Charles ignored his partner. He didn't really care what this man chose to believe. "Did you check the computer inventory at the office, Dickson? There's always the possibility that James gave the document to someone else in the firm. Maybe Franklin?"

"I thought of that already," said Dickson. "I couldn't find anything."

"Then I don't see how there could be a new will." Charles hesitated. "That is, unless . . . Did James mention anything to you, Theo, about using another law firm?"

Theo's questioning eyes turned to Dickson. "Do you think that's possible?"

"Doubtful, but I'll check on it."

"Make the inquiries discreet," cautioned Charles. "I don't want anyone thinking James lost confidence in us."

"I know what to do, thank you."

"Now what happens?" asked Theo.

"I'm afraid if we can't find a new document signed by James, there's nothing *we* can do. His last will, the one I just read, is controlling."

"But that wouldn't be fair." Theo looked agitated. "He clearly wanted to change it. He told me so."

"That may very well be, but my hands are tied." Although he didn't want to, Charles had to turn to Dickson for support. "Explain the law to him, Dickson."

"It's too soon to make any assumptions," countered Dickson quickly. His face was grim as he moved away from

Charles and closer to Theo. "Theo will have to consider all his alternatives. Then we'll see."

"See what?" Charles couldn't believe his ears.

"Whether or not we're going to challenge that damn will," stated Dickson.

Charles stared coldly at his brother-in-law. It was hard for him to hide his contempt. "On what grounds, might I ask?"

"You'll see when you're served," advised Dickson smugly.

Charles felt like smashing Dickson in the teeth, but he knew he should try to preserve peace. "Look, Theo, your mother is quite upset. For her sake, you must go back in there. This has all been too much for her. Then we'll meet," he suggested, "and we'll discuss this whole thing like rational human beings."

Theo suddenly seemed to snap. "I can't pretend anymore! My brother never accepted me. I thought he had changed his mind, but it's obvious he didn't. He's still trying to control me, to fucking change me, and this time from his grave." Theo clenched his fists. "It's more than I can take."

"And more than you have to," said Dickson, with a nasty glance at Charles, as he accompanied the younger man from the room.

Bower and Donaldson listened politely to Robert Aimsley, a renowned criminalist for the Los Angeles police crime lab as well as many others throughout the country. He was telling them about the characteristics of the spent bullet extracted from James D'Arcy's head.

"We can determine with microscopic certainty that a bullet has been fired from one and only one weapon. Every gun except a shotgun or other smooth-bore barrel has had rifling machined into the barrel to make the bullet's path truer. These lands and grooves mark the bullet as it passes through the barrel."

Bower smiled to himself as the expert rattled on. The man was a frustrated teacher; he loved to explain things.

"Are you sure now what kinda gun was used, from the bullet removed from D'Arcy?" asked Donaldson eagerly.

Aimsley nodded. "I would say it's confirmed. The bullet was fired from a .22 Ruger semiautomatic pistol."

"We thought so. The wife had a gun like that. Now we have to find it," said Bower. He reached into a bag and produced another gun. "We just retrieved this from the victim's office. It's not a Ruger, but test it anyway."

"Sure." Aimsley reached for the weapon. "But it's not the gun."

"Fine. But I wanna see if it was fired recently. I can't figure why a man like D'Arcy had a gun that wasn't registered." Bower exhaled loudly.

"I'll get on it right away," said Aimsley.

Bower looked glum. "Without the murder weapon, we've got a weak case. We need some other evidence."

"Were there any casings found at the scene or another bullet that perhaps missed the victim?" As Aimsley asked the question, he simultaneously opened the report and began to flip through it.

Bower shook his head. "Only one shot fired. The killer musta picked up the one casing."

Aimsley scratched his beard and closed the report. "I would say then there's a strong probability that the person pulling the trigger knew what they were doing."

"Yeah, we already figured that."

"You think the wife shot him from behind?" asked Aimsley.

"We don't think she pulled the trigger. What we're thinking is a conspiracy of some kind." Bower paused. "Next thing. We made an impression of a footprint we found near the scene. Who's workin' on that?"

"I believe it's Holmes across the hall."

"Great. Appreciate your help." Bower shook Aimsley's hand.

"No problem. Let me know if there's anything else."

As the two officers walked down the hall, Donaldson asked his partner, "What do you think?"

"Whenever a case has gotta rely on a forensics guy, I get

worried. It's hard to get a jury to understand how each weapon marks its bullets in a unique way."

They entered the doorway and Bower asked for Holmes. When they were told he was out to lunch, they left word for him to call. In the hallway again, they headed for the elevator.

"I think the footprint is gonna be the key," said Donaldson. "The gardener says he watered about four P.M. That means the footprint could only've been made between then and the time D'Arcy was shot."

"I think you're right. In the meantime, I wanna find the wife's gun. If it's the murder weapon, it's the answer to proving a conspiracy. Get some men and search the area again," said Bower. "And get fliers out to the people in the neighborhood. Maybe we'll get lucky and catch ourselves a rich young widow."

11

Standing at the helm of the sleek Italian Baglietto, Kate thrilled at the feeling of power that pulsated beneath her. From the vantage point of the fly bridge she saw the sunlight sparkling on the water as the sixty-five-foot yacht cut through the waves, leaving behind it a large wake. The boat was going fast, wind whipping at her hair and face. She breathed in the sea air, closing her eyes momentarily.

She gazed over at Charles, his lean, muscled body clad in tennis shorts and shirt, stretched out on the white Naugahyde cushions. The breeze ruffled his salt-and-pepper hair. He looks well dressed even asleep, she reflected.

As if sensing her stare, he opened his dark eyes beneath

which slight shadows betrayed a lack of sleep. "You're very good at the helm."

"I'm good at a lot of things," she responded, her eyes fastened on the blue and gray water in front of them.

"Believe me, I know." He chuckled. "That's one of the reasons I'm so exhausted!" He looked at her. "You know, Kate, someday you're going to make one hell of a luscious-looking governor," he teased. "But if you ever change your mind about the line of work you want, you'd also make one hell of a delicious-looking boat captain."

"Thanks. But why not a luscious-looking president or a delicious-looking admiral?" she kidded back.

"If that's what you really want, it's yours. Remember, I'm the kingmaker."

She smiled mischievously. "Don't you really mean to call yourself the queenmaker?"

He threw his head back laughing and she smiled too.

"We're almost there." Charles came to stand behind her. Putting his hands under her top, he reached up to her shoulders and nuzzled her neck. His hands gently moved down to cup her breasts and rub her nipples lightly. Through the thin, silky fabric of her swimsuit, she felt him harden against her.

A shiver of excitement shot through Kate. "If you keep this up, I'm going to forget everything you taught me today."

"Don't pay any attention to me, I'm just copping a feel."

"And driving me crazy."

"There's Ship's Rock." He pointed to a huge formation jutting up out of the water. "Better let me take over now."

Kate stepped aside while he skillfully slowed the boat down and shifted into neutral.

"We have to wait for the harbormaster," explained Charles. Then his hand gestured in a wide circle. "But this is it—welcome to the Isthmus at Catalina."

He had warned her not to expect a lush green island. Instead, she saw rolling hills, wheat-colored grass, and palm trees he told her had been brought to the island many years before for the filming of the movie *Hurricane*. Other than a few structures, the land looked untouched to Kate, probably one of the last places in California unspoiled by progress. She sighed and breathed in the magnificently clean air. "It's so peaceful."

"It is. You're going to love it."

"I'm going to love being with you."

His dark eyes met hers and they both smiled.

Fifteen minutes later Kate saw that they were securely fastened on his mooring, H-5. She was amazed by the way Charles sprinted around as he prepared the boat to become a floating condo. She was used to seeing him under different circumstances—at the office, where he delegated authority and wielded power with ease, or at political functions, where there was no doubt that he was a politician by nature as he charmed and cajoled people into doing what he wanted. And then there were the business meetings, where his charisma disarmed his opponents. But here in Catalina he seemed younger, if that was possible, and even more vibrant.

As Charles barked out orders and she scuttled back and forth to follow his directions, she smiled at this side of him she had not seen before. Finally satisfied, he turned off the powerful engines. It was almost eerie, she thought, the way they were instantly engulfed by the silence.

Charles picked up his sunglasses and towel. "Come on," he said. "Cocktail hour."

Kate laughed. "It's only two o'clock in the afternoon."

"In boating, as soon as the engines are off, it's that time." He grinned. He reached into the refrigerator, found a bottle of Raymond Chardonnay, opened it and poured them each a glass. "To us."

"*Salud.*" She lifted her glass to clink with his.

"Come here." His voice was gruff as he pulled her eagerly to him. He kissed her deeply.

Kate suddenly felt as though it were their first time—she was all nerves and need. Her breath was soft and shuddering.

With aching slowness, he began to undo the strap and hook of her bikini top, then let it fall to the deck. Her breasts stood full and firm, the darkness of her nipples pushing against the diaphanous fabric.

"I want you so much," he whispered into her ear.

Even though the heat of her desire immediately suffused her body, she sensed they were in full view of other boats. And without realizing it, she pulled away.

He looked down into her eyes. As if reading her hesitancy, he expertly lifted her into his arms. Her head rested against his chest as he carried her below.

Kate awakened in the dark. She heard the lines creak as the boat swayed gently on its mooring. The small gold clock next to the bedside read 7:40 P.M. and she realized they had slept for hours. Grabbing Charles's robe, she drew it around her and went up to the main salon, where she saw the lights of the other vessels. There were quite a number of boats there, yet it was so quiet. She gazed ashore at the dim outline of hills and campfires on the beach, completely transfixed by the splendor.

For the first time in a long while, Kate felt at peace, as if an emptiness deep inside her had been filled. She relished the tranquillity. Soon, she thought, I'll have everything I've always dreamed of.

"It's beautiful, isn't it?" Charles came into the salon, a towel wrapped around his lower body and his hair tousled from sleep.

"I don't remember ever being so happy," she murmured.

"I'm glad." His eyes drifted over her body, enveloped in his robe. "You look sexy, even though it's too big for you. I'm going to picture you this way at our next associates' meeting."

"Oh you." Kate pushed against him, laughing.

He grabbed her and hugged her to him. "Hungry?"

"Starved."

He turned on some switches and a second later she heard the soft purr of the generator as the lights came on. Then he fastened his robe tighter around her; its roughness scratched against her skin. "Come, I'll show you the galley. The steaks are defrosting. You'll find the fixings for a salad in the refrigerator."

Kate smiled to herself: I might very well be the future

governor of California, but he still expects me to make dinner. "I hope you plan to help me." Her tone was light, but firm.

"Of course—I'll get the barbecue started," he stammered, appearing slightly embarrassed.

The assumption on Charles's part that she would be the one to make the dinner bothered her. She had seen her mother become a slave to her stepfather. That wasn't for her. A relationship had to be equal. Nonetheless, she set about the chore of rinsing and slicing the lettuce and other vegetables.

When she took the salad topside, she saw he had set the table to face the water. Votive candles flickered in the night air and smoke rose from the barbecue grill in the fishing cockpit.

After they sat down to eat, Kate found she was really ravenous. The inky blackness of the water mesmerized her as she stared out at the moorings. "I haven't wanted to say anything before this," she said quietly. "I mean, the last two weeks have been hell. But with James dead, what do you think is going to happen with my candidacy?"

"We convince others to back you. James was, of course, the best there was. But there are others who can help. As for James's contribution, I'll see that the company honors his wishes; however, we need many others. Right now I'm loaded down with extra work. It may be a little longer than I had originally planned before we can officially declare you in the race."

"Well, I'm going ahead with all of my speaking engagements. I'm also going to continue to court the women's political organizations in the city. I've got some momentum going and I think it would be a mistake to slow down now."

"Absolutely."

She decided that now was as good a time as any to confront him with the other important issue on her mind. Clearing her throat, she asked, "And us, Charles? What about us?"

She heard the sharp intake of his breath.

"Kate, I'm planning to talk to Ann about a divorce." He

paused, "But you must understand, it's very complicated."

"Charles, I told you at the beginning, I was not going to be the other woman in a triangle."

"I know, but James's death has turned things upside down. Not only the extra work, but because I can't leave Ann until I am picked as the next senior partner." He turned to look at her, his hands on her shoulders. "I'm sure Franklin thinks I'm the best man for the job, but I can't count on his support if I divorce his daughter. He has a blind spot where she's concerned.

"And there's Dickson. Do you have any idea how much trouble he can cause us? I must be in a position where he can't hurt us. There are many things to consider, Kate. I've told you before, Ann's a rich woman with separate funds from before we were married. We both enjoy the interest benefits, but the capital is hers. So things have to be right for me before I can leave."

"I don't need a lot of money," insisted Kate. "I was born poor and I've worked my whole life and I'll always work. I'm making more money now than I ever dreamed I'd make."

He nodded. For a moment he was silent. "We forget so fast."

She reached for his face, her hand brushing his cheek. "It'll be just the two of us, Charles. Your son and daughter are already in college, and I don't want children. It wouldn't be fair to them. A career in politics is an all-consuming endeavor. We shouldn't need a lot of money, but if we do, so we'll both just work harder."

He pulled his chair over to her and hugged her warmly. "It still has to be the right time for me. There are also the problems with Dickson and Theo. They're talking about a full-scale challenge to James's will."

"I don't care . . ."

Charles put a finger over her lips. "Kate"—his voice was gruff—"please give me some time. First things first." His tone dropped. "Trust me. I don't intend to lose you."

Kate sighed. "I'll try to be patient. But I can't promise for how long."

* * *

Once again, Bower and Donaldson found themselves at Sandra D'Arcy's door.

"We saw Tommy," Bower explained after they were led into the living room. "He said you two were having an affair. You wanna tell us about it?"

"So I was sleeping with him. What difference does it make?" Sandra's challenging question hung in the air as she gazed defiantly into the policeman's eyes. She was obviously expecting this. She walked over to the coffee table, picked up a cigarette, and lighted it.

Bower put on his no-emotion face and asked dryly, "Were you planning on leaving your husband?"

"No. Tommy asked me to," she said, tilting her head proudly. "But I told him I couldn't because of Jimmy."

"What did he say to that?"

"He didn't like it, but there was nothing he could do." Sandra brushed back a wisp of blond hair that had slipped out of her ponytail.

"When was the last time you saw Tommy?"

She inhaled and blew out the smoke. "I already told you."

"Refresh my memory," said Bower.

"Five days before my husband was killed. He brought me home from class."

"Right," said Bower. He took a piece of paper out of his pocket and handed it to her. "You recognize this note?"

Sandra glanced at the paper. "Yeah."

"Would you tell us what it means?"

"I loaned Tommy some money for his rent."

"How much?"

"Five hundred dollars."

Bower and Donaldson exchanged glances. Bartholomew said it was two thousand bucks, recalled Bower. He wondered which one of them was lying—unless, of course, they both were.

As if realizing she needed to explain things further, Sandra went on: "Tommy told me to leave the money with his manager. So I put the note in an envelope with the cash and gave it to her."

"Sure," said Bower. He took back the piece of paper, a copy of the original, folded it and stuffed it into his pocket. He walked to the window and stared out, stalling. Then he turned and looked at her directly. "You sure Tommy didn't know about your gun?"

Sandra bit her lip and twirled her wedding ring for a moment, looking down at her fingers. "Oh," she mumbled. "I did show it to him once. I forgot. I asked him to see if I was loading it correctly."

"Where'd you do this?"

"In my bedroom."

"Was he ever alone in there?"

She shook her head. "Never."

Bower quietly considered whether she was lying. He wasn't sure. "Thanks. Sorry to have bothered you," he said, making his way toward the door.

Lauren left the restaurant and handed her ticket to the valet parking attendant. When the man returned with her Jaguar, she slid in and immediately dialed her car telephone.

"Yes?" answered a strong male voice.

"Daddy, how far away are you?"

"Hello, darling," responded Miles Cunningham from thirty thousand feet up in his private jet. There was obvious pleasure in the man's voice at the sound of his only child. "We're over Las Vegas. We should be there in thirty minutes. You coming to the airport?"

"Of course!" exclaimed Lauren. "I can't wait to see you."

"Me too," he boomed.

Lauren hung up the phone and headed toward the San Diego Freeway. She was excited at the prospect of seeing her father, and even more excited at the prospect of using his power and influence to enable her to triumph over Kate.

Across the water from Catalina in Rancho Mirage, ten miles outside of Palm Springs, Ann Rieman closed the door to the den in her parents' beautiful house. She had just called her home and was furious to find that Charles had given their housekeeper, Mercedes, the weekend off. Damn, she swore. I gave Mercedes strict instructions to report to me on his every movement. How could she fall for something so transparent?

No one was answering Charles's private number at the office either. Although he said he often worked in the library and couldn't hear it ring, Ann's intuition told her that her husband was not there.

Ann opened her purse and searched for a piece of paper she had tucked into the back of her wallet. It was a number she had gotten from the computer at the office. When she dialed Kate Alexander's condominium, a machine answered and Ann quickly hung up. She took out her address book and dialed again.

"Harbormaster, Isthmus," boomed a male voice.

"This is Ann Rieman. Is Mr. Rieman's boat on his mooring this weekend?"

"Yes, it is, Mrs. Rieman. Do you want us to relay a message?"

"No. I'll call him through the Redondo Beach marine operator. Thanks anyway." She hung up, an icy fury gripping her: He's with that bitch and he'll be goddamned sorry.

12

Madeline Gould, having just ended an exhausting rape trial, headed back to her office in the Criminal Courts Building in downtown Los Angeles. As her high heels clicked on the linoleum floor of the hallway, a man sucking on an unlighted pipe came out of one of the offices toward her. Madeline saw that it was Philip White, chief deputy for the D.A.'s office.

Philip looked no different from every other conservatively dressed D.A. across the nation. He was of medium build and height, forty-two years old, with brown eyes and light brown hair parted on the side and thinning slightly on the top. Beyond appearances, however, he was known for being deadly on cross-examination and had a reputation as one of the most astute trial lawyers in the office.

"Hi, Philip," she said.

"Jury out?"

"Yeah. It looks like a long wait, so I decided to come back."

"Good, because there are some people here that want to talk to you." He took her arm and steered her toward the office of the district attorney himself, Ronald Miller.

Once inside, she recognized Detective Doug Bower standing by the window; they smiled at each other. The younger man sitting across from Ron Miller she had never met. She wondered what was going on. The D.A. seldom had time to meet with detectives.

"Madeline," said Miller, "I see you already know Detective Bower, and this is Detective Ed Donaldson. Donaldson, this is Deputy D.A. Madeline Gould."

"How do you do," said Madeline, holding out her hand.

"Pleased to meet you, Ms. Gould," responded Donaldson.

"These men have brought us the results of their investigation into the robbery-murder of James D'Arcy." He gestured at White. "Philip has indicated that you are the best choice for this high-profile murder case."

"Thank you," she said, her excitement beginning to mount. What a plum assignment this would be!

"Sit down." Miller motioned to Madeline and Philip. "Boys, why don't you fill in Ms. Gould on what you've been telling me? You can use my office—I have a meeting to attend."

"Thank you," said Bower as Miller stood up, grabbed his jacket, and went out the door.

Bower took the seat just vacated by Miller, cleared his throat, and began. "Almost from the beginning we suspected we were looking at more than a robbery-murder. Now that certain facts have become clear, we're virtually certain of it. Seems the victim's wife was having an affair with one Tommy Bartholomew, a would-be actor. Tip came from an anonymous phone call. The caller said, quote"— Bower read from his report—" 'Check out Tommy Bartholomew on Sawyer Street in Northridge. He and Sandra D'Arcy were fucking around. He's your killer.' " Bower put down his report and smiled apologetically at Madeline.

She held up her hands as if to say, I'm just one of the boys here. Aloud, she asked, "You get a trace on the call?"

"Tried, but the caller hung up before we could do anything."

"Go on, please."

"Right. Well, the two lovebirds supposedly met in an exercise class. Aimsley at the crime lab has ID'd the bullet removed from the victim's head as coming from a .22 Ruger semiautomatic pistol. Funny enough, Mrs. D'Arcy bought a gun, same make, only a month before the incident. She claims her husband told her to buy it after their home was burglarized. That part of her story checked out. They had a break-in. The interesting thing, though, is that the burglary took place in July of last year, but Mrs. D'Arcy waits six months before she buys the gun. By this time she's seeing Bartholomew. We asked to see the weapon. Mrs. D'Arcy took us upstairs. When she couldn't find it, she acted surprised." He cleared his throat.

"Did you ask her why it took her six months to get a gun?" asked Madeline.

Bower nodded. "First she says she can't remember. Then she says she just didn't get around to it before that."

She nodded and he went on. "A neighbor walking his dog around the time D'Arcy was shot noticed a white car, a late-model Mustang, speeding down the hill. He got a partial on the plate, NKB something. It was dark but he was

119

positive the driver was a Caucasian male and he was alone in the car. While we were running a D.M.V. check, we got the other call and ran a check on this Tommy fellow, too. Came up with a white Mustang, four five three NKB.''

Madeline looked at Philip knowingly as Bower continued.

"There's some additional information about Mrs. D'Arcy's conduct the night of the murder. I'll let you read that yourself in my report.''

"Fine. Go on, please.''

"By the way, both the widow and Bartholomew weren't exactly open about being acquainted, much less about the true nature of their relationship, if you know what I mean, until we got a little insistent. At first, she denied knowing anyone with a white Mustang, but when we told her one of the neighbor's servants''—he checked his report—''a cook at 2400 Rock Canyon Drive, Bel Air, had seen a car of that description parked in the D'Arcy driveway a few days before, she suddenly recalled a friend who drove a white car.''

He put his report down and continued: "Anyway, Bartholomew has no corroborated alibi for the night in question. Says he went to a bar, had a few drinks, got sick and was taken home by a stranger. Bartender isn't sure if he was in or not. No one remembers anyone getting sick and having to be driven home. There was a game on the tube during that time and the bar was real crowded. Bartholomew claims he wasn't drunk but got the flu and was wiped out for days. We checked his place. It was a real mess and smelled like shit.'' Bower grimaced at Madeline. "Sorry.''

"That's O.K., Detective, go on.''

"It was obvious he'd been sick.'' He shrugged. "But it could be killin' someone turned his stomach.''

Donaldson chuckled, obviously liking Bower's stab at humor.

"Anyhow, he didn't come across as telling the truth,'' finished Bower. "We asked for permission to search his apartment—''

"Did you get a consent waiver signed?'' interrupted Madeline, a frown across her brow.

"Yes, ma'am."

"Good."

"We found two things of interest in the bedroom. The first was a note." He handed it to her.

Madeline's eyebrows shot up as she read the contents of the note. Her mind raced. What a case this could be if the evidence bore out that D'Arcy was in fact killed by his wife and her lover. She leaned forward, eager to see what else they might have.

"Bartholomew claims she lent him some money for his rent and her story is the same. Problem is, their stories don't jibe on the amount. Two thousand bucks versus five hundred, cash. Maybe it's nothin'." He shrugged again. "On the other hand, why lie about small potatoes?"

"That is odd," agreed Madeline. "What's his rent?"

"Five hundred and a few bucks. Now"—Bower, pausing for dramatic effect, sat back with a satisfied look on his face—"we got the most critical piece of evidence linking Bartholomew to the crime."

Madeline waited anxiously.

"A footprint was discovered near where D'Arcy's body was found. According to the gardener, he'd watered that area only a few hours before. We checked and it wasn't the gardener's footprint." Bower seemed to be allowing the tension to build for a moment.

Madeline glanced at Philip.

"We just heard an hour ago from the lab. One of the boots we took from Bartholomew's apartment was a perfect match. And the sample of mud from the bottom of the boot matched a soil sample from the grounds of the D'Arcy estate where we found the footprint."

"Wonderful!" she almost shouted.

"Yeah, I thought so too." He grinned.

"So what else do we have on her?"

"Not so much direct evidence, I'm afraid. Mostly circumstantial and a lotta possibilities."

Madeline tried not to appear too disappointed. She would want to try them both if they had conspired to murder D'Arcy. "What are the chances he acted alone, without her?"

"Possible," said Bower. "But I dunno, I don't think he's all that bright."

"How about a motive?"

"According to D'Arcy's will, which was just filed with the probate court, she's quite a rich lady, even though there was a prenup . . ." He gestured with his hands. "You lawyers are much better than me at figuring out those kinda things."

"Did you bring me a copy of the will?"

"Sure did." He reached over and took a thick document from the file.

"Thanks," she said, skimming it briefly.

"We're still investigating. We'll keep you updated on any new developments."

"Fine. I'll look all this over"—she indicated the file they had brought with them—"and I'll want to speak to the crime lab, the medical examiner, and the rest of them."

"O.K.," Bower said.

"Then we'll get together and see if we have enough for an arrest on Bartholomew." Madeline chewed on her pencil. "Perhaps he can be convinced to implicate her?"

"Who knows. Anyway, we don't wanna scare either one off."

"True. Arrest him and she'll have a high-powered lawyer so fast it won't even be funny."

"That's what we figured. We pushed only enough not to cause 'em to panic."

"Good." She appeared pensive for a moment. "Could I see the original robbery report?"

"Sure." Bower handed it to her.

Madeline glanced at it. "It says here that money, a watch, and a ring were taken. I don't suppose the jewelry has shown up?"

"No such luck," said Bower. "Didn't see any evidence of the dough at Bartholomew's either."

"All right." Madeline began to put the papers in order. "It looks like you did a thorough job. Thanks for your hard work." She smiled at them and held out her hand. "I'll be calling you in a few days, if not sooner."

After the two policemen left, Madeline turned to Philip. "Thank you. This could be the trial of the decade if the guy pleads not guilty." She gave a grateful squeeze to the arm of the man who had been her mentor.

"You deserve it," he said proudly. "Ron and I both wanted someone who wouldn't be intimidated by the prominence of the victim, or the voracious media."

She saw a funny look on his face. It didn't seem bosslike. Others in the office had more than once pointed out to Madeline that Philip White was crazy about her, but Madeline insisted it was a purely platonic relationship. In the romance department, she had her sights set on someone else.

"I'll want the widow, too," Madeline stated firmly.

"I knew you would." Philip laughed. "I'm going to lighten your case load so you can spend more time on the D'Arcy case."

"That's great, Philip. I owe you about a thousand and one!"

"But who's counting?" he said good naturedly. He knocked his unlighted pipe against the palm of his hand. "Madeline, you are more than worthy of this challenge."

"I appreciate the vote of confidence."

"Want to have a drink at Clem's to celebrate?"

"Oh Philip, I'd love too, but I can't." She glanced quickly at her watch. "I have two hungry mouths at home to feed."

He smiled. "Another time then."

Madeline drove home filled with excitement. A murder trial involving a celebrated family such as the D'Arcys would be a media sensation. It was the kind of case she had dreamed about. It could give her the voter recognition she would need to run for D.A.

As she exited the freeway at Woodman in Sherman Oaks, her mind raced. It would be hard to raise the necessary capital to launch a competitive race without political connections. This case could help to give her the publicity she needed but couldn't possibly afford to garner on her own. Then she'd have a fair chance against Kate, if they both ended up running.

She glanced at the briefcase on the seat next to her. It would take the weekend to finish her paperwork, and afterward she would have the time to devote to the D'Arcy matter.

Pulling into the driveway of the rambling ranch house she had shared for fifteen years with her husband, Sam, now her ex, Madeline felt a sense of pride. It had been an ordinary tract dwelling, completely bare, with no landscaping, fixtures, or hardware when they bought it, and Madeline had spent several years planting the flowers that were now in full bloom. She had also handpicked the lovely antiques that were mixed in with the overstuffed, comfortable furniture in the cheerful country French interiors. They had had some wonderful times together in this house, she reminisced, as she opened the garage door with her remote control.

When she walked into the kitchen, her ten-year-old son raced to greet her.

"Hi, Mom."

"Hi, Kenny." She gave him a hug. The deafening sound of music blared through the house. "I've got to get Jud to turn that down." She gazed at the dog wagging its tail at the back door. "Did you feed Miranda?"

"I was just going to do it," said Kenny.

She smiled and headed down the hall. She opened the door to her older son's room. "Please, Jud, turn that down. It's going to make you deaf."

"Oh Mom," protested the freckled, fourteen-year-old boy who was lying on his bed reading.

She stooped to kiss the top of his dark head. "Dinner will be in an hour."

"Dad called," said Jud. "He's going out of town for a week."

"Does that mean he's not taking you boys for the weekend?" Madeline tried to hide her disappointment. She needed time to work, and Saturday evening she had a date with Gary.

"Yeah," he said.

Leave it to my ex-husband to fuck things up, she thought.

*   *   *

"To the most beautiful woman at Morton's tonight." Miles Cunningham's voice was rich and full as he looked at his daughter with obvious adoration. "I like that black and red dress. Armani?"

"Yes."

"Looks great on you."

"Thank you, Daddy." Lauren took a sip of her Kir Royale and glanced around at the celebrity-filled eatery. Although her father had been greeted by name and they had been led to one of the best tables, she was depressed. As she gazed back at her daddy, pride swelled her heart. He was still such a handsome man at sixty-three, she thought. She knew from photographs that his silver-blond hair was as full now as it had been thirty-three years ago when she was born.

"Something's bothering my baby, I can tell," he said, scanning her face.

"I'm sorry. I've been really upset lately."

"That's why I've flown all this way. Unload yourself and let's see if we can't fix it." He reached across the table for her hand.

Lauren considered what he had said for a moment. "It's the damn partnership selection. I can't seem to think of anything else."

"A lady shouldn't swear, Lauren."

"Sorry, Daddy."

"You know, Lauren, I wasn't happy about your becoming a lawyer." He gestured to stop her from speaking. "Let me finish, gal. It wasn't that I minded you getting a little education. But I didn't want you becoming one of those feminist women that march around and say bad things about men. The kind that don't want to stay home and have children. Lauren, baby, it's important for a woman to do womanly things."

Lauren sighed. He was about to launch into his usual dissertation on womanhood and Texas. Ordinarily, she would have shushed him up, even if it made him angry. But she needed him to fight for her. She had to have his help.

All of a sudden, she knew how to get around him. She

reached for his hand and looked into his eyes. "Daddy, I wasn't ready to tell you this yet, but I'm dating a wonderful man, and . . ." She forced herself to blush. "I think he may be the one."

"Baby, why didn't you tell me? What's his name? When can I meet him?"

"Whoa there. I said it looked good," she drawled. "I feel it in my heart. He's a lawyer and he's gorgeous." She rolled her eyes and he laughed. "You'll meet him, the next time you're here, I promise. But this time, we must concentrate on the partnership for me."

"Nothing to worry about there," he said confidently. "It's sure to be you." He smiled and his eyes crinkled at the corners. "I'm meeting with Franklin tomorrow like I promised."

Lauren shook her head. "It's more complicated than that. There are four of us, Kate and me along with two male associates. But everybody is sure the next partnership will go to a woman. So it's me against her. And it would be humiliating if I lost to her. I just couldn't stand it."

"She's no competition for my daughter," he said bluntly. "I've already told you that."

"I wish it were true." Lauren searched her father's eyes for understanding. "Kate's the only lawyer at Manning & Anderson who heads a department and isn't a partner. Charles Rieman, the partner who deals with all the political shi—" She caught herself. "All the political stuff as well as mergers and acquisitions—"

"I know Charlie," Miles interrupted. "So what's the problem?"

"He's championing Kate, while Arnold Mindell, my boss, hates me. Arnold's told several of the other partners that I'm difficult, that I refuse to work overtime, and all sorts of other lies."

"How dare he!" Miles's brow furrowed. "I'll speak to Franklin about him also. We have all the connections." He patted his daughter's hand. "I'm sure Franklin will be amenable to my suggestions. I'm also planning to discuss the entire senior partnership matter with him."

Her face showed her surprise. "You are?"

"Certainly. After all, I give Manning & Anderson a good deal of my business. I have a right to say what I think. I admit Charlie Rieman is probably one of the best lawyers around. And he's absolutely brilliant at political maneuvering. But a man should support his own son to take his place, and I plan to tell Franklin that. Then I'll bring you up. The way I see it, if Dickson is chosen over Charles, we'll have an easier time getting you picked over Kate, don't you think?"

"That's complicated too. With James D'Arcy's death, Charles is in a powerful position with the D'Arcy family's business. If he isn't made senior partner, he could very well leave Manning & Anderson and take the fees with him."

"No way, darling." He shook his silver mane. "The Manning and D'Arcy families go way back. Franklin Manning and William D'Arcy were best buddies. No matter how much Abigail might respect Charles, he's not from the same background. She wouldn't allow the business to leave Manning & Anderson with him."

Her eyes brightened. "I should have thought of that. Oh, Daddy, thank you. I already feel better." Lauren took another sip of her drink, thrilled with the knowledge that he would do his best for her, she could count on that. She only hoped it was enough. Just in case, maybe it was time she had a little talk with Dickson.

"What about the gal you said you wanted me to give some political support to?"

"Let me tell you about her." For the next fifteen minutes Lauren told her father all about Madeline.

"She sounds interesting, but I don't know how concerned I am with a D.A. race."

"Please, Daddy, it's really important to me. I'm sure you can find some angle to make it worth your while."

He fingered his chin. "Well, you never know, today's D.A. could be tomorrow's governor or senator. Couldn't hurt to have her in my pocket. Tell you what, next time I'm here, arrange a meeting."

"Thanks. You won't be sorry."

She felt so much better. If only her parents lived in California, life would be so much more exciting. She hated Texas, especially the chauvinistic attitude of most Texan men. Yet she sorely missed the recognition and deference afforded her family there.

"Would you like another drink?" asked the waiter.

"Please," said Lauren, handing him her empty glass. Now that her daddy was here, things were definitely looking up. In fact, she could feel her spirits lifting by the minute.

Charles was upset as he parked in the driveway at Sandra D'Arcy's home. How dare she not tell him sooner that the police had been questioning her. God only knew what she had told them. As soon as they were in James's study with the door closed, he faced her. "Why didn't you tell me before that the police were here?" he demanded sharply.

"I didn't think it was that important." Sandra shrugged. She looked like a teenager dressed in jeans and a black knit sweater, her pale blond hair combed back in a ponytail. Detracting from the youthful effect, however, was the ever-present cigarette.

"Not important? When did you get your law degree? And put that damn thing out. I can't stand it."

"I may not be a lawyer, Charles, but I'm not stupid." Her blue eyes blazed fire at him as she crushed her cigarette out on a paperweight.

Charles grimaced when he saw how she was using James's valuable Steuben glass paperweight.

"I only called you because I thought you should know. If you're going to be so horrible about it, forget it."

"That's great!" he shouted. "The police are questioning some guy you were fooling around with and I should forget it. Sandra, if you know something about James's death you're not telling me . . ." He let his threat hang in the air.

"I didn't say anything—"

"Cut the crap," he interrupted. "This is me, Charlie Rieman, not some stupid cop you're talking to."

Sandra seemed startled by his unexpected outburst as he waved his arm at her. She took a step backward.

"If you hadn't been worried, you wouldn't have called me," said Charles. "So why don't you stop acting shocked and start answering my questions?"

"What do you want to know?" she asked, pouting.

"How long were you seeing this guy? What's his name?"

"Tommy Bartholomew, and it was a few months."

"Did anyone else know about your affair?"

"I'm not sure."

"Well think, damn it."

"Don't shout at me." Sandra glared at him, her hands on her hips. "Some people in my class might have suspected."

"Does this guy have many friends?"

"No, not really. He hasn't lived here that long."

"What does he do?"

"He works for a construction company while he's studying to be an actor."

"Just what this world needs, another fucking actor." Charles rolled his eyes. "Where was this aspiring thespian the night of James's death?"

"I don't know."

"You don't know," he mocked, his dark eyes indignant.

She lifted her chin in the air. "He told me he went to a bar, had some drinks, got sick, and went home."

He ignored her explanation. "O.K. What else do you know about him?"

"He has a mother and one sister back in Kansas City and he's been in the army."

"So let me get this straight. You meet this complete stranger in an exercise class, a construction worker with no friends, no family here, and yet you had all this trust in him?"

"Well . . . yes."

"For all you know, the guy could have been Jack the Ripper. Did you talk to him the day of James's death?"

"No. I hadn't talked to him for about five days."

"Why not?"

"He was pressuring me to leave James. I broke it off." She twisted her wedding ring.

"What made you decide playtime was over?"

"My son."

"How noble," he said. "How did Bartholomew take the news?"

"He was upset. Said he'd get me to change my mind."

His eyes lighted up. "Did that include killing your husband?"

"Charles," she stammered, "that's ridiculous."

"I'll tell you what's ridiculous." He pointed his finger at her. "James married you, gave you his name, a beautiful home and all the trimmings, not to mention a place in society, and you repaid him by taking up with a two-bit hustler."

"You're not going to make me feel guilty," she insisted. "I'm not ashamed of what I did."

"Well, maybe you should," he snapped. "Did it ever dawn on you that this man could have had something to do with James's death?"

"No, of course not." Her eyes widened with fear.

"Do you have any idea how your situation might have looked to someone like him?"

"I'm not sure what you mean."

"Don't you realize your husband was one of the wealthiest men in the country? That makes you and your kid a target."

"It wasn't like that," she protested. He had finally gotten to her. Tears filled her eyes.

"We'll see, Sandra. We'll just see." Charles paced the room, shaking his head as he cracked his knuckles. After a full minute of silence, he turned and stood in front of her. "Did you have anything at all to do with James's death?"

"No."

He appraised her critically. "I hope for your sake you're telling me the truth."

"I am," she said hotly.

"O.K." He threw his shoulders back. "This is how it's going to be. From now on, you're not to speak to the police without me or another lawyer present. If they contact you, tell them you're represented by counsel. Understand?"

"I have nothing to hide!"

"You do as I say or I won't be responsible for what happens to you!"

She glared at him sullenly and bit on her lip.

"And you are not to speak to Tommy."

"I just need to see him for a few minutes—"

"No!" he almost shouted before she could finish her sentence. "This is serious, Sandra. You either follow my instructions or . . ." He gestured. "I won't give a damn what happens to you," he warned, his dark eyes piercing her. "Do you understand?"

"Yes!" she yelled back.

But from the way she angrily shoved her hands into her pockets, he wasn't so sure.

13

Philip White stuck his head into Madeline's office. "What do you think so far?"

She took off her reading glasses and glanced up. "Looks good against Tommy Bartholomew. He had the opportunity, no alibi, and the means, if he used Sandra D'Arcy's gun. His motive was money whether he committed the murder with her or because she told him it was over and he wanted to hold on to her *and* all that money."

Philip ambled into the office and sat in a chair facing her desk. "The *corpus delicti* of a crime."

Madeline rubbed her eyes as if she was tired. "It's Sandra I'm having a problem with. I've gone over the will and the prenuptial agreement. According to the terms, she ended up with the same thing whether she divorced D'Arcy or he died. So if she wanted the money, why didn't she just divorce him?"

"Perhaps she didn't think he'd let her go."

"Come on, Philip, this is California, no-fault divorce, remember?" She smiled at her boss, who loved to play devil's advocate. "He couldn't have stopped her."

"Maybe not, but he could've made it difficult. It's possible she wasn't too sophisticated."

"This prenup says she had independent legal counsel who advised her of her rights before she signed." Madeline pointed to one of the documents on her desk.

"Doesn't mean a whole lot," Philip said, hitting his unlighted pipe against his hand and putting it back between his teeth.

"What we have against her isn't all that strong," continued Madeline. "An affair isn't enough. But we have the note regarding the money, and one of them is lying about the amount. Plus we know she purchased a gun that most likely was the murder weapon, very close to the time of the murder. And we have her saying that even though she bought the gun because of a burglary, she waited six months to make the purchase. She wasn't seeing Bartholomew at the time of the burglary, but *was* seeing him at the time of the purchase." She struck the pile of documents.

Philip smiled. "Not bad."

"Yeah, but it's mostly circumstantial. Philip, my gut tells me she did it. The first thing I learned as a deputy D.A. was to check out the family of the victim. More often than not, it's one of them. An inheritance is usually a good motive."

His clear brown eyes focused on her. "Right. What else?"

"I've got a rap sheet on Tommy Bartholomew." She put on her glasses and read from some papers. "It says he got one year for obtaining property under false pretenses." Madeline gazed at him. "Apparently he separated a woman from her money. To read this, it sounds like he whined and cried every time he was questioned."

"What was the kid's story?"

"That the woman gave him the money to invest. Then, when he screwed a friend of hers and she found out, she yelled thief. At the sentencing hearing, Bartholomew pleaded with the judge not to put him in jail. He was worried that because he was so good-looking he might get raped.'' Her eyebrows arched for emphasis.

Philip laughed. ''What'd he get?''

''Suspended sentence and probation.'' She shook her head. ''But here's my problem. I don't get the sense of a cold-blooded killer here. I don't see him doing something like this.'' She chewed on her pencil. ''Not unless someone else did a good job of talking him into it.''

''The most benign person can be a killer under the right circumstances,'' said Philip.

Madeline shrugged. ''What if D'Arcy's death happened the way it looked? A random robbery, guy got scared and pulled the trigger?''

''That's always a possibility.''

''Yeah.'' She twirled her pencil around. Then, rummaging through some papers, she found what she was looking for. ''Bower said they found a receipt for a bottle of champagne from Bob's Liquor Store in D'Arcy's car. Yet D'Arcy had a fully stocked wine cellar with dozens of cases of imported champagne. Including this kind. And''—she looked up at him—''the owner of the store who was on duty that day couldn't ID James D'Arcy's picture.''

''Wasn't there a rash of people followed home and robbed in the hillside areas recently?'' asked Philip.

''Yeah. It's been going on for several years. Most of the time, people stop at a market or a liquor store and from there the robber follows them home. But most of them don't involve murder, although the robbers usually carry guns.''

''So then maybe it happened like you said. A follow-home robbery and the person got spooked. Who knows, D'Arcy was an important man. He could've told the robber he'd have his balls for this. So the guy gets scared and kills him.''

In spite of herself, Madeline laughed.

''Did the police show Tommy's picture to the liquor store clerk?'' he asked.

Madeline nodded. ''He didn't recognize him either.''

''I see.'' Philip sucked on his pipe.

"Oh, by the way, Bower talked to James D'Arcy's brother, Theo. He may contest the will. Said his brother promised to change it right before he died and that it sounded to him like the new document had already been drafted. The will that was filed with the probate court by Charles Rieman of Manning & Anderson was dated over a year ago."

"Bower check with Charles Rieman?"

"Yes. He handled all of the D'Arcy Company and D'Arcy Foundation matters. He was also D'Arcy's personal lawyer. James never mentioned changing his will to him."

"Hmm," he said. "But the brother thought it was changed?"

"Yeah."

"Maybe the brother wanted to get rid of D'Arcy?"

"That entered my mind," she said. "A contemplated inheritance could also be a motive. However, because of the footprint evidence, I'd say Tommy was our triggerman."

"But you don't think he was acting alone?"

"No. I'm sure there was someone else. I'd say the widow is the prime suspect at the moment as Tommy's accomplice. But don't rule out the brother. I've made a list of things for the police to investigate, including checking to see if there's any connection between Theo and Tommy. In the meantime, we've got to decide whether to risk arresting Tommy now—in which case the widow will get a lawyer and clam up—or wait a few days and see if she and Tommy contact each other."

"You've certainly got some hard decisions to make." Philip stood up to leave. "I trust you'll make the right ones."

"The buck stops here, huh?" Madeline made a face at him as he walked out the door.

In all the years he had known her, Charles had never seen Abigail D'Arcy betray her emotions, not even at her son's funeral. Yet when he broke the news to her about Sandra's affair, her dark eyes blazed with anger.

"How dare she risk the D'Arcy name like that," she

said, straightening her spine. "We are the first family of California and as such we have a position to maintain."

"It was very stupid," agreed Charles. He stirred his tea. Abigail had insisted the butler serve them from the D'Arcy silver. It amused him that even though it was early afternoon, she was dressed in a gray brocade dressing gown, wearing diamond earrings and a gem-studded necklace.

"What an irresponsible girl."

"That's why I believe she needs representation," explained Charles. "Who knows what else might come out. We can't have her talking indiscriminately to the police."

"Goodness no!"

Charles fingered one of the tiny sandwiches on his plate and waited for her to continue.

"I was not happy when my son married Sandra for many reasons, including the fact that she was not from our class of people."

Charles tried not to react to her remark. Maybe she had forgotten he wasn't born into their class of people either.

Abigail continued. "To be truthful, I still do not give a fig about her." She sat rigidly as she talked. "Nevertheless, she is the mother of James's child and we have the D'Arcy name to protect. I do not want a scandal, Charles. You must do whatever is necessary to nip this thing in the bud."

"I'll do my best, Abigail. But until I find out what the police have, I think it's best if Sandra does as I say."

"Of course." A worried frown creased her still-beautiful face. "If this man was involved in my son's death, our name will be in headlines across the entire nation. We have already had too much publicity. We are cursed now, like the Kennedys."

She pursed her lips as she put two lumps of sugar in her tea. "Charles, I want you to contact our friends in the newspaper and television industry. Ask them to . . ." She paused to gaze at him. "I do not have to tell you what to say. Just do what is necessary to keep this from becoming a major scandal."

"You know I'll do what I can. But we can't stop the tabloids."

She frowned. Then, looking at the clock on the mantel, she commented, "I wonder where Theo has been all afternoon. I am worried about him. I am not sure how much more he can take."

Charles was glad Theo was not there. It gave him a chance to approach this forbidding woman on what he feared might be a sensitive subject. Even after all these years, Abigail was one of the few people who could make him feel uncomfortable. He cleared his throat. "Theo's still insisting James changed his will before he died."

"Yes."

"I'm sorry he's so upset. However, I had no choice but to file with the probate court the will James left in my possession. To my knowledge, it was the last will my client wrote." He looked at her. "No matter how much I may want to help Theo, there's nothing legally I can do."

"I understand," she said softly, putting her manicured hand on his arm.

His eyes were dazzled by the famous thirty-carat diamond ring that sparkled against his sleeve. "I appreciate that," he said, then added, "Dickson and Theo have threatened to contest James's will. Without a new instrument to support their claim, I can't imagine that they'll eventually be successful. Nevertheless, they can certainly keep the will from being admitted to probate. Perhaps for as long as several months. I'll have to go into court and get myself appointed as a special administrator so that I can carry out James's wishes."

"Absolutely. Do whatever you must."

"I will." He coughed. "However, I honestly don't think a legal battle would be in the best interests of the D'Arcy Company or the D'Arcy Foundation."

"I agree with you, Charles. More tea?"

He nodded.

She leaned forward to pour. "Let me talk to Theo. We certainly do not need for the company's sales to drop any further. William must be turning over in his grave by now."

Charles was pleased. Abigail was a reasonable woman. He took the steaming beverage from her outstretched hand.

With her on his side, he knew, Dickson and Theo would have to reconsider the lawsuit. They wouldn't go against Abigail's wishes. He forced himself to concentrate on what she was saying.

"Theo is convinced he never measured up like his brother did in his father's eyes; nonetheless, that is no excuse for a D'Arcy to complain in public." She studied him for a moment. "I have always been proud of Theo, but then a mother sees things differently. If only he could have been nurtured along, instead of being left out so much by first William and then James. I know my eldest son was not an easy person to get along with. But I had hoped the two of them could have been friends."

"I know," he murmured, hoping he didn't sound sorry for her. Abigail, like Franklin, hated pity of any sort.

She turned her dark eyes toward him. "I think James made the right decision. You, Charles, are the most qualified person to run things at the moment."

Charles felt vindicated. "Thank you, Abigail."

"However," she added, "I want Theo to do more for the D'Arcy Company and Foundation than he has been allowed to do in the past. If I convince my son to drop this foolishness, I would expect you to train him to take over someday. After all, he is a D'Arcy."

"Of course, Abigail. I'd be happy to help."

"Now, who will be asked to watch out for Sandra?"

"It should be a criminal lawyer, just in case," said Charles. "Do you remember Kate Alexander? She heads our criminal defense department."

"She was here at the reading of the will?"

"Right," he said. "She's very good."

"Very well. I will leave it for you to arrange. Naturally, I will take care of the fees."

Dickson slid into the booth and ordered a Crown Royal on the rocks from the waiter. He then looked at his friend and client, Theo D'Arcy, sitting across from him at Valentino's.

"I'm so glad you could meet me for dinner," said Theo.

"Me too." Dickson loosened his tie and unbuttoned the top button of his shirt.

Theo leaned forward. "Have you spoken to Charles any more about the problem?"

"He's too busy. Since Charles filed James's will with the probate court, he's strutting around like a peacock, running to meetings of the D'Arcy Company and the Foundation as if he owned the world."

"Oh," Theo said glumly, taking a sip of his champagne cocktail. "Alistair Davis, executive secretary of the Foundation, called to tell me Charles was convening a special meeting of the board of directors. He naturally assumed I was now one of them." He laughed bitterly. "I told him James had excluded me from any participation in the Foundation."

"What did he say?"

"He was shocked. He pointed out that James often let me attend the meetings as a member of the family." Theo grimaced. "Of course, the bastard never let me say anything, so I stopped going. It was too humiliating."

"I'd go anyway. What can Charles do?"

"I'm not in the mood to be embarrassed," said Theo morosely.

Dickson glanced at him, worried over how despondent Theo had become since his outburst after the reading of the will. "I've got two associates doing research on contesting the will. In the meantime, we'll file an objection to the will. That keeps the court from admitting it to probate and gives us some time. As soon as I have enough on which to base our case, I'll hire outside counsel to file the lawsuit."

"Outside counsel?"

"Because of the conflict of interest."

"I see. Well . . . I've been thinking it over." Theo's brow was furrowed. "I'm not sure I can go through with it."

"You're not going to back out on me now, are you?" demanded Dickson.

"I might as well tell you. Mother doesn't think I should contest the will."

"Why wouldn't Abigail want you to get what's rightfully yours?" Dickson felt his blood pressure rising.

"Mother doesn't believe James changed his mind. She's also against airing the family's dirty laundry in public. She reminded me of my duty to uphold the D'Arcy name." Theo mimicked his mother's tone of voice and manner of talking. "And she's worried the publicity won't be good for the D'Arcy Company and Foundation. They have enough to contend with already due to James's death."

Dickson was not at all happy with this turn of events. He had to convince Theo to go forward with the will contest. It was the only way Dickson could wrest control of the D'Arcy business from Charles. He spoke gently.

"Your mother's doing a number on you, Theo, can't you see? You'll feel emasculated for the rest of your life if you give up without a fight."

"It's not Charles's fault James chose him over me. And Mother said Charles was being reasonable. He's willing to train me. Gradually I'll assume some control."

"That's no good. It puts you in the position of waiting for Charles to throw you some crumbs."

"Not exactly . . ."

"What about your dreams, your plans?" Dickson urged, trying to stay calm.

"They'd take a little longer to realize," Theo said.

Suddenly, Dickson hit the table with the palm of his hand. "I don't believe you're saying this. You're ready to allow Charles to run things instead of you. It stinks, Theo, and you know it."

"I'm not happy about it. At the same time, I can't bear to cause Mother more pain."

Dickson was more than upset now. He was worried. If he didn't oust Charles from his recently enhanced position of power, he could easily lose the senior partnership to him. "Let me talk to Abigail," he urged. "I'll make her understand why this is so important. It's our only leverage."

"I don't know." Theo ran a fork along the tablecloth.

Dickson gazed at Theo directly. "You've got to trust me. Have I ever steered you wrong?"

"No . . ."

"I've got several theories on which to contest the will, and we have some time yet to bring the action. In the meantime, to protect you, I'll file the objection. Maybe we'll get lucky and the new document will turn up."

"I'm not sure," said Theo.

"Theo, listen to me. I'm your attorney. I have only your best interests at heart. And I'm telling you, you must do this. If not, you'll regret it for the rest of your life."

"You really think so?"

"I know so," said Dickson with conviction.

"I warned you, Charles, but you didn't listen. You went ahead and saw her anyway." Ann Rieman's blue eyes burned with anger as she blocked her husband's entrance to his dressing room.

"Ann, I didn't—"

"Don't lie to me!" she shouted. "You were with her on the boat in Catalina. I checked with the harbormaster." She clutched her robe to her body.

Shit, thought Charles. His mind quickly surveyed his alternatives. Unfortunately, he wasn't ready to make his move—he had to secure the senior partnership first. It was obvious he had no choice at the moment but to stall her.

"O.K., Ann." He held out his hands as if to say, You win. "I didn't tell you because I knew you wouldn't understand. I had to see Kate to explain."

"And it took a whole weekend?" she asked sarcastically.

He flushed, embarrassed by his lack of power. "I could've told her on the phone we were finished, but it wouldn't have been right. I work with her on a daily basis; she handles my corporate clients who are being criminally investigated or charged. I wanted to let her down easy."

"So you fucked her a few times before you gave her the bad news. Kind of a going-away present." Ann's body was rigid as she furiously hurled her words at him.

"It wasn't like that. I had only planned to go over there, tell her, and come right back, but she was pretty upset." He shrugged his shoulders. "It was only fair that I give her time to get used to the idea. We talked a lot. Then she walked on the island alone. I had my work with me and I did it.'' He took a step toward her.

She held up her hand to stop him. "No, Charles. I don't trust you.'' She hesitated. "I'm not sure what to think.''

"Ann, I'm sorry.'' He pleaded with her, begging for understanding. "It's over, you must believe me.''

Ann appeared to be wavering. She thrust out her chin belligerently. "Charles, if you're not telling me the truth, I swear I'll ruin you.'' Her threat hung in the air.

"Ann, you have to accept what I'm telling you.'' He hesitated and then went on. "I was going to surprise you, but since you're so upset, I'll tell you now. I've got tickets for the new Andrew Lloyd Weber show. We're going to fly to New York this weekend and stay in a suite at the Plaza.''

"We are?'' she asked, surprised.

Charles moved toward her and wrapped her in his arms. "I'm sorry, Ann. Forgive me?''

"As long as you never see that bitch again.''

He had no choice but to promise.

Detective Bower answered his telephone. It was Madeline Gould, the deputy D.A.

"How's the search for the gun going?'' she asked.

"We combed the area. No luck yet.''

"Darn. I was hoping it would show up.''

"Wish the news was better.'' Bower meant it. He liked Madeline. She was determined and thorough. Now that his own daughter was in law school, his perspective on women lawyers had changed. While he still worried about his language in front of them, he thought for the most part they did a super job. They tried harder.

"I've reviewed the evidence against Sandra D'Arcy,'' she continued. "There's not enough to issue a complaint. No proof she was in on this thing with Tommy. Just a lot of suspicions.''

"Damn. Somehow I knew you were gonna say that.''

"On the bright side, I'm drafting the complaint against Bartholomew. If you want to arrest him after the warrant's issued, it'll be ready shortly. If not, you can book him on suspicion.''

"I'll wait. You prepared for the media blitz?"

"Yes," she laughed. "I just wish we could take the widow in at the same time. The more I look at the evidence, the more positive I am she's the co-conspirator." She paused. "How about your surveillance team, anything there?"

"Nope. Without a wiretap on Bartholomew and Mrs. D'Arcy's phones, it's gonna be tough."

"I'm sorry. The judge, unfortunately, didn't see it our way."

He heard the genuine sympathy in her voice. "It's these times we live in. Criminals have got more constitutional rights than the frigging victims."

"I really did try."

"I know you did. Win some, lose some." His voice dropped. "Sometimes this job gets to me."

"Me too." She sighed. "By the way, anything of interest yet on the brother, Theo D'Arcy?"

"Just some people who say things were not good between the brothers. D'Arcy says he was home at the time of the murder. That could be. We've got it pretty well nailed down that Tommy pulled the trigger. But who paid him or talked him into it? Don't know yet. I'll phone you as soon as I've got any news." As Bower hung up, he wondered how he'd feel if his daughter ended up in the D.A.'s office around criminals and cops all the time. Better she chose contract law.

Sandra D'Arcy pulled into the parking lot of the Bel Air Hills Market, her eyes searching for the car. Her hands were moist as she clasped the wheel. Thank God Victoria had gone away for a few days. When she saw him coming toward her with that smile she adored, she felt a shiver of excitement travel up her spine.

Tommy's dirty-blond hair fell forward over one eye as he leaned in through the open car window. "Hi, sweetheart. You sure are a pretty sight." He winked.

Sandra felt her cheeks growing warm. "Hi, Tommy." She looked around nervously, then gazed back into his eyes. "You can't call me at home anymore . . . the phone may be bugged." She reached into her purse, extracted an envelope, and handed it to him. "Here's one thousand dollars. That's all I could get on such short notice."

"Thanks." He peered inside, then stuffed it into the pocket of his jean jacket.

She glanced around again. "I gotta go."

"Whoa, not so fast." He reached in, opened the door, and climbed into the car. "First I want my hug and kiss."

While Sandra pulled the car over to the far side of the lot where they couldn't be easily spotted from the market, he let his hand run up her leg. She felt tingles all over as she put the car into neutral, leaving the engine running.

Tommy moved over and put his arms around her. "Aren't you glad to see me?"

"Of course."

"Then show me."

She turned and kissed him on the lips, her body melting into his for a moment. It felt good. He was holding her so tight she could feel the buttons of his jacket pressing into her chest.

"Do you still love me?" he whispered into her hair.

"Yes," she murmured, then pulled away. "Tommy, I've got to go—we shouldn't be seen together for a while. Don't call me. I'll get in touch with you." She craned her neck to see out the window. "You better go now."

He held up his hands in mock surrender. "O.K., O.K., I'm going, but I want you to know I'll be counting the hours until I can be with you forever." He got out of the car and smiled.

Sandra waved and screeched out of the parking lot.

The camera shutter clicked away, recording the meeting.

"I'm coming in," said Detective Harris on his radio. He packed away his long-range camera and started up his car. Then he drove out of the parking lot of the Bel Air Hills Market and back to police headquarters.

14

Miles Cunningham patted his stomach after a three-course meal at the prestigious Wellington Club, near Century City. "That was delicious."

"It certainly was," agreed Franklin Manning as he gazed around the dining room. The interior had always reminded him of an old English pub; he found it very comfortable. As far back as Franklin could remember, he had heard his father talk about the power meetings that went on in the club and how if you wanted to be a success, you had to belong. It was where political alliances were formed and corporate policies with far-reaching effects were resolved. Franklin recalled how proud he had been when his father brought him here after he passed the bar. "It's your turn now," Otis Manning had said to his son.

Miles reached into his pocket and took out a cigar. He unwrapped the cellophane, clipped off the end, and lighted it. He then took a long, languorous puff and blew out the smoke.

"Smells good." The lawyer sniffed the air. "My doctors won't let me smoke since my heart attack, and it's driving me crazy."

Miles nodded absently, his gaze wandering to a shapely blonde who was being ushered to a table near them. "I was dead set against letting the little gals into this club, but they sure do improve the scenery, don't they?"

A polite smile appeared on Franklin's face. He had hoped that Lauren's becoming a lawyer would temper her father's views, but he was the same old chauvinistic Miles. Thinking back to the rowdy Democratic convention where they had first met, he realized his client had not changed one iota in over thirty years.

The Texan stretched out long legs encased in alligator cowboy boots, and turned his gaze back to his lawyer, studying him closely. "So what's this I hear about you stepping down?"

"Because of my heart attack, the doctors have ordered me to cut back."

The other man's bushy eyebrows came together quickly. "Who you going to pass the reins to?"

"It's not up to me. It's a partnership decision."

"Come on. Don't kid me. This is Miles you're talking to." A devious smile played around the corners of his mouth, while the eyes beneath the thick silver-blond hair shone with curiosity. "We both know those partners of yours will go along with anybody you endorse."

Manning shook his head. "It wouldn't be good for the firm if I shoved my choice down their throats."

"Aha!" said Miles. He had a knowing look on his face as he sat forward in his chair. "So there really is going to be a fight between Dickson and Charles?"

Franklin stiffened. "Where'd you hear that?"

"I have my sources, and that doesn't include my daughter, I'll have you know. But I heard you announced your retirement, then changed your mind."

Franklin appraised the Texan carefully. He didn't trust him, but he didn't want to antagonize him either. "After James's death I reassessed my decision. It was no longer a good time for me to leave. As far as a fight between Charles and Dickson, they both want what's best for Manning & Anderson. They know clients get nervous when they hear about dissension in a firm. So whatever differences may exist between the two men, I'm confident they'll work them out."

"And don't forget banks also get worried about their loans while headhunters start calling the best and the brightest of your lawyers." There was a malicious glint in Miles's eye; it was as if he enjoyed imagining what might happen to Manning & Anderson if word of their problems surfaced. "Well, you can trust me, old buddy, but just between us, who's it going to be, Dickson or Charles?"

"We'll just have to wait and see," said Franklin. He would be damned if he was going to tell Miles how much he personally wanted to see Charles in his place. Charles was far superior to his son at assuming leadership and making sound business decisions. If only there was a way to get Dickson to step back gracefully. Franklin couldn't afford to have a power struggle plunge the firm into a full-scale war, nor could he run the risk that Charles might take his business and leave, especially now that Charles had the final say in who did the legal work for the D'Arcy Company and Foundation.

Sadly, Franklin realized that Dickson didn't share his feelings on how Manning & Anderson should be run. He prayed that the other partners would pick Charles without his vote, because if Franklin was forced to choose between his son and Charles, he didn't know what he would do.

"O.K., O.K., I won't press you anymore." A cagey smile brightened Miles's face. "However, I certainly have a right to know who the hell's going to take over my work. You're the only one I trust."

"Don't worry, we'll find someone you feel comfortable with, and I promise to oversee things."

"That's good." Miles chewed on his cigar. "Listen, I need a favor from you."

"You only have to ask."

"My little gal Lauren is worried sick over this here partner selection you have coming up."

Franklin's eyebrows arched in surprise. "Tell her not to worry. She's a good lawyer. If she doesn't make it this time, she can try again next year."

"A man can't tell his daughter not to worry," said Miles. "Being passed over for partner this time would be a real humiliation. She's my baby. I don't want her upset."

"I understand." Franklin smiled. "I feel the same about Ann. However, the other three candidates are all good lawyers too."

"Word has it the new partner will be one of the ladies."

"I don't know where you're getting your information, but Kate Alexander is a darn fine lawyer too. Either of them would be a good choice."

"You're putting that gal Kate in the same league with my Lauren?"

"Don't get so worked up. Lauren's been with us seven years—hired right out of law school. Kate was hired laterally three years ago from the district attorney's office. She heads our criminal defense department. Both of them are on the same partnership track. In fact, I believe they graduated from law school together."

"Surely Lauren can offer a lot more than a moneyless nobody like Kate? Hell, with my connections my daughter has the potential of being a big rainmaker for your firm."

Franklin bristled at the suggestion, but he smiled graciously. "I'm not one to undervalue an attorney's ability to bring in the clients. However, I think the tendency of some of the newer firms to consider volume more important than good lawyering is wrong. As for your observation of Kate, I think that's unfair of you, Miles. Kate wasn't born rich, but she graduated at the top of her class and she's a brilliant lawyer. Clients rave about her, and Charles thinks the world of her too."

Miles cocked a suspicious eyebrow at his friend. "I guess it depends on what you think is more important." He drummed his fingers loudly on the table. "Is something going on between Charles and Kate?"

"Absolutely not!" chafed Franklin, startled. "Charles is devoted to my daughter, Ann, and he's going to stay that way."

Miles held up his hands in mock surrender. "Just kidding, old buddy, just kidding." He leaned back in his chair, puffing on his cigar while he assessed the other man. "You know, I've been thinking. Up until now you've only been representing my business interests on the West Coast. I'd like to give you a shot at my global empire."

"I'm flattered, of course," said Franklin, mentally calculating that the added business could be worth millions in fees to the firm. "But there can't be any strings attached."

"Of course not, Franklin," chuckled Miles.

* * *

Defense attorney Andrew Stewart smiled at his image in the mirror. Straightening his tie, he winked at himself. "You handsome devil, one woman is never enough for you, is it?"

He grabbed his sports jacket from the suede-covered, king-sized bed. The bedroom was a mess. The bed was still rumpled; fifteen minutes earlier Andrew had ushered his latest conquest out the door.

Outside, he got into his black Ferrari. His eyes roamed over the low, sloping roof line of his house and then took in the sparkling lights of the city below. Buying this house had been one of the best moves of his life. It had made him an instant millionaire on paper, although he now had a staggering mortgage. Owning his home had other advantages too, he mused. Women were immediately impressed.

Gunning the motor, he backed up, then streaked down the hill toward the flats of Beverly Hills that lay beneath a sky flooded with stars. The day I saw my house was a lucky one, he thought, remembering how he had come to own his hilltop haven. He had received a call from Janet, a pretty young woman at a local real estate office. She had let Andrew see the house before anyone else even knew it was on the market.

He had bought cheap, then fixed it up using all his contacts and calling in all his outstanding debts. Being a criminal attorney had many pluses. What he couldn't afford he bartered for. There was that plumber he had gotten off on a drunk driving charge. The man had been so relieved he had installed new copper plumbing throughout the entire house as well as all new fixtures, at cost. It had been worth calling in the favor owed to him by a deputy D.A. He reminded himself that he had to get a few more favors lined up. He didn't have many left.

The house was now worth at least several hundred thousand dollars more than he had paid, including the money he had spent fixing it up. Janet had been richly rewarded on the plush carpet of the empty house for her part in finding it.

Andrew smoothly handled his sleek car as it made its way down curving Benedict Canyon. On Sunset Boulevard he turned right. A few minutes later he pulled in at Lauren's condominium in Westwood.

Handing over his car to the parking attendant, Andrew mused that since that night at L'Escoffier and his subsequent promise to take her to Hawaii, he and Lauren had made love three times. She was insatiable, but he wasn't complaining. Each encounter had been thoroughly enjoyable.

Andrew exited the elevator on the penthouse floor and rang the bell. The door opened and Lauren stood in the vestibule. "You look beautiful," he said, gazing admiringly at her clinging dressing gown and the faint outline of her nipples protruding underneath the soft, filmy fabric.

"Come on in."

Andrew marveled that years of living away from Texas had not removed the traces of a southern drawl from her speech. As she led the way, he noticed her slim legs faintly visible beneath the flowing white robe while her satin mules clicked against the hardwood floor. He felt himself stir.

"Martini?"

"Please."

Lauren went behind the mirrored bar and he surveyed the room, where a fire was softly glowing on the opposite wall. He had been quite impressed the first time he saw her condominium, a richly furnished penthouse with a spectacular view of Westwood and beyond. It was probably worth millions.

In the middle of the large room, two white silk couches faced each other; floating between them, a black ebony coffee table rested on an exotic zebra skin rug. The wood of the table caught the light from the fire. In the center of the table sat a Baccarat crystal vase filled with peach roses, along with a figurine of jade and a carved ivory tusk from the Orient.

"My daddy was in town." She handed him his drink and sat down next to him.

"How is he?" Andrew had heard much about the wealthy and flamboyant Texan who was a staunch supporter of the

Democratic party. Some of the stories about his wealth were outlandish, while others nailed him as nothing more than a crass, oil-rich cowboy.

"He's fine. He wanted to meet you, but I called and called and there was no answer at your place last night."

"I forgot to pick up my messages," he lied, and silently cursed. He had hoped to meet her father; the Texan's vast range of contacts could be helpful. Andrew wanted more of a shot at getting appointed to certain task forces known for their political influence, assignments that would give him more visibility and name recognition. Translation: bucks. The more attorneys who recommended him to clients in need of a criminal lawyer, the more his name would be bandied about . . . and so on. Oh well, next time, he thought.

Andrew took a sip of his drink and smiled lazily at Lauren. "God, I'm beat," he sighed, hoping she would think his exhaustion work-related.

"Rest for a few minutes," she suggested softly.

He closed his eyes and luxuriated in the comfort of the surroundings. He must have dozed off for a few minutes. When he awoke, he felt a flicker of something against his skin like someone's breath and realized her lips were brushing against his.

"Tell me one of your sexual fantasies," she whispered.

Andrew opened his eyes slightly and gazed into hers. He could read nothing behind the thick lashes. A faint smile curved the corners of her lush mouth as she ran her tongue lightly over her bottom lip.

"To have you make love to me and be unable to move," he said without blinking or even thinking.

"Come on," she said.

Inside her bedroom, he ambled over to the huge bed and quickly peeled off his clothes. Then he pulled away the cream satin bedspread and lay back on the huge bed, watching as she rummaged through her drawers throwing scarfs and other silky garments onto the thick shag carpet.

She came toward him, a wicked smile on her face. "Trust me?" she teased.

He felt a momentary tickle of fear run down his spine. He couldn't back out now; she would tease him unmercifully. "Is there some reason I shouldn't?" he kidded back.

"I don't know. You tell me." She tilted her head coyly while she tied a long pink scarf around his wrist.

Andrew found the combination of the silken fabric against his skin and Lauren's musky scent enticing. His pulse quickened as he focused on the magnificent body above him. Voluptuous breasts above a waist tiny in comparison to the full hips. All this complemented by slender legs. With her reddish-golden hair and blue eyes, she was every man's dream—and rich too. What a combination.

With his free hand, he reached up and undid the pins holding her hair. It cascaded down around her shoulders and onto his stomach as he ran his fingers through it. He brought her closer and pressed his mouth to hers.

"Mmm." She pulled back and grabbed his other wrist to tie a scarf around it. Then she hopped off the bed and tied the ends of each scarf to the headboard.

Andrew pulled against his restraints and realized she had fastened him more securely than he had thought possible. She certainly didn't appear to be that strong. A shiver of apprehension coursed through his body, causing waves of ecstasy to roll deliciously over him. For a moment he worried he might come right then and there.

When she went for his legs, he protested, moving his feet away from her hands. "No, I want to be able to move."

"It's better if you can't," she insisted firmly. She wrapped a silken garment around each of his ankles, then deftly secured his legs to the footboard.

He wondered what kind of fabric she had used. It felt like silk but had the strength of rope. He sensed that maybe it wasn't the first time she had tried this.

"Now you're in my control," she whispered, running her fingers lightly over his legs, then his groin, not stopping but continuing up over his stomach and chest until they rested on his lips. He quivered beneath her touch.

Slowly, very gently, she began to run her moist tongue over him, tracing the same path her fingers had followed a minute before. His body arched; his breath quickened. He felt her tongue lighting small fires wherever it touched. Desire pulsated through him as she straddled his body and put her mouth on him. His cock responded as it took on a life of its own. Higher and higher his passion rose while he twisted and pulled at the scarves. When she bit him ever so lightly on his nipples, he felt as if he would die from the pleasure—and the pain.

He began to throb as the tension built inside him. For the next several moments he knew she could do whatever she wished. Nothing could stop the explosion that was coming.

Dickson had been asked to come to his father's office. As he walked in, he was again struck by how incongruous the furnishings were with the rest of the distinctly modern offices. Years before, Franklin had been impressed with William Randolph Hearst's castle and had decorated his own office in the same dark and heavy carved woods and ornate fabrics. Dickson found his father's tastes, like his father himself, an anachronism; it was time for both to be replaced.

Franklin was seated behind his desk and gestured for Dickson to take one of the client chairs facing him. Dickson knew it was his father's habit to address people from behind the massive fortress of his desk. It made them feel smaller and Franklin appear wiser. "I'll sit over here," he said, going to the couch instead.

Now Franklin was forced to get up and join him. This pleased Dickson. He wasn't sure what his father wanted, but he instinctively knew it would help to have the old man on equal footing. "Father, you don't look good. I thought the doctor didn't want you back at work yet."

"Not now, Dickson." The older man held up his hands in protest.

"Does Mother know you're at the office?" Dickson was determined to keep his father on the defensive.

"My health is not why I asked you here," snapped Franklin. "The potential of a lawsuit over the will of one of this firm's biggest clients is what's on my mind."

"I see," said Dickson, his tone noncommittal.

"I've talked the situation over with Abigail. She's not happy about the prospect of a lawsuit either. And you realize it would have to be handled by outside counsel?"

"Of course. I've already advised Theo there's a conflict-of-interest situation. In fact, it might be best if we don't discuss it either."

Franklin paid no heed as he shook his head. "James wouldn't have drafted a new will without Charles knowing about it."

Dickson glanced at the wedding picture of Ann and Charles sitting prominently on the credenza behind the desk. From their wedding day on, it had seemed to him that Charles had taken his place in his father's affection. "How can you be so sure?"

"Because he trusted Charles with everything. Why, James practically turned over the entire operation of the D'Arcy Company to Charles during the last several years. As for the D'Arcy Foundation, Charles was pretty much making all the major decisions there, too."

"Has it occurred to you that Charles may have destroyed the new will?"

Franklin stiffened. "That's not worthy of an answer. And why would he do such a thing? Charles isn't even a beneficiary under the will."

"Not in a direct monetary sense," agreed Dickson, "unless you want to count the legal fees earned under the terms of the will. On the other hand, maybe he didn't want to give up control of the D'Arcy Company and Foundation."

"Being named executor and trustee is nothing but a big headache to Charles, as well as a lot of responsibility. He's already overburdened. As for any fees, they belong to this firm."

"Maybe there's something else he *didn't* want."

"This conversation is foolish. Charles has too much on his mind already without the added headaches of the D'Arcy business. There's the tender offer by Suni Industries. The deal has attracted an antitrust suit as well as charges of industrial espionage and insider trading. Charles also has the next election to think about. He's way behind in his fund-raising efforts for the party's candidates. I think it's fair to say that Charles works harder and brings in more fees to Manning & Anderson than any two lawyers combined.''

As Dickson listened to his father, he smoldered inside. He could see he was going to need something substantial to prove his own value to the firm, a value his father didn't seem to recognize. ''By the way, Father, I'm working on getting a new client. One worth at least two million in yearly fees.''

''Who?''

''I can't tell you yet. The lawyer who is recommending me is taking this client away from another firm. He said if word leaks out before it's a done deal, I'll lose them.'' Dickson gave his father a look that said, That's it for now. He hoped he had said just enough to whet his father's appetite.

Franklin tapped his knee with his hand. ''I'm not through discussing the will situation. Are you giving Theo sound advice on this matter?''

''With all due respect, what I tell Theo is none of your business. However, I can assure you he's being very insistent on going forward with a will contest. I'll lay out all the pros and cons for Theo, but it will be his decision in the end, not mine.''

''We can influence those decisions whichever way we want, and you know it. It's the first skill they teach in law school.''

''Theo's interests come first with me,'' retorted Dickson, sitting up straighter. ''What I want has nothing to do with it.''

Franklin peered at Dickson, a skeptical look on his face. Finally, he said quietly, ''I have to tell you that for the good of Manning & Anderson, for the good of everyone, you shouldn't encourage Theo in this. And remember, you also have a duty to your partners and to me.''

His father's words irritated Dickson, but he didn't let on. ''Father, my duty to this firm is always uppermost in my mind. But I have a responsibility to Theo also.''

Franklin went on as though he hadn't heard what his son had said. "I've talked to Charles. He's willing to help Theo become familiar with the Company and the Foundation. Eventually, he'll give Theo more responsibility. Abigail agrees it's the best solution."

Dickson's eye began to twitch. It was always the same story. His father wasn't interested in what he had to say; he only listened to Charles. "I'll tell Theo your concerns." He stood up to leave. "I have a client coming in."

"By the way, Dickson. Your wife's been complaining to Mother. Says you're never home. What's going on?"

"Charles isn't the only one who's working hard!" As Dickson left his father's office, he was really seething. How dare his father ask him about Alana or tell him how to advise Theo! Theo's concerns *were* important to him. Could Dickson help it if his own agenda also happened to be benefited by Theo's fighting for control of the D'Arcy estate?

15

Madeline caught Philip as he was ready to leave the office. "Got a minute?" she asked.

"What's up?" He stopped to look at her, nodding his head absently as others called out their end-of-day good-byes.

"The investigators have been digging around on James D'Arcy. I wanted to run a few things by you."

"Grab your coat. We'll get a drink."

"Be right back." Madeline hurried off.

Fifteen minutes later she was seated with Philip in the

lounge of the Westin Bonaventure Hotel. After ordering, he turned to her. "So what's the inside scoop on the man?"

"Perplexing," she admitted. "People were more than willing to talk about James D'Arcy, the public man. They all seemed to be impressed by his charm, his concern for the world around him, his prominent family, his enormous wealth, the D'Arcy business empire, especially the Foundation." She paused.

"And the private man?"

"They were more reluctant. The investigator got the impression James D'Arcy was intensely disliked by an awful lot of people. In fact, hated might be a better word."

Philip raised his eyebrows. "Hated?"

Madeline nodded. "Seems he had a vicious tongue. Often lashing out at employees, humiliating them in front of others."

Philip sucked on his pipe and thought for a moment. "He picked on folks who weren't able to fight back?"

"Right. Little people. The few who talked said D'Arcy was impossible to get along with. He was demanding. Insisted on perfection. Always wanted everything to be done his way and only his way. He was also known to carry a grudge and be totally unforgiving." She chewed on her lip for a moment before continuing. "Many of them were also worried about retribution from the D'Arcy family. If they talked, that is."

"Not quite the smiling man we saw in the media."

"Right. That was the image D'Arcy wanted to portray. But there was definitely another side to him. One employee told our investigator about a supplier who insulted James in front of two other people. James ruined him. Didn't stop till the man lost his business, his house, everything."

"A real Dr. Jekyll and Mr. Hyde."

She nodded her head in agreement.

"The obvious question seems to be," said Philip, "did any of those people hate him enough to kill him?"

"That's what we're trying to find out."

He twirled the ice in his glass. "So, you're definitely

looking for a connection between Tommy and someone else?"

"Absolutely. Bower and I are both convinced Tommy didn't plan this himself. There had to be a co-conspirator, or even co-conspirators."

"Three of them?"

"Why not? According to several sources, Theo D'Arcy was the only one of the D'Arcy clan to welcome Sandra into their midst. Who was it that wrote, 'Greed makes strange bedfellows'?"

He laughed. "I don't remember. But whoever it was was right." Philip seemed to study her face for a moment. "How're the boys?"

"Fine." She smiled. It was nice to have a boss who remembered you had a personal life beyond the D.A.'s office. "Kenny's involved in Little League. I'm juggling a bunch of car pools for it. Jud's into his music—his stereo blasts day and night. He also plays the drums in a band. I'm going crazy from the noise." She rubbed her temples in mock pain.

Philip smiled sympathetically. "Sam taking them regularly?"

"Unfortunately, no." She thought about what a disappointment her ex-husband had turned out to be for the boys. It was a shame Philip's wife had died before they had children. He would have been a good father. She sighed. "He seems to have less and less time for them. When he does take them, he invariably has some nineteen-year-old bimbo with him."

"Oh?"

Madeline saw the curious expression on Philip's face and realized he thought she was jealous. "It's not me, Philip." She paused. "It's the boys. They're the ones that don't like it."

His shoulders relaxed as he exhaled inaudibly. "Divorce always ends up being the hardest on the kids."

"True. I knew Sam was selfish and egotistical where I was concerned. I just never figured him for acting that way with his sons."

Philip reached out and squeezed her hand. "I'm sorry."

Madeline glanced at him gratefully. What a nice person he was. "Thanks, Philip. I didn't mean to bend your ear."

"If I hadn't wanted to hear it, I wouldn't have asked," he said firmly.

Dickson pulled into the courtyard of the D'Arcy mansion. Looking into the rearview mirror, he smoothed back his hair and got out of the car. Upstairs, Arthur, the butler, showed him into Abigail's sitting room.

"Dickson, how nice to see you." Abigail held her cheek out for a kiss.

He obliged. "It's nice to see you too, Abigail. I hope you're well?"

"I am fine." Her voice, as usual, was strong and firm. She motioned toward the chintz sofa. "Please sit down. May I offer you something?"

"No thanks." He crossed his legs. "I can't stay long."

"I'm glad you are here. I want to thank you for all the support you have been giving Theo. He is taking his brother's death very hard."

"We're all taking his death hard. And I do want to help."

"We must go on. James would want that."

Dickson wondered at the source of this woman's apparent strength and resolve as he nodded.

"So what brings you to see me?"

"I wanted to talk to you about Theo."

"Is something wrong?"

"It's about James's will."

"I see." Her black eyes gazed at him shrewdly.

"Theo is absolutely sure that James changed it before he died," explained Dickson.

"Yes. My son has indicated that to me also. But there is no evidence to support such a claim."

He judged her carefully before choosing to be direct. "Abigail, do you trust your younger son? Do you have faith in him?"

She bristled as if to say, What impertinence! "Of course."

158

Although he knew Abigail was not the kind of woman who appreciated being told what to do, he decided to chance it. "Why not encourage him to contest the will if that's what he truly believes?"

"Because no good could possibly come of it."

"But if—"

"Let me finish," she said, holding up her hand as if to stave off the rest of his speech. "Perhaps James did intend to change his will. We will never know. However, I sincerely doubt he did anything about it. It is not the sort of thing he would have done without consulting me."

"But not impossible?"

"Nothing is impossible. My son was a grown man, Dickson. He did, nevertheless, like to discuss such matters with me. On several occasions, James and I discussed the prenuptial agreement Sandra signed as well as the will he made after they were married."

He tried to hide his surprise. Theo had never told him that James and Abigail might have actually discussed James's will. "I didn't know that," he said solemnly.

"James counted on me to tell him what my late husband, William, would have said." There was a meaningful tilt to her head at the mention of her husband. "James and I were very close."

This was a complication Dickson had not counted on. Abigail could be a maddening old woman and a formidable foe. He couldn't afford to anger her, yet he didn't plan to give up, either. There was too much at stake. He coughed. "I appreciate that, Abigail. And I'm sure there's a great deal of truth in what you're saying."

"Then why do you persist in encouraging Theo in this foolishness?" she asked sharply.

He felt himself bristle. He was not going to see Theo end up with nothing but a few crumbs. That would not be good for his own future. Dickson took a deep breath. He obviously had no choice. "Because I saw the new will." He waited a second for his words to sink in. "And there were two witnesses."

For the first time during their talk, Abigail seemed genuinely taken aback. Her eyebrows shot up and the look in her eyes turned hard. "Two witnesses? Theo did not mention that to me."

"He didn't want me to say anything yet."

"Why?"

"First, we wanted to see if the document itself showed up. Second, we wanted to give you time to adjust to your loss. Third, we hoped everyone could be convinced to honor James's wishes without the necessity of litigation. But now that doesn't seem even remotely possible."

She laid her palms on her lap. There was an almost menacing expression on her face. "I see."

He hastened to explain. "As a lawyer, I know how unpleasant litigation over a will can be. Often things the family would rather not have made public come out."

"I will not have it!" she said suddenly, her back absolutely rigid. "Who are these so-called witnesses?"

He shook his head. "I'm sorry. I can't remember."

"This sounds more ridiculous every moment, Dickson." Her voice rose. "I demand to know who these witnesses are."

"Unfortunately, I didn't recognize either of their names."

"We had best call Charles."

"No," he said hurriedly. "I don't want him involved."

"Dickson, I'm not a woman who appreciates the word no."

"I'm sorry. I'm doing my best to remember. In the meantime, I'm hoping the lost document will surface." He stood. "Thank you for seeing me." He smiled his most gracious smile as he waved goodbye and walked out of the room.

Theo seemed surprised to see Dickson at his front door. Then a worried frown creased his forehead. "What's wrong?"

"I just met with your mother. I've come to tell you the facts of life. Attorney to client."

"And?"

"It appears your mother, my father, and, most of all, Charles do not want *you* to take over as trustee."

"What do you mean?"

Dickson straightened his shoulders. "I've come to the conclusion that one of them has the new will. And for their own selfish reasons, they have decided to act as if it doesn't exist."

Theo turned pale. He made his way to his couch and sat down. "I'm afraid I don't understand."

Dickson strutted across the room to the bar. "I'm going to fix myself a drink. I think you need one too?"

"Make it a double."

After pouring two stiff drinks, Dickson joined Theo on the couch. "It's time for you to go on the offensive."

"Want to explain what you mean by that?"

"We must act like we know the will was drafted. Period. In fact, I am going to say I saw it."

"Why would you say that?"

"It's called a legal fiction. We have to flush out the person or persons who do not want the existence of the real will to be known. It's the only way."

"I'm having a difficult time understanding what you're talking about."

"It's all a bunch of legal mumbo jumbo, but basically, it's this: Without the written document, the only chance we have is to say we actually saw the document, which was witnessed, and now it's been lost or destroyed."

"Let me get this straight. You're going to say something is true, when it's not, for the legality of the matter?"

"Yes. I'm not going to go into all the legal problems, but those are the facts we have to present to get us through the first legal challenge."

"I see. And you want me to say this?"

"No." Dickson got up and started to pace. "It will be more credible if it's someone who is not a beneficiary." He turned to Theo. "Do you trust me?"

"Of course. You know that."

"Good. Then leave it to me. If anyone asks you anything, and I mean anyone . . . your mother, Victoria, Franklin, Charles, you tell them you're represented by counsel on the matter. Refuse to discuss it with them."

"I thought you couldn't represent me on this. You said there was a conflict of interest."

"Right. Tomorrow I'm going to retain outside counsel for you. I'll then give them my statement in the form of an affidavit. It'll get the ball rolling."

"I don't see how—"

"Theo," Dickson interrupted, "I know what I'm doing. It's done all the time to get past the legal maneuvering, the hurdles that could get your case thrown out before it even starts. Don't worry. Let me handle it."

Theo looked at Dickson skeptically, but Dickson insisted.

"I've seen it done lots of times before. Don't worry. I'll take care of it all."

After he hung up the phone from Abigail's call, Charles hurried to find Dickson, but his secretary said he wasn't back yet. "Let me know the minute he shows up," he demanded.

An hour later he accosted his brother-in-law as he got out of the elevator on the twenty-sixth floor.

"A welcoming committee?" said Dickson caustically. "You shouldn't have bothered."

"It's time we talked."

"Sure, why not?" Dickson followed Charles back into his office. "So talk."

Charles forced himself to be pleasant. "Would you like a drink first?"

"Crown Royal straight up."

Charles fixed two drinks and handed one to Dickson.

"It's not poisoned, is it?"

"Take a sip. If you don't drop dead in two minutes, you can drink the rest."

"Very funny." Dickson swirled the liquid with his finger.

"Here. Take mine if you're worried."

Dickson hesitated, then lifted his own glass to his lips and gulped.

"Now that we've seen to the preliminaries," said Charles, thinking to himself what an ass Dickson was, "let's go on. I think it would benefit us both if we talked things over."

"What would you like to discuss first—our differences

162

over James's will, the D'Arcy Company and Foundation, or the future of this law firm?'' Dickson's voice was acerbic and clipped. "After all, it's rather amusing, isn't it, that we really have so many subjects on which we disagree. It makes us almost compatible, wouldn't you say?''

"I'm not sure amusing is the right word. But then we never did agree on what was funny either." Charles sipped his drink. He was thinking about how best to bring up the subject of the will without telling Dickson outright about Abigail's call. "In spite of what you may think, I swear I never saw a new will. James did discuss with me some changes he was considering, but he wasn't sure yet what he wanted to do.''

"What changes?" Dickson asked, his eyes suddenly alert.

"We debated revoking the prenuptial agreement, but I talked him out of that.''

"I can't believe James would even have considered something so stupid. What else?''

"James talked about giving Theo more of a role in the D'Arcy Company and Foundation. In fact, I was to think about it and get back to him with suggestions.''

"Just a role?''

"That's all he mentioned.''

"Well, just because he didn't tell you about it doesn't mean James didn't make a new will," retorted Dickson.

"True, but if he did, I don't have any idea where it is. Do you?''

"If I had it, you'd know by now.''

"In that case, shouldn't we concern ourselves with doing what's necessary for the D'Arcy Company and Foundation?''

"You'd like for it to be business as usual.''

Charles heard the bitterness in Dickson's voice but went on. "I think we've an obligation to keep things going. The D'Arcy Company sales still have not stabilized. And for the sake of everyone else, the firm, our partners, I believe you and I should try and work out our differences.''

"I'm sick and tired of everyone worrying about the firm," said Dickson. "It's *my* firm too. *My* father built it and it will be *mine* one day.''

"Shouldn't we let our partners decide that?" Charles purposely tried to keep his voice light.

"When the time comes, you'll see, they *will* pick me. Blood will win out and the other partners will follow my father's lead." Dickson's eye began to twitch.

"Fine. Let's not belabor the point. I'd rather talk about Theo. I'm more than willing to help him learn all about the business—"

"Big fucking deal," interrupted Dickson.

"Why don't we just cut the crap," snapped Charles, his anger surfacing. "You have no legal grounds on which to contest James's will and you know it. At best, Theo had a verbal promise. If it wasn't in writing, it's unenforceable."

"You're wrong there, dear brother-in-law. I saw the document and there were two witnesses." Dickson's eyes held a gleam of triumph.

"That's a damn lie!"

"No it's not."

"Then who are these secret witnesses?"

"I can't remember their names, but don't worry, I will."

Charles shook his finger in Dickson's face. "You're lying. You and Theo have made it up."

"You'll just have to prove that, won't you," taunted Dickson, getting up and striding to the door. "See you in court, Counselor." He slammed the door behind him.

Before he headed back to Texas, Miles Cunningham had told his daughter about his meeting with Franklin Manning. While her father seemed to be positive Manning would think things over and favor Lauren, she was not so sure.

Christ, she thought to herself. When Daddy offered to give the firm his global business, that should have done the trick. She considered it for a few minutes. Daddy's global business was worth a lot of money. Certainly it would mean something to somebody else. Maybe somebody who wasn't an ole stick in the mud like Franklin Manning.

She twirled her letter opener in her hand. Suddenly, she sat forward. "Of course! Why didn't I think of it sooner?" she said out loud.

In a flash, she was out of her office and running up the stairs to the main floor. She heard a door slam and saw Dickson, his face flushed, storming out of Charles's office. Good. Maybe Dickson could figure out a way to use her father's promised business to advance both their causes.

16

Kate punched the intercom button and heard Charles's voice.

"Can you come in here?" he asked. "I need to talk to you."

"Sure." She hoped he meant to explain why they hadn't seen each other since Catalina. "I've got one call to make and I'll meet you in your office."

A few minutes later she closed the door behind her and sat down in front of his desk. "Shoot."

"What I'm about to discuss with you is extremely confidential." Charles fiddled with some papers, then looked directly at her. "When the media finds out about it, I don't want the source to be traced to us. O.K.?"

"Of course." She studied his handsome face, wondering why he was behaving so mysteriously all of a sudden. Whatever he was talking about didn't sound like it had anything to do with her and the fact that they weren't spending any time together.

"Remember I told you that we had learned Sandra was having an affair with some construction worker? Well, it seems there's a good possibility Sandra's little affair was more serious than I first thought," he said. "It appears the police have found some evidence that links Tommy Bartholomew to James's death.''

"I see."

"It's not a pretty picture," he confided. "I've spoken to Abigail D'Arcy at length. She and I don't want Sandra to speak to the police unless she's represented by counsel."

"That's good advice, even essential. But why hasn't she already been told that?"

"No one dreamed she'd shoot off her damned mouth. And she foolishly insists she's got nothing to hide." He shook his head. "She's not an easy person to deal with or tell anything to. In fact, I warned her not to see or contact that young man again. She didn't take kindly to my suggestion."

Kate's mind formed the picture of the young widow she had seen several times since the fateful party the night before James's death. She definitely looked like she'd married James for his money, but was she capable of murder? And in cold blood? For this certainly did not have the earmarks of a crime of passion. "Do you have any information that leads you to believe the police think Sandra is involved?"

"Not really," he admitted. "I was hoping maybe you could find out."

"I'll try."

"Abigail, of course, is worried about the publicity. Even if Sandra doesn't know anything, it still looks rather bad. I can already see the headlines screaming, 'Young Wife Romantically Linked with Husband's Murderer.' It's not going to be pleasant."

"No," she agreed, "it won't."

"Anyway, Kate"—he gazed into her eyes—"Abigail D'Arcy wants you to represent Sandra."

Kate caught her breath. She was already overloaded with work. Didn't he realize that? "Charles, I'm flattered, but what about the heavy case load I've got?" She glanced at him critically. "Three of your major corporate clients are being investigated at the moment. One for insider trading, one for leaking fraudulent information, and one for illegal toxic waste disposal. Don't you think I should focus on what's already on my plate?"

He got up and perched on the edge of his desk in front of her. "Darling, everything you say is true. But I'm also overburdened. I really need your help with Sandra. Isn't there anyone in your department who can help you?"

"Of course they can help!" she said, more sharply than she had intended. "But you and Franklin have insisted that I deal with certain clients personally. And Sandra obviously needs special handling too. I'm tireless, but even for me there's a limit." She shook her head. "There's a big difference between four hours of sleep and no sleep."

"Don't I know it! Tell you what. Look around for someone to hire. Laterally, if need be."

"Charles," she laughed. "I don't have time to breathe, let alone look at résumés."

"Call that headhunter we used before."

"I still have to interview the potential candidates, and that can take hours and hours I don't have."

"Just do your best. O.K.?"

Kate sighed. She knew another reason not to take on any additional work. Their relationship was taking a beating lately.

"I know you're being asked to do a lot, but think about what this could mean." His voice rose with excitement. "Kate, there's bound to be a lot of publicity associated with this case once word gets out about the affair and Bartholomew's possible involvement. It couldn't hurt to have your name and picture in the papers or on television, especially for a future in politics. That kind of free publicity's hard to get."

"That's the first thing you've said I like." Suddenly, her mind raced with the possibilities a big case like this might hold for her career. The prospect was seductive.

"There's one other issue. It's conceivable the police might say Sandra solicited the murder of her husband or, even worse, conspired to bring it about. If this ends up in a trial, her defense could be worth hundreds of thousands of dollars, maybe even a million dollars in fees. Abigail has already promised to foot the bill. We can't afford to have fees like that walk out the door."

"I don't know . . ." She hesitated.

"Kate, in a few months Manning & Anderson will be selecting its next partner. Handling Sandra will give you even more of an edge on Lauren. After all, Sandra is a *D'Arcy*." He turned and smiled at her. His implication became obvious as he continued. "Partners are expected to be capable of generating enough fees to pay for themselves and others. You shouldn't refuse something that's good for the entire firm."

Kate wasn't sure she liked the double message. Do *this* if you want *that*. She peered out at the buildings of Century City while she considered his words. There was a great deal at stake here. Not just her future but Sandra's.

As a prosecutor, Kate's choices had always been relatively simple: working for the state, she sought justice for the victim. In private practice, the lines in criminal defense work were not as clearly drawn. More often than not, a lawyer was forced to defend someone who was guilty. And what if Sandra was guilty? What if she really did conspire to kill her husband? Kate wasn't sure how she felt about that. She didn't need to defend a guilty client just before an election, one of whose issues was tougher crime legislation.

"How do you think losing this case would affect my career?" she finally said.

"All you can do is your best," he pointed out.

Kate thought that Charles was doing a masterful job of avoiding the issues.

"By the way," he added, "Dickson and I had a terrible row before."

"What happened?"

Charles related the details of the meeting with his brother-in-law.

After he finished, Kate sat pensively for a moment, digesting the information. "Charles, maybe Theo had something to do with James's death."

"What makes you think that?"

Kate held out her palms. "I'm not sure. It just seems to me he's making a big fuss about this will thing. Maybe something more's at stake."

"Could be. All I know is that this firm needs you on this case—and so does your career."

Philip White walked behind Madeline into the waiting room of the D.A.'s office and watched as she stopped to chat with a policeman. He saw the cop's face light up with pleasure and marveled at how easily Madeline got people to talk. All it seemed to take from her was a smile, some warmth, and they opened up. When he remarked about it once, she had explained that everyone had a story to tell.

She looks so pretty today, he thought, eyeing her curvy shape in a red dress, a dark blue jacket draped over the briefcase she carried.

He knew of witnesses who arrived hostile, unwilling to testify and angry over a long wait, who found themselves discussing things with her that they'd had no intention of talking about. He had also seen battered and abused victims trust her instantly.

"It's a real gift," Philip often told others. "Madeline could get conversation out of a stone."

Philip's thoughts returned to the present. He rushed to hold open the door that read "Authorized Personnel Only."

"Thanks, Philip." Madeline smiled at him warmly.

As the two of them walked down the hall, Gary Sutter stuck his head out his door and called, "Madeline!"

"I'll see you later," she said.

Watching her disappear, Philip felt a strange sadness. It was one thing to wait patiently for her to realize how much he cared, hopeful she would return his feelings someday. It was another thing to see her get involved with someone who didn't deserve her.

Philip had been the sole voice against hiring Gary Sutter, who had worked as a prosecutor in the D.A.'s office in San Francisco before coming to Los Angeles. Philip's objection wasn't anything specific—it was just a gut feeling. Sutter didn't have a sense of humor; he always seemed so serious, almost brooding. Philip considered a sense of humor essential to work in a place like this; things could get pretty grim. But aside from all that, he simply didn't like the man.

* * *

Inside Gary's small and cluttered office, Madeline collapsed into a chair. Her purse landed with a bang on the floor the same instant as her briefcase. "I'm beat." She pointed to the overstuffed case. "I can't seem to get finished."

"We do have large case loads," he agreed.

"It's also the lack of support staff. This morning I came in early to type my own pleadings."

"That's hardly fair."

"It's easier than telling the judge my secretary went home sick." She frowned, mimicking. "My secretary's got the flu, Your Honor, may I please have another continuance?"

He grimaced.

Gazing at him, she thought Gary was the sexiest-looking man she had ever known. His hooded green eyes, tousled brown hair, and full, sensuous mouth sent her pulse racing. Not to mention his superb physique. "Besides, I've got to clear my calendar. Philip assigned me the D'Arcy murder."

"I heard." There was a slight frown on his face. "Some people have all the luck."

Madeline wondered if that was envy she heard in his voice. "Philip's very fair," she hastened to explain. "You're on the list, I'm sure."

"I better be." For a moment the frown turned into a scowl. "So how's the plum assignment of the year coming?"

"We're about to arrest the lover. Nothing yet on the co-conspirator. At the moment, the wife's the leading contender for the spot. And if I were a betting person, I'd lay odds on her. She's got to be guilty."

"Without the lady, the kid's got no motive."

"That's the way I see it too. But don't worry. I'm going to get her."

He reached across the desk to take her hand. Rubbing it gently, he put it to his lips. "I'm sure you will. Anyway, I'm looking forward to Saturday night."

"Me too." Madeline felt warm all over and she knew her face was flushed. Glancing at her watch, she reluctantly grabbed her briefcase and purse. "I've got to run. See you later."

Armed with an arrest warrant, Bower and Donaldson drove over to Tommy Bartholomew's apartment in Northridge. Bower rang the bell. After another minute he rang it again, twice.

"Coming," called a voice. When the person inside got closer to the door, he asked, "Who's there?"

"Police, open up."

"Shit. I've told you guys all I know."

"Open up, Bartholomew, or we're coming in after you."

The door quickly opened. Tommy stood there with a look of surprise on his face. "What the hell?"

"You're under arrest for the murder of James D'Arcy," stated Bower. He breathed a sigh of relief when Bartholomew offered no resistance as they hooked him up and read him his rights.

"O.K., let's go." Bower moved with Bartholomew to the door.

Outside, Donaldson got into the front of the car to drive while Bower sat in the back seat with the kid. Although Bower and Donaldson made small talk, Bartholomew remained silent.

When they arrived at headquarters, the two officers waited while Tommy was booked. Then, after placing a call to Madeline Gould to tell her of the arrest, they took the kid to an interrogation room.

"You wanna give us a statement?" asked Bower.

"What for?" Tommy shoved his hands into the pockets of his jeans. "I didn't have anything to do with killing D'Arcy."

"If you didn't kill him, should be no problem to answer some questions."

"Like what?"

"We'd like to tape your statement."

"I don't know."

"You just said you didn't do it. You wanna change that?"

"Hell, no. O.K." Tommy shrugged and Bower nodded to Donaldson, who set the machine up to record.

After Bower stated the names of those present and the date he asked the young man. "What involvement did you have in James D'Arcy's death?"

"I didn't have anything to do with his death."

"But you were in love with D'Arcy's wife, weren't you?"

"Yeah. So what?" Tommy's brown eyes glared at them defiantly.

"Didn't you want her husband out of the way?"

Tommy fidgeted in his chair. "What do you mean?"

Bower placed his gun on the table. "You ever say to Sandra D'Arcy you wished her husband was dead?"

"Can I have a smoke?"

"You gonna be straight with us?"

"Yeah, sure."

Bower handed him a cigarette and bent over to light it. "I want the truth, Bartholomew. Even if you didn't mean it, did you ever say those words: 'I wish he was dead'?"

"Yeah. But it was a joke. We didn't do anything."

Bower exchanged a surprised glance with Donaldson. "So you talked about getting rid of D'Arcy?"

"Yeah, but so what? There's no law about just talking, is there?"

"When was the last time you saw Mrs. D'Arcy?"

"The other day."

"Where was that?"

Tommy proceeded to tell them about meeting Sandra in the market parking lot.

"Why'd you have to meet her in a parking lot?"

"She said her sister-in-law was giving her a hard time." Tommy shrugged again. "It was O.K. with me."

"She give you anything at that meeting?"

The kid's brown eyes couldn't quite meet Bower's. "What do you mean?"

"She give you some money? An airplane ticket? Anything like that?"

"Yeah." He nodded. "She gave me some money."

"How much did she give you?"

"A thousand."

"Did you and Mrs. D'Arcy talk about her divorcing her husband?"

"Yeah. We always talked about it, but it was no use."

"Why not?"

"He said he'd take her kid away from her."

"How'd she feel about his threats to take her kid away from her?"

"Not good, I can tell you that. She was real unhappy."

"Could you be more specific? Did she say what she'd like to do to him?"

Tommy gave a half-smile. "She said she'd give anything to be out of the crummy marriage she was in."

"And did Mrs. D'Arcy ever show you her gun?"

"Yeah, once."

"Where'd she keep it? You remember?"

Tommy paused. "In her room, I think. Hey, I don't like where this is going. I—"

"You take it with you when you left her house?"

"No!"

"When did she give the gun to you, Bartholomew?"

"What're you talking about?" His voice rose with alarm. "She never gave me a gun."

Bower sat on the table, his face friendly. "Bartholomew, why don't you tell us about the night D'Arcy was killed. Where you went, what you did."

"I told you. I went to a bar about four o'clock. I had some beers. I was upset 'cause Sandra said we couldn't see each other."

"Bartender see you?"

"Yeah."

"He doesn't remember seein' you that night."

"Well, I was there! Ask him if he remembers the guy sitting next to me. He bought me a few beers. He can vouch for me."

"What was the man's name?"

Tommy hesitated. "I'm not sure. I think it was Vincent."

"Then what happened?"

"I felt really sick, like I was gonna pass out. This man, this Vincent, was kind of nice about it. He said he'd drive me home. I gave him the keys to my car. He helped me into the bedroom and that's the last thing I remember."

"Now why don't you tell us the truth?" said Bower, suddenly becoming confrontational. "Why don't you tell us how you drove up to the D'Arcy place, waited for the man to come home, and then shot him? Why don't you tell us how Mrs. D'Arcy helped you to make sure the man would have to stop and get outta his car? Why don't you come clean?"

Tommy's wary expression changed to one of fear. "I think I better have a lawyer," he stammered.

"Sure, if you want one, you got a right," said Donaldson, stepping in. "But you've been doing a good job of telling us what happened. Why not finish?"

Bower flashed a worried look at his partner. Donaldson must know he was out of bounds. Once they asked for a lawyer, a cop had to stop the questioning or risk violating the accused's constitutional rights.

"I think I should have a lawyer," Tommy repeated stubbornly.

"O.K.," said Bower, knowing he had no choice but to do as requested.

Donaldson glanced at Bower as if to say, Fuck, and slammed out the door.

Tommy was scared. This thing was getting way out of hand. The only person he could think of to call was Burt, the guy who worked in the exercise place.

Burt promised to ask around and find a lawyer for Tommy. He asked a bookie he knew downtown. After the usual runaround, the guy gave him a name.

Andrew Stewart heard the beeping of his pager and went to the telephone. When he found out what was up, he was ecstatic. As luck would have it, he was already on his way to the jail to see another client.

Of course, he wouldn't be the only one trying to get through to Tommy Bartholomew. A case like this attracted a lot of criminal defense lawyers. Some of them wanted a high-publicity case. Others wanted to champion the underdog. Still others wanted the money they could get for defending him. Andrew personally thought all three reasons were perfectly valid.

However, if Tommy was indigent, then the state would have to pay for him to have a lawyer. Usually, these were public defenders. But once in a while, they farmed the case out to a private lawyer.

There was also the possibility that Tommy had family. It was surprising what parents, sisters, brothers, would do when one of their own was arrested. Families were usually in complete denial, not understanding how their own flesh and blood could have committed murder. Often they were willing to put up their houses, cars, or whatever else they had to pay for a lawyer.

The media were already going crazy, especially the tabloids, speculating as to the causes behind the murder. When they found out Tommy had been arrested, they would have a field day. Andrew thought about taking the case and the resulting publicity. He knew that once he was on record as Tommy's attorney, a judge would not let him out of the obligation unless Tommy asked him to do so.

In Andrew's mind Tommy would have no chance unless he got a top-notch lawyer. The D'Arcy family would put a lot of pressure on the D.A.'s office to nail James's killer. Tommy could become a sacrificial lamb.

That was why Andrew liked to even up the odds. He knew he could help Tommy. He always relished a fight like this—especially with the whole world watching.

Coming down the hallway to the jail, he saw that the news of the arrest was already out. The corridor was filled with reporters as he made his way to where they were holding Tommy. One of the reporters recognized him and asked if he was going to be the kid's lawyer.

"No comment yet," said Andrew, smiling as he pushed

through the door. Inside, he brazenly asked to see his client, Tommy Bartholomew. The guard knew Andrew and sent for the prisoner.

When Tommy was ushered into the visitor's room, he looked confused. Andrew smiled his most charming smile and held out his hand. "Hi, Tommy, I'm Andrew Stewart. I'm a lawyer and I've been recommended by a friend of Burt's."

Tommy sighed. Andrew knew he was sizing him up, from his tailored suit down to his expensive leather loafers. "I haven't got any money."

"Don't worry about it," said Andrew smoothly. "We'll work something out. You have any family?"

Tommy nodded. "A mother and a sister. In Kansas."

"Your mother live in a house or an apartment?"

Tommy looked confused. "A house. Why?"

"Just curious. She own it?"

"Her and the bank. Hey, you got a cigarette?"

Andrew handed him one from a silver case he kept in his briefcase for his clients.

The young man lighted it and handed back the matches. "You going to ask her to pay you?"

"I'd like to call her and discuss it."

"I don't know." Tommy inhaled deeply. "My mother and I don't get on so great."

"Give me her number and let me find out what she says."

"What if it's no?"

Andrew patiently explained to Tommy how a judge would appoint a lawyer from the public defender's office if Tommy was indigent.

"What's that mean?"

After Andrew told him, Tommy seemed worried. "Are those lawyers any good?"

"Some are, some aren't," said Andrew. "Of course, they do have very big case loads. If I take the case, I'll devote most of my time just to you."

Tommy took a few drags of his cigarette as he stared at the table. "O.K. You better call her."

After giving Andrew the information, Tommy looked up at him. "Now what?" Andrew could see he was nervous.

"I'll see if I can make the financial arrangements with her. In the meantime, you tell anyone who asks that I'm your lawyer. Here's my card with my number. You'll be needing it."

"O.K., so now you're my lawyer," said Tommy, absently fingering the card. "What's next?"

"I don't want you speaking to the police about anything unless I'm present."

"I already told them some shit."

Andrew frowned. "What kind of 'shit'?"

"Just about the affair and things."

"Sit down, Tommy. We need to get one thing straight. If I'm going to represent you, you've got to pay attention. This could mean your neck." Andrew gestured with his finger across his throat. "Now I want you to think for a moment, then repeat to me every word you told them."

Tommy's brashness disappeared, and a scared kid sat there. He started talking. When he was finished, Andrew got up and walked around the room.

"They read you your rights?"

"Yeah."

"When? Before or after you told them those things?"

"Before."

Andrew fingered his chin thoughtfully for a moment, then grinned at Tommy. "Well, you must not have understood them, I guess." He sat down and furiously wrote some notes. "We'll see if we can't get the judge to suppress your statements."

"O.K. But I didn't kill him."

"Sure, kid, whatever you say."

Reporters started calling Manning & Anderson. Charles heard about it and walked into Kate's office. "Can you reach someone at the D.A.'s office and find out what's going on?"

"Sure." Kate made a call, asked some questions, and hung up.

"Tommy Bartholomew's been arrested for James D'Arcy's murder. There are no immediate plans to charge anyone else."

"I better tell Franklin and Abigail. Then I'll call Sandra. I'll tell her you'll be phoning to set up an appointment."

"Remember, until I meet with her, I'm not agreeing to represent her."

Charles nodded absently. Back in his own office, he buzzed Franklin on the intercom. The senior partner's secretary explained that he had gone to the doctor. Charles left a message. Now he had no choice but to telephone Abigail with the disturbing news.

"Send Kate up here to meet with me," ordered Abigail. "I want to talk with her before she sees Sandra."

"Of course, Abigail. I'll tell her right away."

He dialed Sandra next.

"Oh God!" she cried when he told her about Tommy's arrest.

"It'll be O.K. By the way, you remember my associate, Kate Alexander, don't you? She was at the reading of the will."

"Yeah."

"She'll be calling you today to arrange an appointment. I want you to be totally honest with her."

"Why aren't *you* going to be my lawyer?"

"Sandra, I'm not a criminal lawyer."

"I'm *not* a criminal. I want you!"

"I really can't. Abigail and I already discussed it and we decided that Kate would be the best one to represent you."

"I don't want some damn woman for my attorney!" Sandra shouted at him.

"Look, you're in no position to be giving orders!" Charles retorted; then, in a calmer voice, he added, "Come on, Sandra, be reasonable. Kate and I discuss everything. I'll know what's going on at all times, I promise. And if you need me, just whistle."

From the other end of the telephone came only a sullen silence.

"I'll expect you to make yourself available for Kate," he said. "O.K.?"

"Shit," she said, and hung up.

17

On her way to the D'Arcy mansion, Kate wondered why the older woman wanted to see her alone without Sandra. After all, Sandra was the potential client and the person Kate was most anxious to talk with. As for the case itself, Charles was right about one thing. Publicity was good for Kate's political future. But she still didn't know, if Sandra was guilty, how that would affect her career.

When she was shown into the upstairs suite, Kate found Abigail sitting in a high-backed chair instead of a wheelchair. Her bearing, her facial expression, the faultless silver waves that crested her head, all made the woman appear regal. Especially the glacial look with which she assessed Kate.

Seeing Abigail's formal dress, Kate was glad she had worn her classic navy-blue suit. She peered around. In one corner of the grand room was a beautiful Chippendale couch covered in a chintz that reminded Kate of a summer garden. Against the far wall was what she assumed to be a genuine Louis XIV desk and matching chair.

Abigail motioned for Kate to sit on the small love seat next to her, covered in the same flowery chintz as the couch. "Tea?"

"Please."

Kate took the cup and saucer from the woman, trying not

to stare at the huge diamond ring on her aging, manicured hand.

"I thought we should get acquainted," Abigail said as she appraised Kate. "I am sure you have heard I do not give a hoot about Sandra. I do not deny there is no love lost between us. After all, my son could have married any woman he chose."

"I had the privilege of meeting Mr. D'Arcy," Kate said softly.

"Then you know what I mean," said Abigail. "I want you to know I do not condone my daughter-in-law's affair with that construction worker . . ." Her voice trailed off as she shuddered. "My son did not deserve a wife who acted in such a common way, so beneath him." Abigail sat quietly for a few moments, her hands folded in her lap. "If I thought Sandra was involved in James's death, I would not hesitate to destroy her."

The old woman's threat sent an involuntary shiver up Kate's spine.

Abigail waved her hand, the diamond flashing. "However, there is James's child to consider. Along with the D'Arcy name, my grandson is the most important thing in my life. Someday he will vote his father's shares and take his rightful place at the helm." A momentary softness crossed her features.

"I'm sure he'll do a fine job," said Kate, not knowing what else to say.

The matriarch seemed to be in a world of her own. "It will be hard for anyone to step into James's shoes. However, I will see that James junior is ready when the time comes." She paused. "What I *am* worried about is the effect of all this notoriety on my grandson. Heaven only knows what the child might see on the television." She shook her head in disgust. "I do not know what is happening to our world. The media used to tread more carefully around people like us."

"I can understand your concern. It's not an easy situation for a four-year-old to handle."

Abigail graced Kate with her first smile of their meeting.

"That is why I must see that my grandson never forgets what a great man his father was."

"I'm sure you'll keep his father's memory alive for him."

The old woman's eyes bored into Kate unmercifully. "In order to accomplish that, I will need your help."

"I'll do whatever I can, Mrs. D'Arcy."

"Good. I was counting on that."

Kate noted Abigail's tone was now one of a conspirator, and she wondered what exactly the woman was getting at.

"My grandson must come to live with me." There was a slight smile on Abigail's thin lips. "And Sandra must think his coming to live at D'Arcy Oaks is your idea."

Kate squelched her irritation. This woman was trying to manipulate her. If Abigail expected her to represent Sandra, then she had to realize the well-being of her client would always be paramount to Kate.

Listening to Abigail, Kate recalled how James's family had treated Sandra at the funeral. She felt a twinge of pity for the young widow who obviously had a formidable opponent in this old woman. "Mrs. D'Arcy, before I can recommend anything, I have to meet with Sandra."

Abigail glanced at Kate sharply. "Of course." She raised her regal eyebrows a notch and her voice became saccharin sweet. "Charles has assured me you will be made a partner soon."

Kate felt her color rising. "I hope so."

"A situation like this can make or break a career." The voice was still pleasant, but now it had an icy undertone.

"True." Kate was guarded.

The woman folded her hands together and straightened her spine. "For my grandson's sake, I expect you to prove his mother had nothing to do with his father's death."

Kate was becoming exasperated. One moment this woman issued veiled threats and demanded her grandson be brought to live with her. The next minute she dispensed ridiculous orders. "Mrs. D'Arcy, if Sandra is not charged with a crime, we don't get a chance to prove anything in a court of law. But if she's tried, my job is to destroy the prosecution's case by convincing the jury they can't prove, beyond a reasonable doubt, that Sandra had anything to do with your son's death. Absolute proof of innocence doesn't really enter into a criminal case.''

"I see." Abigail studied Kate for a moment. "Well, then I expect you to do more than your job. I want Sandra cleared. I do not want my grandson to grow up believing his mother is a murderess.''

"I'll certainly do my best," said Kate, deciding that this was not the moment to argue with Abigail D'Arcy.

"Then your best must be very, very good, Miss Alexander.''

After Kate left, Abigail called Charles. "She is gone.''

"I trust all went well," he said.

"That remains to be seen." Abigail was silent for a moment. "I will say one thing for Kate, she has spunk. She stood right up to me and that is no easy task.''

"That's true," he said, chuckling to himself at Kate's audacity. Even he didn't stand up to Abigail very well.

"Nevertheless, it will be your responsibility, Charles, to see that she does as expected.''

"You know you can count on me," Charles responded.

Driving back to the office, Kate realized that Abigail hadn't even asked her if she wanted to represent Sandra. She had merely treated it as a foregone conclusion. What nerve. In fact, the whole interview had gone quite differently than expected. Kate had assumed Abigail would ask her questions about herself and her background, then give her a chance to ask some questions also. Instead, the woman had tried to coerce her. Well, Abigail D'Arcy might think that her becoming Sandra's lawyer was a *fait accompli*, but it wasn't.

One other thing bothered her. While the woman insisted Sandra be proved blameless, she also wanted her grandson brought to live with her as though his mother had already been found guilty. Very strange, Kate mused, unless Abigail's assertion that she believed in her daughter-in-law's innocence was merely an act.

Back at the firm, Kate marched into Charles's office to tell him she was still undecided. "I'm a defense lawyer, not a miracle worker. In my humble opinion, there's a good possibility that Sandra's guilty!" She drummed her fingers on her briefcase.

"Calm down," he urged. "Let's talk this over."

She ignored his suggestion. "I'm not at all sure this is a wise career move for me. I've all kinds of speeches to give, meetings to attend, not to mention the cases I told you about. If Sandra's charged, there will be a trial." A frown brought her brows together. "I don't know if I'm willing to make that kind of a time commitment. I've got an election to get ready for."

"You'll get help," he said hurriedly, motioning her to sit. "I'll be right back."

Where was he going? she thought impatiently. When he returned a few minutes later, Franklin Manning was with him. Damn. Why did he have to involve the senior partner? She really wanted to discuss this matter with Charles first. She braced herself, realizing that even more pressure was about to be put on her.

"Sit down, sit down," the senior partner directed Kate when she rose to greet him. "Charles has told me your concerns, and you have my word that you'll have all the help you need."

"Thank you, Mr. Manning. I appreciate that." Kate wondered why it was so important to all of them that she become Sandra D'Arcy's lawyer. In the three years she had been at Manning & Anderson, she'd barely spoken to the senior partner. True, he was rarely at the office since his heart attack, but still it was odd for him to come to Charles's office to see her instead of the other way around. "However," she added, "it's possible Sandra would be better off represented by an independent attorney or defense firm—one that's not entangled in her dead husband's life and business."

"My dear Kate, we've considered that," said Franklin. "But Abigail D'Arcy wants Sandra's defense to stay with us. She doesn't trust another firm to be as discreet, if you know what I mean."

She looked from him to Charles, trying to decipher the true meaning of that statement. "Sandra will have to sign a conflict-of-interest waiver."

"Of course," said Charles.

"You know, Kate, it isn't every day one gets a chance to do something important," Franklin added.

Her face impassive, she waited quietly for him to explain.

"As senior partner, I must consider what's best for Manning & Anderson. Does that mean anything to you?"

"Of course. . . ."

"Good. Glad we understand each other." He patted her hand. "Doing as the D'Arcy family wishes is usually good for Manning & Anderson and therefore good for business. What's good for business is also good for Kate Alexander's future."

The import of his words couldn't be any clearer, she thought. If I represent Sandra, I've a better chance at the partnership and a better chance to run for D.A. If I don't . . . She refused to let her mind wander in that direction. It was evident to her that at Manning & Anderson, the wishes of their high-powered clients came before any personal concerns a mere associate might have. No, that wasn't true. She guessed that even as a partner, her decisions would never be entirely her own.

She cast a surreptitious glance at Charles. Although she wanted his support, she sadly realized that because of his own agenda, Charles couldn't be expected to oppose Franklin Manning to help her. The ball was clearly in her court.

"May I have a day or two to think things over?" she asked. "I haven't even had a chance to meet with Sandra D'Arcy about all this."

Franklin frowned ever so slightly. "It would be best for all concerned if you could see your way clear to a decision now."

"I see." She stalled for time, but in her heart she knew if she wanted them to back her for D.A., she was going to have to pay their price. She only hoped there weren't too many other hidden costs she didn't know about. For whatever reason, the powers that be had decided on her representing Sandra. But if Sandra was charged with murder, and Kate was not able to get her acquitted, she might find herself and her own future sacrificed for the good of Manning & Anderson.

"I'll do whatever the firm asks of me," she said reluctantly.

"I knew you'd see it our way." A faint smile played around the older man's lips as he nodded approvingly at her. "I consider it a personal favor to me, my dear."

After Manning had left, Kate turned to Charles. "Did you have to get him involved?"

"You needed to know where the real pressure is coming from."

She took a deep breath, determined to regain some lost ground. "I'll want Marty to start some investigative work for me right away."

Charles hesitated. "We have a fine private investigator on our staff, Frank Jones."

"If I'm going to have to fight you for every additional expense . . ." Her voice had a definite edge to it. "I don't intend to put up with penny-pinching at this point. Marty's the best there is."

He walked over to the window and glanced out. "I'm not going to fight you at all. I just heard that Marty got fed up with the rat race, closed his office, and left town."

Kate's face registered a look of annoyance. "He couldn't have. He had several ongoing cases."

He shrugged. "I'll check it out if you want."

"I'd appreciate it. I'm swamped."

At eleven the next morning, Tommy Bartholomew was brought before Judge Harry Jackson in Division 5 of the municipal court in the Criminal Courts Building in downtown Los Angeles.

Kate had been told about the appearance and arrived early. Glancing around, she saw that the courtroom was so packed with reporters and spectators that not one more person could have been squeezed in.

Tommy was wearing ill-fitting jail clothes and looked uncomfortable. Next to him Kate was surprised to see Andrew Stewart. He was quite a striking man. She fleetingly recalled having the same impression the day they had met briefly at the Century Plaza Hotel.

Kate saw Madeline at the prosecution table and made a note to find out if she was going to be the deputy D.A. assigned to the case.

Tommy was arraigned. The judge set his preliminary hearing in ten days. Andrew requested a continuance and the judge asked Tommy if he was willing to waive his right to a preliminary hearing within ten days of his arraignment. Tommy, looking pale, said yes. The postponement was granted. As to the question of bail, this being a special circumstance murder case involving what Madeline labeled "murder for profit" and "lying in wait," bail was denied. Tommy was led back to jail.

Kate went up to Madeline. "Hi. You assigned this case?"

"Yes." Madeline was all business. "What brings you here today?"

"I've been asked to advise Sandra D'Arcy." Kate's tone was matter-of-fact, following Madeline's lead.

The deputy D.A.'s eyebrows rose slightly. "I see. Well then, we could be on opposite sides in this one."

"What are the chances of that?" Kate knew Madeline could be forthcoming or not as she chose, but as a rule, prosecutors tried to cooperate with former prosecutors. Kate was hoping that would prove true in this case.

"If I could, I'd arrest her tomorrow." Madeline's brown eyes were clear and direct.

"I see." Kate sighed, relieved Madeline had been frank. "Can you tell me anything more?"

"No. Not right now, I'm afraid."

"O.K. Thanks for your candor."

"You're welcome."

Kate walked out into the hallway and saw Andrew speaking into a microphone as the glare of bright lights shone in his face and the crush of reporters pushed to get at him.

"It's my belief the D.A.'s office doesn't have a case against my client," he said, smiling.

As she watched him, he looked over, caught her eye, and motioned for her to wait. She strode to the end of the hall and peered out the window. A few minutes later she heard his voice behind her.

"Hello, Kate. Nice to see you again."

"Hello, Mr. Stewart. How are you?"

"*Mister* Stewart," he mocked. "Please call me Andrew. Now that you're here, I'm great. You come to see the arraignment or just in the neighborhood?"

Kate had a hard time concentrating, he was smiling at her in such a teasing way. "I came to see the arraignment."

"Any particular reason?"

She did her best to keep her voice as light as his. "I heard you'd be performing your unique brand of magic and wanted to see for myself."

His laugh resonated deeply. "Hope I didn't disappoint you?"

"Well, I see you weren't able to get your client out on bail." She smiled to soften the blow of her words. "But I would have been surprised if the judge *had* allowed that. Otherwise, I was quite impressed."

Again he laughed, showing her he had a nice sense of humor. "Well, now that you've told me royally how I failed, how about joining me for lunch? As a consolation prize." His eyes flirted with her unmercifully.

Kate was dismayed to find herself tempted. The last thing she needed was to have her life complicated by this arrogant man. She looked at her watch. "I'm afraid I have another engagement. Thank you anyway."

"I'll walk you to your car."

"That's not necessary." She felt the color rising in her cheeks when he looked at her, questioning.

"I promise not to bite." He grinned mischievously.

It was her turn to smile. "I'll take your word for it. Anyway, I'm in a rush. It was nice seeing you." Before he could register a protest, she walked quickly away, a bit unsettled by the way her heart was hammering in her chest.

Andrew watched Kate leave, amused. He liked a challenge and this beautiful woman, with her ivory skin, flashing green eyes, and black hair, was definitely not falling for his charm.

He wondered why she was here today. He knew that she was at Manning & Anderson, so she could have been here on behalf of the D'Arcy family to report back on how justice was being served. Or, a much more interesting possibility, she could be planning to represent Sandra D'Arcy. In that case, if Sandra was charged as a co-conspirator, he and Kate would probably be seeing a lot of each other in the future.

He checked the time. He had to get to the bank. Tommy's mother was wiring him the first installment of his fee today. She'd promised to work on arranging a second mortgage on her home as soon as possible. Ordinarily, he'd have demanded a guarantee up front. But this case was too good to pass up. And if Kate Alexander was going to be a part of it, he'd enjoy it even more.

Kate paced back and forth in Sandra D'Arcy's small sitting room off the large drawing room. She was annoyed at being kept waiting. It was fifteen minutes before her client finally appeared. The young widow was wearing a pink leotard, black tights, and sweatband. Kate noticed that Sandra's face was flushed.

"I'm so sorry," murmured Sandra sweetly. "I thought the housekeeper said you were calling from your car phone."

"Oh, really?" Kate knew damn well Sandra was lying and had kept her waiting while she finished exercising. "Where can we talk privately?" Her voice was cool. "I need to take notes."

"The solarium." Sandra led the way. "Want some iced tea?"

"No thank you." Kate gazed around at the sunny room

filled with wrought iron and glass furniture. Its lush greenery and brightness appealed to her.

"What do you want to know?"

"What the police asked you and what you've told them." Kate opened her briefcase and took out a yellow legal pad and a pen.

Sandra shook her head. "I can't even remember it all. They were here four times."

"I suggest you try. This is very serious business."

"I've already told Charles," Sandra said hotly.

"Mrs. D'Arcy, or may I call you Sandra since we're going to be seeing each other quite a lot?"

"Sure, why not?" Sandra shrugged.

"Good. Call me Kate." She twirled her pencil. "I know you've told Charles. But since I'm the one who'll be advising you in this matter, I need you to tell me also."

"Why do I have to deal with you? Charles was James's lawyer. He's supposed to take care of me, too."

"I understand how you must feel. But first off, this is a criminal matter you're involved in. I'm the firm's criminal lawyer. Secondly, Charles is handling quite a lot since your husband's death. The D'Arcy Company and D'Arcy Foundation are both full-time jobs."

Sandra crossed her legs and stuck out her chin stubbornly. "I don't care."

"Maybe you don't, but this is the way it is." Kate looked Sandra directly in the eye, her voice even. "Mr. Rieman and your mother-in-law expect you to cooperate with me. So let's both make the best of it."

"Fuck!" Sandra pulled off her sweatband and shook her hair loose. "I'm so tired of that damn family running my life. What the hell do you wanna know?"

"Start at the beginning and tell me everything," said Kate.

Sandra was explaining things to Kate, although her manner and attitude were still rude, when Kate heard the doorbell ring.

A minute later Victoria D'Arcy Mandeville burst into the room, angrily waving a newspaper. "I just got back from

Aspen''—her nostrils flared and her thin mouth was pinched with fury—''and I find headlines screaming about some jerk my sister-in-law's been screwing who's been arrested for my brother's murder!''

"I didn't know you were back," said Sandra lamely.

"How dare you disgrace this family?"

Sandra sat there, mute.

Victoria wagged her finger at Sandra. "You better not have had anything to do with my brother's death or you'll wish you had died with him!"

Kate couldn't help but notice the effect of Victoria's tirade on Sandra. The young woman blanched. Here was someone Sandra was definitely afraid of. Why? she wondered.

18

Kate was upset as the entire week passed and Charles made one excuse after another not to come over to her place. It seemed he was avoiding her, and his coolness was baffling. In the past, even though he was always careful in public, he'd slip her little love notes or secretly wink at her. Lately she felt no warmth of any kind from him.

He was also making it impossible for her to talk to him by having a continual procession of people going in and out of his office. When he broke his promise to take her to the Joffrey Ballet, even though the tickets had been purchased weeks in advance, she knew his actions were deliberate.

She was rushing back from her office with some papers Charles had requested on the Suni criminal investigation, when, without meaning to, she overheard his secretary on the telephone.

"I'm confirming the honeymoon suite for Mr. and Mrs. Charles Rieman for this weekend. Right. They'll be arriving on American Airlines, flight number two hundred at Kennedy."

A wave of nausea swept over Kate. Reaching out to steady herself, she felt the secretary's words reverberate in her ears. As soon as she was able to move, she raced for the ladies' room and slammed the door behind her. She soaked some paper towels in cold water, then held them against her flushed face. Tears stung her eyes as she pressed the heels of her hands hard against her eyelids, trying not to cry.

Doubt filled her. Then rage. Yanking dozens of paper towels out of the holder, she ripped them apart and rolled them into a wad which she threw against the mirror. I hate him, she fumed at her reflection.

Why had he lied to her? Determined to have it out with him, she marched toward his office. But she was stopped cold by the sight of Charles standing in the hallway with several men she instantly recognized as political honchos. Damn, I'll never get him alone now, she swore to herself as the door to his office closed.

She knew she had to calm down or she'd blow it all— him, her entire future, everything. Grabbing her purse, she called to her secretary, "Mary, I'll be back in an hour— something's come up."

Running to her car, her high heels clacking loudly on the pavement, she jumped in, gunned the engine, and roared out of the garage, leaving a startled attendant in her wake. She headed for Holmby Hills, where she knew she could drive fast and avoid traffic.

Pain seared into her, making her feel as if she'd been smashed in the stomach. She beat her fist against the steering wheel so hard her hand throbbed. Finally, she pulled over to the side of the road. As her head rested against the wheel, sobs racked her body.

Why was he doing this? Hadn't he promised her in Catalina to ask Ann for a divorce as soon as possible? True, he'd said he couldn't leave yet, but he'd made it clear that he and Ann were barely speaking to each other, let alone sleeping together. The words "honeymoon suite" echoed in her mind. How could he?

After a while, taking deep breaths, she asked herself why men were so hateful, so selfish. As she searched her heart for the answers, she remembered another time in her life when she thought her heart would break.

She had been eight, and her parents had been separated and then divorced for over three years. She hadn't seen her father for a long time, when one day he arrived unexpectedly with lots of gifts. He scooped her up in his arms, calling her Katie and telling her she was beautiful. She felt so special. Then came the best part when he sat her on his lap and told her where he had been and what he had been doing. It sounded so exciting to her young ears.

When he said he had to leave, she was devastated, begging to go with him. Gently he explained he was going on a cruise and "little girls can't come." Promising to write, he had swept out of her life. He had never returned. To this day no one was allowed to call her Katie.

Damn Charles! she thought as she hit the steering wheel again with her fist.

When Andrew's secretary told him Lauren Cunningham was on the telephone, he realized it was the third time she had called and he had not called her back. "I'll take it. Hello."

"I was beginnin' to think you were avoiding me." Lauren's slight southern drawl didn't hide the peevishness in her voice.

"I've been really busy. Tommy Bartholomew retained me to represent him. He's the kid accused of murdering D'Arcy."

"I probably know more about it than you do. Our firm represents the D'Arcy family."

"I forgot." He hadn't, but he didn't want her to realize it. Lauren could be a valuable inside source, but he'd have to be careful. "Is that why Kate Alexander was at the arraignment?"

"You saw Kate?"

He heard the jealousy in her voice. "Yeah. I asked why she was there, but she didn't say."

"So what *did* you discuss?"

He laughed. "Small talk, Lauren, like people usually make when they've met but have nothing to say to each other." He heard her exhale, but he didn't want to give her a chance to change the subject before he found out what he needed to know. "Is Kate representing Sandra D'Arcy?"

"She hasn't been charged, has she?"

"No. But she's bound to be a witness."

"Charles Rieman was James D'Arcy's attorney. Kate's the firm's criminal lawyer. So make of it what you will." Her voice was edgy.

"That's probably why she was there. Wonder why she didn't want me to know."

"Who cares! I didn't call to talk about Kate. What's happening about Hawaii?"

Andrew sighed. "I'm afraid I won't be going now." He heard the sharp intake of her breath.

"You can't be spending all of your time on that one case?"

He chuckled. "I am. But all work and no play makes one a bore, doesn't it?"

"It certainly does."

"Then we'll have to rectify that. Listen, I've got another call coming in that I have to take. I'll call you tomorrow."

"Don't forget."

"I won't." When he hung up, he wrote down her name in his calendar. *Call Lauren to find out if she knows anything more about Kate representing Sandra D'Arcy.* Lauren was a beauty, and sexy too. And he couldn't very well forget all that money, he reminded himself. The only problem was that he liked to be the one who did the pursuing. Not the other way around.

* * *

Reporters mobbed Victoria D'Arcy Mandeville as she arrived at her brother Theo's house. Once inside, she barked, "Theo, get some of the company's security people here right away!"

Her shrill, demanding voice reminded Theo his sister was sounding more like James every day. "Hello, Victoria," he said soothingly.

"Don't be condescending," she snapped. "Call them. And why do you refuse to live behind gates like the rest of us?"

He sighed. It was impossible to win an argument with his strong-willed sister. After he made the call, he joined her in his living room, where he saw she had already poured herself a drink. "When did you get back from Aspen?"

"Did you know about the affair?" she demanded, her face twisted with anger.

"No, I didn't, Victoria."

"It was bad enough when James married that little tramp. Now she's brought further disgrace upon us. Why couldn't she fuck around quietly? How dare she do this!"

"We both know James was hard to live with."

"Who cares! I can tell you this, if she had anything to do with his death, she'll pay for it."

Theo watched his sister's anorectic body fidget nervously. "Don't be silly, Victoria," he said, trying his best to calm her down. "Sandra wouldn't have killed him."

"Ha! I bet you anything that bitch did it! She wanted it all. Sandra knew James wouldn't let go of her. Not after she produced the long awaited, precious heir to the D'Arcy fortune." She stopped pacing long enough to face her brother. "Somehow the rest of us have managed, or should I say mismanaged, not to produce an heir."

Her words sounded like an accusation to him.

"What does Mother say about all this?" Victoria demanded.

"Her first worry is the D'Arcy name. Her second concern is for her grandson." Theo tried, but couldn't keep the bitterness out of his voice.

"Mother can't seriously believe Sandra's innocent?"

"She chooses to believe the boyfriend murdered James to get Sandra for himself."

"I don't believe it for one second. Mother must be up to something. That construction worker, actor, whatever the fuck he is, wouldn't have murdered James without the tramp's help."

Theo shrugged. "Best to stay out of it. Mother wants us to be above it all. Remember, we're this city's answer to royalty."

"Aren't we though," she said with disdain. "By the way, where were you when James was murdered?"

"Home . . . alone."

Lauren walked gracefully in front of Dickson as the waiter showed them to a table in the Lobby Lounge of the Regent Beverly Wilshire. When they were seated, she smiled at him. "This lunch was my idea, so it's my treat." Before he could protest, she ordered a good bottle of wine.

After the waiter was gone, she put her napkin on her lap. "I'm so glad you could come." She started to bat her eyelashes, then changed her mind. A direct approach would be best. "You know, Dickson, our fathers have been friends for a lot of years."

"So they have."

"When Franklin retires, my daddy and I both think you'd be the perfect senior partner."

His eyes brightened. "I appreciate the vote of confidence."

The waiter appeared with the wine. While Lauren tasted it, her mind rehearsed her next words. She held her glass toward Dickson. "Here's to Manning & Anderson's next senior partner."

He clinked his glass to hers. "Thank you, Lauren."

"You're welcome," she drawled. She sipped her wine. "Did Franklin mention his lunch with my daddy the other day?"

"No, he didn't."

"Daddy told Franklin he should insist you take his place."

A dark cloud seemed to pass over Dickson's face. For a moment she worried she had said the wrong thing. "Daddy also feels as one of the firm's largest clients, he should have a say in the choice. And he wants you."

Dickson sat up straighter in his chair, obviously pleased by her words. "I respect Miles a lot."

"You know, Dickson . . ." She drew a painted fingernail along the tablecloth. "Daddy only gives a part of his legal business to Manning & Anderson. He gives the rest to firms with offices in major U.S. cities and abroad."

Dickson's immediate grin told her she had hit pay dirt. "That's exactly what I've been saying. We need an international presence to attract global clients like your father, and the only way to get it fast is to merge with a firm that's already there."

"Right. But Franklin seems to be against a merger of any kind. So's Charles."

"Father and Charles live in the past. I should meet with your father to discuss this further."

"No need for that. I have his unofficial proxy." She smiled. "That's why I asked you to lunch. From now on, I'll be the one deciding on who gets Daddy's business."

Dickson seemed to peer at her with newfound respect and Lauren mentally patted herself on the back. She had certainly found the way to this man's heart.

"If I had the promise of your father's global legal work in my hands, I'd be in a very strong position. Quite a few of the partners are still sitting on the fence between Charles and me. And the subject of a future merger seems to weigh heavily in the decision. Those who think I'm right are behind me. And of course"—he waved his hand in a dismissive gesture—"those who are crazy enough to think Charles is right are behind him."

"We need to get the word out that clients like my daddy are for a merger."

"Absolutely." He smoothed back his hair. "Lauren, I don't know how to thank you for bringing this to my attention."

She looked down at her fingernails for a second. Then her

blue-green eyes gazed at him. "There's a little something you could do . . ." She let her words trail off as she wrinkled her nose. "We'll talk about that later. Let's order."

By the time the waiter served them, Lauren could see Dickson was about to burst.

"Tell me what you need. Whatever it is, I'm sure I can help."

"Why, Dickson, how gallant of you to come to a poor girl's rescue. You know, you're not the only one whose future is threatened by Charles."

"Has that man done something to you?" His eye twitched.

"No, not directly. But I'm sure you're aware he favors Kate Alexander to become the next partner in the firm?" She was relieved to see a knowing look come into his eyes. Good, she wasn't going to have to spell it all out. She rushed on with her argument. "Now I know you like Owen a lot," she said, referring to one of the other associates up for the slot, "but I've got more potential as a big rainmaker."

"I agree. You're a natural."

Lauren was almost home free. She had one more hurdle to overcome. "But you know," she said coyly, "Arnold doesn't much like me."

"Why do you think that?"

"He says I don't work hard enough. But he's wrong. Why you should see my latest time sheets. My billing hours are way above what's required." She raised her eyebrows. "It's personal with Arnold."

"I'm not sure I follow you."

"Well . . ." She sighed. "Arnold resents the fact that my daddy helped get me into the firm. And he allows that to determine my value rather than my brains. Were you aware I was the one responsible for the new disclosure forms our broker clients are using?"

"No, I wasn't."

"See. What did I tell you? You know, Dickson"—she lowered her voice—"a smart person uses every little bit of help she or he can. Don't you think?"

"Absolutely." He nodded in agreement. "That shouldn't be held against you." He fingered his chin. "Arnold and I are very close. Let me talk to him. I'm sure I can convince him to change his mind."

"Well, if you could do that, I'd be ever so grateful. So would Daddy."

He smiled confidently. "Just leave it to me. There's no reason we both shouldn't get what we want."

"Thank you, Dickson. You're a prince of a man."

Dickson couldn't believe his good fortune. Lauren's little proposition was an answer to his prayers. Back at Manning & Anderson, he wasted no time in locating Arnold Mindell. He cornered the man in the john and related his meeting.

"I don't want Lauren for our next partner," said Mindell stubbornly as he shook himself off and zipped up his fly.

"Why not?"

"She's a know-it-all."

"Her father's business is worth millions of dollars in fees." Dickson squinted at Mindell. "Isn't her work up to par?"

The other man washed his hands. "It's fine."

Dickson hurried on. "You want us to merge with Livingstone & Kenter, don't you?"

"Yep."

"Then I've got to become senior partner." Dickson put his arm on Mindell's shoulder. "Once that's locked up, I'll repay the favor."

"I've wanted to be head of litigation for years, but Charles wanted Lester, and Franklin took his side."

"It's yours. Look, we need to meet with Emery and Ornstein, using Miles as the carrot to lock up their support. If we get those two partners to back me, there's a chance I can become senior partner on the first ballot." A sardonic grin pulled at the corners of Dickson's mouth.

Mindell studied Dickson's face for a moment as if deciding. "Let me think about it."

Dickson tried to hide his annoyance. "Don't think too long. We have to make our plans."

19

Kate gazed around at the throngs of people gathered in the Westside Room of the Century Plaza Hotel. She usually looked forward to these political get-togethers for candidates and their causes. Tonight, however, was different. All she could think about was Charles going to New York with Ann.

A waiter passed and Kate reached for another glass of wine, her third of the evening. I must be trying to get drunk, she mused. The numbness caused by the alcohol felt good as it spread throughout her body. It eased the pain and helped keep a smile pasted on her face.

She felt someone's gaze on her and looked up to see Andrew Stewart staring at her. As he made his way toward her, she was struck again by his stark blondness and his muscular body, discernible under the beautifully tailored suit. He moved like an athlete, she thought, and certainly had the body of one, wide at the shoulders, narrow at the hips.

She took a sip of her wine, conscious of the quickening of her pulse. It had been a long time since any man other than Charles had had any effect on her. But why does it have to be this one? she asked herself. If I want to take my mind off Charles, the room is certainly filled with handsome, eligible men. I don't need to mess with one Lauren's already staked out.

"Excuse me." Andrew grabbed Kate's elbow and steered her away from the crowd. Once they were out of earshot, he whispered, "I finally found you."

"So you have." As Kate looked into his laughing eyes, she felt a heat in her body, a sudden tension at his touch. She watched his tanned fingers reach for two wineglasses as a waiter passed by them with a tray, then hand one to her. "For you."

She held up her glass. "I already have a drink."

"Well, finish it and start on this one," he teased, a smile playing at the corner of his mouth.

"I'm already a little tipsy."

"That's the best news yet."

"Mr. Stewart, are you trying to get me drunk?"

"If that will make you more amenable to my dinner invitation, then by all means drink up." His blue eyes danced. "And please don't call me Mr. Stewart, it excites me."

"I'll try to remember." She smiled.

"Am I moving too fast for you?"

"That's a very leading question. Of course, one couldn't expect less from a prominent defense attorney." She laughed softly.

"Please say you'll have dinner with me."

"Aren't you seeing a friend of mine?"

"If you mean Lauren, the answer is not really."

Her eyes momentarily clouded over. "I thought you were."

"We've dated a few times, that's all. Nothing serious."

Kate wondered if Lauren viewed it that way. Recalling her friend's string of romances, first in law school and then at the firm, she knew Lauren never stayed interested for long in any man. But how Lauren could pass on this gorgeous creature was beyond her. "Perhaps another night," Kate said. "I've got a previous engagement." She looked at her watch. "Would you excuse me?"

"Not again," he protested. "You did that to me the last time I asked."

"I need to make a phone call."

"Promise me you'll come back." He gave her a crooked grin.

She laughed. "I promise."

Kate made her way to the ladies' room, where there was a telephone. She had slipped a note to Charles earlier saying she'd call him at seven. The few minutes she'd spent in

Andrew's company had been pleasant, distracting enough to give brief relief to the pain she had been feeling since that afternoon. Now she felt the apprehension settle in on her again. Please God, let me have heard wrong. I don't want him to be taking his wife to New York.

Charles's impatient voice answered the private line on the first ring. "Yes?"

"It's me, Kate."

"How's the cocktail party?"

"Still going. We had a large turnout."

"Good." He paused. "Well, I've made a dent in one pile, but the other side of my desk is as high as ever."

"There's always tomorrow." She forced her tone to be casual. "Charles, I have to talk to you tonight."

He sighed. "I can't. Warren called. He needs me to come to New York immediately."

The mention of Warren Thornton, head of Suni Industries, caused Kate's antenna to go up. "New York?" There was a sickening, dull ache in the pit of her stomach.

"Yes. Seems the board of directors is having trouble approving our figures for the takeover. He thinks if I talk to them, it'll help."

"When did you say he asked you to do this?"

"Just a couple of hours ago, and that's the problem. I've got to fly out tonight."

"Tonight?" So he was going to offer no explanation for Ann, she thought, touching the diamond pin he had bought her to pledge his love.

"I know you wanted to talk to me." He lowered his voice, his tone becoming intimate. "I miss you. Believe me, the last few weeks have been hell for me too." He hesitated. When she didn't reply, he continued. "James's death has certainly complicated our lives. I've lost my best friend right in the middle of the biggest takeover Suni has ever attempted. And Warren won't let anyone else handle things."

Kate knew he expected her sympathy. Only this time, he wasn't going to get it.

"Kate, are you there?"

"Yes, I'm here, Charles."

"I thought the line had gone dead." He coughed and cleared his throat. "If it were feasible, I'd ask you to come with me. It just isn't possible this trip, sweetheart." After another silence, he asked. "Kate, did you hear me?"

Her voice was barely audible. "Yes, I heard you."

"Then why aren't you answering me?" There was a slight edge to his voice. "I feel like I'm talking to myself."

"I need to see you tonight, Charles. Even for an hour." Why was she begging like this? It was so demeaning.

"I need to see you too, darling. Please be patient a little longer. If I grab the red-eye, I can meet with Warren before talking to the board in the morning."

Damn him, thought Kate. She knew absolutely that Warren Thornton was here in California for the weekend. She had even talked to him only a few hours ago. I'll give him one last chance, she decided. "It's seven o'clock now. You could meet me for an hour and still make the plane. I'll even drive you." Say yes, Charles, she thought, for God's sake, say yes.

"If it's so important it can't wait, talk to me now."

"Not on the telephone."

"Christ! I expected you to be more understanding."

"I'm the woman you love and want to marry, remember?" She raised her voice. "But you can't spare one lousy hour?"

"Kate, I don't know what's gotten into you, but I can't come over tonight. That's all there is to it."

"Goodbye, Charles," she said firmly. As she hung up the phone, she heard him yell, "Kate!"

She looked around, relieved that the ladies' room was empty and that no one had overheard her conversation. She was shaking. How dare he lie to me like that she fumed, her eyes glaring at her reflection in the mirror. Screw him, playing with me as if I'm some idiot, some stupid bimbo. I'll show *him*. She dabbed her wrists with perfume, freshened her lipstick, and made her way back to the ballroom.

Andrew was leaning against the bar watching the doorway. "You came back." He sounded pleased.

"I said I would. Now where were we?" She softened her pointed remark with a smile.

"I was begging you to go to dinner with me. You were telling me you had another engagement."

"I just canceled my plans," she said, with a touch of defiance. "But if I say yes, you must promise not to talk about the D'Arcy case."

"No problem." He smiled charmingly. "Where would you like to go?"

"I'm not really hungry. I filled up on hors d'oeuvres," she lied. She didn't want to tell this handsome man she'd been too upset to eat and that the idea of food sickened her at the moment. "I'd rather do something physical."

He grinned. "Now you're talking my game."

"Are you trying to take advantage of me?"

"I was hoping to talk you into taking advantage of me."

It was Kate's turn to laugh. "What I really meant was a game of tennis or maybe a run on the beach."

He seemed surprised. "I didn't figure you for a runner."

"I am. That's how I keep my sanity." She gestured toward her dress. "I'm really much happier in sweats than I am in clothes like this."

"Then let's go. I work out several times a week, so my things are in the car. Where do you like to run?"

"On the beach by my house. I live in Santa Monica."

Kate suddenly became wary. What was she doing? She hardly knew this man, and besides, he was such a flirt.

"Hey," he said, as if reading her mind. "What could be friendlier than the two of us jogging?"

He was right, she thought. "Let's." She smiled impishly.

He grabbed her arm and they went up the escalator to the lobby. "I'll follow you to the beach," he called out as she got into her car.

At her condominium, he parked next to her and was out of his car like lightning to open her door. When Kate walked into her place and snapped on the lights, Andrew whistled. He opened the sliding door and went out onto the patio. "This is wonderful."

She pointed to her den with its adjoining bath. "There are fresh towels in the bathroom. Help yourself to whatever you need."

Kate came out of the bathroom in baggy gray sweats to find Andrew waiting for her in a yellow sweatshirt and black shorts. She noticed that his legs were thick, muscular, and covered with blond hairs. She walked next to him down to the stretch of wet sand where the tide had already gone out.

She was surprised when Andrew told her he'd been one of eight children. "A good Catholic family," he said laughingly, relating how he'd grown up in the San Fernando Valley. His family sounded rather normal in a traditional sense. His mother had stayed home to take care of the kids, and his father had worked at the General Motors plant in Van Nuys. He was the first one to go to college. She had mistakenly thought Andrew was just another arrogant rich boy; somehow she felt better about him now.

"My father died when I was eight."

"I'm sorry." He looked at her solemnly.

She shrugged. "It's hard on a kid. My mother remarried when I was ten. I hated my stepfather. I have two stepbrothers but I never see either of them. I only talk to my mother. I was the first one in my family to go to college too. In fact, I had to leave home to do it because my stepfather objected."

"What did your mother say?"

"She felt bad, but wouldn't stand up to him for me. And when I went to law school, they both thought I was crazy." She made a face.

He laughed. "They must be proud of you now, though. I know my folks are."

She suddenly became quiet as she picked her way through the sand. "If my father was alive, he'd be proud." She exhaled loudly. Thinking of her father made her think of Charles and his betrayal. The pain was back. "Shall we get to it?"

They started to run, side by side. Kate set the pace, opting for steady, long strides rather than the shorter jogging steps. After a few minutes, they were puffing hard, inhaling and exhaling in long, controlled breaths. The only sound Kate heard was their feet on the sand and their breathing as she pushed herself to her limit. She didn't intend to allow Andrew to slow down for her sake.

Kate ran with a vengeance, as though she were trying to rid her body of some deadly toxins, her life dependent on it. With each stride, she screamed inside her mind. You fucker, you lied to me! she shouted silently to Charles Rieman. I hate you, but I hate myself more for believing you. I should have known better than to get involved with a married man.

Up until Charles had said he wished he could take her with him, she had prayed there was a logical explanation for Ann's going to New York. Maybe someone had died. Of course, that wouldn't have justified the honeymoon suite, but she was open to any excuse he could offer.

Why couldn't he have leveled with me, trusted me with the truth? she thought. Even if I hadn't liked it, I would have respected his honesty. No, the man had to lie, pretend he was seeing Warren Thornton, and sorry she couldn't go too. She felt tears stinging at the back of her eyes. She ran faster, intent on exorcising both Charles and the anger she felt at him.

After they had gone nearly two miles, Kate suddenly stopped. Her heart was pounding and she was breathing so hard it hurt. Her sweatsuit was completely drenched.

"Giving up on me," he teased.

"It must have been the wine," she admitted. "I think I've had enough." She started to walk in place.

Together, they started back at a cool-down pace. After a few minutes, they reverted to a walking pace, flexing and shaking their limbs. The beach was deserted. Kate stopped and bent forward at the waist, bracing her hands just above her kneecaps, hanging that way, trying to catch her breath. She was winded.

Andrew put his hands on his hips and leaned backward. She straightened to find him facing her, a strange look on his face.

"Forgive me for doing this, Kate, but I have to." He

pulled her to his damp, warm body, burying her lips beneath his in a passionate kiss.

Her entire body felt as if a scorching, deep heat were rising through it. She let her body melt into his, wanting to forget all the hurt and pain Charles had caused her.

Something inside stopped her, forcing her to pull back. Her sudden movement caused him to lose his balance and he fell to the sand, taking her with him. After they landed, he pulled her close and kissed her again, taking her breath away. This time she returned the kiss. When it ended, she felt his warm breath as he kissed the nape of her neck, around her shoulders, up to her ear, all the time murmuring low, throaty sounds.

"I want to make love to you," he whispered softly, soothingly, stroking her arm.

His words sounded far away. Oh God, why had Charles lied to her? A stab of pain raced through her and she forced herself to concentrate on the man she was with. The chemistry between them was palpable, but was this what she wanted? Lust? Why not? she thought. Maybe it will wipe out the agony.

His body felt hard and muscular against hers. When he slipped his hand under her sweatshirt, she felt shivers race up her spine. Then she ran her fingers under his shirt. Warmth, dampness, and rigid muscle greeted her caress.

She felt his hand move up her bare back to her shoulders, where he rubbed the tense muscles. Then he broke away to gaze at her. "I knew it would be like this when I kissed you."

No matter what she was feeling now, she knew tomorrow she would feel guilt. Yet she didn't want to stop.

"Let me stay with you," he whispered.

"For tonight only, if that's all I have to give?"

"Yes." He caught her hand and rolled to his feet, pulling her up with him. "But don't let's think about anything beyond tonight, for now at least. There's always time for that."

Kate stood in the shower, letting the spray wash over her, her eyes closed, her face uplifted. She felt a trifle foolish for having insisted they shower separately, but he had not blinked. She knew there were reasons that had nothing to do with Charles that should stop her from doing this. After all, Andrew represented Tommy Bartholomew in a capital case and Tommy's interests might differ greatly from Sandra D'Arcy's. But she didn't want to think rationally tonight.

I can handle it, keep it all separate, she thought. I have a right to this. Andrew's a handsome, eligible man who desires me, wants me, pursued me tonight when he could easily have had virtually any woman he wanted.

She dried herself, combed her hair back, and slipped into a silk nightgown. Back in her bedroom, she turned the lights off, leaving just the moonlight flooding the room.

There was a soft knock. Her heart pounded as Andrew made his way to where she was standing. When he got closer, she saw that he was naked except for a towel around his waist. His body was as beautiful as she had imagined.

He reached for her, holding her close as though it were the most natural thing in the world. Then he drew back, studying her face, which was covered in shadows. "You're so lovely."

As she read the desire in his eyes, her body trembled. His grip tightened around her. "It was a good run," she said tensely as his fingers grazed her face.

"Mmm." He kissed her lightly, continuing to imprison her body in his grasp. "This is better."

Her body stiffened against him.

"Something wrong?"

"No, not really." She hesitated. "I guess I'm nervous."

"Don't be afraid of me," he whispered, his mouth pressed against her hair. He led her to the open window. "Look at that moon." Standing behind her, he nuzzled the back of her neck.

She felt his body stir against her as she willed her mind to turn off, to let this happen: I need so badly to be loved, caressed, cherished—it feels so right.

"Kate, ever since we met, I haven't been able to stop thinking about you. You've bewitched me."

"I must have wiggled my nose more than the prescribed

three times,'' she teased softly. Content for the moment to be in his strong arms, she breathed in the masculine smell of his skin, liking its essence, grateful for the way he was giving her time to relax.

"I promise to stop if you say so, but I want to make love to you so badly it hurts."

She turned, seeing his handsome features clearly in the moonlight. Her breath shuddered. "I'd like that." She was trembling as he kissed her passionately, then led her to the bed. Lying next to her, he traced her mouth, her eyes, her nose, and then her neck with his fingers, causing shivers to run up her body. Tears unexpectedly filled her eyes. "I don't . . . ," she started to say.

"Shhhh." He put his finger on her mouth. "No words, no explanations . . . The only thing that matters is you, me . . . now." Stroking her lightly with his palm, he kissed her throat, then slid his hand down her bare back.

She arched, thrusting her breasts toward him, relishing the nearness of his body, his touch, his smell.

"You're so beautiful." He rubbed his cheek against her skin. Then his lips found hers.

Her lips parted, her moist tongue met his, searching, tasting. She heard him moan, felt the racing of his heart against her own. The silence surrounded them, relaxed her, an urgency fueled her so quickly it seemed to take total command. There was nothing but him, his arms, his lips. Touch me, love me, make me forget, she cried silently, her fingers locked in his thick hair, so blond it looked white in the moonlight.

Feeling his sleek, hard muscles, she experienced a familiar stirring in her loins. Her hand groped for him, felt him straining against the towel. The nubs of the material bit into her skin like tiny little stab wounds as their bodies pressed together.

She was filled with a sense of unreality, as if the whole scene were taking place in a dream. Her body urged him on as he traced the tautly erect tip of her nipple with his tongue. When he put it in his mouth, his delicate bite sent shock waves of ecstasy blazing through her.

A small gasp escaped her lips when he slid the wisp of silk from her, leaving her naked beneath him. Slowly, almost imperceptibly, she became aware of his hand probing between her legs where she was wet and moist, aching for him. For a moment their bodies were suspended. She felt him throbbing against her, against the pressure of the condom as he ran his tongue along the line of her ribs. When his mouth brushed low over her stomach, she moaned again, her nails digging into his shoulders.

With one hand, he lifted both of her hands above her head and linked her fingers with his. Putting his other hand under her buttocks, he lifted her pelvis up, and plunged deeply into her as their bodies came together.

"I wanted you so much," she heard him whisper as over and over he submerged himself into her, each thrust long and deep. Her hips rose to match each stroke until she embraced him totally.

As the tempo increased, she felt her muscles contract in exquisite pleasure, her legs tightening around him, seeking to contain the fire ignited by his powerful thrusts. When it happened, she couldn't stop the shudders, they continued to race through her long after she heard him cry, and felt him burst forth into her. A sense of peace engulfed her.

Later, unable to sleep, Kate carefully eased Andrew's arm from her and slid noiselessly from the bed. She drifted to the window. I'm not sorry, she mused. I wanted him to make love to me. She gazed at the stars and sighed. I wonder where Charles is at this moment and if he's even missed me at all.

"Operator, ring that number one more time." Charles held his hand over his mouth so as to muffle the sound of his voice. He gazed out the window, the early light, a bright New York morning, creeping under the closed shutters. From the marble bathroom, he heard the water stop and knew Ann was out of the shower.

Kate's machine picked up again. Damn, he thought as he slammed the phone down angrily. Where the hell is she?

20

"**G**uess what I have?" Madeline's brown eyes were alive with excitement.

"What?" asked Philip.

"Pictures of Tommy and Sandra, together, taken by the cops the day before he was arrested."

He raised a cynical eyebrow. "How'd you manage that?"

"Bower had them followed. He was sure they'd meet."

Philip flipped through the photos.

"Looks like he was right." He handed them back to her.

"According to Bower, Sandra said she'd stopped seeing Tommy five days before her husband's death and hadn't seen him since. He's going to call her in for a statement, and this time we'll get it on tape. I only hope she lies again." Her face brightened. "Sandra's voice on tape lying to the police, along with the cop's testimony about the pictures he took, will sway a jury much faster than Tommy's testimony. The photos will also corroborate Tommy's story."

"Just be careful how you and Bower handle this."

She was surprised. "What do you mean?"

"The D'Arcys are important people with friends in high places. If Bower records her statement, he'll have to read her her rights. Sandra's sure to have an attorney who will realize she's a suspect, and you may be tipping your hand too soon."

"She's already got an attorney—Kate Alexander. She was at Tommy's arraignment." Madeline chewed on her lip. "It makes sense that Sandra and Tommy are in this together. Tommy's not bright enough to have planned it himself. The way I see it, Sandra was the stronger one in the relationship and she coerced him into killing her husband."

"That's very possibly the way it happened. Still, I wouldn't rule out the likelihood someone else put Tommy up to it. But in either case, you need proof. Who else stood to benefit?"

"The sister and the brother. Both of them are quite wealthy, but not in comparison to James. The father left the majority of the shares in the D'Arcy Company to James, which gave him control. Now James has left everything to his son."

"Uneven distribution," warned Philip, "makes for angry heirs."

"We've also been told by quite a few people, too many to ignore, that Theo D'Arcy hated his brother for not letting him into the family business and especially the D'Arcy Foundation."

"What's the brother's alibi for the night in question?"

"He says he was home, alone."

"Interesting. Any connection between Bartholomew and Theo D'Arcy?"

"Nothing yet. We're still investigating."

"Well, the family's politically connected, so use even more caution with the brother."

"Why?"

"The D'Arcys might throw Sandra to the wolves if they find it expedient. She's not really one of them. But Theo, that's a different ball game. If he's arrested and charged, they'll fight us tooth and nail."

"Aha, one kind of justice for her and another one for him." Her tone was mocking.

He nodded. "Look, I'm just telling you the realities. By the way," he asked, "isn't the brother contesting the will?"

"Yes."

"What's all the fuss about?"

"Theo D'Arcy told Bower he's positive his brother changed his will before he died to make him the trustee. When Bower spoke to Charles Rieman, the victim's lawyer, he said there were no documents to support the brother's claim."

"Anything on the lawyer?" Philip eyed her critically.

She shook her head. "Basically, he gets a load of responsibility. There's no financial gain for him under the will except for certain fees he's entitled to. Of course, on a billion-dollar estate, we're talking about a lot of money. Nevertheless, Bower ascertained that the fees go to the firm, and I can't imagine an entire law firm committing murder for the purpose of increasing their fees."

Philip grinned at her. "I can."

She laughed. "Very funny. We all know how much you love large law firms. You think anyone who works in the private sector is a crook."

"Well, I wouldn't say everyone. But from the books I've been reading lately, I'd say most. You know why a lawyer doesn't have to worry about sharks?"

"Professional courtesy," she said, laughing.

He smiled ruefully. "You heard it. So, what are the chances this whole thing was a random robbery and killing?"

"Bower doesn't think so." She repeated the detective's reasoning. "And I'm inclined to agree with him."

"What about that guy D'Arcy supposedly ruined?"

"Nothing yet. Everything keeps pointing back to the D'Arcy family or at least someone in James D'Arcy's inner circle. For my money, the widow's still my best shot."

"Even though she could have divorced James and gotten the same money as if he had died?"

"I think so. Sandra may have been afraid James would make it difficult for her to divorce him. Or perhaps Tommy was pressuring her." She smiled because she was now arguing the position Philip had taken the last time they discussed the case.

"So we're back to the two of them. Well, love does strange things to people."

"Love?" she scoffed. "I can see why he fell for her, but why on earth would she jeopardize her status for him?"

His brown eyes gazed at her. "Maybe he was great in bed."

Madeline was taken aback by Philip's comment. It was so unlike him that for a moment she could think of nothing to say.

"Well"—he smiled sheepishly—"who knows?"

Madeline chuckled. "I already assumed he was good in that department or the affair wouldn't have gone on for six months. But I can't figure out why she'd take up with a kid like that in the first place."

"Maybe Sandra was lonely and he made her feel special."

Madeline gazed at him, puzzled. He could show such empathy, such kindness. But there was another side to him. The lawyer. During cross-examination Philip turned into a barracuda. His favorite technique was to lull a witness into a false sense of security, then go for the jugular.

She wondered what Philip would be like in bed. Would he be as good as Gary? Hoping he couldn't read her thoughts, she turned away from Philip toward the window. "I still want to understand what appealed to Sandra about Tommy."

"Some people thrive on danger. It's exciting."

Turning around, she found Philip looking at her in a strange way. His words unnerved her. Had he sensed the feeling of danger yet indescribable excitement that overwhelmed her whenever she was with Gary? "Could be."

There was a knock on Philip's door and his secretary stuck her head in.

"Excuse me, Mr. White. The reporters are here and the D.A. wants you and Ms. Gould to join him."

"We'll be right there." The door closed. "The circus is starting. Better hurry."

"Aren't you coming?" Madeline asked.

"No." He smiled. "It's your turn to shine."

"Philip, you should be in the spotlight with me."

"Not this time."

"Why?"

He shrugged but said nothing further.

"You're the logical choice for D.A. when Ron moves on to something bigger," she insisted, knowing in her heart it was true. "Instead of pushing me out there to gather all the glory, you should take some of it for yourself."

"No thanks. I'd rather be the one behind the scenes. More privacy that way."

"But you'd be so good at it."

"I couldn't stand living in a political fishbowl."

"And I think it would be thrilling!"

"That's why you're a better choice." He grinned at her. "And we need someone ethical like you in the top job. So get going. The publicity will be good for you."

"Think I'm totally crazy?"

"No, just ambitious," he laughed. "We both know how glitz, money, and sex get the media and public all worked up. It's the stuff careers are made from, Madeline, so go." He gave her a playful shove toward the door.

She turned to face him, her eyes filled with gratitude. "Thanks, Philip."

"Good luck," he called as she hurried out.

Mary, Kate's secretary, told her that Sandra D'Arcy was waiting on the phone. "Yes?" said Kate, picking up the line.

"Detective Bower called and wants me to come down to the police station today to give them some kinda statement. I said I'd be there at one."

"I thought I told you not to speak to anyone unless I was present." Kate couldn't keep the annoyance out of her voice.

"Why do you think I'm telling you!" snapped Sandra. "You can meet me there if you want."

"I meant for you not to talk to the police at all. You were supposed to say you're represented by counsel, give them my name and number, and hang up."

"Jesus! How the hell was I supposed to know that?"

"I told you the other day," Kate said testily.

"You didn't say those exact words. I'm not stupid. I didn't get that from our conversation at all."

Kate reminded herself to count to ten before responding to her new client. If she didn't, their relationship would be impossible. "O.K. Let's start again. You're not required to give the police a statement."

Sandra was quiet for a moment. "But if I don't, they'll think I've got something to hide, won't they?"

"Don't be concerned with what they think."

"But I haven't got anything to hide! If I tell them my story once and for all, maybe they'll stop bothering me."

"There's no guarantee of that."

"You going to meet me there or not?"

Kate paused. "If you insist on doing this, at least postpone it until we can meet and discuss it more fully."

"I'm going today." Sandra's tone was firm.

Kate sighed. "I'll meet you in front of Parker Center at twelve-thirty. Don't be late. And remember what I've told you." Kate briefly related some of the dos and don'ts for Sandra's interview with the police.

Before Kate could even finish, Sandra interrupted: "O.K., you've already told me." Her voice was sullen as she slammed down the receiver.

Kate rubbed her ear. Her relationship with Sandra D'Arcy was getting off to exactly the start she had feared.

Sandra hung up the phone and hurried to finish dressing. She was due at Abigail's in fifteen minutes.

Half an hour later she was seated in her mother-in-law's sitting room. Victoria was there too. Sandra tried not to let her sister-in-law's dirty looks upset her.

"Sandra, I do not want to discuss details," explained Abigail. "That is why we have hired a lawyer for you. However, I want to remind you of a few things." A faint smile played about the thin, parchment-paper lips as she spoke.

Sandra was not fooled by the old woman's smile. James's mother hated her.

"I want you to remember the *honor* my son bestowed upon you when he gave you the D'Arcy name," said Abigail. "For better or worse, what you do and how you act will reflect on all of us. I expect you to conduct yourself in a manner befitting a D'Arcy. And that means you are to hold your head high at all times."

"I'll try."

"Do more than try," ordered Abigail. "Also, Sandra, I expect you to divulge nothing, not even to your attorney, that would reflect badly upon the D'Arcy name. Do I make myself clear?''

A sense of helplessness bubbled up in Sandra. She started to speak, but Abigail gestured regally.

"There is nothing to discuss. I believe I have explained our position."

A malicious grin appeared at the corners of Victoria's mouth, giving her an almost grotesque look. Sandra recalled James's telling her that Victoria had submitted to the surgeon's knife at least six times, fixing everything from her prominent new cheekbones to the newly rebuilt chin. All of it done to make up for a philandering husband and to attract lovers, the average age of whom James had said was getting younger every year.

"Make sure you do as Mother asks," said Victoria, "or you'll be sorry."

There it was again, thought Sandra. The unspoken threat. She needed advice. She had to find out if they could take her kid away from her. But who was she supposed to ask? Certainly not Kate, who would probably tell Abigail everything Sandra said. She nodded and remained quiet.

"We shall stand beside you, Sandra," warned Abigail, "as long as you follow our rules. If not . . . ."

She didn't need to finish. Sandra knew what Abigail meant.

Franklin Manning looked out the window of his study and then turned to his daughter. "Have a good time in New York?"

"Yes." Ann's eyes refused to meet his. "How are you feeling, Father?"

He ignored her question. "I thought the trip was supposed to be a second honeymoon?"

"Charles had a great deal of business to attend to." Her face had a hard look that even her smile did not soften. She looked out the leaded-glass window to the garden.

"You patch up what was bothering the two of you?"

She turned to face him. "Yes."

"I'm glad."

"It was nothing really," Ann hastened to add. "Charles has just been working too hard. He's spread too thin."

"I know that, Ann."

"Can't you do something to alleviate it?"

As he sighed, his posture slumped. "So much has happened at once. James D'Arcy's death. The Suni takeover." He frowned. "Then there's my health. And . . . well, it's a lot . . ."

"I didn't mean for you to do any more. It's my brother I'm talking about. Why can't Dickson do more to help Charles?" She came to stand in front of her father.

He looked uncomfortable. "I'm afraid Charles has to attend to the D'Arcy matters himself. As for the Suni takeover, Warren Thornton won't let anyone but Charles handle it. I know he's overloaded, but that's the way it is. Give it a little time."

"Father, if you depend on Charles more than Dickson, then Charles should be rewarded."

Franklin eyed his daughter shrewdly. "With the senior partnership, you mean?"

"Yes."

"I wanted to make sure things were good between the two of you."

"They couldn't be better."

"I hope so." He gazed at his daughter, wondering.

Having told her client to dress conservatively, Kate was appalled when Sandra walked toward her at five minutes to one in a white knit minidress. She should have picked Sandra up. Then she could have made her change. Now it was too late. Kate forced herself to smile. Every curve of Sandra's body was accentuated by the tight-fitting garment. As they walked down the corridor, police officers on all sides did double takes.

When Bower and Donaldson joined them in the room, Kate saw that Donaldson was unable to keep his eyes off Sandra. Kate wasn't pleased. Sandra was purposely flaunting herself as a sex object—not something that was likely to help her case.

They exchanged greetings; then Bower explained to Sandra that he wanted to tape their conversation, to which Kate agreed. Bower asked Donaldson to read Sandra her rights.

So, thought Kate, she's definitely a suspect. While she listened to Bower ask Sandra a few basic questions, she noticed that her client could not meet his gaze. Not a good sign.

"Would you please tell me what your relationship was to the deceased?" asked Bower.

"I was his wife."

"You know the man accused of killing your husband, Tommy Bartholomew?"

"Yes."

"Tell us when you first met him and the nature of your relationship."

"Why do you have to ask me all this again? I've already told you this stuff."

Bower's eyebrows arched in surprise as he looked over at Kate.

"May I please have a minute?" asked Kate.

The detective nodded.

Kate leaned over to talk softly to her client. "Sandra, since you wanted to do this today, forget what they've asked you before and answer their questions. As I've already explained to you, if it's something I don't want you to answer, I'll tell you."

"He looks at me as if I'm guilty of something," whispered Sandra through clenched teeth.

"Forget what he's thinking. Look past him and respond as simply as possible."

Sandra looked exasperated as she began to relate how she'd met Tommy at exercise class and then how their friendship developed until it became intimate.

Kate listened to her client's words. Unfortunately, Sandra's affair with Tommy sounded tawdry and cheap as she explained it to Bower. But it didn't make her guilty of murder.

Bower showed Sandra a piece of paper and asked her to identify it.

"It's a note I wrote to Tommy . . . when I loaned him some money for his rent."

"How much did you loan him?"

"Five hundred dollars."

"You absolutely sure?"

"Yes."

"Any way you could be mistaken about the amount?"

"No."

"I see. Was this money you gave him a check, cash, or what?"

"Cash."

"Remember the denominations?"

"Five one-hundred-dollar bills."

"You sure?"

"I said so, didn't I?"

That attitude is going to get her nowhere, thought Kate. "One moment," she said, taking her client's arm.

"Sandra, it's O.K. not to remember."

"But I do," insisted Sandra.

Bower next had Sandra recount how she had come to own the gun and then how she had shown it to Tommy. Kate listened intently while Sandra went into detail, explaining about the burglary that had occurred the summer before James's death. When her client explained why she had waited until six months after the burglary to buy the gun, Kate imagined how Sandra's excuse would play to a jury. Unfortunately, not very well, she knew.

The session had been going on for almost forty minutes and Kate wondered how much longer Bower intended to continue. She crossed her legs and shifted positions in the stiff-backed chair.

As if reading Kate's mind, Bower shuffled some papers as though he were done. Then, looking up, he asked another question. "You're absolutely sure you haven't seen Bartholomew since your husband's death?"

"That's what I said."

Kate was alarmed by Bower's triumphant smile. What did he have on her client? She put her hand on Sandra. "If you're not sure, it's O.K. to say so."

"Aren't you listening?" snapped Sandra, loud enough for them all to hear. "The last time I saw Tommy was five days before James's death."

Damn, thought Kate, it's as if everything I told her went in one ear and out the other.

"Let's go on," Bower said. "Besides the five hundred bucks you said you gave Tommy, did you loan or give him any other money?"

"No."

"You sure?"

"What's the matter with you guys anyway? If I say no—it's no!"

"Fine." Bower looked pleased. He checked his notebook. "Mrs. D'Arcy, did you and Tommy ever discuss getting rid of your husband?"

"I'm going to advise my client not to answer that question on the grounds of self-incrimination."

Bower gazed at Kate, then back to Sandra. "Tommy Bartholomew told us you and he joked about getting rid of your husband."

Sandra turned white as Kate interrupted. "Again, I must advise my client not to answer . . ."

"You ever wish your husband was dead?"

"Again, I'm going to instruct her not to answer." Kate's voice was firm. "I suggest you change the subject."

Bower rubbed his chin for a moment. "O.K."

Kate wasn't happy. Something about the way Bower looked when he repeated what Tommy had supposedly told him made Kate suspicious. She was positive Sandra had not leveled with her.

To make matters worse, Kate knew that if Sandra was tried for her husband's murder, it would be tough to discredit Tommy without putting Sandra on the stand. And Sandra taking the stand was not a pleasant prospect. In two minutes, the young widow would alienate the prosecutor, the judge, the jury, and, Kate thought grimly to herself, probably me.

Bower closed his folder. "That about does it for now. Thank you for coming in, Mrs. D'Arcy." He stood up and turned to Kate. "I'll be talking to you."

"Of course," Kate responded.

Afterward, on their way to the elevator, Kate spoke her mind. "Look, Sandra, I know you're upset. God knows, if I were in your shoes, I'd be too. However, your belligerent attitude with the police has got to stop. In my opinion, you're treating this whole investigation too lightly."

Sandra stared at her attorney with unmasked hostility. "You don't have any idea how I feel."

The elevator arrived, but Kate ignored it, turning instead to Sandra. "Let's get a cup of coffee."

The elevator doors closed.

"I can't. I've got to be somewhere." Sandra brushed back her hair, which was falling into her eyes, and pressed the elevator call button.

Kate felt her frustration rise again. She had to reach this woman. "Sandra, the way I see it, as soon as we walked out of that room, Bower was on the phone to the D.A. Mark my words, they're preparing a case against you."

"They can do whatever they like."

Kate wanted to shake Sandra. Instead she issued a firm order. "Be in my office tomorrow morning at nine A.M. sharp, and be prepared to work."

"Sure," said Sandra as she got into another elevator filled with people.

As Kate followed her in, she couldn't remember ever feeling so nervous about a client. Sandra was like a ticking time bomb, and Kate couldn't predict what might set her off.

When they stepped out of the elevator, flashes went off. A microphone was shoved at the young widow, newspeople moved in for the kill. "Mrs. D'Arcy, what did you tell the police?" asked a dark-haired newswoman.

Kate reached for the mike, giving Sandra a look that said: Keep quiet. Sandra glared at Kate. "Mrs. D'Arcy answered the questions put to her by the police to the best of her ability."

"Ms. Alexander, what did the police want to know?"

"You'll have to ask them." Kate smiled. "We're merely trying to cooperate in any way we can."

"Do you expect your client to be charged in the murder of her husband?"

"I can't answer that," said Kate.

"She going to attempt to see her boyfriend?" asked another.

"No comment."

"Have they offered Mrs. D'Arcy immunity in exchange for her testimony?"

"No comment."

Newspeople were pushing closer and Kate looked around worriedly. A wave of relief washed over her when she saw Frank Jones, the black investigator who worked for the firm. With his six-foot-five frame, he was able to push back the crowd.

"We have nothing further to say," said Kate. "Now if you would please excuse us."

Frank grasped the arms of both women and guided them out of the building.

Gary came into Madeline's office, closed the door, and put his arms around her. "I missed you," he murmured.

"How much?" she teased. She felt the hardness of his muscles pressing against her through his shirt. It felt good.

"Too much. You miss me too?"

"Uh huh."

"Can I see you this weekend?"

"I don't know yet." She pulled back and gazed into his eyes. "Unfortunately, I'm not sure if Sam's taking the kids."

"Why not?"

"He says he may be going out of town."

There was a sharp narrowing of his green eyes. "Again? What's his problem anyway?"

She heard the irritation in his voice and tried to minimize Sam's conduct. "He said he'd let me know by tonight."

"So we're supposed to hold our breath while he decides if it's convenient to baby-sit his own kids?" A flush of anger crawled up his neck.

"It may look that way to you, but—"

"It seems to me this ex-husband of yours gets first choice and we get leftovers. It's bullshit!"

She felt a momentary twinge. This was her first serious romance in years and Sam was managing to screw it up for her.

"Your agreement says every other weekend," he insisted.

"I know. It wasn't always like this. In the beginning, Sam wanted the kids all the time."

"So he's doing it on purpose?"

"What do you mean?"

Gary's chin jutted out belligerently. "You told that bastard you were serious about someone and now he's trying to keep us apart."

Madeline wondered if Gary could be right. It was true that Sam had never forgiven her for wanting to have a career when he was already so successful. He'd made her life miserable from the time she entered law school until the day she asked him to move out. Yet he had also begged her to reconsider when she asked for a divorce. Was it possible he was still in love with her?

"If this scumbag ex-husband of yours was a defendant, you'd ask the jury to hang him." Gary's fist slammed into the desk so hard it shook.

Madeline jumped. "Gary!"

He stuffed his hands in his pockets, his eyes hooded.

"What on earth's the matter with you?" she said sharply.

Gary studied her silently for a moment. "Sorry."

"You're making too much of this," she said, only a bit relieved at his apology.

"I don't like to share you." Gary smiled at her in that special way he had. He put his arms about her again. "You can't blame me for that, can you?"

"No." She liked the way his arms felt around her, but she was still upset at his sudden outburst. "I thought you liked my boys," she said warily.

"I do. I just hate going home before dawn or having you leave my place at the stroke of one." He rubbed her back. "It gets so lonely without you."

She hesitated. The last thing she needed in her life was a man who lacked understanding. At the same time, she couldn't help but be flattered by the obvious intensity of his feelings for her, an intensity that made her do things in bed with him she had never dreamed of doing with Sam.

"Don't be angry with me," he pleaded softly, nuzzling her neck with light kisses that sent her blood racing.

"O.K. I'll call Sam." She reluctantly pulled away and glanced at her watch. "Right now, though, I've got to be in court. I'll see you later." She picked up her briefcase and headed out the door.

"Be tough with him," he called after her.

21

Lauren was seeing red. She'd just run into a friend who wanted to know why she hadn't come with Kate to the political get-together Friday night at the Century Plaza. Then the friend told Lauren how she'd seen Kate leave the hotel with a handsome blond man, someone who sounded just like Andrew Stewart. Lauren picked up a Baccarat paperweight from her desk and clenched her fingers against its coldness. So Kate was now trying to steal Andrew away from her. That bitch, that fucking bitch! Over my dead body! vowed Lauren.

As for Andrew, no wonder he'd been so evasive. How dare he lie to her about work keeping him so busy! She felt like flinging the piece of crystal against the wall.

On second thought, maybe it wasn't Andrew's fault. Hadn't Kate said how gorgeous he was, that day in the lobby of the hotel? I never should have introduced him to her. In all fairness to Andrew, this whole thing's probably Kate's fault, Lauren rationalized. And men will be men.

She replaced the paperweight, but couldn't rid herself of the image of Andrew and Kate together doing God only knew what. Her rage growing by the minute, Lauren headed down the hallway and up the stairs. When she barged into Kate's office unannounced, she found her on the telephone. "Get off," she ordered loudly, slamming the door behind her.

There was a look of astonishment on Kate's face as she put down the phone.

"Who the fuck do you think you are going out with my boyfriend?"

Kate turned pale. "Your boyfriend?"

"Don't play stupid with me. I know you and Andrew left the Century Plaza together Friday night!"

"We went for a run on the beach," explained Kate. "Andrew told me there was nothing serious between the two of you and I just—"

Lauren cut her off. "I don't believe you. You're only trying to excuse your despicable behavior."

"No I'm not," said Kate curtly. "He came up to me at the Women's Political Action cocktail party and we started talking. When he invited me out to dinner, the first thing I did was ask if he was still seeing you."

"How big of you," said Lauren in a mocking tone.

"I wouldn't have gone if I'd thought you were still seeing each other."

"You should have asked *me*, not him," Lauren challenged sharply. "Why didn't you tell me about the cocktail party in the first place? I would have wanted to go."

"I wasn't sure I was going myself until the last minute."

"A likely story."

"No. It's true." Kate gestured toward her desk. "I'm swamped. But when I called to back out, the chairperson had a fit. Said she was counting on me. So I raced out of here."

"I don't believe you! You wanted to be alone with him!"

"I didn't even know he'd be there. I've never seen him at a W.P.A. affair before."

"You must have told him!" she shouted. "I'm warning you, Kate Alexander, leave him alone. He's mine." Lauren stormed out of Kate's office, her mind racing with ways to make that cunt pay for what she'd done: I'll find a way to make her lose everything, not just the partnership but her future, everything. That bitch will wish she'd never set eyes on him.

Lauren almost bumped into Charles in the hallway. "Excuse me," she said as she hurried off.

No sooner had Lauren stormed out of Kate's office than Kate found herself facing Charles.

"What was that all about?" There was a puzzled frown on his face as he closed the door behind him.

"She's upset with me." Kate spoke with as much coldness as she could muster. So, he was finally back. And from the looks of things, he was going to pretend their argument on the phone had never happened.

"I missed you." His dark eyes swept over her, his desire unmistakable.

She stiffened. How dare he act as if nothing had happened. What a fool she had been. "No more lies, please," she demanded, staring at him with distaste.

His eyebrows shot up. "What?"

Her face was pinched with anger. "We're through, Charles."

"What the hell are you talking about?"

"Spare me the dramatics. It's over between us."

"Kate." He came toward her confidently. "I love you—don't even joke about something like that."

She held up her hand to stop him. "I've never been more serious in my whole life." Her voice was deadly quiet. "Did you really take me for such a fool?"

"Fool?" He searched her face. "Kate, I've no idea what's going on. Care to fill me in?"

"Did you honestly believe I wouldn't find out about your weekend with Ann?" Although her words were clipped and the look in her eyes hard, she hoped he couldn't hear the thudding of her heart.

"Kate, I can explain . . ."

She summoned all her dignity. "There's nothing *to* explain." She stood and gestured toward the door. "Please go."

Charles nervously ran his hand through his hair. "I told you why I couldn't leave her yet. Ann merely had something to attend to in New York and I had to be there anyway. So we went together."

Kate's eyes blazed with anger. "In the honeymoon suite at the Plaza, of course!"

The color drained from his tanned face. "Kate, please don't do this—I love you." He tried to put his arms about her, but she shook him off violently, backing away.

"God *damn* you, Charles!"

He tried again to pull her toward him. "I know you still love me too."

She wrenched her hand away and struck him across the face as hard as she could.

Charles touched his cheek, a stunned look on his face. "You're making a mistake."

For a moment, as his dark eyes begged her for understanding, she felt her resolve weaken. She could see the handprint whitening his face from her slap.

"I can explain. It's not what it looks like."

Could he? she wondered.

"Please listen to me." His voice was almost pleading. "It was the only suite left."

She felt her burning rage turn into an icy fury. "You're lying, Charles," she said as she glared at him.

"Kate . . ."

"There's nothing you can say. I also know Warren Thornton was in California for the weekend, not New York."

"That's because—"

She interrupted him. "I don't want to hear any more of your goddamn lies. Go back to your wife." Her voice was heavy with sarcasm. "I've nothing more to say."

He stared at her for a moment as if trying to decide what to do. Then he turned and left.

Kate watched him go. She knew the pain would be there when the fury subsided. Tomorrow she'd have to figure out how they were going to work together. She had no intention of resigning or being forced out. Nor would she allow him to renege on his promise to make her the next partner. But it was too soon to deal with these problems. Like a divorce, their separation would take some getting used to.

She took a deep breath, reminding herself she was strong, a survivor. Even if, she thought as her confrontation with Lauren flashed through her mind, she was not always such a great judge of character. Meanwhile, there was a lot of work to do. She forced herself to concentrate on Sandra D'Arcy, making a list of things for herself and Frank Jones to see to.

At the Los Angeles County Jail, Andrew told Tommy about the news conference. "Sandra's lawyer told the media her client was cooperating with the police and D.A.'s office. You have any idea what that's all about?"

Tommy stared at Andrew as he nervously chewed on his lip. "No." He hesitated. "Just . . ."

"What?"

"I owe some guys money and Sandra . . . was going to help me."

Andrew glared sternly at his client. "Don't lie to me, Tommy. Who do you owe the money to and for what?"

Tommy looked at his shoes. "I lost some bucks at the track." He hesitated, then added, "I met some good contacts there but I owe them some money."

Andrew sighed disgustedly. "Well, you may have bigger problems now. What if the D.A.'s office is offering Sandra immunity in exchange for her testimony?"

"What's that mean?"

"If the D.A. thinks Sandra can help make their case against you stick, they can offer to either charge her with a lesser crime or not charge her at all in exchange for her testimony against you."

Tommy's boyish face became a mirror of fear. "I don't understand."

"Sandra may be planning to nail you," explained Andrew. "Think about what she knows that could hurt you."

"Listen, man, I'm innocent. I keep telling you that. Why don't you believe me?"

"That's what they all say. Did you do it for the money you owe?"

"I didn't kill her old man," insisted Tommy.

Andrew sized up his client. "It's going to take a lot more than that to convince the D.A. you're not involved."

"Shit," said Tommy.

Andrew motioned to a chair. "Sit down. I'm going to tell you what kind of evidence they have linking you to this murder. Then I want some straight answers."

Detective Bower paced back and forth in Madeline's small office as he waited for her to return. He liked the small things she did to make the office homier. Pictures of her kids, a few plants. He had even seen flowers the other day. Many women D.A.s tried to act tough, as if they didn't want anyone to notice they were women. He knew some of it was because cops weren't comfortable around them either. Madeline was different, though. She seemed to like being a woman.

At that moment, Madeline walked in. She threw her briefcase on her chair and turned to greet him.

"I see the Bartholomew kid's got himself a fancy lawyer," he said.

"A case like this always attracts them."

"I doubt he's got any money," said Bower.

"We both know that's not the only reason they do it."

"I forgot." He snapped his fingers. "Love of country, the Constitution, justice, and all that patriotic garbage."

"Right, not to mention all of the 'disgusting' publicity." She made a face.

They both laughed.

"Stewart's a sharp operator," she added. "I wouldn't be surprised if he finds some family member to put up the dough."

He scratched his head. "Yeah. You're probably right. Well, I just stopped by to bring you up to date."

"What do you have?"

"We looked to see if the victim was mixed up in any gambling or shady deals. But this was a guy who had lots of legitimate money. I didn't expect to find anything unkosher."

"And?"

"I was right." He shook his head. "The only thing we were told again and again was, the guy had a really bad temper."

"I assume he didn't kill himself?"

Bower laughed again. She was a funny lady. He liked that. "No. He didn't kill himself."

She fiddled with one of her earrings as if lost in thought. "Bartholomew did it," she said.

"I agree. But it's doubtful he acted alone."

"The big question still remains . . . *who* helped him?"

"Dunno."

"I'm sure it was Sandra who coerced him."

"Could be."

"Any leads on the stolen ring or watch?"

"Zero."

"What about the murder weapon?"

"No luck finding the piece."

"Hell!"

"Wish I had better news to report."

"Me too. How'd the interview go?"

He took a cassette out of his pocket and put it on her desk. "It's all on here. Mrs. D'Arcy pretty much told us what she's said before. She's still telling a different story from the kid. She says the loan was five hundred. He says two thousand. She says no other bucks and he says she gave him another thousand. She swears the last time she saw him was five days before her husband died and she hasn't seen him since. Of course, he says he saw her and we've got the photographs to prove it." He glanced up at her with a hopeful expression. "Any luck getting Bartholomew to admit who helped him?"

"I'm meeting with his lawyer later today. But so far, he denies any involvement with the murder."

Bower straightened his tie. "I'll keep my fingers crossed."

"The part I don't like is what we may have to offer Tommy to get him to talk. I hate making a deal with the one who pulled the trigger."

He knew how she felt. He too hated to make a deal with a killer. "I'd sure like to see you offer as little as possible. I won't feel very good if he doesn't serve a long time." He stood and hiked up his pants. "I've got to be in court now. Let me know what the mouthpiece says."

"I will. And I appreciate where you're coming from. Thanks for stopping by." She smiled, holding out her hand.

"No problem," he said, shaking her hand. "I'll call you if anything new comes up."

Andrew Stewart gazed around Madeline's office. It was quite small and littered everywhere with papers, books, and periodicals. Besides Madeline's large wood desk and the two leather chairs in front of it, there were the credenza and several bookcases. Interspersed among these things were a mini-refrigerator, a coffeepot with hot water, and numerous pictures. In fact, every spare inch of free wall space in the office was covered not only with framed diplomas and certificates but also with newspaper articles on the various cases she'd handled.

He was glad he'd gone into private practice. He knew that these surroundings would depress him. Although many prosecutors claimed that helping to rid the world of criminals was the most satisfying job in the world, he for one didn't understand it. How could they feel good when they were paid so little compared to what they could earn on the other side of the courtroom?

He faced her, his voice firm. He liked to start out aggressively. "I'll be making a motion to suppress all of the evidence taken from my client's apartment."

"On what grounds?"

"The usual." He flashed her his most charming smile.

She wasn't amused. "Your client signed a consent waiver to our search."

He held out his hands as if to apologize. "Obviously, he didn't understand what he was signing."

"That's a lot of hogwash and you know it. I was told it was all fully explained to him."

"You'll have to prove that, won't you?"

"I expect to."

"We'll see." He studied her for a moment. She is certainly an attractive woman, he thought. Not my type, though. She's got a dynamite figure, but she's too small. He liked them tall and leggy.

"My client says the police roughed him up to get him to sign the waiver."

Madeline shook her head impatiently. "Spare me, Counselor! Every defendant claims the same thing."

He became serious. "In this case it happens to be true."

"You don't know Detective Bower very well then. He's one of the best on the force and he wouldn't be likely to leave a legal loophole like that for your client to wiggle out of. I can always count on Bower to do an outstanding job of meticulous police work."

"Even the best officer can lose his temper. Anyway, after I knock out those boots of Tommy's as well as the note, you won't have enough evidence for a case."

"I think you're forgetting something," she said. "Your client has already admitted to the police that he and Sandra D'Arcy discussed killing her husband."

He shrugged. "My client was merely kidding."

"That's not going to get him off the hook, Mr. Stewart," she warned. "We have a very strong case against Mr. Bartholomew, and we intend to go for, and get, the death penalty."

"You'll first have to prove there were special circumstances."

"Well, last time I checked, 'murder for profit' and 'lying in wait' got you the death penalty."

Andrew could see that he was getting nowhere with her. She was being more difficult than he had anticipated and he wondered why. It was time for him to change tactics. "I believe you're trying to railroad my client because of who the D'Arcy family is."

Madeline was outraged. "That's ridiculous and you know it!"

"Is it?" he asked smugly. "This case is getting a lot of play in the media. Your office is under pressure to show the public you've got the guy that did it and to convict him fast." He snapped his fingers in the air. "Boom, end of story. Everyone can get on with their lives except my client."

"That's not true. We're still investigating. In fact, we don't think he acted alone."

"Yeah, sure."

"It's no secret," she said. "We're leaving no stone unturned. We intend to find the person he was in on this with."

"So you think there was a conspiracy?"

"I didn't say that."

He rubbed his chin. "I see."

"We are sure of one thing," she stated emphatically. "Your client killed James D'Arcy."

"And what if your investigation shows Tommy's been set up?"

"We're looking at every angle."

"As long as it doesn't tarnish the D'Arcy name?"

She glanced at him angrily. "If you have something to say, say it."

"O.K. I will," he fired back, equally curt. "I think the D'Arcy family is putting pressure on your boss. They want my client convicted as fast as possible so that their precious name won't be dragged through the mud any more than necessary and all the nasty skeletons in their closet will stay put."

"Mr. Stewart, am I to understand that you are accusing this office of wrongdoing?"

He flashed a patronizing smile. "The D'Arcy family has a lot of important and influential friends. Let's just say I think there's a tendency on the part of certain persons to put their own political futures first."

"If you have anything specific to tell me, I'll listen," Madeline asserted stiffly. "If not, I'm going to ignore your insinuations."

Andrew realized that none of his arguments or ploys were making any impression. She was certainly a plucky broad. Perhaps he had pushed her too far. It was time to back off and find out what his client's alternatives might be.

He picked a piece of lint off his suit before posing the most important question. "So, in case my client's interested, are you prepared to offer him anything?"

Madeline was quiet for a moment. "That all depends on whether or not he's willing to implicate her."

"I assume you mean the wife?"

"Yes, I'm speaking of Sandra D'Arcy."

"If he does, what then?"

"How about life without possibility of parole?"

"You've got to be kidding." Andrew's mouth twisted into a grimace and he was unable to hide his astonishment at her response. "That's not worth considering."

She raised her chin proudly. "It's your client's life."

God, but sometimes this was a hard game to play. He allowed a trace of impatience to enter his voice as he got back his equilibrium. "I'll talk to my client. However, in my humble opinion, you'll have to do a lot better than that."

"I doubt if there's anything about you that's humble," she shot back, smiling sarcastically.

A few minutes later Madeline ran into Philip in the hallway. "I just had the most infuriating talk with Bartholomew's arrogant lawyer." Her eyes were blazing with indignation.

Philip smiled as he sucked on his unlighted pipe. "What happened?"

She repeated the highlights of the conversation. When she finished, he chuckled.

"He's pulling out all the stops. Don't let it get to you."

"It makes me mad when they accuse us of not being impartial. I hate his tactics."

"It's all part of the game."

* * *

The sweat was pouring from Kate as she walked back to her condominium after a run on the beach. She heard someone call her name and glanced up, surprised to see Frank Jones bounding toward her.

"Your machine kept answering." He caught up with her. "So I decided to take a chance you'd be out here."

She had been reluctant to use Frank instead of the more experienced Marty, who Charles now said was out of town on an extended assignment. But Frank was proving to be very astute and she was pleased. "Had breakfast yet?"

"Depends on what you call breakfast. I eat all the time."

She laughed. "I'll scramble us some eggs while you tell me what you've found out."

In her kitchen, Kate poured him a glass of orange juice and started breakfast while he sat on a barstool at the counter and watched.

"Tommy Bartholomew's got a rap."

"You're kidding!" Kate turned to face him, a skillet in her hand.

"Nope. Fleeced a rich lady out of some dough."

As he explained in more detail what Tommy had done, she popped out the toast and poured him some coffee. Putting the eggs on his plate, she yawned.

"Am I boring you?" he joked.

"No. I just didn't sleep very well." Her hair was still damp from the run. "I twisted and turned all night long."

"You letting this case get to you?"

She shook her head. "It's personal."

"Oh." He looked like he wanted to say more, but took a few forkfuls of his eggs instead. "Delicious."

"Thanks," she said, smiling. "I'm not much of a cook, but eggs I can do."

"That's all my wife can do too."

"Kids?"

"Yep. Bobby's ten and Lita's six. You ever married?"

"Once, years ago. It was brief. Ended when I started law school." She saw the question on his face and added, "He was my poli sci professor."

"One of those guru types?"

She nodded. "He seemed so worldly, so forward-thinking."

"What happened?"

"My supportive freethinker wanted his dinner waiting and his shirts ironed. I was also expected to accept his affairs with other students. Part of their consciousness raising." Why am I telling him this? she wondered. Something about Frank made him easy to talk to.

He grinned at her. "Sounds like a real jerk."

"Yeah."

"You want kids?" he asked, reaching into his wallet and taking out his pictures.

"Me?" she laughed. "No." She looked at his pictures. "Nice. I love kids. But there's so much I want to do. It wouldn't be fair to a child." She sipped her coffee and went back to talking about the case. "Were you able to find out anything?"

"You know that from my years on the force I've got my sources." He winked, and filled her in on the evidence they had against Tommy, including the footprint. "But as to Sandra, everybody's playing it real close to the vest."

She paused, drumming her fingers on the counter. "What I really need to know is whether or not Tommy has implicated Sandra."

"The security around that information's tight. My gut says they want her bad and don't want any leaks screwing up their chances."

"Damn." Kate knew if Sandra was ever charged in her husband's murder, she'd get to see everything the prosecution had against her client. But for the time being, with Sandra merely a suspect, neither the cops nor the D.A. had to tell her anything.

When Andrew laid out the deal the D.A. might offer him, Tommy turned pale. "They can't convict me of something I didn't do." His voice quavered.

Andrew sighed. "Look, Tommy, they have a fucking

footprint. It shows you were there *after* the gardener watered.''

''I wasn't.''

''So your foot was there without you.''

''You said you'd get all their evidence thrown out.'' Tommy looked like he was about to be sick.

''I said I'd do my best. I can't promise anything. The prosecutor, Ms. Gould, is being a hardass.'' He glanced at Tommy shrewdly. ''You sure there's nothing else you haven't told me?''

''I've told you everything.''

''Remember, death is permanent,'' warned Andrew. ''Don't be a hero to protect Sandra, because she'll sing if she has to, to save her own neck. They always do.''

22

Kate, hurrying through the subterranean garage of her office building, was surprised to see Andrew's muscular frame leaning against the door of her car.

''How'd you know I'd be leaving now?'' she asked.

''Your secretary's nicer to me than you are.''

''Oh.'' She silently scolded Mary for her indiscretion.

''Why haven't you returned my calls?'' His blue eyes were questioning.

''I've been really busy.''

''That's bullshit.''

Kate was startled by his angry tone of voice. It was almost funny. She was the one who had a right to be mad.

Andrew reached out and touched her arm. ''I know what happened between us wasn't my imagination.''

She felt her cheeks burn and couldn't meet his gaze. With the toe of her high-heeled shoe, she pushed a piece of paper out of the way as she waited for him to say whatever he'd come to say.

"What's happened between then and now?"

"I warned you it might only be for one night." Her voice was low.

"That doesn't explain why you won't take my calls."

Kate looked around the parking structure. More people were getting into their cars. Noise and fumes filled the garage. She took a deep breath, deciding to get the nastiness over with. "Lauren found out we left the party together Friday night."

"So?"

She tilted her head as she gazed into his eyes. "She came into my office like a wild woman, warning me to stay away from her, quote, 'boyfriend.' "

"That's absolutely crazy," he said, with a vigorous shake of his blond head. "I only saw the woman a few times."

"Well, she obviously thought there was something more between the two of you than you did."

He stood there with his jaw clenched. "I can't help that."

Kate shifted from one foot to the other, then asked quietly. "Were you sleeping with her?"

For the first time he looked uncomfortable. "What difference does that make?"

"A big difference . . . to me."

Andrew shrugged lightly. "So I went to bed with her. I'm not in *love* with her."

"Maybe you never bothered to tell *her* that!"

A woman getting into her car gave them both a funny look and Kate felt momentarily embarrassed.

Instead of answering her, he gestured in the direction of the exit. "Let's get out of here and go somewhere we can talk without dying from carbon monoxide."

"I don't think that's a good idea."

"You're not being fair."

Kate sighed with exasperation. "Andrew, I've had a rough day. I'm tired. And to be really honest with you, I don't need this kind of aggravation in my life. Besides, until this D'Arcy matter is behind both of us, it might be best if we didn't see each other.''

He drew in a sharp breath. "I promised you we wouldn't talk about the case, didn't I?''

"Yes.''

"Haven't I kept my word?''

She paused. "Yes.''

"Then there's no reason for you not to have dinner with me.'' He smiled at her as if he had just won a point on cross-examination.

Kate realized she was getting nowhere. "I'm really beat.''

"Tomorrow night?''

"I don't know.'' She looked pensive for a moment. "Lauren was quite upset.''

"Let me handle her.''

"I don't want you to end something with her on my account. I think you should first explore your relationship with her. Then, if it's not to be between the two of you, we can see about us.''

"But I want to be with you.'' He leaned over and brushed her lips with his, quickly, before she could protest.

A tingle raced down her spine. Why not go with him? she thought. She was too tired, her body complained. It wasn't love, or even lust, at this moment, her mind responded. It was something else. Being wanted, desired, felt good and she could certainly use some tender, loving attention. Her mind flashed on the last few days. Charles. Sandra and Madeline. Lauren. She truly was weary. Being alone was probably best.

"Right now all I can think about is going home and soaking in a hot bath. Then I'm going to crawl into bed and watch television until I fall asleep.''

He examined her face briefly. "I guess I have no choice but to let you go.'' He stood aside to allow her to open her door. "I'll call you tomorrow.''

She didn't answer or even look at him as she got into her car. Her mind in turmoil, she screeched around the underground maze winding out of the building. Once on Avenue of the Stars, she headed for Santa Monica and the beach.

I shouldn't have started with him in the first place, she thought. It was too soon. I need time to get over Charles. It wasn't fair to Andrew or me. As for Lauren, I didn't mean to hurt her. But even if Lauren cared for Andrew more than he had thought or realized, and Lauren was in fact devastated by what we did, her conduct was still appalling.

She flipped on the radio, wanting to put a halt to her thoughts.

"It's six o'clock in Los Angeles and the temperature's going down to forty-nine degrees tonight," said the newscaster. "Now for the latest news.

"Sandra D'Arcy, widow of the wealthy real estate magnate who was gunned down outside his lush Bel Air home, was questioned by the police yesterday. With her was prominent criminal defense attorney Kate Alexander. So far, the police have had no comment on what transpired. Prosecutor Madeline Gould, who is handling the case against Tommy Bartholomew, the young man accused of killing James D'Arcy, would only say that the police were interested in learning what light, if any, the young widow could shed on the murder.

"And now on the national scene, the President arrived in Washington earlier today . . .''

Kate was pleased to hear herself described as a prominent attorney. Charles had been right about that. The media were on top of this story at every turn. Chances were this same item would be carried on television. She'd have to program her VCR so she could catch herself on the news from now on in case she didn't get home from work in time to see it.

In Sherman Oaks, Madeline watched the television news with her two boys.

"You looked great, Mom," said Jud proudly, after seeing her interviewed by the reporters on the six o'clock news.

"I can't wait to go to school tomorrow," squealed Kenny. He was excited as he jumped around on the couch.

"Get down from there," Madeline said, laughing.

"All the guys are going to think this is great. My mom's a TV star."

Madeline felt good. It was nice to see how elated her boys were over her sudden fame. She too was thrilled. She thought once again what this kind of media exposure could mean to her chances of running for elective office.

She couldn't expect any monetary help from her family because they didn't have it. Nor would there be any contributions from her ex-spouse or his well-to-do family. This free publicity was a gift from heaven. Silently she thanked Philip for assigning her to this case. It would certainly help make her dream of becoming the first woman D.A. in Los Angeles a reality.

In her penthouse condominium in Westwood, Lauren also watched the news. When she saw Kate fielding the reporters' questions, jealousy gnawed at her. It wasn't fair. She was as smart as Kate and every bit as beautiful, if not more so. With her family money and social connections, Lauren should be the one who reaped the benefits of a celebrated trial. Not Kate, who had come from nowhere. Christ, even Madeline was going to be famous after this case, and as far as Lauren was concerned, Madeline had been nothing but a middle-class housewife when she got to law school.

Lauren had to think of some way to make this case backfire on Kate. She couldn't take a chance on Kate's becoming famous, because then Manning & Anderson would be forced to back Kate in her partnership bid. Even Dickson and his support might not be enough to stop it. And now that Kate had tried to steal Andrew, she truly needed to be taught a lesson.

Madeline dabbed a drop of perfume behind her ears and on her wrists. The coolness felt good against her hot skin as she glanced in the mirror, pleased at the way the suede dress showed off her curvaceous figure. The soft taupe color accented the highlights in her chestnut hair and gave her face a warm glow.

"Hi, Gary," she said, waltzing into her living room. He

whistled at her, and her pulse raced as she noted how handsome he looked in a light gray sports jacket, white turtleneck sweater, and black slacks. She smiled, then gazed at her younger son, who was watching television. "Okay, Kenny, Jud's in charge tonight, so you listen to him. I'll be home by one A.M."

"Why so early," asked Gary, looking surprised.

"Sam isn't coming to get them and I don't like to leave Jud alone any later than that. He's only fourteen."

"Damn! That ex-husband of yours is running our lives." Gary's voice was gruff.

His comment startled both Madeline and Kenny, but she chose to ignore it. She turned to her son. "Come give me a kiss."

Kenny got off the couch and slouched over to his mother, his eyes still on the screen. Madeline bent down to kiss him. "Good night," she said, waving as she and Gary went out the door.

When Madeline and Gary arrived at his friend Lenny's house in Westwood, the party was already in full swing in the crowded backyard. The patio and pool area were gaily decorated in the style of a Mexican fiesta. The tables, covered with multicolored cloths, were stacked with food and dotted with flickering candles. Bright piñatas hung from the rafters. Gary introduced her to a few people. They both had a margarita and then danced to the mariachi band that was playing in the corner of the patio.

An hour later someone recognized Madeline from the news and she was suddenly surrounded by people asking questions. It amazed her how quickly she relaxed, realizing she enjoyed being the center of attention. When she looked around for Gary, she saw that he had backed off and stood a few feet away, leaning on one of the patio posts. He had a drink in one hand, a cigarette in the other, and a scowl on his rugged, good-looking face.

She excused herself and strode over to him. "Hi there, I missed you."

"You've enough admirers around you," he said dryly.

"People are fascinated by murder, sex, and money," she joked.

"It's going to make you a celebrity." His mouth was twisted downward as he smiled, so it looked more like a grimace.

"I admit it's a great case for my career." She shrugged as if apologizing. "But I've worked hard. I deserve it."

"Sure." He calmly poured his drink out on the ground.

Her eyes narrowed. "And just what's that supposed to mean?"

He looked at her as if deciding whether or not to proceed. "I've heard rumors Philip White's in love with you."

"Don't be silly! Philip's a dear friend and a wonderful man to work for."

The mocking expression on his face upset her. "Are you suggesting there's more than a professional reason for his choosing me?" Her voice rose.

"Forget it," he said lightly. "Let's dance."

At first, she was stiff in his arms. But when he began to rub her back and brush his lips against her cheek as they glided over the floor, the tension began to leave her body. He had powerful arms and was a graceful, easy dancer. When the music stopped, he kept his arm about her possessively, as though he wanted everyone to know she was his.

"My friends are envious," he whispered into her hair as the music started again and she floated into his arms.

"They are?" His penetrating glance sent tingles up her spine.

"Because the sexiest lady here is mine." He hugged her to him.

One of Gary's friends came over. "Do you mind?" he asked Gary, indicating that he'd like to dance with Madeline.

"Bring her directly back," Gary told him, almost gruffly.

Madeline laughed. She hadn't felt this desirable in a long time. The band was playing a samba and they both moved to the rhythm. Then the music changed to a slow tune. The friend was an accomplished dancer who liked to do a lot of turns and swoops. Madeline hoped she wasn't making a fool of herself as he twirled her around the patio.

When the dance was over, the friend kissed her cheek. The next thing she knew, Gary had pulled her away. "Thanks," she called out.

"We're going."

"Why?"

"I'll tell you outside. Get your coat."

She walked into the bedroom and retrieved her things, wondering what had happened to change his mood so suddenly. She waved good night as Gary practically shoved her out the door. "Gary, what's going on?" she demanded when they were in the car.

The tires screeched as he pulled away from the curb. "I don't like to share you."

She studied his profile in the moonlight, his posture rigid, his jaw clenched tight. "It was only a dance."

His tone was biting. "You certainly appeared to be enjoying yourself."

Madeline glanced at him sharply. "Gary . . ."

He pulled the car over and jammed it into park, then grasped her closely. "I'm sorry. I acted like a jerk," he mumbled into her hair. "It's just that I care about you so much."

"I care about you too," she said. The heady aroma of his cologne, combined with the uneasy feeling in the pit of her stomach, was making her a bit light-headed.

Gary covered her face with light kisses, his breath warm against her skin.

Within minutes they were at his place. They had barely closed the door when he half dragged her to the bedroom, his arms about her, his lips and hands everywhere.

They fell onto the bed, but he gave her no time to think, his mouth immediately claiming hers again. She twisted under him, answering his kiss deliriously as his hands moved expertly over her. There was a tangle of sheets beneath her, the soft fabric of his slacks against her legs, but she was aware only of the storm he caused inside her and the surge of yearning that threatened to engulf her.

His ragged breath shivered into her ear before his tongue darted in. Her arms twined about his neck. Together, they struggled with the clothing that kept them apart. Finally, she felt his firm, muscled body against hers. The nakedness of his skin burned through her, until she felt nothing but him.

His mouth possessed her breasts, one and then the other, while her head fell back, her eyelids closed. He took her savagely. She gasped from the power of their combined passion. Soon the deep growl of his release was joined by the cry that shuddered from her throat.

Her body ached and glowed at the same time, long after Gary lay silent. Did we make love or war? she wondered dizzily.

23

Lauren hung up the telephone. Her father was coming to Los Angeles in two weeks and had agreed to meet with Madeline. She hoped it would work out. Miles liked to have influence in places where he did business and he especially liked to have people beholden to him. He had promised that if he was satisfied with Madeline's positions on the issues, and if she agreed to run her campaign in a way he could live with, he'd give her a large sum of money. Then Madeline could hire the kind of professional team she'd need to mount an effective campaign for D.A.

Next on Lauren's agenda was to stop the favorable publicity Kate was getting as well as to put an end to Kate's relationship with Andrew. She dialed Andrew's private number, hoping this time she'd get through. When he answered, she asked him in a teasing voice, "Interested in what Kate Alexander and the police talked about the other day?"

"You know I am," he responded, sounding wary.

"Then meet me at eight o'clock in the new restaurant on top of the Williams Street Office Building in Santa Monica."

Andrew stepped out of the elevator into the restaurant. This was a new place, one he hadn't been to yet. When he was escorted to the table by the window, he found Lauren waiting for him. She was dressed in a pumpkin-colored outfit that clung to her body as if painted on. "You look ravishing," he said.

"Thank you, Andrew," she cooed, lifting her hand.

He kissed it gallantly and sat down across from her, praying she wasn't planning to make a scene over Kate.

Lauren ordered a bottle of champagne, then turned to him. "You've been a very, very naughty boy."

"Well, I've—"

She didn't let him finish. "I don't want to hear any explanations. I've decided to forgive you, because . . ." She hesitated. "Well, let's just say I know you're only human." She laughed softly. "And after all, boys will be boys."

Andrew was surprised. After hearing from Kate how Lauren had reacted to the news of their tryst, he had expected Lauren to be totally unreasonable.

"Momma always said men had these . . . well, needs, which didn't mean they didn't love us."

The waiter arrived with their champagne and held it up to Andrew for inspection. "Yes," he nodded, wondering where this conversation was going.

The man popped the cork and poured the bubbling liquid. After placing the bottle in the silver bucket next to the table, he discreetly disappeared.

Lauren lifted her glass. "Anyway, here's to the future and to your success in the D'Arcy case."

He cocked his head, his eyes twinkling with amusement. "Hear hear." He clinked his glass to hers, took several sips, then put it down. "So, tell me, what did Kate and the police discuss?"

Her eyes clouded over for a moment. "Oh, Andrew, don't

be so impatient. It's boring. I'll tell you when I'm ready."

Andrew drummed his fingers on the white tablecloth. He really needed to find out what she knew. The D'Arcy case was generating a lot of media attention and he was beginning to have his doubts about Tommy. I need every edge I can get, he thought. His gaze traveled over her. There was no denying that she was a gorgeous lady, in a very sexy, showy way. Hell, what did he have to lose? He sat back in his chair, lifted the glass to his lips, and decided to let her set the pace.

When they had eaten and finished the champagne, she leaned toward him, her voice breathless. "Let's take a walk."

He called for the check, and when it arrived, tried to act nonchalant at the astronomical amount. Lauren had ordered a hundred-dollar bottle of champagne. He whipped out his credit card and paid, hoping her information would be worth the steep price. At any rate, he'd take it as a business deduction.

Out in the hallway, Lauren sauntered past the elevators to the door at the end marked "Exit." She opened it, motioning for him to follow.

A few steps later they were on the roof. Andrew noticed the condominium structure next door that loomed above the office building. Through some of the windows he could see the flickering blue lights of television sets, while in others there was only darkness.

"Let's sit." Lauren pointed to some lounge chairs.

He sat on a chaise and she chose the foot of the same chair. "It's beautiful out here," he ventured.

"Yes." A smile played across her lovely face as she blithely rested her hand on the inner part of his thigh.

He grinned. "Here?"

"Why not?" she teased.

He shrugged and peered quickly around. The thought of her touching him in clear sight of anyone looking out their window caused a surge of excitement in his groin. This woman was something else.

She leaned toward him, her coat falling open. Her hand massaged him through the fabric of his slacks. Andrew felt his body respond. His breath quickened as he reached out to stroke her breasts straining against the velvety material of her dress.

"Mmm," she murmured, swiftly unzipping him. In a second she had him maneuvered deftly out of his pants.

The shock of the night air caused him to shiver involuntarily.

She leaned forward and took him into her warm, moist mouth. He groaned. While his body throbbed with exquisite pleasure, he found himself looking around again desperately. He hoped no one was watching. At the same time, he almost came at the thought that they might be.

She moved her mouth back and forth expertly, sucking him gently and then harder, until he thought he would burst. Finally, the intensity was more than he could bear. He grabbed her head to him while he exploded into her. "Oh my God," he cried. At that moment, he heard the door onto the roof open.

He was grateful her coat obstructed the view of his genitals from the dark figure that approached. He thrust himself quickly back into his pants while Lauren lifted her head and grinned mischievously at him.

It was a guard. "Everything O.K. up here?"

"Yes, Officer," drawled Lauren. "We were just enjoying the lights." She pulled her coat around her tightly.

"Got a report something indecent going on up here."

"Indecent?" She laughed. "Perhaps someone across the way thinks a kiss in the moonlight is indecent."

He shrugged. "Takes all kinds."

Andrew found his voice and jumped up. "We were just leaving," he announced.

"That's O.K.," said the guard. "Take your time."

"Let's go back to my place," said Lauren sweetly. "We have some unfinished business to attend to."

When Kate answered the door, Charles was standing there. "What do you want?" she asked testily.

"To talk."

"I've heard all the lies I want to hear, thank you."

"Kate, after all we've been through, meant to each other, you owe me a chance to explain."

"I wasn't aware I owed you anything," she said coldly, and started to close the door in his face.

He grabbed her arm, his voice gruff. "Damn it, Kate, I love you! You're throwing our entire future away!"

She shook her head as she yanked her arm back. "No, Charles! You want it all."

"That's not true." His handsome face was tired and drawn, with an expression she'd never seen before. Could it be pain? She felt her heart thudding. God, why did he have this effect on her?

"Kate, I've never apologized for anything in my life. I've always had to fight, the same as you. That's why I understand you so well." His dark eyes swept her face. "But I'll say it if it will make you feel better." He paused. "I'm sorry."

My God, she thought, the invincible Charles Rieman is actually apologizing. After that horrible scene in her office when she'd slapped him, she hadn't thought he'd ever say he was sorry. She stepped back far enough to let him into the entry hall of her condominium, but she made no move to invite him beyond that.

"I should have told you the truth. But in my own way, I was trying not to hurt you."

"Trying not to hurt me?" she scoffed.

His neck reddened slightly. "Ann found out about Catalina. She threw a fit."

Her eyes widened. "Why didn't you tell me?"

"I thought if I took her away for the weekend, she'd back down."

"You must really think you're special!" Her voice was filled with sarcasm.

He didn't seem to catch her meaning. "I was wrong. It turned out to be a terrible weekend. All I did was call and get your damn machine." He peered at her suspiciously. "Where were you anyway?"

She ran her fingers through her short black hair. "None of your business."

A momentary flash of anger crossed his face; then the pained expression was back. Kate had never seen Charles remorseful before. There was no question in her mind he shouldn't have lied. At the same time she wasn't sure what she might have done in his place. She hesitated.

He seemed to sense that she was vacillating, and pressed on. "Kate, we're this close to getting everything we want!" He held his two fingers a quarter of an inch apart. "Don't you want to become Manning & Anderson's next partner?"

She stiffened. "I expect that to happen anyway. It should have nothing to do with our relationship," she said icily.

He opened his mouth, then appeared to change his mind. "Of course."

"And while we're on the subject," she continued, "I expect things to be business as usual at the office." She knew she sounded harsher than she felt at the moment, but she'd be damned if he or anybody else was going to stop her now. "Our clients shouldn't suffer because of us."

"I agree," he said softly. "Now, may I come in?"

"No. I don't think so."

"Kate . . ."

"Don't push me," she stated simply.

Charles gazed at her, his dark eyes questioning. Then he gestured with an upturned palm. "O.K. You win . . . for now." He turned to open the door. "Good night."

"Good night," she answered quietly. She closed the door firmly behind him and fastened the bolt. Only after she heard his car drive away did she allow herself to breathe easily. Even if she could somehow forgive him, would it ever be the same between them again? She shook her head bitterly. The pain was still there.

Dickson sat in his car. He had followed Charles tonight because he suspected his brother-in-law was having an affair. Worried that he couldn't win the will contest on the legal issues, Dickson needed to find some dirt on Charles. With the right leverage, Charles might be forced to give up more control in the D'Arcy Company and Foundation than he wanted to.

His heart quickened. There was Charles walking hurriedly out of the building. He watched him cross the street to his car. If his brother-in-law did have a girlfriend, would his visit have been that quick? Charles had been inside for less than fifteen minutes.

After Charles pulled away, Dickson took his parking spot and headed for the building. It was a security condominium, but the names were on the mailbox. One name jumped out at him. K. Alexander. He tried the door. It was locked. Did Charles use a key to get in, or did Kate buzz him through? Shit! Dickson hadn't been close enough to see.

Of course, Charles could have been dropping something off. But then, Dickson hadn't seen him carrying any papers. Besides, there were messengers to do things like that. He doubted Charles would have driven twenty-five minutes out of his way for business. Still, he needed more. He'd have to keep a closer watch on them. Wouldn't that be an interesting development if Charles and Kate were having a fling?

Andrew woke up in the plush bedroom of Lauren's penthouse, his mind fuzzy. It had been a night of heavy drinking and wild lovemaking. Now he wanted to hear whatever it was Lauren had to tell him.

She stood by the bed in her flowing white negligee. Her hair was tousled and her makeup gone, but she was still pretty though, he noted, somewhat hard-looking.

"Kate's making a deal with the D.A."

"A deal." He shook his head as if to clear it.

"Yep. Immunity for Sandra in exchange for her testimony against Tommy."

"No . . ." he said in disbelief. "She would have said something to me."

"Don't be silly," she snapped. "Kate Alexander's only interested in looking good on the evening news."

He chewed on his swollen lower lip while a thousand questions raced through his muddled head. "What's Sandra's story?"

Lauren shrugged. "I can't tell you anything more. You'll have to find out the rest on your own."

Her negligee fell open to reveal her breasts, but his mind wasn't on her body. "Come on, Lauren, don't come this far and then hang me out to dry."

"That's all I could get."

"But I need to know what—"

She put her hands on her hips. "I'm putting my job on the line for you as it is, you know? If anyone at Manning & Anderson were to find out, I'd be fired on the spot."

"I'd never tell where I got the information."

"You better not." She peered at him warily. "You plan to confront Kate?"

"Of course."

"I wouldn't if I were you. I know Kate. She'll only lie. She'll deny it."

His eyes narrowed. "Why would she lie?"

She didn't respond directly. "Does it shock you to find out how devious some people can be?"

"Well . . ."

"I think you've really fallen for her, hook, line, and sinker!" She angrily tossed her head of reddish-golden hair. "I've known her a lot longer than you have. Our little Miss Alexander has plans, big plans! They aren't going to be sidetracked by niceties such as worrying about you." Her voice was spiteful.

He sat there silently, his mind racing. Only a short time ago he had been trying to scare Tommy by warning him that Sandra could implicate him. Now it might actually be happening. Was this why Kate wouldn't see him? Why she had cut it off so suddenly? After their night together, he'd been so sure she'd want to see him again. Lauren's voice brought him back.

"If you're smart, you'll make a deal for Tommy first."

My God, he thought. Was it possible that Kate had been using him for information? He knew the way the D.A.'s office operated. The first defendant willing to deal was the one they worked with, often shutting out the other defendant. He needed to find out what was going on. He rubbed his face. "I have to shave and shower. I'd better go."

"What's the hurry?" Lauren thrust out her chest seductively. "My guest bath has everything."

"Thanks, but I also have to change clothes."

"Will I see you later?" Her voice was sulky.

He was exhausted. "Lauren, we just spent the entire night together. We hardly slept at all. I've got to go to work now." When he saw the jealous glint in her eyes, he realized she'd try to suffocate him if he gave her half a chance. He forced himself to smile. "Tonight I'm going home to sleep. You wore me out." He brushed her cheek with a quick kiss.

"All right, then leave," she said in a huff.

He went into the bathroom. A few minutes later he came out.

"I'll call you," he promised. "And thanks for the information." He grabbed his jacket off the chair. "Think you can find out anything more?"

She tossed her mane. "And . . . if I do?"

"You know I'll be grateful." He reached for her hand and started to kiss her fingers, one by one.

"How grateful?"

"Very."

"I'll see what I can do." She smiled.

"Great," he said as he left.

24

As soon as Andrew was gone, Lauren reviewed their conversation. She'd be thrilled if Andrew raced straight to the D.A.'s office and made a deal for Tommy to testify against Sandra D'Arcy. That would certainly put a crimp in Kate's favorable publicity.

But a more likely scenario would be for Andrew to ignore her warning and go see Kate. He'd want to ask her if she was in fact making a deal with the D.A. If that happened, Lauren was sure Kate, who was a real stickler about client confidentiality, would refuse to discuss the matter with Andrew.

Even if Kate denied she was making a deal, though, the seed of doubt would still be planted in Andrew's mind. He wouldn't be able to stop thinking about it. Soon he'd be back asking Lauren for more information and it would be her job to convince him a deal was imminent.

A quick glance at the clock on the mantel told Lauren her personal trainer would be here any second. Four times a week she exercised rigorously. She wondered if Andrew realized how much time and effort she expended in order to keep her breasts high, her waist small, and her thighs firm.

Pleased with the way things were going and still enjoying the memories of the preceding night's activities, she decided she deserved the day off. She left a message at the office that she was feeling ill and would not be in. Next she called her favorite salon in Beverly Hills and made an appointment for hair color, a blow dry, a facial, a pedicure, and a manicure. Finally, she arranged for her masseur to meet her back at her penthouse at five o'clock.

When the doorbell rang, Lauren rushed to get it. It was going to be a very busy day.

Kate reached for the envelope tucked into the beautiful roses that had just been delivered to her office. She read the card inside.

I'm going to keep calling you until you agree to have dinner with me. Andrew.

She smiled. He had already called her numerous times, both at home and here. She sniffed one of the buds. He'd remembered she loved yellow roses.

Impulsively she picked up the latest message from Andrew and dialed the number written on it.

Andrew sounded excited when he heard her voice. "Kate! I don't believe it."

"I wanted to thank you for the beautiful yellow roses."

"You're welcome. I hope this means you'll have dinner with me?" His voice was warm.

"How about a compromise?"

"Great! Then I'll have dinner with you."

Kate laughed. "What I had in mind was perhaps lunch."

He hesitated only briefly before responding, "You're on. Name the day and time."

"Say tomorrow at one o'clock?"

"Wonderful! How about I Cugini in Santa Monica?"

"I'll meet you there," she promised.

Theo finally escaped the reporters and managed to pull his car inside the gates to Sandra's property. As they closed behind him, he drove up to the house.

Sandra opened the door for him. Her pale blond hair hung softly about her face. "Thanks for coming."

Theo assessed the worried frown on her brow. "I came as soon as I got your message. What's wrong?"

She held her fingers up to her mouth in a shushing sound and then cupped her ears as if to indicate someone was listening. "Let's go outside. It's such a beautiful day."

Theo followed his sister-in-law as she quickly led the way to the patio off the dining room. Could the house really be bugged, he wondered, or was Sandra merely being paranoid?

Once outside, she seemed to breathe easier. She turned toward him and in the bright sunlight he could see the toll this whole gruesome mess was taking on her. Her young face looked haggard. Hell, he thought, it was taking its toll on all of them.

"What's going on?"

"I can't take a chance on anyone hearing what I have to say." She took a pack of cigarettes from her pocket. "Mind if I smoke?"

"Not as long as we're outside."

She lighted a cigarette and inhaled deeply.

"I need to get word to Tommy." Her tone was almost a whisper.

"That's crazy."

Her face crumpled and he thought he saw a glimmer of

tears in her eyes. Sometimes she acted tough and streetwise. At other times she seemed to be nothing more than a young, scared kid.

"I have to find out what Tommy's told the police." She gazed downward and twisted the diamond ring on her finger.

"Sandra, I think—"

"Please don't tell me what to do," she whispered fiercely, her hands over her ears. "Abigail orders me around all the time, telling me what I should do and think. 'Don't say this.' 'Do that.' " She mimicked her mother-in-law's voice. "I'm sick of it."

"I can imagine." On that score he truly did sympathize with her.

"I need someone I can trust to get a message to Tommy," she implored.

"Sandra, there are reporters out there dogging our every step. The tabloids would just love to get their hands on something like this. And then there are the police. How do you think it's going to look if I show up at the jail and ask to see my brother's killer?"

She turned away, appearing to stare out toward the gardeners busy at work on the grounds.

"Have you discussed this with Kate Alexander?" Theo asked.

"She told me I couldn't see him." Her voice was very low.

"And she's right," he said forcefully. "You could be putting yourself in jeopardy. I don't—"

"Look, just forget it, O.K.?" She whirled around to face him. "I'm sorry I asked."

"Sandra, be sensible. It's dangerous. Listen to your attorney."

"I said forget it, didn't I?" Her eyes blazed with anger.

He tried to reach for her hand, but she shook it off. "I assume you can find your own way out!"

As she strode away, he stood rooted to the spot. His stomach was churning and he was upset. Sandra seemed ready to explode, he thought.

* * *

Franklin Manning had been experiencing some angina pain and his doctor had ordered him to bed. He was having trouble sleeping and had been irritable and uncommunicative for days. When his wife, Irene, came in to see how he was doing, he grumbled at her.

"Oh my, we are out of sorts today, aren't we?" she said sweetly.

"I hate being sent to bed like a naughty child."

Her eyes softened as she looked at her husband of forty-eight years. "I know."

"I've got to be at the office," he said resolutely. "I need to settle the senior partnership matter. Until then I can't think of retiring."

She busied herself fluffing his pillows. "Have you decided what to do?"

"I'm not even sure it's up to me anymore." His voice was tinged with the bitterness he felt.

"That's not true. You're the senior partner. Everyone in the firm looks up to you."

He shook his head sadly. "I've been out so much lately, things are getting away from me. I know I have their respect, but it's not the same as the support I used to have."

"Oh dear," she murmured. "You're obviously still having trouble deciding between Charles and Dickson?"

"Yes."

"It's an unfair choice for a father to have to make."

He peered at his wife gratefully. "I love our son, but I'm afraid he's not the right person to head the law firm. The first thing on Dickson's agenda would be to push for a merger with a big New York firm."

"But he knows you've been against that for years," she said, sounding shocked.

"As soon as he had my voting rights, he'd do what he damn well wanted."

"There must be some way to protect the firm."

He studied her face. "I've been toying with the idea of giving Dickson and Charles each half of my shares and recommending that the two of them share the helm."

"That sounds like a Solomon type of solution."

"Yes," he said wryly. "The only problem is that instead of splitting the baby, it'll probably split the firm." He shook his head. "I'm afraid Dickson's not the right man for the job."

She reached out to squeeze his hand. "And Charles?"

"We see eye to eye on most things." He sighed. "He could have been my son, he's so much like me. Yet I'm afraid Dickson will never forgive me."

"Never is a long time."

Kate noted the beautiful tropical flowers placed around the room in large Chinese porcelain vases as the hostess escorted her down the middle of the noisy restaurant and through the double French doors to the table in the enclosed patio.

Andrew stood and pulled out her chair. "It's good to see you, Kate." His glance swept over her. "You should wear yellow more often. It's a beautiful color on you."

She smiled as she sat down and removed her sunglasses. "Thanks."

"So how's the world treating our famous lady lawyer?"

Kate laughed. "Very well. And thanks again for the beautiful roses. They've started to open and my office is filled with their lovely smell." She found herself squinting. The sun was so strong she decided to put her sunglasses back on.

"I'm glad." His eyes crinkled at the corners as he smiled at her. His hands, tan against the snow white of the tablecloth, fiddled with the silverware.

The waiter arrived, poured their bottled water, and Andrew held his glass up in a toast. "To being friends."

She smiled as she clinked her glass to his. "Friends."

Behind her dark glasses she was able to study him without his realizing it. With his blond hair, golden tan, muscular build, and light eyes, he looked more like a movie star than a defense lawyer. She bet his looks gave him an advantage with female jurors, though the males probably found themselves jealous.

After they ordered, Andrew gazed at Kate. "Been to any political fundraisers lately?"

"I usually go to one or two a week."

His eyebrows arched. "If I go to one a month, it's too much. How do you stand it?"

Kate shrugged her shoulders and smiled. "I love it."

"I bet most people go to be seen and written up in the columns."

"True. But I believe in what Eldridge Cleaver said. If you're not part of the solution, you're part of the problem."

"In other words, if I'm not helping others, I'm a bad person?"

"Bad's a strong word. Passive is more like it."

"I better get my act together or you won't approve of me?"

"That's right," she teased, smiling again and sipping her water. The waiter arrived with their lunch and Kate took off her glasses before tasting the pasta. "Delicious."

"Yes." He took a few mouthfuls, then peered at her. "Tell me, is it true what I hear about you running for D.A. in the near future?"

"It's a strong possibility."

"And from there you have your eye on the governor's mansion?"

"Why not?" she said cockily.

"Well"—he held his fork in the air—"I think you'd be very good at anything you did."

"I think so too."

He laughed. "Spoken like a true politician."

Kate concentrated on her lunch for a few minutes, as did Andrew. Finally, he put his napkin down and looked at her. "Kate, I know we made a pact not to discuss the D'Arcy matter."

A look of wariness came into her eyes. "Andrew, I don't want to ruin—"

"Please let me finish . . . I don't want to upset you. But I must ask you one question because I've been told something that troubles me greatly. I'd just like a simple yes or no. O.K.?"

"Go on," she said testily.

"Is it true you're making a deal for Sandra D'Arcy to testify against my client?"

Kate stiffened. How dare he bring this subject up after he had promised not to! "Andrew, I don't intend to discuss the D'Arcy matter with you."

"For God's sake, Kate, I have a right to know if the answer to that is a yes or a no!" The color rose in his face.

"And I refuse to debate it with you!" she said through gritted teeth. Damn him. She would never have agreed to meet him if she had known this was what he intended.

His blue eyes seemed to be assessing her. "I heard it from someone at your firm."

"That's not possible," she blurted out before she could stop herself.

"Forget what's possible." His voice rose. "Damn it, Kate, just tell me if it's true!"

Kate threw her napkin down and stood up. "If this is why you asked me to lunch, you can go to hell!" She stormed out of the restaurant, oblivious of the many stares her outburst had caused. She felt incredibly stupid falling for the oldest trick in the book. Charm.

25

"**R**achel, is something the matter?" asked Kate, picking up the receiver, a worried frown on her face.

"Nope," answered Rachel. "Just wanted to remind you about the monthly luncheon tomorrow."

"Oh." Kate had noticed the date in her book, but had planned on having her secretary call at the last minute to say she'd been unavoidably detained. As much as Kate dearly loved and missed her friends, she didn't want to spend an hour in the presence of that insufferable Lauren, who was making her life miserable because of Andrew. "Rachel, I'm really sorry, but I can't. Something important's going on."

"A trial?"

"No."

"We promised a trial was the only excuse we'd accept."

Kate sighed. Rachel had outmaneuvered her. "Where?"

"Jade West. One o'clock."

"Fine. See you then." Kate swiveled around in her chair, determined to ignore Lauren tomorrow as best she could.

She glanced out the window at the verdant grounds of the Los Angeles Country Club, and the deep blue sky with white wisps of clouds floating by. It was so easy to forget what a beautiful day it was when your desk was covered with mountains of work.

Madeline hung up the phone after speaking to Rachel. She had tried gracefully to get out of tomorrow's luncheon, but Rachel had reminded her that the only excuse was a trial. Now Madeline wished she had told a little white lie.

She didn't want to spend an hour in Kate's presence when all she could think about at the moment was arresting Kate's client. Madeline adored Kate and didn't feel comfortable not being able to tell her about the ongoing investigation of Sandra. She'd have to watch what she said, and if Sandra was arrested . . . She caught herself—no, *when* Sandra was arrested, she'd try her hardest not to let her friendship with Kate interfere with both of them doing their jobs.

I hope it happens soon, Madeline thought, sighing. She was irritated that it was taking so long to get the evidence to arrest Sandra D'Arcy. She needed either Tommy's testimony implicating Sandra or some other evidence. Her eyes fell on her desk, strewn with papers and case files she couldn't seem to get to. She was so behind—sometimes she thought she'd never catch up.

* * *

"Of course I'll be there, darling," drawled Lauren. She wrote down Jade West in her alligator skin datebook. After hanging up, she gazed around the room with all its expensive accessories and plants. If it weren't for the costly things that surrounded her and helped make her ordinary office special, she would have been even more miserable at Manning & Anderson than she was. They'd given her the worst associate's office in the entire place. She looked out on nothing.

All that would change, however, when she became a partner. Then she'd move to the next floor and could furnish her new office exactly as she pleased. If the budget was insufficient, and she already knew it would be, she could supplement it from her own pocket. That, of course, meant that no expense would be spared; thank God she had money. She'd already promised herself it would be the plushest office in the entire firm. She couldn't wait.

Kate and Madeline arrived in the parking structure at the same time. "Hi. How are you?" called Kate.

"Working hard as usual," Madeline replied lightly. "You?"

"Good."

Inside the restaurant, the Chinese maître d' bowed and showed them to their table. Kate smelled the delicious aroma of Peking duck. When they got to the table, she saw that Rachel and Lauren were already jabbering away.

Lauren pulled out the chair next to her. "Sit here, Madeline," she insisted.

Kate watched as Lauren leaned forward and whispered in Madeline's ear.

"Hey, guys, no secrets," kidded Rachel.

"It was just a little personal tidbit," said Lauren.

"Wait till you hear about Lauren's Andrew," said Rachel. "She's been filling me in on the details, and he sounds like a real hunk."

Kate stiffened ever so slightly. Andrew had certainly wasted no time in hightailing it back to Lauren. But then, for all she knew, he had never left Lauren.

"I think," observed Madeline, "that Rachel gets a vicarious thrill hearing about our love lives."

"Absolutely," agreed Rachel. "I've been married too long to remember what it's like to date or have someone court me."

"Oh, come on now," Kate cut in, "you and Darren have a great relationship."

"That's true, but after seventeen years and two children, it's hard to remember the adventure and romance of dating. Sometimes when I listen to the rest of you, I feel I'm missing out."

Kate's smile was more of a grimace. This was going to be torture. She couldn't wait for lunch to be over. Hearing about Andrew and Lauren for an hour was more than she could take.

After they had ordered, Rachel turned to Lauren. "Isn't your beau defending the man accused of killing James D'Arcy?"

"Yes." Lauren shook her head emphatically.

"So," teased Rachel, "what's the inside scoop on the case?"

Madeline spoke quickly. "Listen, guys, I hate to be a party pooper, but since I'm prosecuting the D'Arcy case and Lauren's boyfriend is defending the accused, this could get sticky. Also, Kate represents a possible suspect who, at the very least, will be called as a witness. It'd be best if we didn't discuss the matter at all." She glanced at Kate for support.

Kate nodded. "I think that's best too."

Rachel appeared embarrassed. "Of course. Please forgive me. I had no idea you were all involved."

"No problem," said Madeline.

"Well, Kate and Madeline might not be able to discuss the case," declared Lauren. "But I'm not directly involved. I can discuss anything I damn well please."

Kate frowned. "Sandra D'Arcy's a client of Manning & Anderson. The last time I looked, you were on the letterhead."

"Oh, bullshit," said Lauren. "I give them twelve hours

a day, five to six days a week. That's all and that's enough.''
She turned to Rachel. ''What do you want to know,
honey?''

Rachel looked uncomfortable. ''Let's just forget it.''

''You're all a bunch of worrywarts,'' accused Lauren.

More than ever, Kate wished she hadn't come. Lunch
couldn't be over too soon. Between the discomfort she felt
around Lauren because of Andrew, and her inability to
speak about the D'Arcy case in front of Madeline, she was
a bundle of nerves. Most of the time she was good at keeping things separate, but today she couldn't seem to stand
back and be objective.

Later that day Madeline saw Detective Bower standing in
the doorway to her office. ''Come in. You in the building to
testify or to see me?''

He grinned. ''Both.''

''Sit down.'' She motioned him to a chair.

He looked at his watch. ''I can't. I stopped by to tell you
I finally spoke to that guy I mentioned. The one who was
practically ruined by D'Arcy.''

Madeline was immediately interested. ''What did he have
to say?''

''What didn't he say is more like it! The guy obviously
hated D'Arcy. Made no bones about it.''

''Interesting.''

''Yeah. Seems the D'Arcy Company owed him a nice
chunk of dough. He was doing some work on one of their
developments. So he goes to their office where the book-
keeper gives him the usual runaround. 'We only pay twice
a month. Go away.'

''As he's leaving, he sees D'Arcy in the hall talking to
some lady. He introduces himself, apologizes for interrupt-
ing but he's got a family problem and would appreciate it if
D'Arcy could bend the rules and pay him ahead of time.
D'Arcy turns to him and says, 'What the hell do you think
I am, a fucking bank?' Guy's totally embarrassed. Tells
D'Arcy he's a fraud who doesn't give a damn about little
people. D'Arcy turns red as a beet and orders the guy to

leave. Says he'll never work for the D'Arcy Company or any other firm in California again.''

''Nice guy,'' said Madeline, shaking her head.

''And,'' continued Bower, ''D'Arcy stuck by his word. He saw to it that no one would hire this guy or his company for anything.''

''The man lost everything?''

''Had to move outta state. Start all over.''

''That's terrible. Besides, it sounds like D'Arcy lost his temper first.''

''He did, according to this guy. Anyway, he was glad D'Arcy was dead.''

''I'm not sure I blame him.''

''Especially when you hear why the guy needed the money.'' He rolled his eyes. ''Seems his wife was having cancer surgery.''

''How awful that D'Arcy never even asked.''

Bower nodded in agreement. ''I checked out the guy's alibi. He was with several other people at the time of the murder. Anyway, I still say we've got our killer in Bartholomew.''

''One of them,'' she corrected.

''We'll get 'er yet. Don't worry. The kid'll crack.''

''I hope you're right.'' Madeline frowned as she wondered about James D'Arcy. Philanthropist or fraud? Good question.

There was a knock on his door and Charles looked up from the papers he was reading, a scowl on his face.

''I'd like to talk to you for a minute,'' said Lauren sweetly as she stuck her head in.

''I'm in the middle of drafting an agreement,'' he explained irritably. ''Can't it wait?''

''No. It's something you need to know.''

''Very well.'' He sighed with resignation. ''Come in then.''

She closed the door behind her and sashayed across the elegantly furnished room to his desk.

''Sit down.'' He indicated the chair in front of his desk.

"Thank you." She flashed him a winsome smile and crossed her slim legs as if hoping to attract his attention to how shapely they were.

Charles was oblivious to her charms. This woman did not appeal to him at all. "What's so important it can't wait?"

"Do you know who Andrew Stewart is?" Her tone was sugary.

He gazed at her impatiently. "He's a defense lawyer and he's representing Tommy Bartholomew, isn't he?"

"That's right." She smiled as she toyed with a lock of her reddish-golden hair. "Well, I've been seeing him on a social basis and—"

Charles interrupted with a chortle. "If you're worried about a conflict of interest question, Lauren, I would hardly think that qualifies."

"It wasn't me I was worried about."

"Oh?"

"It seems Andrew's also seeing Kate Alexander."

Charles felt his heart thud as he jolted forward slightly in his chair. He forced his voice to be calm; he couldn't allow her to see how upset he was. "Are you speaking of seeing as on a social basis"—his voice caught—"as opposed to a professional basis?"

Lauren laughed out loud. "My," she drawled, "you are being so gentlemanly. Yes. I'm talking about the male-female thing."

"I see. You're sure?"

"Absolutely. Why, I even confronted Kate and she just up and admitted it."

"How long has this been going on?"

She looked at him coyly. "All I know is that they left the Women's Political Action party at the Century Plaza Hotel last Friday night together and saw each other over that weekend."

Charles felt his hands become clammy. He quickly stood and walked across the room to the window, giving himself a minute to gain control over his emotions.

"I came to see you, Charles," she went on, "because in light of the fact that Kate is the attorney assigned to handle

266

Sandra D'Arcy, it seems to me she's engaging in a relationship with Mr. Stewart which could certainly be viewed by some, especially the tabloids"—she hesitated for a moment—"well, as lacking in propriety."

Charles wanted to run down the hall and strangle Kate, but first he had to handle this conniving little bitch. He turned and smiled. "I'm sure nothing involving the D'Arcy matter was discussed. Kate's a very ethical lawyer," he said. "However, I do appreciate your bringing this to my attention." He peered at her with a stern gaze, his brow furrowed. "I trust this will not go any further."

"Of course not." Lauren's thick dark eyelashes lowered coquettishly.

"Good." He clapped his hands together. "And don't you worry about it anymore. I'll speak to Kate right away."

"It'll be our little secret," cooed Lauren, standing up to leave. She waggled her fingers at him. " 'Bye now."

After the door closed behind her, Charles slammed his fist in his hand. God damn it! So that's where Kate was last weekend. He had known something was wrong when he kept calling from New York and couldn't reach her.

He started to pace his office, his mind working feverishly. Andrew Stewart was a formidable foe. Not only was the man outrageously handsome, he was also a damn good lawyer and a bachelor to boot. All that aside, though, he was a stupid choice on Kate's part. She should have known better than to get involved with someone when there was a possible conflict of interest.

I've worked my ass off to position her for a brilliant political future, he fumed, and when I turn my back for one second, what does she do? She throws the whole thing away.

Charles wasn't sure he trusted himself to act rationally. To steady his nerves, he walked over to his bar, poured himself a stiff drink, and took a big gulp. After a few minutes, the shaking inside stopped. He drank the rest, then put his glass down. Somehow he had to straighten this mess out.

* * *

Theo waited impatiently in his parked car for Dickson to show up. His long copper hair brushed the back of his shirt every time he turned around to gaze out the rear window. He was extremely upset over his visit to Sandra's and the way she was behaving.

He saw a Mercedes pull into the parking lot of the Federal Building in Westwood. As soon as he recognized Dickson, he breathed a sigh of relief. He got out of his Jaguar and locked the door while his lawyer drove over to where he was.

"Hi." Theo opened the passenger door and slid in.

"What's so urgent?" Dickson maneuvered his car out of the lot and headed down Wilshire.

Theo related his conversation with Sandra, ending with, "She says it's important she find out what Tommy told the police."

"Shit, I can't believe she'd put you at risk that way. The kid obviously murdered your brother. Sandra should keep her fucking mouth shut! She's messing where she shouldn't be."

"What's that supposed to mean?"

"Forget it." Dickson turned to Theo again. This time he had a placating smile on his face, which made the cleft in his chin appear even deeper. "Look, Theo, the important thing is that you told her no. My advice to you is, don't get involved. Let me handle it from here on out, O.K.?"

"Sure." Theo was relieved to have Dickson take over. Now he had one more concern. He cleared his throat. "The police asked me again where I was the night of James's murder."

"What'd you say?"

"Home, alone." Theo's palms were damp. "What if they find out?" He waited for Dickson's response, but Dickson stared straight ahead, saying nothing.

26

Lauren fluffed her hair in the mirror; under the lights of her dressing table it shone in reddish-golden waves. She dabbed some mascara on her lashes and hurried to slip on an alluring silk caftan. Her heart was beating rapidly. Andrew had just telephoned from the lobby and was on his way up.

The doorbell rang. Before she opened the door, she took a deep breath, her hand on her heart. You can do it, she promised herself. "Why, Andrew, what a pleasant surprise."

Andrew stepped into the foyer, seemingly oblivious of how sexy she looked. A quick glance at his handsome face as he strode past her and into the living room told her he was troubled. "You were right. Kate's making a deal."

"She admitted it?"

"No." His blue eyes clouded with anger. "She refused to discuss it with me."

Lauren felt a surge of triumph. Her prediction that Kate would refuse to discuss anything that had to do with the D'Arcy case had proved correct. This was wonderful news. She did her best to disguise her glee. "Oh dear," she managed to say sympathetically, adding, "But I'm hardly surprised. Kate obviously doesn't intend to tip her hand to you in any way."

His brow furrowed. "I'm still having trouble believing it."

"Andrew, I gave you confidential information because . . ." She looked down, a faint blush on her cheeks. "Well, because I care for you." She reached out for his hand and smiled. "I didn't want you to lose such a big case just because someone was playing dirty behind your back. But it was wrong of me to tell you." Her voice dropped

269

almost to a whisper. "I could lose my job over this, you know?"

He nodded.

"What I've done is somewhat unethical," she hastened to add, "but I wanted to help you."

"I appreciate it." He smiled and squeezed her hand. "By the way, were you able to find out anything more?"

"I did overhear something, but . . . maybe I've already said more than I should." A secretive, knowing look slid across her face.

"Lauren, please," he implored. "It's so important to me."

She took a deep breath. "All right. I heard Kate talking to Charles Rieman about a deal she'd been offered. She was promised that if Sandra would agree to testify that Tommy killed her husband with her gun, they would give her immunity from prosecution for murder and allow her to plead to a lesser charge. Kate was hoping for solicitation."

"That only carries a two-to-six-year sentence! It's unbelievable," he muttered.

"Not really. The D'Arcys are a rich, prominent family and Tommy Bartholomew is a nobody. Who really cares what happens to him anyway?" Lauren's tone was sarcastic.

"If what you're saying is true, Tommy and Sandra are both guilty! Why should his punishment be so much greater than hers? It's not right."

"Exactly," she said coyly. "I gathered from the conversation between Kate and Charles that the case against Sandra is weak. Apparently, the thinking is that if Sandra's testimony makes the case against Tommy ironclad, it's worth it. And a guilty plea from her on a lesser charge would suffice."

"I've got to stop this!" The muscles in Andrew's cheek moved.

Lauren hurried on. "Yes. You've got to make a deal for Tommy first. If he agrees to testify that Sandra was the mastermind behind the plot to kill her husband . . ." She didn't have to finish.

Andrew leapt in. "Then that strengthens their case against her. If they have a good chance at convicting Sandra, they'll go forward with it. Those people hate to lose." He chuckled. "Lauren, you've been an enormous help. I don't know how I'll ever repay you."

She smiled knowingly. "I'm sure we'll think of a way."

He pulled her to him. "You know what? I'm going to make one of *your* fantasies come true."

"Which one?" she joked playfully.

"You'll see," he said in a teasing voice.

Lauren was feeling pretty mellow after she and Andrew had smoked some grass. When the doorbell rang, he went to open it. A young woman wearing a beige wool coat entered. Andrew brought her over to Lauren.

"This is my friend Paula," he said. "Paula, I'd like you to meet Lauren."

Lauren gazed at the woman critically. She was quite pretty, with honey-blond hair and large brown eyes. Lauren guessed her to be about thirty. There was a softness to her face, and when she smiled her eyes were filled with warmth. "Here, let me take your coat."

When Paula removed her wrap, Lauren saw she was full-figured, definitely too lush to be a model or even an actress in today's thin-obsessed world. Underneath she was wearing a pair of beige wool slacks and a matching silk blouse.

"We've already started." Andrew held out a joint for Paula. "Great stuff." He winked. "From Maui."

"Thanks." She put it to her mouth, inhaled deeply, and slowly let the smoke out. Then she took another deep puff, holding the smoke longer in her lungs before exhaling. "Good."

"A friend gets it for me," explained Lauren. "Want some wine?"

"Sure."

Lauren filled another glass and handed it to Paula. Then

she did a little dance around the room. "Wow, am I ever feeling good."

"You're going to feel even better soon," promised Andrew, a mysterious smile on his face.

"Much better," agreed Paula softly.

Lauren became moist just from the tone of their voices. Andrew held out his hand and led her to the bedroom. Quivering at his touch, she found herself being gently undressed by him. He kept kissing her throat and murmuring to her softly as he removed her caftan, then her bra.

"Just relax, this is going to be so good and I'll be here for you all the way."

Andrew bent down to slip off her panties, planting a warm kiss where her soft hair met her leg. She was now totally nude. She shivered. Surprisingly, she felt no embarrassment as the other woman's soft brown eyes swept frankly over her body.

"You're lovely," Paula said, smiling.

Andrew guided Lauren backward until she was lying on the bed.

With her head on the pillows, she felt slightly dizzy as Andrew continued to stroke her, nuzzling her neck with his mouth while Paula moved around her room lighting several fragrant candles she had removed from her bag. She also put rose-colored scarfs over the lampshades and set the music on the stereo. In the rosy glow of the room, Lauren watched fascinated as Paula removed her clothes. It was so sensuous. She was amazed at how voluptuous yet firm Paula's breasts and body were.

When Paula took a bottle and a vibrator from her bag Lauren tensed.

"Relax, baby," whispered Andrew.

Lauren heard Paula's soft voice. "I'd like to rub some of this lotion on you while Andrew takes his clothes off."

Lauren nodded, too mesmerized to speak. It felt strange to have another woman rubbing her body in such an intimate way; she had always insisted on a male masseur. Yet there was a definite gentleness to the way Paula touched her. To her surprise, she liked it. Warmth began to spread over the surface of her skin.

She felt the weight of Andrew's body sink onto the bed next to her, his hardness against her thigh. His mouth nibbled her breast while Paula continued to rub the lotion down Lauren's leg and up the other one. Then Paula turned the vibrator on and ran it over Lauren's body. Everywhere it passed, a surge of heat suffused Lauren. Her body was on fire.

As Andrew kissed her deeply, thrusting his tongue into her mouth and stroking her breasts, Lauren felt a moist kiss on the inside of her thigh. When she realized it must be Paula's tongue on her, she tried to sit up, but Andrew gently restrained her.

"Take it easy, baby," he whispered, his breath warm in her ear.

Part of Lauren wanted to tell them to stop, yet at the same time, another part of her didn't want it to ever end. It felt so good. Paula's tongue had softly worked its way inside and Lauren was instantly inflamed.

Never, in all her life, had she been made love to like this, and it was wild. Her heart quickened, her breath caught in her throat as a spark of excitement traveled from her stomach to her legs, then up between her thighs to her spine. "Fuck me, Andrew. Please. I want to fuck."

He smiled down at her indulgently. "We'll get to that, I promise. Just let yourself enjoy this." His voice was soothing.

Soon Lauren felt the familiar waves of ecstasy starting to build—the heat inside her thighs was almost unbearable. She tried to forget that it was a woman between her legs as her body began to spasm. "Oh," she cried out, unable to stop. "Oh!"

The sensations were too intense. "Stop," Lauren pleaded, "just for a minute, let me catch my breath."

Mercifully, she felt Paula move away. Andrew continued to restrain her as he kissed her on her neck and around her ears.

The softness of a woman's hand began to stroke her legs

and then to massage her feet. After a few minutes, she felt the woman's caresses back between her legs and the heat was instantly back. "I want to fuck," she called out. "Please!"

"Anything you want," said Andrew. He drew her legs up and entered her, and she realized that the mouth now suckling her breast belonged to Paula. The thought of it excited her even more. While Andrew thrust himself into her repeatedly, Lauren cried out in pleasure as again and again she flowed forth with passion.

Finally, he pulled out and she saw he was still hard.

"Want to watch me fuck Paula or do you want more?" There was a grin on his face.

"More," she cried.

Andrew forced her hands above her head while he plunged into her, impaling her with his strong body. "Tell me what you want."

"To have you fuck me," she responded, breathing hard.

"I didn't hear you. Tell me again, what do you want?"

"I want you to fuck me!" she screamed.

At last, he seemed to sense her exhaustion. "Had enough?" he asked, pummeling her.

"Yes," she almost sobbed as Andrew exploded inside her. After he pulled out, she still felt the warmth of his body in her. She was drenched with perspiration. "I want to see you fuck her now," Lauren said, sure he wouldn't be able to.

Andrew disappeared into the bathroom for a moment. When he came back, Paula reached for the condom and slipped it on him, then put him into her mouth. It excited Lauren more than she could believe.

When he was hard, Andrew pulled out of Paula's mouth and lowered himself onto her.

At the sight of his body inside the other woman, a wave of panic washed over Lauren. "No," she cried. "I changed my mind. I don't want you to fuck her!"

Andrew grinned at Paula. "Our little Lauren is jealous."

"Poor baby," Paula murmured.

"What should we do about it?" He drew slightly out of and teasingly entered her again.

Lauren couldn't help herself, she became wild with fury.

Paula's soft brown eyes were sympathetic. "I think you should do what she wants, Andrew."

He turned to Lauren, a mocking smile on his face. "And what's that, Lauren?"

"More," she said. "I want more."

"More what?" he demanded.

"I want you to fuck me more."

Hours later, when she awoke, it was as if the entire thing had been a dream. Both Andrew and Paula were gone.

As she moved languorously on her bed, her body remembering the things that had been done to it, she couldn't shake a feeling of unease. Had they taken pictures or tape-recorded anything she said? She shook her head. That was silly. Andrew wouldn't do that. She wanted to marry Andrew. In fact, she was going to talk to her daddy about it. Yet the image of Andrew entering Paula's body bothered her more than she cared to admit. And even though she tried not to think about it, pictures of Andrew and Kate making love together also flitted through her mind.

Up until a few hours ago, she was sure everything she'd done was going to get her exactly what she wanted: Andrew. But now she sensed they had somehow humiliated her. She recalled how she had begged him to make love to her. She definitely liked it better when it was the other way around.

Kate looked up as Charles came barging into her office, slamming the door shut behind him. He strode over to her desk and, with a flick of his hand, turned off the dictating machine she was using.

"I've always considered you a smart lady, but you may have just thrown your entire future away!"

Kate's eyes widened in surprise. "I'm not sure I'm—"

"You've been seeing Andrew Stewart," he spit out.

"Charles . . ."

"Save it. We may say things we'll regret." His jaw was rigid. "Right now I'm your boss and what I'm about to say is for the good of your career as well as this firm." He glared at her. "You're not to see that man again while the D'Arcy case remains open."

Kate blanched. "Just like that. I'm accused, tried, given no chance to say anything in my own defense, and then convicted?"

"If you can't comply with my request, I'll expect your resignation on my desk immediately." His tone of voice was cold and brutal.

"I see." Her eyes flashed angrily at him. "And who's speaking? My boss or my jealous lover?"

Charles clenched and unclenched his fists.

"Is smashing in my face," she taunted, "going to solve something?"

He glowered at her. "It'll make me feel better."

She rose and came quickly toward him. "Go ahead, I dare you."

"Kate, don't push me."

"Let me tell you something, Mr. Rieman. What I do in my free time is my business, not yours and not this firm's! I've *never*"—she almost shouted the word—"*never* compromised a client or this firm and I don't intend to start now." Her nostrils flared as she spoke and her breathing accelerated.

"You may not have meant to, but don't you understand how bad this could look?" He grabbed her shoulders, his fingers digging into her flesh.

"Charles, you're hurting me." She tried to get away, but his hands gripped her firmly. He pulled her to him and the next thing either of them knew, his mouth was against hers, kissing her fiercely.

She pushed against his chest, but he wouldn't let go. Suddenly, Kate was overwhelmed with longing. She couldn't help herself as she responded to his kiss with all the passion she had tried to pretend was gone.

When she finally found the strength to break away, she saw that Charles was still scowling. She gazed directly into his eyes and he glared back at her. Kate didn't know what she felt. She was angry, hurt, upset, and at the same time, she realized, still very much in love with him. It was obvious from the look on his face that he too was suffering from indecision.

He finally broke the silence that hung between them like a leaden weight. "You've certainly gotten back at me in spades, if that's what you intended."

"It wasn't that," she fumbled, unwilling to admit she had succumbed to Andrew because of what Charles had done to her. If he only knew how Andrew had manipulated her at lunch yesterday, she'd look so stupid.

"Look," he said gruffly. "I'm willing to forget everything that has happened." His eyes seemed to be pleading with her. "I love you, Kate."

She shrugged her shoulders and bit her lip to keep from crying. He reached out and pulled her to him again. She yielded to his strength, letting him hold her close as her mind sprinted over the events of the past few weeks. How could she admit to him what a scoundrel Andrew Stewart was, merely using her to get information on the case? What a fool she'd been! Was her judgment of men so seriously flawed? She hoped not.

It felt so good to have his strong arms around her again. This was the man she had wanted to spend her life with. Maybe he truly was sorry about the incident with Ann. Maybe she'd been too harsh. Maybe she should forgive him.

Charles drew back and cupped her chin tenderly. "You're the only one I love." He kissed her lips gently and stroked her hair away from her face.

Kate looked deeply into his eyes. Perhaps he deserved another chance. "I'm willing to try again. But first we need some new ground rules."

"Anything you say."

"No more lies."

"I promise, no lies."

"Starting from this moment on, no matter how awful, you must tell me the truth. And I'll do the same. But I don't want to hear what went on in that hotel room, and I don't want you to ask *me* about Andrew Stewart.''

He started to protest but she put her fingers on his lips.

''If you can't accept these conditions, I don't want to even try to get back together again.''

Charles gazed at her for a few moments. Finally, he said, ''I accept.'' He tried to kiss her again but she resisted.

''One more thing. You've got three months to secure the senior partnership. That's all. Then you can choose to leave Ann or not, but I won't spend the rest of my life in a clandestine relationship.''

''You drive a hard bargain, Kate.''

She shook her head. ''I should have done this long ago.''

''Very well, I agree.'' He took her into his arms again.

The door to Kate's office suddenly opened and Dickson sauntered in. When he saw Kate in Charles's arms, he grinned. ''I see I'm intruding,'' he said facetiously.

Charles glared at his brother-in-law.

Kate tried to maintain her dignity. ''Yes?''

''When you're through with Mr. Rieman, please come down to *my* office.'' Dickson walked out, slamming the door behind him.

27

Andrew paced anxiously, his mind in a quandary, while he waited for Tommy. If Kate really was making a deal for Sandra to testify against Tommy, wouldn't he have detected at least a glimmer of something in her eyes? Or was she capable of hiding her emotions that well? It was amazing how little he actually knew about her.

She had seemed so passionate, almost vulnerable, the night they had spent together. Then, suddenly, she had refused to see him again, blaming it on Lauren. Was it the truth or a plausible excuse? Wasn't it more likely she didn't want to see him because she had something to hide?

He replayed in his head his conversation with Kate at lunch the day before. If she was in fact making a deal, she was one hell of an actress.

Lauren, on the other hand, was as readable as the marquee on a movie theater. She clearly had one thing on her mind: sex. He'd never met anyone like her; she would do anything. But was she believable? She had no reason to lie. The fact that she was willing to risk her future at Manning & Anderson for him said something. No, she had to be telling the truth.

He pulled his thoughts back to the problem at hand. He had to make a decision regarding Tommy. If Sandra was ready to point the finger at him, that fact, along with the evidence the police already had, would most likely seal Tommy's fate. No amount of brilliant lawyering could save him then.

He was also worried because he hadn't heard yet from Tommy's mother about the second mortgage on her house. He reminded himself to call her when he got back to his office. Andrew wondered if it might be better to cut his losses and convince Tommy to cop a plea. He was sure Tommy was guilty, anyway. Weren't most of them? Andrew had learned it was sometimes better not to know the truth. It was easier to defend them if you didn't think about guilt or innocence. His job was to force the prosecution to prove their case beyond a reasonable doubt. If they couldn't, his clients walked. It was that simple.

Andrew looked up as Tommy was ushered in. The kid was starting to look pasty and swollen. He'd put on a few pounds. It was no wonder with all the starchy, greasy food he was getting in jail. "Sit down," Andrew said. "I've got something important to tell you."

Tommy looked up hopefully. "Good news?"

"Sorry," said Andrew, his face glum. "It's not."

"Oh man, what's happened now?" Frown lines appeared on the young man's face as he gazed worriedly at his attorney.

"Your girlfriend's about to confess to the cops how you killed her husband." Andrew watched carefully for Tommy's reaction. He had to hand it to him, he was putting on a good show. He looked genuinely shocked.

"She wouldn't do that!" Tommy reached nervously in his breast pocket for a cigarette.

"Don't kid yourself." Andrew offered a match. "When the boat's sinking, it's every man for himself."

"Why'd she want to lie like that?"

Jesus, thought Andrew, if a client ever actually proclaimed the truth when confronted with the evidence, he'd go back to church. "It's a lie" was their favorite expression. "Who knows?"

"But I didn't do it. I thought you believed me."

"Look, Tommy, it's not important what I believe." Andrew sat down opposite his client and spread out his hands. "My job's to do the best I can for you. Right now I've got to tell you that if Sandra testifies, you've got troubles, big troubles, my friend."

"How'd you find out she was going to do that?"

"I've got my sources. Inside sources, I might add." Andrew leveled his gaze at him. "The only chance you've got to cut a deal for yourself is *now*."

"I don't wanna cut a deal. I didn't do it."

Andrew sighed. Sometimes he got so tired of hearing their spiel. "Listen, let me tell you the facts of life." He started to count on his fingers. "They've got your footprint at the scene. You've got no alibi. You were in love with her and wanted her old man dead. Remember all the things you told the cops in that recorded statement." He sighed again. "Added to that, there's the money she gave you—"

"Loaned," interrupted Tommy.

"Whatever. At any rate, the gun that killed D'Arcy was probably hers and she'll say she gave it to you. Your car was seen leaving the scene." Andrew's eyebrows arched pointedly. "Shit, if she takes the witness stand and says the two of you planned to kill him, who do you think they're going to believe?''

"She'd never say that," protested Tommy.

"Let's cut the crap, O.K.? Look at it from the jury's point of view. Sandra D'Arcy's a rich broad. The D'Arcys are a prominent family. They have a lot of juice. If she's willing to get on the stand and say you did it—"

Tommy cut in. "But if she says I did it, won't she be found guilty too?"

"Not necessarily. She can say she talked to you about killing her husband, offered to pay you, showed you her gun." Andrew shrugged. "Then she changed her mind. Didn't want to see you anymore. And I can guarantee you, the whole time she's telling this to the jury she'll be crying. The upshot is, she used you to kill her husband and you end up paying for the crime." He gave his message a chance to sink in. "Pretty neat, huh? So she pleads to a solicitation charge. Big deal.''

"What's that?"

"In simple terms, it's asking someone to kill for you. Only carries a two-to-six-year sentence. She'll be out on parole in a couple of years." He looked at Tommy gravely. "While you'll die in the gas chamber."

Tommy blanched; his whole body started to tremble. "No way. I didn't do it."

"If the jury believes you're guilty, Tommy"—Andrew ran his fingers across his throat—"you're a dead man."

Tommy's eyes filled with tears, and his hand shook as he took out another cigarette and lighted it from his stub. "So what do I do?"

"Want my best advice?"

"Yeah."

"O.K." Andrew leaned forward. "You tell the cops Sandra did it, in exchange for a lesser sentence for yourself."

Tommy inhaled deeply. Although his eyes seemed to assess Andrew warily, he remained silent.

"Tommy, I'm going to tell you what I think happened, O.K.? Then you say if I'm right or all wet."

After a long pause, Andrew continued. "The way I see

it, you were crazy in love with a beautiful lady, and you were dead broke. Killing her husband was Sandra's idea. She worked on you day and night until you couldn't think straight. You were terrified of losing her. Finally, in desperation, you agreed." He paused again. "She planned the entire thing. It was her gun, she gave it to you and told you when her husband was coming home. She gave you a bottle of champagne to plant in the car after you killed him to make it look like James stopped and was followed home. She made sure the tricycle was blocking the gates so he'd have to stop the car and get out. You waited for him, killed him, and when it was over, you threw the gun away. The next thing you remember is waking up sick in your room."

A look of terror passed over Tommy's face. "Shit," he muttered, putting his head in his hands.

"Listen, Tommy, do you even remember what happened that night?"

Tommy shook his head.

"So you can't honestly tell me you didn't do it, can you?"

All of a sudden, Tommy began to sweat and Andrew could see he was about to pass out. "Put your head between your legs, kid. Let the blood rush back into your brain."

Tommy did as he was told, while Andrew waited patiently. After a few minutes, the shaking stopped. Then Tommy looked up. "Now what?" His voice was barely audible.

"You'll plead guilty. The cops will arrest Sandra, put her on trial, and you'll testify against her. In exchange for that, you'll get maybe twenty years."

"Twenty years!" gasped Tommy, his eyes nearly bugging out of their sockets.

"It's better than the gas chamber. That way there's no coming back. Besides, you behave and you'll be eligible for parole after maybe eight, ten years. You'll still be young."

"I don't know . . . ."

"Every second you wait, there's more of a chance Sandra's making a deal. And if she does, the D.A. won't give a damn what you have to say. They'll only deal with one of you. It's you or Sandra. First one to pass Go collects the reward; the other one dies. Better make up your mind and fast. You wait one minute too long, it'll be too late."

"I don't want to make things worse for her," Tommy muttered.

"Jesus fucking Christ!" yelled Andrew. "The broad's about to say you pulled the trigger. You're going to fucking die, man, and you're worried about her? What are you, a masochist?"

Tommy looked grim but said nothing.

Chief Deputy Philip White looked up and saw Madeline standing in the doorway to his office.

"Got a minute?" she asked.

"Sure, come on in," he said, smiling.

She closed the door behind her and took a chair.

"What's up?"

"Just got off the phone with Andrew Stewart."

"Oh?" Philip's eyes filled with curiosity.

"He's coming to see me at four o'clock. I think he's ready to make a deal."

"Well, well." Philip leaned back in his chair.

"What do you think?"

He stuck his unlighted pipe in his mouth. "It's still hard for me to accept making a deal with a triggerman."

"I know," she sighed. A frown appeared on Madeline's brow. "I hate the idea too. I'm just afraid without Tommy's testimony, we'll never get her. She'll get away with murder." She stood up and paced the room a few times, then turned to look at him, her brown eyes serious. "If *we* don't get justice for the victim, who will?"

He studied her face as if weighing her words, then sat forward abruptly. "Let's meet with Ron and get his parameters. I'll see what his schedule is."

Philip picked up the phone and spoke to the D.A. "He wants to see us now," he said, hanging up.

District Attorney Ron Miller sat behind his desk in his large and well-furnished office, while Philip and Madeline took the two chairs facing him. Madeline quickly brought him up to date on the D'Arcy matter.

"What are your feelings about a deal like this?" the D.A. asked, when she was through.

Madeline gestured toward Philip as she spoke for the two of them. "We're convinced Tommy pulled the trigger and we're not crazy about making a deal with the shooter . . ." She paused, then continued, "We also realize Sandra couldn't have done it without Tommy."

She chewed on her lip for a moment. "On the other hand, we doubt if Tommy would have killed D'Arcy if Sandra hadn't talked him into it. She must have worked on him day and night until she got him to say O.K."

Philip nodded in agreement as the D.A. gazed from one of them to the other, a thoughtful expression on his face. "Let's see if I understand. You've got the triggerman, whom you'd really like to see get the death penalty. But in reality, you don't even know if you can convict him. The worst scenario is, you don't make a deal with Tommy, he goes to trial and gets off. Then he won't have any reason to snitch-off his girlfriend and you'll never get the woman who talked him into killing her husband. Is that your reasoning for wanting to offer Tommy a deal?"

Madeline nodded. "Exactly."

Miller interlaced his fingers, put his hands behind his head, and leaned back. "I don't like making deals with shooters either. Yet it's not right for the wife to go free." He sat forward suddenly.

"Because of the witness/accomplice rule, we need more than the uncorroborated testimony of the co-conspirator to convict."

She nodded again. "Right."

"I usually like to leave the sufficiency of the additional evidence up to the prosecutor. Any other case, I'd say O.K., go ahead, even if it isn't airtight. But this is the D'Arcy family. I don't want problems on appeal."

"We're sure we can overcome that," she said.

"Any chance Stewart will go for life without possibility of parole?" Miller asked.

"I doubt it."

The D.A. paused. "O.K. What if you offer life with possibility of parole, he testifies at trial, and she walks?"

"That's the risk we have to take," Madeline said. "We can never guarantee the outcome."

Philip spoke up for the first time. "Are we free to deal, even if Stewart can't deliver anything more than Tommy's testimony?"

"Think you've got enough to convict her?"

Madeline reiterated the evidence.

"All circumstantial," the D.A. pointed out.

"Yes, but with Bartholomew's testimony, it'll be enough." Madeline's voice was firm.

Miller clasped his hands in front of his knees. "O.K. I'll go along on life with possibility of parole. But you're the trial attorney. It's your decision. And I'd like you to feel out the guys at homicide and call the victim's family, too."

Her eyes became wary. "They don't have to agree, do they?"

"It's your call. But I don't want to see the D'Arcy family crying on TV about how we let the killer escape the gas chamber. I want them fully briefed."

Madeline had no choice but to agree. She knew only too well the political realities of a situation like this. The D.A. was looking toward the next election. He couldn't afford to appear soft on crime or to make enemies of the D'Arcys, who were a force to be reckoned with in the party. This way, if the family was angry they could take it out on her, not Ron Miller. Great.

At precisely four o'clock, Madeline escorted Andrew Stewart into her office. "Coffee?" she offered.

"Sure. Black."

She prepared two cups and handed one to him.

He wasted no time. "If my client's willing to say Sandra D'Arcy was the mastermind, that he was hopelessly in love with her and unable to say no to whatever she asked, would you make some kind of recommendation?"

Madeline felt her skin tingle with excitement, but she

appeared cool. "That depends." She picked her words with care. "I'd have to be convinced I couldn't get her any other way. I'd also like to see how homicide and the D'Arcy family feel about it." She drained her cup of coffee and looked at him.

He didn't seem pleased with her response. Perhaps he thought I'd roll over and be grateful, she thought, perturbed. "Your client ready to do this?"

Andrew's expression was cautious. "He's not sure. I told him I'd feel you out."

"You mean you're fishing for a deal without your client's consent?" Suddenly, she didn't like the whole situation.

"I'm just testing the waters."

Madeline checked her angry reply. "It all depends on what your client gives us besides his testimony. We might be interested. But in no case will I go for less than a life sentence."

Andrew smiled. "You're being a little harsh, don't you think?"

"That's my position, Counselor."

He seemed to be considering her words for a moment. Then he shrugged. "With possibility of parole?"

She paused.

"Without possibility of parole, my client's not interested."

Madeline hated to do it, but she didn't want to blow the deal. "O.K. Possibility of parole."

"I'll talk to him."

"Fine."

After he left, Madeline walked to the window and looked out on the downtown traffic. She disliked making a deal with that arrogant man. If Tommy went to trial, she was sure she'd win—she had one of the most impressive trial records in the office. And she'd enjoy wiping that smug smile right off Andrew's face. But she also wanted Sandra D'Arcy, and this was the only way to make it happen.

A lot of deputies put in their time and then left to go into private practice as defense lawyers. But although the money could be phenomenal, especially compared to the salary of a county employee, it was something Madeline knew she could never do. Kate Alexander had once said she felt the same way, but then she had left. Of course, she apparently now wanted to come back. Maybe Kate had the right idea; maybe she was going about it the right way.

In Madeline's opinion, the primary objective of defense lawyers was to make money. Their sole obligation was to serve their clients and walk them out of the courtroom, even if they had, in fact, committed heinous crimes.

The idea of fighting to free a guilty person made Madeline sick to her stomach, even though she knew the adversary system was necessary to a democratic society. No, she definitely didn't like Andrew Stewart. She didn't even respect him. But this was the way justice worked. He was merely a cog in the wheel.

Madeline called and asked Bower to stop by. When he did, she laid out the possible deal.

"Hey, lookit," he said, "we're not in the business of killing people. It's our job to find 'em, convict 'em, and put 'em away. We got to remember, this way it'll be both of 'em."

She nodded. "I'd like the family to understand also, but under the circumstances, that may not be easy."

"Who knows?" He hitched his droopy pants up over his bulging stomach. "For ordering the murder, they may want to see her get hers."

Kate was worried as she entered Dickson's office and closed the door. Charles had tried to convince her to let him sort out the messy situation they'd found themselves in, but she'd insisted she could handle it. Now she wondered if that was true.

Dickson's smile was more of a smirk. "So, Kate, seems you and my brother-in-law are having a little, what shall we call it . . . fling?"

She wanted to shout at this obnoxious man that she and Charles loved each other, but she knew it was neither the time nor the place. Best to act like it had been nothing. "I'm afraid you jumped to the wrong conclusion. I'd just had some bad news. Charles was merely comforting me."

"Do you think I'm a stupid man, Kate?"

"Of course not."

"Then why feed me such a line of rubbish?"

She felt herself become flustered. "I'm not sure I understand."

"I'm very well aware that you and Charles have been involved for . . . a while."

Her stomach dropped. How had he found out? She said nothing—she would wait and see what he wanted.

"Not going to deny it?"

"I've said all I have to say. I believe you totally misinterpreted what you saw."

"I don't think so." Dickson strode around to the front of his desk as if to peer down at her at closer range. "The wisest thing for you to do, unless you want this little matter to get out, is resign."

Kate looked at him, incredulous. He couldn't be serious. Resign after all her years of hard work? "I've no intention of resigning. It was a hug between friends. Charles will back me up."

"Perhaps you're not aware of my brother-in-law's reputation as a ladies' man. No one will believe him, or you for that matter. Besides, these things often have a way of getting out."

"Why are you doing this to me?"

He pulled on his cuffs. "I have my reasons."

"I realize you haven't liked me since our first unfortunate dealings, but I never expected you to try something like this."

He winced at her words. Then he smiled. "Kate, Kate. You represented me as counsel in that matter. As such, need I remind you, everything was privileged?"

What a bastard, she thought. He thinks he can blackmail me and I'll go quietly to my own funeral. Well, he can think again! She straightened her spine. "I propose we sleep on this, no pun intended. We may both realize we've more to gain by forgetting the whole thing."

"Are you threatening me?"

"Hardly. I thought that was your game."

His eyes narrowed into slits. "It would be a breach of ethics on your part to say anything."

"*I* wouldn't dream of saying *anything*." She paused. "But as you've already mentioned, sometimes these things have a way of getting out."

He glared at her, then walked to the window and looked out. When he turned around, his jaw was rigid and his eye was twitching. "You're playing a dangerous game, *little girl*. Be careful you don't get burned. Remember, when I'm senior partner, Charles won't be able to protect you."

She peeked at her watch. "I'm late for an appointment. Have a nice evening, Dickson." As she walked out with her head held high, Kate's knees were shaking. Had she convinced him to say nothing or had she merely overplayed her hand?

28

At eight-thirty that evening, Madeline was seated with Philip in The Grill, a restaurant in Beverly Hills. Throughout the meal they had discussed their strategy in the D'Arcy case. By the time coffee arrived, there was little more to be said about the matter. A period of awkward silence followed, during which Madeline noticed that Philip seemed preoccupied. His face was strained as he fiddled with a spoon. She wondered what was wrong.

Finally, he spoke. "I understand you're seeing Gary Sutter?"

Madeline was floored. Philip was never one to pry into

someone's private affairs. "We've gone out a few times," she responded.

"Is it serious?"

"It's too early to say." She was puzzled. "Something the matter?"

"Well . . ." He hesitated. "Ordinarily, I wouldn't even mention something like this. But since"—he turned crimson—"since you've been seeing each other socially . . ."

Madeline peered at him curiously. It wasn't like him to struggle for the right words. "Go on," she urged.

"Gary came to see me about you."

"About me?" she asked with disbelief.

"Yes. He didn't think you were ready to handle the D'Arcy trial."

She was stunned. "What exactly did he say?"

"That it was a big case with lots of pitfalls and that the media would be watching every move."

"And?" she prodded, knowing there had to be more.

"That we couldn't afford to make any mistakes and that we needed a prosecutor with more experience on the case."

"Did he recommend someone?" Her voice cracked as she spoke.

"He said he was more qualified."

Madeline's face turned white. "I can't believe it."

"It shocked me, too."

"But why would he say a thing like that?"

"I don't know. I thought you could tell me."

She shook her head. "I have no idea." A frown appeared on her brow. "Philip, you're not having second thoughts about me, are you?"

"Course not."

"Good," she mumbled, still visibly upset. What on earth could Gary have meant?

"Has Gary ever acted like he was jealous of you?"

"Jealous? In what way?" Her heart started hammering in her chest.

"Professionally."

"Oh." A wave of relief washed over her. Then her pulse quickened again. "I'm not sure." She searched for the right words so Gary wouldn't look bad in Philip's eyes. "We were at a party the other night. Some of the people recognized me from TV and asked a bunch of questions, made a fuss. You know how it is." She smiled. "Gary walked away. When I went over to him afterward, he seemed a little irritated."

"What did he say?"

She blushed as she remembered Gary's insinuation that she'd gotten the case because Philip White was in love with her. How was she going to tell her boss that? "Something about your playing favorites."

"I see." Philip looked pensive for a moment.

Madeline ignored the warning bells that were going off in her head. "Maybe he meant he was worried for me. The case is going to be played out in the media and all that . . ." She paused, not knowing what else to say.

"Well"—his mood brightened—"perhaps I read too much into it. I hated to bring it up, but . . ." He shrugged.

"I'm glad you did, Philip. That's what friends are for."

"Unfortunately, I've seen competition ruin friendships."

"I understand." She smiled at him with a bravado she didn't feel. In the pit of her stomach she had a sinking feeling that Gary Sutter might not be the man she desperately wanted him to be.

Seated on the couch in his oak paneled study, Franklin Manning removed the plaid flannel blanket from his lower body. He didn't like to appear too ill when his son was around, and he was expecting him momentarily. Dickson always tried to use his father's failing health to his advantage and Franklin intended to have the upper hand today.

His eyes surveyed this room he had always loved, furnished in dark woods, the walls lined with bookshelves. A fire blazed in the fireplace; he was always cold lately. The doctor said it had to do with his heart not pumping the way it used to. Getting old was horrible, Franklin thought. Especially when the firm's future wasn't settled. He dreaded the confrontation he knew he was going to have with Dickson.

On the mantel above the fireplace was a family photograph of him and Irene with Dickson and Ann when they were children. He sighed. What had gone wrong? Why did he and Dickson always butt heads? There was a knock and the door opened.

"Hello, Father. Mother said I could find you in here."

"Come in, Dickson. Sit down." Franklin's voice was gruffer than he had intended. Dickson sat in the club chair as Franklin went on.

"I've had a rather nasty shock."

"About what, Father?"

"I've been told you're claiming now you saw a new will for James and that there are two witnesses."

"So?"

Franklin pointed his finger at Dickson. "Who are these witnesses?"

"I'm sorry, Father. I can't seem to remember their names."

"That's rubbish and you know it!" The elder Manning glowered.

"They were not names I recognized."

"I'll tell you what I think. I think you're making it up. Trying to put Theo into a position his brother never intended."

Dickson's right eye began to twitch. "And I'm telling you James decided to make Theo trustee of his estate so he could head both the D'Arcy Company and the Foundation."

"I doubt it." Franklin shook his head. "James was turning things over more and more to Charles. He wanted to take time off because of his child and he knew he could trust Charles to handle things as if they were his own."

"Maybe Charles disappointed him," snapped Dickson.

Franklin wondered for the hundredth time why Dickson always had to say derogatory things about Charles. They used to be such good friends. But that was a very, very long time ago. He peered gravely at his son. "Dickson, it pains me to say this, but I believe you're lying."

A flush appeared in Dickson's cheeks. "That's your opinion."

"Well then, since you don't seem to want to cooperate, let me make my position clear." Franklin sat up straighter on the couch. "Either you give me the names of these two mystery witnesses now, or else . . ."

Dickson turned crimson. "Are you trying to intimidate me?"

"Damn right!" Franklin slammed his fist down on the couch.

"Father, your heart . . ."

"Shut up," warned Franklin. "I want this will contest dropped immediately or I'm prepared to throw my weight and influence behind Charles for the senior partnership."

"Why do you always stick up for Charles?"

"Maybe it's because he's never lied to me."

"Ha! That's what *you* think."

Dickson bit his lip, thinking quickly. He wanted to tell his father what he'd seen between Kate and Charles, but he had no real proof yet. And besides, he was worried. What if Kate decided to breach the privilege? He'd better wait. It was too risky.

"What did you mean, Dickson?"

"That Charles is two-faced, that he is not the saint you believe him to be."

"I had hoped to remain neutral, but you're making that impossible."

His mind racing, Dickson realized he couldn't afford to antagonize his father at the moment, not when things were so close to working out for him. He just had to maintain the status quo until he knew what Mindell and the other two partners were going to do. Then maybe he wouldn't need his father's help. However, he couldn't take a chance on his father's openly supporting Charles. That could be disastrous; it could sway others. He needed to buy time.

"Listen, Father, let me talk to Theo again." Dickson cleared his throat. "Maybe I can convince him to forget about contesting the will."

"I asked you to do that weeks ago."

"I tried. Really I did, but Theo was adamant." Dickson

forced a smile to his lips. "I'll try again. Theo usually listens to me."

"Good. See that he does."

When Charles was ushered into Governor Ned Brandon's suite at the Century Plaza Hotel, his friend was standing at the large picture window looking out. "Hello, Ned."

The governor turned around, his brown eyes lighting up with pleasure. "Charles." Grasping Charles's hand, he half embraced his oldest and dearest friend. "Thanks for coming on such short notice. I know how pressured you are."

"For you, Ned, I can always make time."

"Thanks, buddy. Want a drink?"

"Please."

Charles watched Ned at the bar, aware of how tired his friend looked. He could see that the other man's hair, once so full, was now sparse, and that he had put on weight. Even though he and Ned were the same age, Ned looked ten years older. Charles mentally congratulated himself for keeping fit, thankful that he made himself run five miles three times a week.

Charles raised his glass. "A toast to California's next United States senator."

Ned grinned, then clinked his glass to his friend's. "Thank you." He took a deep swallow. "So how's it going?"

"Well, I'm right on schedule with my fund-raising."

"Good, good. You're one of the few people I can count on to do what you've promised, and on time!"

"I try."

"Let's sit down." The governor indicated the couch in one corner of the suite's richly furnished living room. When they were both settled, he started to talk. "As we all know, Vince will go for the governor's chair in the next election as soon as I take myself out of that race and declare for the Senate."

"Right." Charles moved his shoulders slightly under his well-cut suit.

"And the D.A., Ron Miller, will go for Vince's spot as attorney general."

"That's what we've always planned," agreed Charles.

"That leaves one important place open. You still feel Kate Alexander's the best choice for that spot?"

"Absolutely. You're not changing your mind, are you?" There was a wary expression in Charles's dark eyes.

"Well, some of the men are balking," the governor stated candidly. "They hate to see such a plum go to a woman. So many qualified men also want the spot."

Charles felt his temper flaring as he leaned forward. "I've got news for you, Ned. I've gathered enough information on the two potential male candidates to bury them before the nomination gets to the table, to say nothing about jeopardizing their current professional situations. And I'll do it— that's a promise."

The governor drew back and set his drink down. "You want her that much?"

"Damn straight. We need more competent women in office and you know it. And Ned, while we're talking, you owe—"

"Say no more," said the governor, paling. "You don't need to remind me."

"Good, then it's settled."

"She know you're playing hardball?"

"She'll learn that side of it soon enough."

Kate heard the excitement in Charles's voice when he called her from his car.

"I'd like to come over. I've got some good news."

"Sure."

Ten minutes later she opened the door to her condominium. Charles grabbed her by the waist and whirled her around.

She laughed. "What's going on?"

"I just left the governor."

"He's in town?"

"Yes." He put her down and kissed the top of her nose.

"What did he want?"

"To ask a bunch of questions." There was a teasing smile around the corner of his mouth. "Basically, though, he wanted to know if I still thought you were the best choice to run for D.A. in the next election."

Kate's eyes sparkled with excitement. "What did you tell him?"

His handsome face turned serious. "Absolutely not."

"You didn't?" She punched at him playfully.

He reached for her, nuzzling her ear with his lips. "I told him you'd be great."

"That's wonderful," she cried, hugging him with all her might.

"What happened with Dickson?" There was a slight frown on his face.

"Piece of cake," she said lightly, hoping it was true. She took his hand and pulled him toward the living room. "Tell me everything the governor said."

As she listened to Charles, Kate couldn't help but feel his magnetism. When it came to politics, no one played the game better than he did. But her excitement was mixed with a sense of unease. It wasn't that she didn't love Charles. She did. And she was glad they were back together again. Still, something nagged at her. The hurt, the pain—they were still needling, right beneath the surface. She sighed. It would take time to forget.

And then there was the problem with Dickson. She prayed he'd back down, but if he called her bluff, she didn't know what she'd do. Ethically, she couldn't even tell Charles what she knew about Dickson. It was confidential.

Andrew hung up the telephone, furious with himself. Tommy's mother had just said she couldn't get the rest of the money she owed for Tommy's defense. Hell. He'd been around long enough to know he should have gotten his entire fee up front. He'd let his desire for publicity cloud his otherwise astute judgment. Of course, he had still been paid twenty thousand dollars, he reminded himself, but that wasn't what he'd expected. A defense like Tommy's if it went to trial was worth hundreds of thousands of dollars.

He'd bet Kate Alexander and Manning & Anderson were getting a million dollars to represent Sandra.

On the way to talk to Tommy, he thought about the conversation he'd had with his partner yesterday. After his partner had reviewed all of the evidence the state had against Tommy, he'd taken the position that Andrew should definitely convince his client to plead guilty in exchange for a deal. It was better to save Tommy's life.

Andrew thought about all the media attention. He loved the circus atmosphere surrounding a big, star-studded trial. His theory was, whether you won the big case or lost it, what people remembered most was that you were in it. Oh well, if Tommy made a deal, he'd still be the prosecution's star witness and there would still be media interest in Tommy and his attorney. He made his decision. Tommy had to testify against Sandra. Now all he had to do was convince Tommy.

When Tommy was brought in, Andrew went over the same ground he had the day before.

"You really think I'll lose?"

"Doesn't look good." Andrew gazed at Tommy meaningfully. He could see he'd have to walk his client through his case one more time. "You can't account for the time when James was murdered. No one saw you at the bar, no one saw you leave with a man named Vincent, no one saw you at home sick. They have your footprint at the scene at the right time. The mud from your boot matched the soil near the body. Your car was seen racing down the hill afterwards. You got money from Sandra. You knew she had a gun and where it was kept. The gun was the kind used to kill D'Arcy. And, you said you talked with Sandra about getting rid of her husband so you and she could be together." Andrew ticked the points off on his fingers. "You had the motive, the opportunity, and the means. Now, if you were sitting on that jury, what would you think?"

"It sounds pretty bad when you put it that way," admitted Tommy.

"Jurors are just human beings and you're betting your life on the roll of the dice. Remember, if you don't get to the D.A. first, Sandra's going to be on that witness stand someday telling the jury you killed her husband.''

Tommy's eyes widened in fear. "You really think so?"

"I know so."

"What should I do?"

"Make a deal, Tommy."

"I plead guilty . . .''

"You give them Sandra, and you get your life."

"I can't.'' Tommy's breath grew ragged.

"You want to die?''

"I sure as shit don't want her to die in my place,'' Tommy snapped back. "What kinda person you think I am?''

"Listen carefully. You plead guilty to murder, with no special circumstances, and you'll get life.''

"The special circumstances means the part about killing someone for money?''

"That and lying in wait. The D.A. has indicated they won't be asking for the death penalty against Sandra, either. So probably the worst she'll get is life too. With luck, you'll both be out in eight to ten years.''

Tommy chewed on his lip. "But if I don't testify, they don't even try her, right?''

Andrew sneered. "Maybe not this month, or even this year, but don't kid yourself. There's no statute of limitations on murder. The police'll keep investigating no matter how long it takes.'' He shook his finger at Tommy. "And when they find the evidence, she'll be tried and sentenced to die, just like you.''

"Say I agree to a deal. Tell me what happens then.''

Andrew went through his checklist for Tommy—what Tommy would be expected to say in front of the judge who would have to approve the deal and what the judge would do then. He also filled Tommy in on the kinds of questions he would be expected to answer when he testified at Sandra's trial. When Andrew was through, Tommy still seemed undecided.

"I don't want to make things worse for Sandra.''

Andrew began to pace the room. Either his client was

stupid or he just wasn't getting it. Well, maybe denial was Tommy's way of dealing with the situation, but Andrew damn well knew that if Sandra was getting ready to say she and Tommy did it, they probably did. He could see he was going to have to get tougher.

Andrew stopped and planted his feet squarely in front of Tommy. "You know how they do it to you in the gas chamber?"

Tommy shook his head, tears starting to roll down his face.

"They put you in a room with glass all around it. Outside, there are rows and rows of seats. That's for the people who watch while you die. They tie you into this chair and they put the cyanide tablets into the container that releases the gas into the room. You start to choke and gasp for air. It is *not* quick and it is *not* pretty. At the end, you will feel like your lungs are being seared and you'll scream for mercy. You'll wet your pants and probably shit, too. And all this time, there are people staring while your eyes pop, your skin turns purple, and you begin to drool. You'll writhe in agony. Who knows, maybe you'll get lucky and they'll televise it . . ."

Andrew didn't have to finish. Tommy had his head in his hands, his body racked with sobs. Andrew waited patiently. He wasn't leaving this jail until Tommy had agreed.

29

Madeline tried to hide her excitement when the call came from Andrew Stewart that she should proceed with the deal for Tommy to testify against Sandra. As quickly as she could, she arranged to meet with Abigail, Theo, and Victoria at Abigail D'Arcy's home.

After the guard checked her identification and the large gates opened, Madeline drove up the tree-shaded drive. My God, she thought, I knew they were rich but this looks like a castle.

Her ex-husband's parents had been well-to-do, but this was more than mere wealth. The pastoral beauty of the green lawn gave her the feeling she was in the English countryside. It was hard to believe she was only minutes away from U.C.L.A. and Westwood Village.

A butler answered the door. From the massive entry she was ushered upstairs into a sitting room. She saw an elegant woman she recognized from her many photographs as Abigail D'Arcy. She was in a wheelchair, and sitting next to her on a flowery chintz sofa was a dark-haired, painfully thin, yet attractive woman. Madeline judged her to be in her late forties. It was hard to tell her age since the woman's face looked stretched—it didn't match her hands.

Standing at one of the draped windows was Theo D'Arcy, whom Madeline had met before. He was the only one in the room to smile at her, as he came over to shake her hand.

"Thank you for coming," he said politely. "It makes it so much easier for my mother."

"You're welcome."

Theo introduced his mother, who offered her hand but still didn't smile. He next introduced his sister, Victoria D'Arcy Mandeville, who merely nodded and fixed Madeline with a stony gaze.

"Please sit down." Abigail pointed to the chintz couch opposite the one her daughter was sitting on.

Madeline felt acutely uncomfortable as Theo D'Arcy's sister continued to appraise her from head to foot. She was glad she had worn her best suit, especially after seeing how formally Abigail was dressed. Victoria as well looked ready for a society photographer. Only Theo appeared more casual in his baggy slacks and silk shirt.

Madeline laid out the elements of the deal. Tommy would plead guilty to murder and receive a life sentence.

"Will he get paroled?" asked Theo.

"It's likely, but not until he's served at least sixteen years. Our prisons are very overcrowded."

"I see," said Theo glumly.

"Of course, it's up to a parole board," she pointed out.

"In return for the life sentence, Tommy will agree to testify against Sandra at her murder trial." She paused to let it sink in.

"Will *she* get the gas chamber?" Victoria said abruptly.

Madeline rushed to explain. "We won't be asking for it. It's hard to justify life imprisonment for the shooter and the death penalty for the co-conspirator, who didn't pull the trigger. If Sandra's convicted, the judge will probably give her life also."

"I see," said Abigail.

"This deal isn't on the table because we don't have a good case against Tommy Bartholomew," Madeline pointed out. "In fact, we feel we have a very strong case against him. A request for a plea bargain was initiated by Bartholomew's attorney, and the D.A. wanted me to get your feelings on it."

Abigail lifted her eyes toward Madeline. "My dear, would you be so kind as to give us a few minutes to discuss this?"

"Of course." Madeline stood up and Theo took her to another room. He closed the door behind her in what seemed to be a library and Madeline walked over to survey some of the shelves. Removing one of the books, she realized she was holding a rare and beautifully bound first edition of *Wuthering Heights*. Yet she found it impossible to concentrate on anything but what she imagined was going on in the next room.

Theo, looking upset, spoke up as soon as he came back into the room. "I'm going to call Dickson."

"Very well," agreed Abigail.

The call was brief. "Dickson said we shouldn't oppose a deal." Theo's fine-featured face had turned pale. "The publicity would be bad if it got out that the D'Arcy family was trying to protect Sandra from prosecution. It'd make it look like the rich don't expect to pay for their crimes.''

"I am very worried about the publicity," said Abigail. "I do not know which is worse for us—to have her tried and convicted, or not.''

"I don't care what happens to that tramp," seethed Victoria.

"No need to be crude," Abigail chided. "Let us try to discuss this reasonably. After all, we have James junior to consider." She smoothed back her hair. "Of course, I will be the one to raise my grandson.''

"I don't see how we can just throw Sandra to the wolves," said Theo, momentarily surprised to find himself disagreeing with Dickson.

"It's seeing that justice is done," snapped his sister. "Why should that whore be above the law?''

"I had better call Charles," said Abigail. On the telephone, she related to him what had happened.

Charles didn't respond immediately. At last, he said quietly, "We need to be certain the state doesn't ask for the death penalty.''

"Ms. Gould already assured us of that.''

"I'd like to speak to her and make sure your position is clear on that," he said.

"Certainly." Abigail rang the intercom in the library. When Madeline answered, Abigail asked her to speak to Charles.

After Madeline had hung up and Abigail was again on the line with Charles, he said, "They're positive Sandra was involved, but at least they won't be asking for the death penalty. I recommend you tell Ms. Gould you're not opposed.''

"Thank you, Charles." Abigail put the phone down and asked Theo to fetch Madeline.

When Madeline reappeared, the matriarch gazed at her. "We will not oppose the arrangement. However, my daughter-in-law will have the best defense there is and it will be your job to prove she is guilty.''

"Of course. Thank you for your input. I'll let you know what happens."

"Sandra is represented by Manning & Anderson. You can deal with them," Abigail advised her.

Madeline drove as fast as she could toward her downtown office, her mind filled with all the cases she had to clear in order to make room for the case against Sandra. But the very first thing she had to do was to formalize the deal with Tommy Bartholomew. She wasn't about to let Sandra slip away from her now.

Back at the D.A.'s office, Madeline saw Gary standing in the corridor. He was talking to another deputy D.A. and she vowed to walk right past him without saying hello. Since Philip's revelation, she'd been in turmoil. In fact, she hadn't slept a wink the previous night. Why had Gary said something like that to Philip?

"Madeline, you're just the one I was looking for." Gary excused himself from the other person and came over to her, a wide smile on his face.

"I can't stop to talk, I've got an appointment."

"Whoa, just a minute." He reached out to grab her arm. Madeline reacted violently. "Let go of me!"

He seemed stunned. "Hey, what's the matter with you?"

She peered around, hoping no one had overheard their exchange. "I really can't talk now," she stammered.

"Obviously something's bothering you." He looked at her closely, still holding her arm as he steered her toward the door of her office. "Let's go in here for just a minute."

"Gary, I've—"

"Please, Madeline."

She might as well get the entire unpleasantness over with. "All right," she sighed, "but just for a minute. And let go of my arm."

He released her immediately and Madeline could feel the soreness where the pressure of his hand had been.

Inside her office, he closed the door behind them and turned to face her. "What's going on? You act like I'm contagious."

"I heard something about you that upset me." She went to stand behind her desk as if that would give her some protection from him.

"Want to fill me in on what it was? Or is this a Star Chamber?" he asked mockingly.

Madeline's face was serious. "Philip White told me that you questioned my ability to handle the D'Arcy trial. That you didn't think I had enough experience."

Gary's eyes remained unwavering. "Not true."

"You're saying Philip's lying?"

"He's too smart for that. He just took what I said and twisted it around to suit his own purposes."

"You're not denying you went to see him?"

"No."

"And you didn't tell him you were more qualified than me?"

"No."

"Why would Philip say what he did?"

"Because he's in love with you!" A sardonic smile pulled at the corners of his sensuous mouth.

"That's not true."

"The man loves you, Madeline. Stop being so blind."

"I find that hard to believe. And it's beside the point. What exactly did you say to him, then?"

He leaned forward, his hands on her desk. "That the D'Arcy case was going to be big, with a lot of media attention, and it warranted two attorneys. I wanted him to know I'd handled high-profile cases like it before in San Francisco, and if he was thinking of assigning a second attorney, I'd like to be the one."

Madeline listened. He was certainly presenting a different scenario than Philip had. A part of her wanted desperately to believe Gary. Wasn't it possible Philip had misunderstood?

Gary went on, his green eyes crinkling at the corners. "I thought it'd be kind of fun working together." He winked.

His nearness was making it hard for her to think clearly. The sexual tension between them was palpable. "I'm still confused," she said, biting on her lower lip. "Let's go see

Philip together and get this straightened out. It sounds like a simple misunderstanding.''

Gary drew himself up. ''I'm not putting myself in that position. The man'll do anything to make me look bad in front of you.''

''Don't you think you're being a little paranoid?''

His jaw jutted out belligerently. ''I've told you what happened. Do you believe me or not?''

''You're not being fair.''

''No, Madeline. You're the one not playing fair. I thought you cared, that we had a future.'' His face tightened. ''Guess I was wrong.''

Madeline's stomach lurched as her thoughts swirled through her mind. ''I do care. I just don't know what to think.''

''Then I'll remove myself from the competition. Call me if you change your mind.'' He walked to the door of her office and opened it. ''Goodbye, Madeline.'' He arched his eyebrows. ''It's been nice.''

As soon as Sandra was ushered into Kate's office, she asked, ''What was so important that you had to see me immediately?''

''Come sit down and I'll explain,'' Kate said.

Looking annoyed, Sandra perched on the chair in front of Kate's desk.

''Charles spoke to Madeline Gould a little while ago. She's the deputy D.A. in charge of Tommy's case. It appears Tommy is planning to change his plea to guilty.''

''Tommy didn't kill James!''

''He says he did.''

Sandra clasped her hands together. ''It makes no sense for Tommy to say that.''

''Look, Sandra, I can't tell you what Tommy's reasons are. All I know is, Tommy says you were involved in James's murder too.''

''What?'' Sandra's face was incredulous.

''As I understand, it's part of a deal between Tommy and the D.A. Tommy enters a plea of guilty and says you were in on it, and in exchange he escapes the death penalty.''

"This is some kind of a joke, isn't it?" The young woman stood and began to pace the room.

"No joke."

"Tommy wouldn't say that. It's a lie."

"Why would he want to lie?"

"Can't you find out?"

"Sandra, please listen to me, this is serious—"

Sandra cut in. "How do I know you're telling me the truth?"

Kate shook her head. "I've no reason to lie."

"Someone's lying." The color in Sandra's face rose and there was a wild look in her eye.

"The police and D.A.—" Kate started to say.

Again Sandra interrupted. "The police are a bunch of assholes. Why should I believe them?"

"I understand you're upset . . ."

"Upset! This whole thing is fucking crazy."

"No one—"

"Take me to see him. I've gotta find out what's going on."

"That's not possible."

"But I've got to see him." Sandra's voice was almost a wail. "I've got to find out why he's doing this."

"Sandra, we're wasting time. I've asked you to come here so I can prepare you for what's going to happen next. Now please sit down."

With exaggerated movements, Sandra took the chair in front of Kate's desk. "I can barely wait to hear this!"

Kate did her best to hold her temper. "I haven't been able to get anyone at the D.A.'s office to call me back, so I can't be sure yet how this is going to be handled."

"Some criminal attorney you are."

Without skipping a beat, Kate went on. "They can either arrest you now and hold you on suspicion or they can wait, formalize the deal with Tommy, and arrest you after. I wish I could promise you that they'll give me advance warning so I can be with you, but I can't. So I want to prepare you for what to do in the event they just show up at your front door.''

"I don't have to go with them, do I?''

"I'm afraid you do. Just tell them you want to call your lawyer. They'll probably take you to jail before they let you make the call.''

"Jail? You've got to be kidding.''

"No. I'm not.'' Kate glanced at her client. From the look on her face, Kate could tell she had gotten through. An hour later Sandra left the office looking as white as a sheet.

The next morning, Madeline entered Judge Harrison's courtroom and saw that he was still going through his docket. A thin man with graying hair, he was one of her favorite judges. She noticed that his ebony face looked more tired today than usual. Rumor had it that his wife was sick. Stress like that, added to a constantly overcrowded calendar, could weigh anyone down. As for herself, her confrontation with Gary had not helped her mental state.

In the courtroom, she smiled at several people she knew. Bower was also there. "Morning. How are you?'' she greeted him.

"O.K. You?''

"I'll be better when this is a done deal,'' Madeline said. Her eyes were somber as she gazed up at him.

A few minutes later she saw Andrew Stewart, his hand on Tommy's shoulder, guide him into the courtroom. The bailiff walked behind them. Madeline waited in the well at the front of the room where several other attorneys were standing. Bower stood toward the back. When the case was called, Andrew escorted Tommy in front of Judge Harrison.

"Your Honor,'' said Madeline. "I believe there's a plea.''

Andrew approached the bench, flanking his client.

The judge peered over his thick black-rimmed glasses at the young defendant standing before him. Then he spoke to Madeline. "Proceed, Counselor.''

Madeline put on her glasses. Slowly, so that the court reporter could take down every word, and solemnly she asked Tommy if he had agreed to change his not guilty plea in this matter to guilty, in exchange for a promise that the state would not ask for the death penalty against him. He said he had. She then asked him if he had murdered James D'Arcy.

Tommy nodded.

The judge instructed him to answer yes or no.

"Yes," Tommy said quietly.

Then she asked him if he had conspired with Sandra D'Arcy to murder her husband.

"Yes."

"Do you promise to testify truthfully on behalf of the people at both the preliminary hearing and the trial of Sandra D'Arcy?"

"Yes."

"And is it your understanding that the people have agreed to allow you to plead guilty to first degree murder and life with possibility of parole in exchange for said agreement?"

Again he answered yes.

Madeline next asked Tommy if he waived his right to a trial by jury, and if he was sure that he understood what was happening.

To both of these questions Tommy said yes.

"Your Honor, the people move to strike the special circumstances allegation as alleged in the complaint reducing the charge to first degree murder," said Madeline.

"So ordered."

The judge asked Tommy how he pled to the new charge.

Tommy was shaking as Andrew nudged him. "Guilty, Your Honor." He was clearly nervous.

Judge Harrison accepted the plea, referred the matter to the probation department for its report, and set the sentencing hearing.

Tommy blinked back tears as the bailiff escorted him back to jail.

Madeline handed the judge her complaint against Sandra and asked him to sign the warrant for her arrest. She stood quietly while he read her documents.

With the signed documents, Madeline headed for the rear

of the courtroom. Outside in the hallway, she stopped to shake Andrew's hand. "Thank you, Counselor."

"I still think I could have beat this at trial," he boasted. At the same time, Andrew practically undressed her with his eyes.

She ignored his unsolicited leer to glare at him with disdain. "Then why did you advise your client to make a deal?"

"To save his life, just in case." He smiled.

"We all have to do what we think's best. Now, if you'd excuse me."

Farther down the corridor, Bower caught up to her. "You did a first-rate job."

"Thanks. If it hadn't been for your fine police work, we wouldn't be here."

As she walked back to her office, she felt good. This was what it was all about. Justice for the victim.

It was afternoon when Bower headed up the hill to the house in Bel Air. It was pouring, and the rivulets ran down the windows faster than the windshield wipers could clear them. "Don't look so glum," he said to Donaldson, who was slumped down in the seat next to him.

"Can't help it. I feel sorry for her." He pointed to the rain. "Even heaven is sad."

"Like I've said before, you young cops all think with your cocks," grunted Bower.

At the door, the housekeeper went to summon Sandra. When she finally appeared, there was a look of apprehension on her face. "What is it?"

Bower took out a paper from the inside pocket of his coat and formally stated, "Sandra D'Arcy, I have a warrant for your arrest for murder and conspiracy to commit murder."

Sandra's face turned white and she took an involuntary step backward.

"Please get your things and come with us."

"Now?" she blurted out.

"Yes, ma'am, 'fraid so." He turned to Donaldson. "Please read Mrs. D'Arcy her rights."

Donaldson tried not to look at Sandra as he mumbled the familiar words. "You have the right to remain silent . . ."

When he was finished, Sandra took a deep breath and seemed to regain her composure. She put her hands on her hips in a gesture of defiance. "I can't go now." Her tone was firm, with a rapier edge to it.

"You have no choice," said Bower.

"I'm not supposed to talk to you unless my attorney is present," she snapped, giving him a dirty look.

"Ma'am, we've read you your rights. You don't have to talk to us, but you've gotta come with us. Now." He had raised his voice just enough to let her know he meant business, while at the same time, he put his hand on his gun in a meaningful gesture. "You can call your lawyer at the jail." He told Donaldson to go with her to get a coat.

Five minutes later a surly and tight-lipped Sandra got into the back seat of the police car with Donaldson next to her. Bower got behind the wheel. As he turned around, he saw the frightened face of the housekeeper framed in the doorway.

Kate was in a meeting in Charles's office when she heard the page operator announce an urgent call for her. Excusing herself, she picked up his telephone. "Kate Alexander. Hello? Sandra? . . . When? . . . I'm on my way. Remember, you're not to answer any questions unless I'm with you." Kate put down the phone. "They've arrested her."

Charles scowled. "Bastards. They could've given you the chance to surrender her voluntarily or at least be with her."

"Yeah. But it's done, so I better get going." She headed for the door. She too was upset that Madeline hadn't telephoned her.

"Call me as soon as you know something."

"I will."

His voice stopped her before she went through the door. "I'll need to keep Abigail D'Arcy posted." It was a statement, not a question.

She turned. "I wish you didn't, but . . ."

"I'd better make sure Jimmy is taken there right away."

"I suppose under the circumstances, that's the best place for the child," she said reluctantly. Inside, she bristled. She hated to see that woman get her way.

"Anything I can do for you?"

"Get Frank for me. He's at the Hall of Records downtown. Ask him to call me in my car."

"Right away."

Charles called Abigail. He informed her that Sandra had been arrested and Kate was on her way to the jail.

"Where is my grandson?"

"At home with Maria."

"I want him brought to me immediately."

"I've told Maria to get him ready," Charles assured her. "I'll bring him to you myself."

"I will be waiting."

"I'll bring Maria also."

"No. The sooner we remove that kind of influence from my grandson's life, the better."

"Maybe it would be best for just a few days," suggested Charles. "Give the boy a little time to handle the transition."

"I said no, Charles," she said sharply. "I will get Theo's old governess to help me until a proper one can be hired. From now on, it will be only the best for my grandson. I will personally supervise everything. He will turn out to be a proper D'Arcy after all."

30

The drive to Sybil Brand, the Los Angeles County women's jail in East Los Angeles, was nightmarish. Heavy rain pelted the freeway and traffic was at a crawl. Sandra had told Kate she was charged with murder and conspiracy to commit murder, but Kate didn't know much else. She'd tried to reach Madeline before she left her office, but had been informed the deputy D.A. had gone for the day.

She flicked on the radio. After announcing several traffic alerts, including an advisory to avoid the traffic jam Kate was in, the newscaster went back to the day's events.

"And on the local scene, the widow of James D'Arcy, scion to the multibillion dollar D'Arcy empire, was arrested earlier. Tommy Bartholomew formally changed his plea to guilty in court today, claiming he and the wealthy, young socialite planned the murder together. The D.A.'s office issued a statement saying Bartholomew has agreed to testify against his former girlfriend in exchange for the state's not seeking the death penalty against him. In other news, the mayor today met with several representatives . . ."

Her car crawled past a bad traffic accident and she finally pulled off the freeway. A few minutes later, she turned into the parking lot of the women's jail. Damn! She realized she didn't have an umbrella in the car. She tucked her briefcase under her raincoat, put her head down, and raced for the entrance.

Before she could get the door open, flashbulbs went off in her face. Several reporters, all holding umbrellas, clustered around her. "Is Sandra D'Arcy going to plead guilty?" asked a tall woman.

"I'm sorry, I've no comment as yet." Kate smiled, then pushed her way past them.

Sandra's first words to Kate were angry. "What took you so long?"

Kate started to apologize, but caught herself. She wasn't going to allow her client to put her on the defensive. "Hello, Sandra."

"Why the fuck do I have to be in this place?"

"I explained that all to you last night."

"You said they'd take me into custody. You didn't tell me it would be a shit place like this!"

"This is the women's jail." Kate's voice was even and controlled.

"You sure took your damn time getting here."

Kate felt the hair on the back of her neck rise. Sandra was making no attempt to be civil. She had expected her client to be somewhat subdued. After all, jail was a humbling experience. "Sandra . . ."

"Can't you get me out now?"

"I haven't been able to—"

"What the fuck have you been doing while I've been in this hellhole? There were photographers outside waiting to take my picture when they brought me here! It was embarrassing!" Sandra's angry voice rose to a high pitch.

"I can't help you unless you calm down. That includes being civil to me." Kate's nostrils flared in spite of her intention to remain composed. She snapped shut her briefcase.

"You're my attorney," Sandra shot back. "You can't leave."

"Watch me!" Kate picked up her briefcase.

A flicker of fear crossed Sandra's face. When Kate walked over to the door to knock for the guard, Sandra backed down. "Don't go," she mumbled, without any apology.

Kate studied her for a moment, then put the briefcase back on the table and sat down. "O.K. Let's get to work. I want you to sit down. We have to talk."

"I don't want to talk! I want out!"

"You're making it impossible for me to defend you." Sandra gave her a dirty look but quieted down.

"Remember when I told you last night that Tommy may have killed your husband?"

"Yeah." Sandra's face was sullen.

"For the moment, we're going to have to assume it's true so we can prepare for the preliminary hearing."

"It's a mistake." Sandra's blue eyes challenged her attorney.

Kate knew she had to penetrate Sandra's blindness where Tommy was concerned before she could even think about preparing her for the hearing. "They found Tommy's footprint near James's body," she reminded her. "And the mud from Tommy's boot matched the soil in front of your house. That puts him directly at the crime scene."

"But Tommy visited me before. How can they be so sure it was that night?"

Kate sighed with exasperation. They had gone over this before. Patiently she explained it all again.

"It doesn't prove anything!"

"It puts him at the scene at the right time. Also, a neighbor heard the shot and saw Tommy's car pulling away."

"There are lots of white cars in Los Angeles."

"With Tommy's license plate? Come on, Sandra, be realistic. We have to prepare for reality. If you think I'm being hard on you, wait till the prosecutor starts tearing you apart."

"Can they do that?"

"If we decide to put you on the stand." She lowered her voice. "Isn't it possible you don't want to see the truth because you love him?"

Sandra glared at her with unmasked hostility.

"If Tommy says he did it, Sandra, he probably did."

Sandra's eyes filled with tears, but she bit on her lip to keep from crying. "I don't believe it," she said finally.

Kate couldn't allow her client's tears to move her; pity must not get in the way of her job. "We have to concentrate on *you* now, Sandra. Not Tommy."

"I didn't kill my husband!"

Kate wasn't at all sure she believed her, but what had she expected her to say? I did it? Fat chance. "Then we have to find out why Tommy's lying,'' she said automatically. "Maybe he saw it as the only way to save his own skin."

Sandra turned pale. She jumped up and started to pace the room again. "You have to get me out of here," she pleaded. "Jimmy needs me."

"He's fine," Kate assured her. "Charles has taken him to Abigail's."

"No! I don't want my kid with that bitch!"

"He can't stay at your house with someone who can't drive. What if there's an emergency?" She paused. "We had no choice."

"You had no right. Whose side you on anyhow?"

Sandra's accusation bothered Kate. She hadn't wanted the child to have to go to Abigail's either. Unfortunately, she had no other option at the moment. "Maybe we can make other arrangements for him. Do you have any family?"

"Not really."

"Are your parents alive?"

"Yes." Sandra refused to meet Kate's gaze. "They live up north."

"Perhaps we can get them to come and stay." Kate poised her pen to write. "Give me their name and phone number and I'll call them."

"They wouldn't lift a finger for me." A trace of bitterness crept into Sandra's voice.

This was the first crack Kate had seen in Sandra's armor. "We don't know what people will do for us until we ask. Why don't I give them a call anyway?"

"I haven't talked to them in seven years. They never cared before. Why should they care now?"

Something in Kate stirred. Sandra's estrangement from her parents touched a chord within her. Maybe she could help. "Can I try anyhow?"

Sandra looked annoyed. "Go ahead, call them. It won't do any good. Nora and Ed Denton in Bakersfield. It should be listed."

"Fine," said Kate, writing down the information. "Now, since the D.A. already filed the complaint and the charges against you, and the judge issued an arrest warrant, you'll be arraigned either tomorrow or the next day. Do you remember what I told you about the arraignment?''

"Sort of."

"It's where you appear in front of a judge to hear the charges against you and you officially become a defendant."

"Then you said something about a hearing?"

"Right. At the arraignment, the judge will order you back to court for a preliminary hearing, which is supposed to be ten days after arraignment unless you waive the time."

"I'm not giving them more time for anything."

"Let me finish. I really didn't explain the preliminary hearing last night. It's where the prosecutor presents the evidence to a municipal court judge, through both testimony and exhibits. Then the judge decides if the evidence is sufficient to bind you over for trial."

"Fine! Now when do I get out of here?"

"I'm not sure." Kate started to put her things in her briefcase.

"Where you going?"

"To find out what I can. I'll be back tomorrow and we'll talk more."

"You mean I've got to stay here overnight?"

"I'm afraid so. For the moment there's no bail."

Sandra looked at Kate with disbelief.

"I'm sorry." Kate shook her head sympathetically, as she summoned the jail matron. "I'll see you tomorrow."

Kate ran to her car from the jail, holding a newspaper over her head. Even though the rain had let up a little, she still got wet. She was grateful to find that the reporters had left. Inside, she started the engine and immediately called Frank Jones, her investigator, and asked him to meet her at the Westin Bonaventure Hotel.

In the lobby of the hotel, she found a telephone and arranged to meet Charles later. He was worried about how tired she sounded and offered to pick something up for dinner. She felt warmed by his concern. As she and other female lawyers always joked, what she needed was a wife.

While Kate sipped her tomato juice in the bar, the memory of Sandra in jail kept intruding on her thoughts. She would call the parents to see if they'd take Jimmy. No matter how rotten a daughter Sandra had been, they'd care about their grandchild.

Her reverie was broken by Frank sliding into the chair next to her. There were drops of water shining in his dark hair. "Sorry it took so long."

"No problem."

"Was Sandra moaning because they didn't have satin sheets?"

"She came unglued when I told her there was no bail." Kate was pensive for a moment. "No matter how many times I've been to Sybil Brand, I always remember the night I spent in jail."

He raised his eyebrows quizzically. "You?"

She nodded.

"Tell me about it." He quickly ordered a beer.

"I was in college at the time. A bunch of us went to a civil rights demonstration. Just because we were blocking an entrance, they called the cops and we were all arrested and taken to jail."

"Shocked you, huh?"

"Yeah. They locked us up with the drunks, prostitutes, and whoever else they had hauled in that night. When I got out the next morning, I was a wreck. But there were never any charges or records, so for that I'm grateful."

Frank looked at her. "It takes courage to stand up for what you believe in."

She shrugged and smiled. "I was young. Later, when I went to law school, I was terrified that the incident would keep me from practicing law."

"They must have asked about prior arrests?"

"Of course. When I saw the question, I quaked in my boots."

"What'd you do?"

"The only thing possible. Wrote it down in the proper blank and attached an explanation. The dean warned us that the worst thing we could do was not mention something."

"Then what happened?"

"I got a letter asking for more information. And that was it. Guess they decided it was the sowing of wild oats, or at least not a matter of moral turpitude." She smiled. "Anyway, here I am—fortunately, it didn't stop me from becoming a lawyer."

He took a swig of beer. "If it had been a felony conviction that would have been the end of you."

"For sure. So what did you find out?"

"As you heard on the news, Tommy's made a deal. He's going to testify against her."

"Do they have any new evidence against Sandra?"

"Yeah. They caught her in some lies."

"What kind of lies?"

"Sandra apparently claimed that the last time she saw Tommy was five days before the murder, period. And that she definitely didn't see him after." He peered at her before continuing. "They've pictures of her meeting Tommy in the parking lot of a market, just before his arrest."

"God damn it! She didn't listen to me. I could tell from the look on Bower's face when he questioned her that he had something on her. I wonder what else she hasn't told me."

"Scary ain't it?" Frank finally asked the question she'd been avoiding. "Think she did it?"

"She claims she's innocent."

"If she said anything different, I'd be surprised, wouldn't you?"

"Yes." She stared off into space, pondering whether or not Sandra had been acting. "Too soon to know yet."

He nodded sympathetically. "I hear from my buddies she's a difficult lady."

"Impossible."

He grinned. "So what do you want me to do next?"

Kate told him about Sandra's parents. "She hasn't heard

from them in seven years. I want to talk to them personally. In fact, we may have to go up there. They live in Bakersfield.''

"No problem.'' He adjusted himself in his chair. "What else?''

"We have to get the initial discovery from the prosecution. What we get will determine what we have to do next.''

"Need my help?'' He tossed a fistful of nuts into his mouth.

"Not with this, no. You and I have enough else to do.'' She drummed her fingers on the tabletop. "I'll put some of the staff on the legal end, while you and I start trying to piece this thing together.''

As she drove home, Kate kept thinking about the hot shower she was going to take when she got there. Then she'd eat whatever Charles had picked up. She was starved.

After dinner, she brought her wine over to the couch in front of the blazing fireplace. She could hear rain pelting the roof. "That sauce was hot but I liked it,'' she said to Charles as he too sat down.

"I tried a new Thai place tonight.''

Kate stared thoughtfully into the fire. "Do you know anything about Sandra's parents?''

Charles seemed to consider her question for a moment. "James once told me she'd run away from home and spent some time in a juvenile facility.''

She leaned forward. "A juvenile hall or a foster home?''

"I don't remember. But if I'm not mistaken, she was only sixteen.''

Kate's hands became clammy as she suddenly recalled how it had felt leaving home at seventeen with nowhere to go. That had been one of the roughest times in her life. A feeling of panic washed over her. She took a deep breath. "Did James know what the problem was between her and her parents?''

"Not that I can recall. Why?''

She didn't want to tell him. There was no sense arguing

about who Jimmy should live with until she had a viable alternative. "Just the usual." She shrugged. "Trying to find out everything I can about my client. When I asked her about her parents, she said they wouldn't care what happened to her."

"She was probably being dramatic."

"No. Kids are usually the helpless ones."

He put his hand on her leg and whispered, "Let's go in the other room."

"No, not tonight," she said, feeling agitated but not understanding why.

31

The ringing of the telephone at six A.M. jarred Kate. She had finally fallen asleep after twisting and turning for hours and she didn't want to wake up. Not yet. She reached for the phone, almost knocking it over. "Hello," she answered, groggily.

"This is Leonard Ames from *Los Angeles World* . . ."

Kate slammed the phone down. How on earth had that tabloid gotten her phone number at home? It was unlisted. She switched her phone machine on and tried to fall back to sleep.

When the phone rang again, she listened. Another reporter. Now her mind was racing. Everything she had to do today crowded in on her. She gave up and got out of bed. The papers she had been working on spilled onto the floor. She must have fallen asleep working on the case. The memory of Charles's unhappy face as he went home last night filtered into her thoughts. He hadn't been thrilled when she didn't want to make love. She had pleaded exhaustion, which was certainly true, but it was something more than that. What, though, she wasn't sure.

Her neck felt tense and she massaged it with her hand. Finding out that Sandra had left home at sixteen bothered her more than she wanted to admit. It brought back too many unpleasant memories of her own.

A run will do me good, she decided. It'll get some of the tension out of my body. She pulled on her sweats and made her way out onto the beach. The rain had stopped but the sand was still wet. She would have to run on the pavement. Slowly, giving herself time to warm up, she started down the street.

In Westwood, Lauren was busy doing her morning workout. Her trainer was unable to come today, so she was pedaling away on her exercise bike while she watched the morning news.

The story about Sandra D'Arcy's arrest came on. She was tickled. It was all going according to plan. Having no doubts that the two star-crossed lovers had killed James D'Arcy, Lauren assured herself that all she had done was to speed up the slow process of the law.

She watched as a jubilant Madeline held a press conference. A reporter asked when the state thought Sandra D'Arcy would go to trial.

"In a few months, we hope," said Madeline.

No way, thought Lauren. By her calculations, Kate would soon realize that a plea bargain was the best way for Sandra to go too. How could Sandra hope to get off when Tommy was going to point the finger at her? In spite of those who thought the D.A. only made deals with one defendant, in reality that wasn't true. It made sense in this kind of case to send both defendants away without an expensive trial.

When it was all over, Andrew and Madeline would be the heroes—he because his client had caused the cheating wife to go down in flames, Madeline because she had obtained two convictions without spending a lot of the taxpayers' dollars. Kate would be all but forgotten.

Lauren's only regret was that she couldn't tell Madeline

how she'd maneuvered Andrew into making the deal for his client. Even though Madeline undoubtedly was happy with the results, Lauren knew that her friend wouldn't approve of how it had been accomplished. Some things were better left unsaid. I'll be rewarded in the afterlife, she thought to herself jokingly.

A picture of Kate arriving at Sybil Brand flashed across the screen. A stab of envy pierced Lauren. Fuck. She hated to see Kate get any publicity at all.

She pedaled faster, the sweat beading on her forehead. An unpleasant thought crossed her mind. Suppose Kate insisted on trying the case? No, it wouldn't matter. Sandra would be found guilty and Kate's winning streak would be over.

The first thing Kate did when she got to the office was to call Madeline. "I thought you'd let me surrender my client voluntarily or at least tell me what time you were going to arrest her so that I could have been with her." Kate's voice held a tinge of anger.

Madeline sighed. "I'm sorry."

Her speedy acknowledgment surprised Kate. "What happened?"

"You'll have to trust me on this one. I couldn't. That's all I can say."

Kate swiveled around in her chair. "That's not good enough. Did the decision not to notify me come from higher up?"

Madeline hesitated. "I can't answer that, either."

"I see." Kate paused, then added in a matter-of-fact tone. "I'd like to meet with you today."

"How about three-thirty?"

"See you then." Kate hung up. Former prosecutors extended courtesies to one another, and as far as she was concerned, Madeline had been out of line.

"Let's go somewhere nice for lunch," said Philip White.

Madeline raised her eyebrows in mock horror. "Since when is our cafeteria not considered nice?"

322

"Since yesterday," he laughed. "Want to go to Little Tokyo?"

"I haven't been there in a long time. Sounds good."

Walking next to her on the street, Philip noticed that Madeline, ordinarily extremely talkative, was unusually quiet. He glanced at her profile. She looked so pretty today, he thought.

"A penny for your thoughts?"

"Just thinking."

When they reached the restaurant, he wondered, as he had so many times before, what it would be like to be out on a real date with her—without the pretense of business. He glanced at her. She still seemed to be very far away. "What's weighing so heavily on your mind?"

"Nothing much . . ." She looked sheepishly at him. "Everything."

"Why don't you start at the beginning?" There was a look of genuine interest in his eyes.

She reached out and patted his hand affectionately. "You're always there for me, Philip. I appreciate it."

Appreciation. That wasn't what he wanted. "So . . ." He let the words hang in the air.

"I have so little time to spend with the kids." She looked at him guiltily. "I don't want to complain to you. You're wonderful about them as it is. Besides, it's not like I didn't know how it would be when I started."

"A big case is bound to make things worse. Something wrong or just the usual?"

"Jud only wants to be alone lately." She frowned. "He doesn't confide in me like he used to. Just lies on his bed and listens to his music, turned on so loud it's driving me crazy."

"He's a teenager now. Probably thinking about girls. I remember doing the same thing."

"Maybe that's it. Still, why won't he confide in me?"

"There are some things a boy would rather not tell his mother." His eyes twinkled with mischief. "He probably needs to discuss things with another man."

"Good luck. Sam's always too busy for him! I don't

often regret the divorce, but when it comes to the kids, I wonder if I should have just looked the other way and stayed married for their benefit."

"That's the age-old dilemma. Stay for the sake of the kids and they know it and suffer, or leave and they suffer."

She nodded. "It stinks, either way. I wish I had a brother. Then I could ask him to talk to Jud."

Although his feelings were far from brotherly, Philip couldn't help himself. "Would I do?"

Her eyes lighted up. "How nice of you to offer, but . . ." She grew thoughtful. "The few times we all went to the ball game together, Jud said he thought you were cool, which means he really likes you. Do you think he'd talk to you?"

"Let's find out. How about dinner this weekend?"

When she hesitated for a moment, he could have kicked himself for asking. He wondered if she was still seeing Gary. He hoped not, but couldn't bring himself to ask.

Suddenly, she smiled. "Why don't you come to our house Saturday night?"

"Great." He couldn't believe it. He felt like a kid again.

Kate arrived at the Criminal Courts Building and parked behind the structure that housed the criminal courts and district attorneys' offices. Her heart sank when she saw the huge line of people snaking around the building. It didn't matter if you were a defendant coming to court, a juror, an attorney, or just a spectator—everyone waited in the same line. The only exceptions were the officers and employees. With their badges and other identification, they were allowed in a separate entrance. I used to have that identification, she mused as she stepped to the back of the line.

Glancing at her watch, she swore. She'd be late now. She was irritated that the world had become the kind of place where people had to be checked for weapons or bombs before they could enter a courthouse.

Finally, it was her turn. She took her keys and change out and laid them on the tray, while she put her purse and briefcase on the conveyer belt. Then she stepped through the detector. On the other side, she picked up her things and raced around to the elevators. She got off on the eighteenth floor.

As Kate waited for Madeline, she reflected on the four years she had spent in these offices as a prosecutor. They'd been good years. She had loved being a deputy D.A. But for a future in politics, she'd known she stood a better chance of getting the financial backing she needed out in the world of private law firms. Only occasionally did she truly regret that decision.

"Come on in."

Kate looked up to see Madeline standing at the door. She followed the prosecutor into the maze of corridors. "You've got a different office," she remarked as she put her briefcase down on one of the brown leather chairs.

"Yes." Madeline smiled. "Finally moved up in the world." Her phone rang. After she answered it, she mouthed to Kate, holding her hand over the mouthpiece, "I've got to take it. Help yourself to some coffee."

Kate went to the credenza behind the desk and made herself a cup of instant. The thought of the elegant coffee room at Manning & Anderson flashed into her mind. There was nothing fancy about a deputy D.A.'s office.

She walked over to the window and looked out at downtown Los Angeles. It was hard to believe this was earthquake country. So many new buildings reaching high into the sky, surrounded by dilapidated and run-down areas.

Madeline ended her conversation and explained the charges and her reasons for not wanting Sandra to get bail.

"But she's not going anywhere," protested Kate. "Besides, she's got a little boy of four who really needs her."

"I feel bad about that," Madeline said. "But I think she'd leave the country if she could."

"Look, we'll post as much bail as you want."

"Money means nothing to the D'Arcy family. Even if the judge set five million dollars, the family would put it up. And if Sandra took off, they'd never miss it."

"She was left a certain sum of money, but she doesn't have access to it all at one time," said Kate quickly. "Her husband set up trusts for her and the child. Under their terms, she can't get her hands on enough cash to live permanently out of the country.''

"When they're facing a lifetime in prison, you'd be surprised at how clever they become."

Kate was frustrated by Madeline's stubbornness. "I'll have to request a bail hearing then."

"I understand." Madeline fingered her pencil. "And I'll have to oppose it."

"You're being unreasonable."

"I'm sorry."

She could see that Madeline's mind was made up. Within a few minutes Kate left. She didn't look forward to telling her client about her unproductive meeting with the prosecutor.

32

When Kate arrived at the jail and told her client about the D.A.'s position on bail, Sandra was predictably upset.

"You've got to get me out of here!" she wailed.

"I'm working on it. Unless by some miracle the judge decides to give you bail anyway, after the arraignment tomorrow morning I'll prepare a motion for a formal bail hearing."

Sandra gazed at her attorney with her usual sullen expression, one that Kate was getting used to. "When can I get this hearing?"

"Depends. So let's get to work." Kate put her briefcase on the table and opened it. She took out a pad of yellow paper, some pencils, and then peered at her client.

"First, the charges. One count of murder in the first degree—"

"I'm not a murderess!" protested Sandra.

"Let me just tell you the facts, O.K.?"

The young woman remained quiet.

"The first charge can carry a penalty of twenty-five years to life."

Sandra blanched. "That's crazy!"

"At least they didn't attach special circumstances, so there's no death penalty involved."

If Kate had expected Sandra to be grateful on hearing this news, she had miscalculated. Her client merely scowled. "I don't even know what that means."

"Special circumstances refers to the types of cases in which the death penalty can be asked for as mandated by the California legislature and the courts."

When Sandra still looked confused, Kate made it simple: "It means they're not asking for the gas chamber."

Her client turned pale.

Kate went on. "Then there's another count for conspiracy to commit murder. That carries the same sentence." She saw the puzzlement on Sandra's face. "In plain language," she explained, "the charges mean that plotting or planning with another person to kill someone can have the same consequences as actually pulling the trigger yourself."

The impact of her explanation apparently hit home, because Sandra clutched her stomach, her eyes fearful. "They can punish me for something Tommy says he did?"

"That's right." Kate's tone was matter-of-fact. "O.K., let's get started. First, the ground rules. In court, if you take the stand, you must swear to tell the truth. If you lie, it's perjury."

"I know that!"

Kate looked at Sandra solemnly. "Fine. Now, there's no penalty for lying to your lawyer. But if you don't level with me, you could spend the rest of your life in prison for murder."

"What do you mean?"

"I can't defend you properly unless you tell me the truth. I have to know what to expect and what the prosecution is liable to hit us with."

Sandra's eyes narrowed. "How do I know I can trust you?"

"Whatever you tell me stays between us. It's a matter of privilege between an attorney and her client. I can't tell anyone without your permission. No one."

"O.K., I get it." Sandra nodded. "But I'm still innocent. I didn't kill my husband."

"Did you ever discuss with Tommy wanting your husband dead?"

"Yeah." She shrugged. "So what?"

"Tell me about that conversation."

Sandra's face hardened. "I don't remember it."

"Of course you remember it," Kate snapped. "If you don't talk to me, I can't help you." She paused, and a sigh escaped her. When she finally spoke, her tone was softer. "I truly want to help you, that's my job. Also"—a faint smile came to her lips—"I don't like to lose. But you've got to believe me. I'm going to need to know everything about you before we're through." Her voice rose. *"Everything."*

"What if I want another attorney?"

Kate stiffened. She thought that issue had been laid to rest. Obviously, it hadn't. Trying not to show her annoyance, she explained, "Sandra, now that you've been arrested for murder, if you don't want me, you're free to choose someone else."

"How do I get another lawyer?"

"Tell me and I'll arrange it."

"Abigail won't like that."

Kate heard the bitterness in Sandra's voice. "It doesn't matter anymore what Abigail wants!" Her reply came out harsher than she had intended.

A look of surprise crossed Sandra's face. "You don't like her either?"

Kate leaned forward. "If you promise not to tell, I'll answer that."

The beginnings of a smile played around the corner of Sandra's mouth. "I promise."

"I can't stand the old witch."

Sandra grinned and Kate smiled back. She knew the war

with her client was far from over, but maybe sharing a common dislike was better than nothing at all.

"In all seriousness, it's important your lawyer be someone of your own choice. But if you can, you should decide before tomorrow morning."

Sandra nervously chewed on her lower lip. Her face, even paler today than usual, appeared strained.

Kate imagined the first night in jail had not been a pleasant experience. She stood up. "I'll give you some time to make up your mind." As she started to close her briefcase, Sandra's hand shot out to stop her.

"I don't need any time."

"You want me to be your attorney?"

"Yes," mumbled Sandra. In a louder voice she added, "But I don't want a lawyer who doesn't believe I'm innocent."

"It's not important what I believe."

"It is to me."

"I'm on your side, Sandra, whether you're innocent or not. But telling the truth does not start and stop with guilt or innocence. I need to know your whole story from the time you were born if I'm going to help you beat this thing."

"My life?"

"Yes. Think you can find a way to tell it to me honestly?"

"I guess."

"That's all I ask," said Kate, sitting back down and taking out a legal pad. "Begin anywhere you find comfortable."

Picking at her fingernail, Sandra seemed reluctant to start. Finally, she coughed. "Would you do something for me?"

Kate was surprised at the hesitancy in Sandra's voice. "I'll certainly try."

"When I called to talk to my son, Abigail was on the extension." Her voice rose. "She made him get right off."

"I'll speak to her," promised Kate.

"Thank you," said Sandra, looking immensely relieved.

"O.K. Let's do it."

* * *

After Kate left, Madeline made some notes. When she finished, she leaned back in her chair, fiddling with her glasses. It bothered her that Kate felt she was being unreasonable. She really believed Sandra would flee the country if given the chance. Just because the D'Arcys were prominent and rich didn't mean they should be treated differently. Her job required her to be hard-nosed when the facts demanded it.

What she did feel bad about, though, was not telling Kate just when her client would be arrested. Still, she couldn't go against the D.A.'s express wishes. It would have been political suicide.

She put the D'Arcy case out of her mind for a moment and reflected on her lunch with Philip. She'd only told him a partial truth. Jud had been on her mind, but so was Gary; she still hadn't decided what to do about her relationship with him.

Last night, leaving work, she'd seen Gary get into a car with a secretary from the sixteenth floor. The two of them had not seen her, but she'd watched as he gave the woman a quick kiss. It obviously hadn't taken him long to get over *her*.

"Well, fuck him," she mumbled out loud. "If he could forget me that fast, who wants him."

She had believed him when he said he wanted a future with her. As for all the things he had said about Philip being in love with her? No. That was just Gary's insane jealousy talking. He's making up shit to justify his rotten behavior. Besides, she just didn't think of Philip that way. Gary never understood her relationship with Philip. Philip respected her, cared about her, asked her about her children. In fact, he was the only male colleague she had who had been a really good friend to her. Why should she listen to a guy who was two-timing her?

As Kate was on her way back to her office from court, she dictated the motion for bail into her recorder. Once at the office, she ran into Charles in the hallway.

"How'd the arraignment go?" he asked.

"As expected." She grimaced. "The judge followed the prosecutor's request for no bail."

"That's the way it goes in capital cases." He sounded sympathetic. "How's Sandra holding up?"

"Not great. She's mad about still being in jail."

"I can imagine. Did you speak to her about a deal?"

"She almost tore my head off. Swears she's innocent. There are to be no deals, no continuances, no delays! She told me flat out she doesn't intend to spend one extra minute in jail."

"She's got a great defense lawyer. You'll get her off."

"Or die trying," joked Kate.

"In the meantime, you're going to file a motion for a bail hearing, aren't you?"

"Yes."

"Good. Keep me apprised."

She started to walk away, when he restrained her with his hand, then looked around to make sure no one was listening. "I'd like to come over for a while tonight."

"Make it about eight?" she said as she went off down the hall to see Frank.

"Any luck contacting Sandra's parents?" Kate asked when she found him at his desk.

Frank shook his head. "The Dentons hung up on me three times. Wouldn't even give me a chance to explain."

"We've got to get through somehow." She drummed her fingers on the desk. "How about a telegram?"

"Good idea. What do you want me to say?"

"That we're Sandra's attorneys and need to see them." She flipped his desk calendar. "Tell them we'll be there tomorrow morning about eleven and to expect us."

"I'll give it the old college try."

"Oh," she said, "and you better make us reservations to spend the night in Bakersfield. It'll take at least two days to interview her parents and anyone else we might hunt up who remembers her." She paused. "Pick Bakersfield's finest." She smiled.

"Your expense account?"

"Naturally."

He burst out laughing. "Too bad there's no Bakersfield Ritz Carlton."

She chuckled. "After you do those things, meet me back in my office and I'll fill you in on my meeting with Sandra yesterday."

Fifteen minutes later, with Frank sprawled out on her sofa, Kate told him what Sandra had said, periodically consulting her notes. "First, Sandra told me about the night of the murder. She said she'd been expecting James home and had been planning a romantic, candlelit dinner for two, when the neighbor came screaming up the hill to say something had happened to her husband. She went back down with him, and when she saw James lying there, she almost fainted. The neighbor insisted she call the police from the car phone and Sandra said she just followed his instructions without thinking. After that, she rushed back to the house."

"Did she even know if her husband was alive?"

"No. I know it looks bad," said Kate. "But she claims she couldn't think. If it comes up at the trial, I'll liken it to the way Jacqueline Kennedy tried to climb out of the car when her husband was shot. It's a panic reaction."

Kate continued: "The next thing she knew, the police knocked on the door and told her he was dead." She looked at her notes. "She claims she didn't hear any shots, but then the house is quite a distance from the street. About the bottle of champagne in the car, she didn't know. Maybe James wanted to surprise her."

Frank interrupted, "And that's what made the police think he had been followed home from a liquor store?"

"Right. There have been a lot of follow-home robberies lately involving people who stop at a liquor store or a market where the robber sees they are well dressed and/or wearing jewelry and follows them home." She gazed down at her pad. "She said it would be unusual for him to stop to pick up a bottle. There were, after all, bottles of Dom Perignon in the cellar."

"Was the dinner a special occasion?"

"Sort of. Sandra and James had had a small argument that morning—about what, she couldn't even remember—and she wanted to do something nice." She paused. "Next, she spoke about her childhood—"

"Wait," Frank cut in. "That's all she said about the night of the murder?"

Kate nodded and went on. "As for her parents, she said she hated them. They were rigid and strict. Never let her have any friends, go out, put on makeup, things like that.

"Sandra also hated school and her teachers except for one, but she didn't remember her name. Let's see if we can find her," she said.

"Then, when Sandra was sixteen, she ran away from home. After that, she spoke to her parents only once, for the specific purpose of letting them know she was alive but not coming back. Noticeably missing from her story was any reference to time spent in a juvenile facility or foster home."

"I'm sure we'll get some specifics up in Bakersfield. Then she'll have to tell you."

"Exactly," agreed Kate. "Next, she told me about some of the many jobs she worked at after leaving home. They were the usual, minimum-wage things, like take-out food places." As Kate mentioned the names of some of the restaurants, she recalled her own stint at the same backbreaking work.

"With no skills," she continued, "Sandra was unable to find a good job. She made friends with some of the other girls and shared an apartment with two of them. Then, through someone she met she got a job as a cocktail waitress. It was there she met James.

"He set her up in an apartment and took care of her for awhile. When she became pregnant, he was amazed because in twenty years of marriage, his wife had never conceived. James didn't want Sandra to have an abortion. He promised to provide for both her and the baby. She refused, saying she wasn't going to have a baby without being married."

She gazed over at Frank. "As the time drew closer for a decision, James abruptly changed his mind. He obtained a quickie Mexican divorce and married Sandra." Kate paused, then added, "She spoke very little about her marriage or relationship with James. I can't put my finger on it, but my gut feeling is, she was holding something back."

"Gut feelings are sometimes your best guide."

"Yes." She crinkled her eyes. "What she did mention was her dislike of the D'Arcy family in general. She complained that Abigail is barely civil to her and Victoria is openly hostile. The only one who's been decent to her is Theo."

"What did she say about Tommy?"

"Except for repeating the same things she's told us before, she didn't want to talk about him."

"What about meeting Tommy in the parking lot?"

"In spite of my warning, she felt she had to see him once to explain why she couldn't see him for a time. When the police asked her, she got frightened and lied."

"They're all alike," sighed Frank. "They lie to their lawyers and end up making it worse for themselves. Did you feel she was leveling with you?"

Kate was thoughtful for a minute. "No."

"That makes it tough to defend her."

"Yes." Without meaning to, she yawned. "I didn't sleep last night again," she admitted sheepishly.

"Why don't you go home?"

"I think I will," she agreed. "I wish the draft of the motion was ready now so I could read it before I go to bed."

"Want me to check on it?" Frank asked.

"No. It's O.K."

Madeline could not stop thinking about Gary. Finally she made a decision. Armed with the knowledge that she was doing the only sensible thing, she headed for Gary's office to end their relationship. She also intended to have the pleasure of telling him a thing or two.

Later that night, Frank decided to take the draft and drop it off at Kate's on his way home. She could correct it and messenger it back to the office in the morning, before they left for Bakersfield. As Frank was pulling up, he saw Charles Rieman come out of Kate's building. Since it was almost midnight, he doubted it was business.

Frank waited for him to drive away. Then he got out and left the document in the security drop box. He felt bad for Kate. An affair with a married man would bring her nothing but grief.

33

Madeline woke up, and for a moment she didn't remember where she was. Then she felt the body next to her and realized she was lying next to Gary in his bed. Damn, she thought, why did I do this?

She had gone to his office intending to break up with him. She started by telling him she'd seen him with another woman. Then she'd accused him of being unreasonably jealous and totally lacking in empathy. When she finished, he had come around his desk, looked her in the eye, and humbly told her he was sorry. He also claimed there had been only the one kiss, nothing else.

Against her better judgment, Gary had then convinced her to go with him for a drink. When he asked her back to his place to share a pizza, her intention had been to talk through their disagreement, not end up in his arms. But he brought out a bottle of red wine and put some soft music on his stereo. Then he told her how much he'd missed her. The physical attraction she felt for him was as strong as ever, and . . . somehow, with him, her mind always lost out to her body's desires.

It must be hours later, she thought, as she carefully got off the bed, trying not to wake him. She searched the dark room for her clothing and purse and crept into the bathroom.

Inside, she closed the door before turning on the light.

When she caught sight of herself in the mirror, she groaned. Her thick chestnut hair was a mess and her lipstick and mascara were smeared across her face.

She peered at her watch. It was two in the morning. The kids were alone and she had to be in court at eight. She quietly washed and pulled on her clothes, bunching up her panty hose and stuffing them into her purse. Then she crept back through his room.

"Where you going?" The moonlight pouring in from the window fell across his muscled body as he sat up in the bed.

"Home," she said. "I tried not to wake you."

"I don't want you to go." He sounded petulant.

Surprised, she turned toward him. "I can't leave the kids all night."

"They've been alone most of it already."

What was wrong with him? Didn't he understand? "I shouldn't have fallen asleep. I've got to go."

Without waiting for his reply, she let herself out of his apartment and hurried to her car. Gary lived in Venice near the beach, and there was dew on her windshield. She flipped the wipers on and headed for the San Diego Freeway and home.

Driving through the nearly deserted streets, she questioned the wisdom of what she had done. If Gary was the right man for her, shouldn't she feel like singing after a night of passionate lovemaking? Instead, she felt like she'd just made a very big mistake.

As Frank pulled his car up in front of the house where Sandra's parents lived, Kate felt apprehensive. She was coming here to see what she could learn that might help her defend her client. But what she dreaded was finding out something that would make defending Sandra even harder than it already was.

She glanced at the house, a modest stucco structure painted a nondescript beige. The front lawn was well tended and she noticed a Plymouth several years old parked in the driveway. She wasn't sure what she'd expected, but it certainly wasn't anything so plain, so ordinary-looking.

"A far cry from the D'Arcys' palatial home, isn't it?" said Frank, reading her mind.

Nodding, she preceded Frank up the stairs to the front porch, where she smoothed back her hair and straightened her skirt while Frank adjusted his tie, squared his shoulders, and rang the bell.

There was no answer. Kate glanced at her watch. It was exactly eleven in the morning. Frank shrugged and rang the bell once more. Again, no response. Where were they? she wondered. Maybe they were at work. Had they even gotten her telegram?

Frank walked over to the window and tried to peer inside, but the curtains were tightly drawn. Instead of ringing, this time he opened the screen and knocked on the wooden door, softly at first; then, seemingly exasperated, he knocked harder.

A woman's thin, reedy voice called out, "Who's there?"

"Kate Alexander and Frank Jones," he yelled. "We sent you a telegram."

"Go away! We have nothing to say."

Kate whispered to Frank, "This is going to be worse than I thought." She stepped forward. "Please, I need to see you about your daughter. I'm her lawyer and she's in trouble."

"There's nothing we can do to help her," came the response.

"There's a child," Kate said. "You have a four-year-old grandson."

Kate heard some shuffling, then the latch being opened. A small, rather timid-looking woman stood in the doorway, an apron over her cotton housedress. She was wiping her hands dry with a towel. Although Kate could see the resemblance to Sandra, this woman had a washed-out, wrinkled face. It must have been lovely once, she thought.

"A boy?" asked the woman.

"Yes." Kate smiled. "His name's Jimmy. Want to see some pictures?" She held out the photographs she had taken from Sandra's house.

The woman hesitated, then turned around furtively as if to get permission from someone else. She turned back and her hand darted out. "Let me see." She trembled as she gazed at the photographs. Every few seconds she looked around. It wasn't hard to see she was afraid of something—or someone.

"Nora?" a man's voice shouted from somewhere inside the house.

The woman quickly handed the pictures back to Kate, a look of fear in her eyes.

Aha, thought Kate, it's him. She's afraid of him. She spoke softly. "May we come in please, Mrs. Denton? I don't want your neighbors to overhear us."

The woman faltered. "Wait here." She slammed the door in Kate's face.

Kate glanced at Frank, who merely shrugged as if to say, I don't know what's going on either.

A few minutes later the door was opened again. This time a tall, thin man with gray hair and stooped shoulders was standing there. He was quite a bit older than Kate had expected. "Ed Denton's the name."

"I'm pleased to meet you." Kate held out her hand. "I'm Kate Alexander."

He opened the screen door but didn't offer to shake her hand. "Who's the colored?"

Kate ignored the slur. "This is Mr. Frank Jones. He works with me."

"Since you're here, you might as well come in." He stood back to allow them to enter.

Mr. Denton led them down a narrow hallway to a den. The room was filled with trophies. Pictures of award ceremonies and men wearing matching shirts lined the walls. When Kate turned around, Sandra's father was peering at her legs, an odd expression on his face. It made her feel uncomfortable.

"Sit down." He motioned to the sofa.

Kate obliged and Frank took the chair by the window.

"She in jail like the paper says?" There was a scowl on Mr. Denton's craggy face.

"Yes, I'm afraid so," answered Kate.

He grunted. "This here's a small town, people know us.

Having a daughter who's an adulteress and a murderer . . ." His voice trailed off as he shook his head.

"Sandra's innocent until proven guilty," said Kate evenly. It was obvious that Sandra's father was more concerned with what the people in town thought than how his daughter was faring. She wondered where the wife had disappeared to and decided to ask. "Could Mrs. Denton please join us?"

"Nora!" he yelled irritably.

Mrs. Denton rushed into the room carrying a tray of cups and saucers and a jar of instant coffee. They rattled in spite of her attempt to balance all the items on the tray. "I'm making us some coffee," she explained.

Her gesture of hospitality took Kate by surprise as she watched the woman put a teaspoonful of coffee into one of the cups and sit down.

"How long has it been since you've seen your daughter?" Kate tried to be as pleasant as possible.

"I'll do the talking, Nora," said Mr. Denton. He turned to Kate. "Long time, maybe six, seven years."

"That must be very hard on you both?"

Mrs. Denton glanced nervously at her husband.

"It's the way she wanted it!" The father's voice was abrupt as he met Kate's gaze with unblinking, hostile eyes.

She wondered why he was so angry with Sandra. And why was Mrs. Denton not allowed to talk without her husband's permission? While Kate racked her brain to figure out how to get them to open up, the teakettle whistled in the kitchen.

" 'Scuse me." Mrs. Denton scurried out of the room.

Kate turned to the father. "What do you do, Mr. Denton?"

"Retired now. I was a foreman for Blaine Construction Company." He sat up straighter in his chair as he added, "Best foreman they ever had."

"And Mrs. Denton?"

He grimaced. "She stays home where a woman belongs."

Well, thought Kate, he obviously doesn't approve of

women attorneys. She decided to try another tack and pointed at the trophies. "Yours?"

"Yes," he boasted. "I'm a championship bowler."

"How nice." Kate hoped she sounded sincere.

"I like to bowl," Frank put in, "but lately there's been no time."

Mrs. Denton came back into the room carrying the teakettle. She poured hot water into one cup only, put the kettle down, and handed the cup to her husband.

He peered inside his cup and barked, "Where's my cream?"

"Oh!" She appeared flustered. "I'll get it." She hurried out again.

"Would you like to see a picture of your grandson?" asked Kate, trying to cover up the awkwardness that hung in the air. When he made no reply, she handed him the picture anyway.

He gazed at it for a moment, then handed it back. There was no hint of any emotion on his face. It remained as rigid as granite.

Mrs. Denton hastened back in and poured the cream into his cup.

Sandra's father fixed Kate with a suspicious stare. "What is it you people want here?"

Kate smiled. "We'd like to know a little bit about your daughter's childhood. What she was like, that sort of thing."

Mr. Denton nodded at his wife. "Tell her, Nora."

"Sandra was just like lots of other kids." Mrs. Denton's voice was nervous and high-pitched. "Always getting into things, making a mess, you know." She made a weak attempt at a smile.

Kate sensed the woman's discomfort. "Did you have any specific problems with Sandra while she was growing up?"

Mr. Denton gave his wife a look that said, I'll handle this one. "A few," he said cautiously.

"Could you tell us about them?"

His eyes narrowed. "We had problems with her because she told lies."

Kate felt her heart sink. "What kind of lies?"

"Lies about everything," he said brusquely. "I gave my daughter everything a girl could want. She repaid us by lying. Isn't that right, Nora?"

"Yes," mumbled Mrs. Denton.

Kate wondered how to broach what was really on her mind. She tried to sound as casual as she could. "I understand Sandra spent some time away from you when she was growing up?"

The man's chin jutted out angrily. "Yeah?"

"Where?"

"A juvenile facility for a while. Then a foster home."

What Charles had heard was obviously true, thought Kate. "Why was that?"

"Because of her lies!" he said through thin lips. "No one could ever believe her."

Kate stared directly at him. "So you and Mrs. Denton sent her away?"

"What did Sandra tell you?" His face had turned stony and there was a new and cutting edge to his tone.

"Nothing." She paused, sensing that this man was worried about something. "It was actually a friend of Mr. D'Arcy's who said Sandra had spent time in a juvenile facility." He seemed to digest her words for a moment. "Look." She tried to keep her voice light. "I know this is hard on you both, but I need to know everything about Sandra if I'm going to help her."

"Well, let me tell you something, Miss Alexander." He shook a bony finger at her. "Whatever made Sandra go wrong is not my fault. I worked hard. Took good care of my family. Gave them a decent roof over their heads, good food in their bellies. I worked two jobs for a while to buy Sandra nice things. I don't drink or run around like other men. All I ever asked for is a little respect, that's all." His tirade apparently over, he barked at his wife, "Isn't that right, Nora?"

"My husband worked very hard," she agreed in a monotone, her eyes lowered. "Always provided for us. Even used to bring presents home for Sandra all the time, you know. Nothing was too good for his little girl.''

As the two of them spoke, Kate wondered what had really gone on in this house. He was protesting so much it made her uncomfortable. And the way Mrs. Denton deferred to her husband rang a bell in Kate's mind. In her years as a prosecutor, she had seen scores of battered women who had the same nervous, deferential attitude toward their husbands.

"I belong to the Rotary Club, the chamber of commerce, and the church council," bragged Mr. Denton as he continued to defend himself. "On top of that, I'm also a deacon at my church." His face wore a self-satisfied smile. "You can ask anybody in this here town you want. They'll tell you they know me and my reputation as one of the outstanding members of this community."

Tactfully, Kate tried to guide the conversation back to Sandra. "What kind of lies was Sandra telling?"

Ed Denton's eyes smoldered with anger. "That we weren't treating her right. Told that to one of her teachers."

"Did she accuse you of anything specific?"

He glared at her and blurted out, "Said we beat up on her."

Now we're getting somewhere, thought Kate. "Both of you?"

"Mostly me," he grumbled.

"And did you hit your daughter, Mr. Denton?"

"No more than any other father. You got to teach children to respect you." He was turning red. "If not, they grow up not knowing right from wrong. That's the problem with the world today. Not enough people willing to take a rod to their kids."

Her heart in her mouth, Kate looked at the mother. "Was there anything else she accused you of?"

Mrs. Denton paled, took a deep breath, and started to say something.

"Nora," her husband warned. He glowered at his wife, who sat playing with her apron.

His voice chilled Kate.

"I already told you that Sandra made up a bunch of wild accusations against me," he said.

"I see," said Kate, noticing that there was not an ounce of shame in his eyes as he stared defiantly back at her. It was almost as if he dared her to find out more.

"So they took Sandra away from you while they investigated the . . ." She searched for the right word. "Accusations?"

"Yep. But they never proved a thing. It was all lies!"

I bet, thought Kate. "Then what happened?"

"We had all kinds of people poking their noses into our business." The color rose in his face again. "You show me one of them that didn't punish their own kids! Bunch of busybodies, that's all they was!" He was almost shouting.

Kate had seen this type of bully before. A man who enjoyed ruling his home with an iron fist. "Can you tell me the names of any people who were involved?"

"There was a damn stupid schoolteacher, a Mrs. Lewis, that believed Sandra. Our lawyer fellow, George Hall, made mincemeat out of her." He coughed. "But if you really want somebody who knows what they're talking about, speak to our minister, Reverend Smith. He vouched for us."

Kate wrote the names down. "And how long did Sandra live away from home?"

" 'Bout eight months."

She took a deep breath. "What was the outcome of the investigation?"

"They found nothing," he said smugly, "because there wasn't nothing to find."

Kate felt her anger rise like bitter bile in her throat as she forced herself to ask the next question. "And afterwards was Sandra returned to you?"

"Sure was." He smirked.

"How was it when she got back?"

"The lying got worse. In fact, she started getting violent."

"Violent?" Kate was almost afraid to ask. "In what way?"

"Throwing things. Acting disrespectful." He shook his head. "I don't know what she learned in that foster home. Nothing good, I can promise."

"Do you remember the names of the foster parents?"

"Yep. I got nothing to hide."

Again Kate wrote as Mr. Denton continued. "After she got back from that foster home, Sandra got too big for her britches. Then," he added, "when she was sixteen, she upped and ran away."

She probably had no choice, thought Kate. "What did you do to try to get her back?"

"Nothing. There was no use," he replied. "She obviously didn't give a damn about all we did for her. We figured it was best to let her find out how cruel the real world is."

Kate and Frank exchanged hurried glances. She was appalled. Sandra's parents hadn't even cared enough about her to search for her. She felt an overwhelming sense of pity for her client and for Jimmy. A choice between Sandra's parents and Abigail was meaningless. One was as bad as the other.

"I'm trying to get Sandra released on bail," she explained, "but if I'm not able to, how would you feel about caring for your grandson?"

"No!" Mrs. Denton cried out, a look of panic on her face.

She knows something, thought Kate.

Mr. Denton gave his wife a dirty look. "That's enough, Nora." He turned to Kate. "We don't have much money."

"The boy has trust funds . . ." The words hung in the air and Kate wished she could take them back.

He sat up straighter. "Maybe we can work something out after all."

Kate handed him her card with a sinking feeling. "Give me a call."

Outside in the car, Frank peered at Kate with concern. "You O.K.?"

"It was just stuffy in the room." She rolled down the window, feeling sick to her stomach. "I'll be all right in a minute."

As they drove to the motor lodge to check in, Kate voiced her fear. "Do you think it was more than physical abuse?"

"It certainly entered my mind."

"But if Sandra's father molested her"—Kate's voice rose—"how could she even consider letting him watch her child?"

He shook his head. "Beats me."

"And did you see the panic on the mother's face when I asked if they would take care of their grandson? She's hiding something. She doesn't want to take the child because of him. I just know it."

When they were seated at a table in the Wellington Club, Miles Cunningham peered closely at Andrew Stewart. "I'm not a man to mince words, Mr. Stewart."

"Please call me Andrew."

"Very well, Andrew. I'm a modern man only to a certain extent. When it comes to my daughter, I'm as old-fashioned as they come."

Andrew heard the southern drawl in the man's rough voice as he spoke. "I can understand that, sir."

"Well then, what I'm about to say should not come as a shock." Miles leaned forward. "I want to know what your intentions are toward my daughter."

Andrew gulped. He had expected the man to ask him some questions, but nothing so direct. "I like your daughter very much." He held his hands out in explanation. "But we're still getting to know one another."

"You're sleeping together. In my book that means you know each other well enough!"

For the first time in years, Andrew was at a loss for words as he looked at the imposing Texan. "I'm not sure what to say to that." He tried to smile.

Miles didn't smile back. He took a cigar from his pocket, removed the wrapper, and sliced off the end with a gold clipper. Then he lighted it and inhaled deeply. Slowly, blowing out the smoke, he fixed his eyes on Andrew. "I don't appreciate a man using my daughter . . ." His words drifted off.

"I'm not using your daughter," protested Andrew. "I can assure you of that." The man should only know the truth about his precious Lauren, he thought. Sometimes Andrew felt that Lauren was the one using him, to fill her voracious appetite for sex. Not that he was exactly complaining.

"Well, see that you don't." Miles flicked an ash. "I have a lot of powerful friends in this city. I could cause you some unpleasantness."

"No need for that, Mr. Cunningham. When the time's right, I'm sure I'll be discussing"—he quickly swallowed—"a future with your daughter."

"The time *is* right, and I'm the one you need to discuss it with first." Miles inhaled and blew out his smoke. "Are you asking for her hand?"

"I hadn't quite meant to, yet," Andrew stuttered.

"I don't like being made a fool of, young man." Miles sat up straighter in his chair, his ruddy complexion darkening.

"I can assure you there's no disrespect intended."

"I'm a wealthy man, Andrew. Has my daughter mentioned to you the trust fund she comes into upon her marriage?"

"No. She hasn't."

"Well, I can tell you it's a significant sum. Somewhere in the neighborhood of ten million dollars."

Andrew tried not to show his shock. That was more money than he'd ever dreamed of. He wouldn't have to work so hard. Hell, he wouldn't have to work at all. He could pick and choose only the best cases. Lauren was beginning to look better by the minute.

"That's just the first provision," explained Miles. "When she has her first child, there's more, and so on." He pointed his cigar at Andrew. "But I want to make sure you love her and not the dollars."

Andrew made up his mind quickly. He wasn't getting any younger. He focused his attention on Miles, all of his confidence and bravado having returned. "I knew you were a wealthy man, Mr. Cunningham. However, that doesn't influence me either way. I'm the kind of man who likes to take care of his own wife."

Miles puffed on his cigar. "Good, I like to hear that."

"So," said Andrew, with his most winning smile, "if you'll agree to give me your daughter's hand in marriage, I'll ask her to be my wife."

"Son, you have my blessing," said Miles, beaming.

When Frank and Kate met at the motel coffee shop, he told her he'd managed to see all the people on his list, gleaning a great deal of background information on Sandra.

"Me too," she said. "So let's compare notes."

"You go first. I'm starved." Frank took a big bite of his hamburger.

"O.K. The lawyer who represented Mr. and Mrs. Denton confirmed our suspicions. Sandra did accuse her father of sexual as well as physical abuse."

"I thought so," he muttered. "What did he say?"

"He painted a very black picture of Sandra, I'm afraid," said Kate bluntly. "Not only did he insist she was known for telling lies, but he said that there wasn't one shred of evidence to support her allegations."

"That's not unusual in that type of case." Frank munched on some french fries.

"True. Anyway, he went on to tell me what an upstanding citizen Ed Denton is and how he's an important member of the church and so on."

Frank looked disgusted. "A real regular guy, huh?"

She nodded and drummed the tabletop with her fingers. "He kept insisting they were not the sort of people who would have allowed any kind of abuse to go on."

"I bet."

"This lawyer explained that Mr. Denton was fifteen years older than his wife. Sandra was their only child and the father doted on her."

"Obviously too much. What did he say about the teacher who supposedly believed Sandra?"

She frowned. "He thought she was meddling where she didn't belong."

Frank shook his head. "Not according to the teacher, Mrs. Lewis."

"You found the teacher?"

"Yes." He wiped off his mouth with a napkin. "She noticed how often Sandra came to school with black and blue marks on her. She could see the girl was smart, but she was listless a lot of the time. She suspected Sandra wasn't getting enough sleep, because she had dark rings under her eyes and fell asleep in class a lot."

"Interesting," said Kate.

Frank pushed his plate away and shook a cigarette out of a new pack.

"I thought you gave that up."

"I tried. I'll quit again," he promised. "Anyway, Mrs. Lewis finally took Sandra aside one day and told her she knew something was the matter."

"Go on," she urged.

"Sandra broke down in tears. Said she'd been having nightmares and couldn't sleep. The teacher got concerned and took Sandra to see the school nurse." He paused as if to emphasize his next words. "They got Sandra to admit her father had been coming into her room at night and sexually abusing her since she was ten."

Kate paled, an uneasy feeling in the pit of her stomach. "You O.K.?"

"Sure. I worked sex crimes as a prosecutor. The stories I heard were so horrible and the children always felt so helpless. You never stop thinking about it. I still can't stand to hear it."

"I know." He nodded.

Kate was thoughtful for a moment. "Remember when Sandra said there was a teacher she liked, but she couldn't remember her name?"

"Yeah."

"I wonder if Mrs. Lewis was the same teacher and if Sandra didn't want to recall her name."

"You're probably right. Anyway, they reported the abuse to the authorities, who took Sandra away from her parents. She was placed in a foster home while they investigated."

"Any word on the foster parents yet?"

"I've left both of our names and the number of the motel on their answering machine. Hopefully, they'll call back. They still take care of foster children." He hesitated, then went on. "Mrs. Lewis told me Sandra used to tell small lies."

"Damn." Kate realized her client had a problem with telling the truth. "I'm going to have to talk to a psychiatrist about it. I think the lying could have something to do with the abuse."

"Could be." Frank took another drag on his cigarette. "If Sandra was molested, how do you plan to use it?"

"Good question. If she's innocent, it's totally irrelevant. But if she killed her husband, I'm going to need to come up with some kind of a defense."

"How does sexual abuse by her father tie into her killing her husband?"

"That's just it, I don't know if it does." Her eyes clouded over. "My gut tells me we don't have the whole story yet. I want to dig a little more. Then I'll confront Sandra with it.

Since the beginning, I've had the feeling she was holding something back, and I intend to find out what it is and why."

"Yeah. It could be important."

"I've got to break through to her if I'm going to help her."

"I know you." He looked at her admiringly. "You'll do whatever it takes to help your client." He glanced at his watch. "Time we checked to see if we have any messages."

"Right," said Kate, signaling for the check.

That night Frank asked around for the best steak house in town.

"This is it?" Kate laughed when they finally found the run-down place.

"Welcome to Bakersfield's finest," Frank said as they entered the restaurant.

After they were seated, and he had his beer and a cigarette, he spoke proudly about his wife, Cheryl, and his two kids, Bobby and Lita.

"Your family sounds so normal, so wonderful."

He saw the wistful look on Kate's face. "You should be married and have kids too."

"Not me." She shrugged. "I've too many things I want to do with my life. It wouldn't be fair to a child."

"Maybe not. But plenty of busy people have kids."

"I think the children suffer. Your kids have Cheryl when you're not home."

"So find yourself a man that likes to stay home," he said earnestly.

Kate laughed. "You're full of the devil tonight, *Mister* Jones."

"I mean it." He smiled. "With the kind of political future you want, you should have a husband who will put you and your career first."

"That would be nice, but not likely."

"Kate, do you consider me a friend?" he asked suddenly, not sure if he should broach the subject or not.

She glanced up at him, puzzled. "Of course."

"Then can I ask you something that's really none of my business?"

She eyed him playfully. "That depends."

His face was somber as the words came tumbling out. "Why are you having an affair with a married man? There's nothing but grief in it for you, both politically and personally."

A flush appeared on her neck. "I'm afraid I don't know what you're talking about."

"You can deny it all you want, but I saw Charles Rieman leaving your place last night."

"It was business," she protested.

"Hey, you want to fool yourself, go right ahead."

"No, it's not that." She looked down at her hands. "I've promised him not to tell anyone."

His eyes flooded with sympathy. "I'm sorry."

"It's O.K." She was quiet for a minute as she fiddled with the silverware. "You know, it's hard not to talk about it."

"I can imagine. You have my word, I'll never say anything."

"Thanks, friend."

"You deserve better," he said.

"I love him."

"He'll never leave his wife."

"He will."

"I hope so. For your sake."

The next day Kate met with Sandra's foster mother. She was a warm, rather large woman with a way of listening to what Kate said with genuine interest.

"I remember Sandra very well," the woman said immediately. "I liked her a lot."

"Did you ever have reason to believe that she lied?" Kate asked at the first opportunity.

"I'm afraid I did. But after a while, after she knew my husband and I could be trusted, it stopped."

"Really?" Kate felt hopeful for the first time in two days.

The woman nodded, smiling.

"Is there anything else you recall?"

The woman squinted. "I remember the first night she was with us . . . when I went to check on Sandra and I found her sleeping fully dressed."

"Oh?"

"I couldn't get her to take her clothes off at night for the longest time. And she seemed so surprised to find a lock on the bathroom door. I finally got her to tell me how her father used to come in and watch her. When she showered, I mean."

"That information could be very important. Would you be willing to testify if we need you?"

"Sure. When I saw Sandra's picture in the paper, I couldn't help wondering if I could've done more for her than I did."

Kate shook her head. "Don't feel guilty. It sounds like you did all you could."

"I remember how terrible I felt when the authorities said she had to go back home to her parents."

"I can imagine . . . Well, I don't want to overburden you with questions. I really appreciate your help." She handed the woman her card. "Please call me if you think of anything else. If not, I'll be in touch."

When she caught up with Frank, he told her that he'd interviewed several classmates of Sandra's.

"Surprisingly, no one knew her that well. I couldn't find anyone who was a close friend or who had even visited Sandra's home." He fingered his jaw. "It's as if school and home were two separate worlds."

On the drive back to Los Angeles, Kate brought up the question of abuse.

"There was no evidence, except Sandra's statement," Frank said, "to back up her story of what her father did to her. No one ever saw the man hit his daughter. No one ever saw him touch her improperly."

"Of course not." Kate could feel the anger building inside her again at what must have been Sandra's sense of helplessness. "He was too smart for that."

After Frank had dropped her off at home, Kate found an urgent message to call the office. When she did, they told her to phone Abigail immediately.

"I need to see you tomorrow in the late morning," said Abigail, sounding agitated.

Kate sighed. Whatever it was that was bothering Abigail now, it probably was not that important. But she had no doubt that Abigail would not think twice about interrupting even the President of the United States. "I've got a very busy schedule tomorrow. I've been out of town for two days on Sandra's case."

"It is extremely important. Be here at eleven."

The phone in Kate's hand went dead. What nerve! thought Kate as she wondered what was wrong.

Early the next morning Frank came rushing into Kate's office. "I just met with the D'Arcy gardener. He told me something that could turn this whole case upside down."

"Tell me," she said eagerly.

"I don't know what made me ask," he said, "but after the trip to Bakersfield, I couldn't stop thinking about Sandra and her father. You know, girls who are abused as children often find themselves in the same lousy situation when they're adults."

"And . . ." Kate asked, suddenly impatient.

"So I asked him if he had ever noticed anything unusual in the relationship between James D'Arcy and his wife."

"What did he say?" She held her breath.

"Bingo!" Frank's handsome face was alive with excitement.

"He saw it?"

"No, but he used to hear a lot of yelling and screaming. He thinks James knocked Sandra around because"—Frank paused for emphasis—"he also saw bruises on Sandra afterwards."

"I knew it!" Kate sat down with a thud. "I had a feeling she was hiding something like this." Suddenly, the full impact of the discovery hit her. "You know what this means, don't you?"

"Sure," said Frank. "That the prominent James D'Arcy was nothing but a lousy wife beater."

"And that she killed him because of it," whispered Kate.

35

As soon as Kate recovered from the surprise of Frank's findings, she started to give instructions. "Find me the D'Arcys' maid. I've got to have someone who can tell us what went on inside their house. If James mistreated Sandra, it could change the entire complexion of the case."

"Self-defense?" Frank asked.

"Perhaps. But it won't be easy. The 'burning bed' defense works best, if at all, when the woman is so frightened she kills the man herself. Not when she gets someone else to murder her husband for her."

Mary, Kate's secretary, stuck her head in the door. "Hey, boss, it's time to leave. You're due at Abigail D'Arcy's."

Fifteen minutes later the butler showed Kate into Abigail's room, where the elderly woman wasted no time getting to the point. "I understand you are planning to bring a motion for my daughter-in-law to be released on bail?"

"Yes."

"I do not want you to do that."

Kate frowned. "I'm afraid I don't understand."

"I do not want Sandra out on bail. She's a murderess. My grandson does not belong with her."

"Mrs. D'Arcy—"

Abigail cut her off. "I will never forgive that woman for what she did to my son."

Kate heard the menacing tone beneath the words. "With all due respect, you're judging Sandra before she's been tried."

"You can spout your rhetoric about justice to the press and even to the jury, but not with me, thank you."

"I thought you wanted me to defend Sandra."

"Because she is entitled to a defense does not mean I am unable to figure things out for myself." Abigail's voice had a razor-sharp edge to it. "On the facts I have heard, I believe my daughter-in-law to be guilty."

"You can't base an opinion on media news and conjecture."

A quick, scornful smile pulled at the corners of Abigail's thin lips. "You underestimate me, Kate. I have access to better information than that."

Kate was unnerved. Was someone in her office supplying Abigail with details from her own files? It was a sobering thought. Who would do that? Could Dickson be filching information off her desk or out of her confidential files and giving it to Theo? But for what purpose? Or maybe the culprit was Franklin Manning himself? The older man's relationship with Abigail went back years to a business and personal friendship with her husband, William. But Kate couldn't think of any reason he'd want to go behind her back. There was also the possibility it was Charles. After all, he seemed to speak to Abigail every day. But he'd ask me first, she reasoned. In reality, it could be any one of these people, but none of the alternatives made any sense.

She focused on Abigail. "If someone's giving you data from my files, it's a violation of the privilege between my client and myself." Kate's voice was curt. "And I really must object."

"My dear." Abigail's expression and tone were those of someone used to patronizing others beneath her. "Why don't you just concern yourself with your job of defending my daughter-in-law. Let me worry about my sources."

Damn her, thought Kate, a nasty retort on the tip of her

tongue. Who did she think she was? Then she quickly reminded herself that she'd come here for more than one purpose. She leaned forward in her chair and tried to be as diplomatic as possible. "My client has complained that you're listening in on her telephone calls with her son and telling him when to get off."

"That is true."

Kate was surprised. She'd expected the old woman to deny it. "Please don't. At least for the sake of the child if not for Sandra. After all, he has to be very confused over all that's happened. His father is dead. He saw his mother taken away by the police. The child's entire world has been turned upside down."

Abigail's surprisingly unlined face wore a look of amused disdain as she lifted her hand imperiously. "Now you listen to me, young lady. Yes, my son is dead, but I have that woman to thank for that. And yes, as a result, my grandson has been traumatized. But as to his world being turned upside down, absolutely not." She sniffed contemptuously. "He is happy and well tended to for the first time in his life. While my son was alive, he would not take my advice as to how to raise his child. He even thought that woman was a good mother. Now, it will be done my way."

Abigail took a deep breath and continued. "Since I have been deprived of my son, I will not be deprived of my grandson. He will have the finest governess and the best schools. James junior will be raised the way a D'Arcy should be raised. And neither you nor anyone else will be allowed to interfere."

Kate squelched her temper even though this woman absolutely infuriated her. "I must remind you that Sandra hasn't been convicted, only charged. As such, she still has rights."

The old woman scowled. "I do not care about *her* rights. Nothing is more important than my grandson. He is the only grandchild I will ever have."

Kate wondered why Abigail would say such a thing. How could she be so sure she'd never have any other grandchildren? She was getting nowhere. She'd better change the subject. "Mrs. D'Arcy, I've got to discuss something of grave importance with you." She paused. She might as well say it. Things couldn't get any worse. "Did you know anything at all about your son physically abusing Sandra?"

Abigail started slightly in the midst of pouring herself a cup of tea. When she raised her eyes to Kate's, they seemed to be filled with hate. "Of course not. That is nothing but a ghastly lie. Did Sandra tell you such rubbish?"

"No, she didn't," admitted Kate. "Still, I have reason to suspect it's true."

"Our meeting is finished," Abigail announced, waving her arm in dismissal. "And you may inform Sandra that if she persists in making up such outrageous stories, she will be hard pressed to pay your legal fees."

"Mrs. D'Arcy . . ."

"Please leave." Abigail's voice was tight with anger.

Kate stood up as straight as she could. "Mrs. D'Arcy, let me make myself clear." In spite of her best intentions, her voice rose. "It doesn't matter who approached me on Sandra's behalf. Only after Sandra asked me to represent her and I accepted did I, in effect, become her lawyer. Therefore, I've been retained by Sandra, not you or anyone else. My first duty is and will continue to be to her, her welfare and her best interests. If you interfere with her talking to her child, I'll ask a judge to intervene. Lastly"—she inhaled, catching her breath—"if I'm able to get Sandra out on bail, her son will go home with his mother."

Abigail's face, contorted with rage, suddenly appeared old. "Get out of here," she choked.

Kate was shaking as she left the house. Her anger felt like a hard knot in her chest. That woman acted as if she were God! She tried to calm herself down; after a few minutes, she succeeded. Anger was counterproductive.

Driving to the jail, Kate thought about how ironic life was. Just a short time ago, she'd been upset as hell about being pushed into representing Sandra. She admitted to herself that she had prejudged her client because she was so young and married to a wealthy, older man. But now that she'd discovered what she had about Sandra's past, Kate could understand why the young woman might have looked for a more mature man. And after seeing how manipulative Abigail was, Kate found herself feeling sorry for her client. What match could Sandra have been for Abigail?

Somehow she had to get her client to tell her the truth. What had really gone on behind the closed doors of James and Sandra D'Arcy's home?

As she pulled onto the freeway, Kate realized she was fighting mad and determined to help Sandra. Somehow, some way, she intended to get Sandra off.

Frank reached Kate on her car phone to tell her the police had searched Sandra's house while he and Kate were in Bakersfield.

"Did they find the weapon?" Kate asked.

"No weapon."

"Thanks," she said, then hung up.

When she saw Sandra, Kate told her about the search of her house.

"I told you the gun was gone," said Sandra.

"Yes. Well, let me tell you about Bakersfield. I saw your parents."

Sandra's chin jutted out defiantly. "I'm sure they told you they didn't want anything to do with me."

"I'm sorry." Kate nodded. "You were right about them."

A derisive laugh erupted from Sandra. "I can well imagine what my darling mother and father had to say."

Kate now recognized Sandra's bravado as an attempt to cover feelings of hurt; anything that made her vulnerable must make her feel like a target. After meeting Sandra's parents, seeing the way the father was a tyrant and the mother meek and submissive, Kate had a clearer understanding of how badly these people had mistreated their daughter. No wonder Sandra had developed such a hard outer shell. A child needed to find some degree of safety from the people she depended on to protect her.

"In all fairness, I think your mother wanted to help us. But she's obviously afraid of your father." Kate waited for

Sandra to agree, but the young woman just played with what looked like a hangnail and refused to meet Kate's gaze.

"She wanted to see the pictures of Jimmy," added Kate. "And when she looked at them, I could see how pleased she was."

"I bet." Sandra continued picking at one of her fingernails.

Kate tried another approach. "We also spoke to some of your teachers and one in particular, a Mrs. Lewis."

A look of wariness came into Sandra's eyes.

"She told us you accused your father of sexually abusing you."

"You had no right!" Sandra jumped up, her blue eyes flashing as her normally pale complexion turned pink.

The commotion caused the guard to glance in with a worried expression on her face. Kate signaled to the matron that it was O.K. and directed Sandra to sit down. "I had every right." Her voice was firm. "I intend to defend you to the best of my ability, and that means finding out everything about you, including things you don't want me to know."

Sandra tossed her shoulders angrily. "What difference does it make now anyway?"

"I'm not sure," said Kate softly. "That's what I was hoping you'd tell me."

"Look. He got away with it! No one believed me."

Kate heard the bitterness in Sandra's voice. "Yes, in a way he did get away with it. But your teacher and the school nurse believed you. Your foster mother believed you . . ."

"You saw her, too?"

"Yes. She sent her love." As the words registered, Kate saw a momentary softness come over Sandra's face. It made her client appear suddenly young, vulnerable. "Please tell me about it," urged Kate.

"There's nothing to tell." The hard shell had slipped back into place. Sandra got up and paced. "When I was ten years old, my father started coming into my room. By the time I was twelve, he was forcing me to have sex with him."

Kate was chilled by the hollowness in Sandra's voice. "What did you do?"

"Nothing. I was too scared." Sandra made a feeble gesture with her hands. "For years he brushed up to me, you know, touching me like it was an accident or something. Mother never seemed to notice. Then he started coming into the bathroom when I was in the shower."

A hardness took over Sandra's demeanor as she talked, as if what she was describing was trivial rather than horrendous. "There was no lock on the door. They weren't allowed. He'd stand there, his eyes going up and down my naked body, a disgusting smile on his face. Sometimes he'd play with himself while he watched me." She paused; then her next words tumbled out in a half-sob. "You can't imagine how dirty I felt."

"I'm so sorry." Kate felt sick to her stomach. "Did you try telling your mother?"

The young woman stiffened. "My mother knew," she said sharply. "And she didn't do anything about it."

"Are you sure?"

Sandra nodded. "One time when she was out, he forced me to screw him on the couch in the den. He was on top of me and I heard a noise. I opened my eyes. Mother was in the doorway. Part of me was glad. Now she'd see what he was forcing me to do, I thought. He'd have to stop."

Kate could hear both the anger and the hurt in Sandra's voice. "What happened?"

"She looked at me like it was my fault, turned, and walked away. She never mentioned it. But I knew she saw us. After that, she acted like she couldn't stand the sight of me."

Kate thought about the woman she'd met in Bakersfield. What had gone through her mind when she saw her husband and her daughter? How could she have stayed with such a despicable man? Kate felt a tremendous need to make things better for Sandra. "You know, I read a book once where a doctor explained that most mothers know about the sexual abuse but feel helpless to do anything about it. In their own sick way they come to hate their daughters for what they themselves are unable to stop."

"Yeah," snorted Sandra.

"It took a lot of courage for you to speak up."

Sandra picked at her fingernail. "For a long time I was afraid to tell anyone. I was sure they'd think I was bad. Then Mrs. Lewis and the school nurse were so nice—" Her voice broke off. "Anyway, it was the only time I felt like somebody heard me."

"I'm hearing you now." Kate hoped her client believed her. "I keep thinking how terrible it must have been for you to be sent back home after they found no evidence to support your claims."

"He was even worse than before. The first chance he got, he pinned me up against the wall and bragged, 'See, I told you no one would believe you.' "

"Bastard." The words were out before Kate realized it. After a moment, she asked. "Is that when the lying really got bad?"

"I guess. It was the only way I had to get even. I started stealing money from my parents, you know, and selling things I didn't think they'd miss. I knew I had to get away before . . ." She didn't finish.

"Before you killed him?" asked Kate, stating out loud what she'd been thinking. She didn't blame Sandra. Parents were supposed to protect their children, not abuse them.

Sandra merely shrugged. "Or something." She refused to meet Kate's gaze, looking instead at the wall. "She should have helped me, you know?"

"Maybe she was afraid."

"I don't care. A mother should protect her child," insisted Sandra angrily. "I'd kill anyone who hurt my child."

What had really happened between James and Sandra? Kate wondered as the anger broke through the shell Sandra used to distance herself. Dare she ask? She had to know all the terrible details, no matter how painful, if she was going to give her client a proper defense. "Was James violent toward Jimmy? Or toward you?"

A veil seemed to come down over Sandra's face. "I don't know what you mean."

"I'm only trying to help you—please don't shut me out

now,'' Kate found herself pleading. ''I need to know if he hurt you.''

Her client turned away. ''I can't answer that.''

''Can't or won't?''

''Leave me alone! We've uncovered enough shit for one day!''

''I've already spoken to the gardener,'' Kate continued calmly, as if she hadn't understood. ''He heard James hurting you. He says he saw bruises on you afterwards.''

Sandra remained silent.

''I'm going to have to insist you tell me.''

''You can do whatever you want, Ms. Smarty Pants Lawyer.''

Kate refused to be baited. This was too critical. ''If James abused you, and you killed him because of it, you're entitled to show the abuse as a defense.''

Sandra turned around, her blue eyes ablaze. ''You're no better than the rest!''

Kate was shocked by her vehemence. ''I'm not following you,'' she said weakly.

''You're saying if he beat me, I probably killed him.''

''I'm only telling you the law.''

''I didn't fucking kill my husband! And I'm sick of no one believing me.''

Why would Sandra try to protect him now that he was dead? thought Kate, her mind reeling. What was she afraid of? With Sandra's history of lying, how was Kate supposed to know if she was telling the truth or not? She steeled herself. She had yet to mention the disastrous meeting she'd had with Abigail and the way it had ended. Taking a deep breath, Kate told Sandra about her visit with her mother-in-law.

''That fucking bitch, I hate her!'' Sandra suddenly burst into tears. ''I knew she'd try and take my baby away from me. I knew it.''

Kate thought Sandra was probably overreacting, but she could understand why. ''Sandra, I feel terrible, but I'm not sure where Jimmy would be better off at the moment. You know there's no love lost between Abigail and myself. But I don't know what other choice we have. You don't want your child to be with your parents, do you? Not if your father abused you, and your mother allowed it?''

Sandra swiped at her tears with her hand. "But I was a girl.''

"That doesn't mean your child's safe.'' Kate handed her some tissue. "There was also *physical* abuse by your father in that house, Sandra.''

Blowing her nose into the tissue, Sandra asked. "So what do I do?''

"We'll just have to get you out of here.'' Kate studied her client's face. The veil of secrecy was back. Even though she wanted to press her on the matter of James, she could see that Sandra had closed off. Better to wait. Tomorrow was another day.

"Sandra, I've got to get back to the office. We'll talk tomorrow. Under the circumstances, I'm going to ask for a continuance for your preliminary hearing.''

"No! I told you. No continuances. No delays!''

Kate sighed with frustration. Sandra's refusal to allow a continuance was reducing Kate's chances of being ready in time for the hearing. But the most serious problem was how to defend Sandra when she refused to tell her what had really happened.

36

After having lunch with Lauren and her father, Madeline left the restaurant in a quandary. She was certain she wanted to run for D.A. She also realized it took a lot of money to conduct a successful campaign. But she wasn't thrilled about some of the things Miles Cunningham had suggested.

Lauren's father had made it quite clear that to win, one had to be prepared to attack one's opponent unmercifully. Madeline hated negative ad campaigns. It was something she had promised herself she wouldn't resort to. Now here was this man promising her millions—but she had to do it his way. She also wasn't sure why Miles had offered to support her; it made her uneasy. He hadn't voiced what he expected in return. She was smart enough to realize she'd be beholden to him—that was obviously true in all political campaigns—but what was this man really expecting?

She wanted to discuss the matter with Philip. She trusted his judgment. Thank goodness Miles Cunningham wouldn't be back in town for several weeks. It gave her a little breathing space before having to commit to him.

What bothered her the most, though, was Lauren's attitude. She had acted positively elated at the prospect of Madeline's media advertisements attacking Kate. Why was that? she wondered.

Victoria paced as Abigail related her meeting with Kate.

"Sit down, Victoria," ordered Abigail. "You are beginning to make me nervous."

Aware she was the only one who dared to ignore her mother, Victoria kept moving. "I can't believe Kate Alexander talked to you that way. She doesn't realize who she's dealing with."

"Then we must show her, because I intend to keep my grandson here with me." Abigail's voice was firm. "It appears he is to be my only grandchild."

Victoria felt the words like a jab in her heart. If only she hadn't had that abortion when she was young, she'd be the one producing heirs instead of that slut Sandra.

Abigail continued. "Sandra is guilty. It would be wrong for her to be out on bail while James lies dead in his coffin. In spite of what that damned woman lawyer says, the child is better off here with me."

Victoria's thin lips curved into a smirk. "Kate Alexander really got to you."

"She is an ungrateful upstart. I already called and told

Charles that I am not happy with Kate. In the meantime, Victoria, make an appointment with the D.A. Get them to offer Sandra some form of compromise. I want Sandra to plead guilty in exchange for a lighter sentence.''

"A lighter sentence?"

"Yes. I want her gone for at least eight to ten years, if not more. That will give me enough time to mold my grandson into a proper D'Arcy. It will also ensure that Sandra does not get anything from James's estate. She is not allowed by law to profit, you know, from her wrongdoing.''

"I think you're absolutely right, Mother. I'll call Ms. Gould when I get home.'' She opened her compact and patted on some fresh powder, smiling at herself in the mirror. ''Do you also want me to give Kate a message from you?''

"She must agree to drop the entire abuse issue. In fact, see her first. Convince her to have Sandra plead guilty to a lesser charge.'' She gazed out the window. ''Yes, let us give Kate one last chance to realign her loyalties before I withdraw my political support. I would like to honor James's commitment but perhaps he saw something in Kate I do not.''

Victoria scoffed, ''She's a beautiful woman, if you like that Mediterranean look. James always did have a roving eye.''

"It is highly inappropriate for you to say such a thing."

Victoria gazed at her mother with amusement. How like her to deny her children's imperfections.

"Explain to Kate she is ruining her future."

"It will be my pleasure.'' Victoria closed her compact and dropped it into her Chanel bag. ''Well, goodbye, Mother. I have an engagement.''

"Goodbye, Victoria. Have a good time. Send Arthur up with my tea.''

Kate again found herself caught in terrible freeway traffic as she left Sybil Brand in East Los Angeles and went through the interchange downtown. She punched in one of the numbers on her car phone. "Charles, I have to talk to you. Can you wait for me? I'm stuck in traffic."

"Sure," he responded. "I've got plenty more to do before I leave."

When she got back to the firm, she found Charles in her office reading some papers on top of her desk. Her eyes narrowed in displeasure. "Do you do that often?"

He looked up and smiled. "Do what? Sit at your desk?"

"Look at my files," she said coolly.

He shrugged. "Sometimes. Is something wrong?"

She threw her briefcase down on the couch and came over to her desk. "Abigail insinuated that someone here is keeping her up to date on the progress of the case and I blew my cool."

"I know. She called. Unfortunately, she's not overjoyed with you at the moment."

"She's an interfering old witch. Is it you, Charles?"

"Is what me?"

"Are you the one feeding Abigail her information?"

His face became grim. "I'm only keeping Abigail informed in a general way."

"From what you read on my desk?"

"Absolutely not!" He glared at her defensively. "How can you even accuse me of that?"

She searched his face as if looking for clues. "I'm sorry," she finally said. "Sandra exhausts me and Abigail infuriates me. This whole thing is getting worse by the minute." She paused. "Could Dickson be leaking the stuff to Theo?"

"I'd certainly hope not!" He paused, rubbing his chin. "But I could be wrong. Maybe we better set up some security measures."

Suddenly exhausted, Kate sat down on the edge of her desk. "I think that's a good idea."

"O.K. We'll put the entire case under a lock code on the computer. Then I'll arrange for your defense team to have a support staff answerable only to you."

"Thanks, Charles, I appreciate it." She brushed a wisp of hair out of her eye. "The D'Arcy family seems to have its tentacles everywhere. And Abigail thinks *she* is God.''

''I know.'' He chuckled. ''When I first came to know them, I was overwhelmed too. I'd never met people like that before.''

''That makes me feel better.'' She sighed. ''At least I'm only one of the many pawns on her chessboard.''

''Glad to oblige.'' He put his arms around her, nuzzling her neck. ''You smell delicious.''

''Better stop or I won't be accountable for attacking you.'' She bit at his ear.

''Go ahead, attack me.''

''Here at the office, Charles?'' she mocked. ''What's the world coming to.'' She heard the noise of a vacuum cleaner; it was coming closer. ''The night staff's still here.'' She pulled away and walked behind her desk. She needed to broach the other subject that had been nagging at her since her meeting with Abigail. ''Charles . . . do you think it's at all possible James abused Sandra?''

He seemed surprised. ''Abused? What do you mean?''

''Could he have physically mistreated her?''

''Not that I know of.'' He shook his head. ''Of course, James did have a vile temper. I saw him lash out at many people over the years. What makes you ask?''

Kate filled him in on what she and Frank had found out in Bakersfield and what she'd learned from her meeting with Sandra.

''Just because her father abused her doesn't mean James did.'' He scowled at her. ''Frankly, I can't see it. James was a prominent man.''

''That means nothing. Abuse stems from the inability to tolerate frustration and pressure, whether you're rich or poor, employed or unemployed.''

Kate could see Charles was still skeptical.

''The gardener heard Sandra and James fighting,'' she added. ''Later he saw her with black and blue marks.''

A shadow darkened his strong face. ''I can't believe it. That's such a cowardly thing to do, hit a woman.''

''I know. It makes my blood boil.''

"If it's true, why didn't Sandra tell anyone? For God's sake, why didn't she come to me?"

Kate found herself jumping to Sandra's defense. "With her background, it's conceivable she was ashamed. In fact, she probably blamed herself. Women victims often do. Besides, would you have believed her?" she asked him with a touch of belligerence.

His eyes met hers with uncertainty. "I'm not sure."

"See?" she pounced. "So what would you have done? Spoken to James?"

He nodded.

"And that's exactly what she was afraid of. Then he would have made her life even more of a living hell."

"You're probably right. But it all seems so crazy."

"When I asked Abigail about it, she got furious and ordered me from her house."

"Now I understand why she was so angry. She didn't tell me what happened, just that she wasn't at all pleased with your attitude."

"I bet. Anyway, I expected her to deny it. Instead, her reaction was very inappropriate, like I had touched a nerve and she jumped." She drummed her fingers on the cushion of the sofa. "You know, it gave me a funny feeling. Like she had something to hide."

"And what would that be?"

"I'm not sure. I worked sex crimes as a prosecutor. Very often with physical abuse, there's a family history of it." She leaned forward. "What was the relationship between Abigail and her husband like?"

"For heaven's sake, Kate, William D'Arcy was an exemplary man!"

Kate watched Charles's face grow somber. "He was one of the few Democrats chosen to be an ambassador during the Republican years. The man was friends with kings and queens. He sat on the World Bank. Why, he had more honors bestowed on him than any other man I can think of."

"That doesn't mean he wasn't a brute."

"Kate, you and I come from middle-class backgrounds.

You don't know the kind of man you're talking about.''

"Charles, I don't care how much money he had, the man could still have been an abuser.''

"An abuser of whom? His wife? His children?''

She shrugged. "Either or both.''

"Well," he sniffed. "Excuse me if I have a hard time seeing Abigail stand still for something like that.'' He paced back and forth and stopped in front of her. "As far as the boys, he was a very strict father. That much I do remember.''

"Strict in what way?''

"He had quite a temper.'' He smiled grimly. "James told me many a time that his father, quote, beat the shit out of him.''

"See, there you are.''

"I doubt it. The world's filled with people who believe in hitting their children. That doesn't make them wife beaters.''

"And it doesn't mean it's right to use corporal punishment on someone weaker and smaller than you. There are also degrees—say, a paddling on the behind as opposed to punching or socking.''

He threw his hands up in the air. "Kate, if I were you, I'd drop it. What difference does it make anyhow?''

"Charles, I'm surprised at you. If Sandra was abused by James and she felt she couldn't get away from him, and if she killed him . . .'' She stopped. "It could make all the difference in the world. I might be able to get her off on self-defense.''

He turned to her, his face grave. "Kate, tread softly. Make sure first, absolutely sure, that something like that really did happen. Angering Abigail could ruin your career. Up until now she's said she'll endorse your campaign. Even though she can't be as vital as James was to us, her name carries a lot of weight, and I didn't like the way she sounded on the phone.'' He placed his hands on her shoulders. "I've worked my ass off positioning you. The governor's all set to back you for the next election. For God's sake, Kate, don't throw it away.''

"I have to do what's right,'' she said softly.

Madeline closed the dishwasher and went in search of her sons and Philip. As she came into the living room, her heart skipped a beat. Philip was on the floor with Jud on one side of him and Kenny on the other, putting together the train set her parents had bought Kenny for his birthday a few weeks ago. It had been a long time since she'd seen either of her boys look this happy.

Damn that ex-husband of hers. Why was he such a louse? Just because their marriage hadn't worked out was no excuse for Sam not to have a good relationship with the boys. But even if you were still married to him, it wouldn't have mattered, a nagging voice inside her said. Sam had always been selfish and self-centered, never helping even when the kids were little.

She thought of Gary. He was such a passionate lover, but so moody, brooding over the least little thing. Would he ever patiently explain something to her sons the way Philip was doing?

Every time she mentioned the kids, Gary seemed angry. He acted like he resented the time she spent with them. Could a grown man be jealous of your children?

Later, she and Philip sat alone in front of the fireplace. He was sipping the coffee she'd just brought out with a plate of oatmeal-raisin cookies. "I can't thank you enough—" she started to say.

He put up his hand. "If it's for spending time with your kids, I'm here because I want to be."

"Thanks." She paused and ran her finger up the side of her cup.

A silence fell. "You know, you've never really told me about your wife, Philip."

"It's still hard to talk about it," he replied softly, then stared off into the fire.

"Then don't," she said quickly. "I understand."

"No, that's . . . that's okay. I'd like to tell you." He paused. "We met in college. When Rosemary went on for a master's degree in business, I went to law school. After my graduation, we got married. We planned to have chil-

370

dren, but first we wanted to get our careers started and save up some money to buy a house. You know, the American dream.''

"I remembered wanting the same thing. What happened?''

"Things went great for about five years,'' he continued. "Then, when she was trying to get pregnant, the doctor noticed a lump on her breast.'' His voice broke and he stopped talking for a minute.

"How awful,'' she murmured. "It was malignant?''

"Yes. We had to stop trying to have a child until she was done with the chemotherapy. After about a year, just when everything seemed to be O.K., it appeared again.'' His words emerged quietly. "This time they did a double mastectomy.''

"Oh Philip, I'm so sorry.''

He shook his head. "It was pretty traumatic. But Rosemary was a fighter and it looked like she was going to make it.''

"And then?''

"Suddenly, it was back.'' He stopped and coughed.

She tried to think of some reply but none came.

"It was the beginning of the end,'' he went on. "She somehow lived another three years, but they were hell for her.''

"And for you too.''

"Yeah. Anyway . . .'' Tears appeared in his eyes and he glanced away.

"I couldn't even begin to imagine it,'' she said honestly. "How long has it been?''

"Five years.'' He put his cup down.

"Are you dating at all?''

"I didn't for almost three years,'' he admitted. "Then people insisted I was being morbid. Actually, they didn't want a nice, single, Jewish lawyer going to waste.''

She chuckled. "But one shouldn't spend his life alone.''

"Funny, that's what I was thinking about you.''

She looked up, surprised. "Oh, but I have the children. Besides, I date.''

"You still seeing Gary Sutter?"

She shrugged. "I'm not really sure."

"Oh?" His brown eyes looked troubled.

"Well, after I confronted him with what you told me . . . he didn't deny it, you know. He just said you had misunderstood."

"And how was that?" he asked, his voice low.

"Gary only wanted to be assigned to the case too. That's what he meant by saying it was too much for me."

"And you . . . you believed him?"

"Honestly, Philip, I don't know what to think."

He chewed on his lower lip for a minute. Then he suddenly stood up. "It's late. I better be going."

She was caught off guard. "I got a couple of videos. It's only ten."

He released a tense breath. "I've a lot of work to do."

"But it's Saturday night." She suddenly wanted to explain how she wasn't sure about her feelings for Gary. On the other hand, maybe Philip wasn't even interested in her explanation.

Gary kept insisting that Philip was in love with her. She watched him as he put on his jacket. For the first time, the possibility that it was true hit her; she felt a momentary sadness. She adored Philip. He was such a dear friend. He just didn't inspire the passion that Gary did. But the last thing she wanted to do was cause Philip more pain.

"Good night," he said, opening her door.

She wanted to ask him if he had meant what he said about doing this again, but the words stuck in her throat.

Philip sat in his car for a long time, not even taking out the keys. He was filled with feelings for Madeline that he thought were dead. At the same time, he found himself trying to push those feelings away. He had suffered so much over Rosemary he didn't want any more pain. But he was also tired of being numb.

With a last look at the lighted window he knew was her bedroom, he took a deep breath and expelled it loudly. Then he started the car and pulled away.

37

Lauren twirled her new diamond ring around her finger as
the elevator climbed to the twenty-sixth floor. It wasn't
quite as big as she would have liked, but then Andrew was
a novice at dealing with someone of her background and
taste. He'd learn. Or better yet, she'd train him. By the time
their first anniversary rolled around, he'd be fully indoctri-
nated into the art of making her happy. She shivered as she
remembered their lovemaking last night. That was one area
in which the man knew how to please her royally.

Stepping into the lobby of Manning & Anderson, she
took a deep breath, excitedly preparing to brag about her
good news. For years she had painted a smile on her face
while poor little secretaries and paralegals flaunted their
engagements and marriages in her face. At thirty-three, she
had begun to feel like an old maid. Although she had done
her best to make people think that was the way she wanted
it, in her heart she'd known all along it wasn't true.

However, things were finally going her way, and as soon
as she was named a partner in the firm, she'd take a leave
of absence. She needed at least six months to plan the
extravaganza she intended to make of her wedding. She
knew her daddy would give her an unlimited budget, and
she was going to do her best to spend it.

One hour later, almost the entire firm had congratulated
her and gazed admiringly at the five-carat diamond sparkling on her hand. Even those who had not bothered to
come out into the hallway to see what all the commotion
was about had not escaped the news of the impending marriage. She had merely flung open the doors to their offices
and announced her good fortune.

Only one person remained to be told. She glanced irritably at the clock on the wall. The nerve of Kate having a client in her office at a time like this: I'm dying to see her face when she hears I'm going to be Mrs. Andrew Stewart. She stopped at Kate's secretary's desk. "Buzz Kate and ask her how much longer," she demanded.

"I'm sorry, Miss Cunningham," said Mary, "but Ms. Alexander said she wasn't to be disturbed."

Lauren sighed with frustration and started to walk away. Shit. Suddenly, she turned around and grabbed the phone on Mary's desk, quickly punching in the number of Kate's intercom.

"Yes?" answered Kate, sounding irritated at the interruption.

"It's Lauren. I know you have a client, Kate, but I need to see you for one quick minute. It's very important. Can you step out to the hallway?"

Kate hesitated. "I'll only be—"

"Please," implored Lauren.

"All right," sighed Kate.

A minute later, Kate came out, making no attempt to hide her annoyance. "What's so important it couldn't wait?"

"This!" shouted Lauren, triumphantly shoving her long red fingernails and the sparkling gemstone in Kate's face.

Kate looked shocked. "Oh," was all she managed to say.

"It's from Andrew," bragged Lauren. "We're getting married!"

"Congratulations," mumbled Kate.

Lauren caught the glance Kate gave her secretary. Her poisoned dart had hit Kate hard.

"I really have to get back to my client," Kate said quickly. She turned and walked away.

Ha! thought Lauren happily. That'll show the bitch not to mess with me or my man.

After her client left, Kate stood at the window. She felt even more foolish now about her indiscretion with Andrew and prayed she had maintained her dignity in front of Lauren.

"Kate?"

She turned. It was Charles.

"You seem thoughtful," he said quietly.

"I was thinking about how the cycle of life keeps going around . . ." Her husky voice trailed off.

"Ah," he said, with a knowing look, "the southern belle's engagement has you down."

She colored slightly. "Well . . . yes . . . I suppose so." Her green eyes lingered on his face for a second, hoping for some kind of reassurance. "You wouldn't believe the way she told me." The moment the words were out of her mouth, she realized she had made a mistake. If Andrew had truly meant nothing to her, why on earth did she give a damn?

His eyes narrowed. "I see. Soon you'll be wearing a ring too," he said gravely. "You have my word."

"I know." Feeling herself near tears, Kate began to sift through the papers on her desk. "This is an article by Brenda Kelsey, M.D., the psychiatrist I'm planning to have see Sandra. She's one of the leading authorities on battered wives. I thought you might want to meet her with me."

"Aren't you putting the cart before the horse? From what you've told me, Sandra has yet to admit James abused her."

She appraised him somberly. "It's only a matter of time, Charles. Trust me, I know it's true. In fact, I'd stake my life on it. And when Sandra breaks down and admits it, I need to have a defense ready for her. I've got to be ready to show the jury she felt trapped, frightened, powerless."

"The Battered Wife Syndrome?"

"If need be. Would you like to be in on the discussion?"

"I can't. I'm swamped. I'm sure you'll do what's right." He glanced at his watch. "I've got a meeting with the curator of the county museum on behalf of the D'Arcy Foundation. I'm going to be late."

"I'll walk you out—I've got to leave something at the front desk."

As they entered the reception area, Charles was called back by his secretary, Nancy, and returned to the inner offices. At that same moment, the elevator opened and coming straight at Kate, tall and blond as ever, was Andrew Stewart.

His eyes brightened when he saw her. "Kate, how are you?"

"Fine," she said coolly, praying he'd walk on by. She didn't want to have to speak to him.

"Aren't you going to congratulate me?" He cocked his head to one side as he smiled at her.

"Congratulations." She looked him in the eye. Then, before she could stop herself, she blurted out, "Odd, though, how quickly you went from having no relationship with Lauren to getting engaged."

His eyebrows arched in wry amusement. "It was the truth at the time." He held her gaze, his look becoming decidedly more intimate. "You could have prevented this, you know."

The man's arrogance was staggering. "Please," she scoffed, "spare me. It's easy to see you were merely using me." She turned to go.

He reached out and stopped her. "That's not true. This all happened with Lauren after you wouldn't see me anymore. Can't we at least be friends?"

As she tried to pull her arm back, she heard Charles at her side.

"Is something the matter?" His voice sounded testy.

"No . . . uh . . ." She was at a loss for words. She hadn't heard Charles come back, but now he stood there glowering at Andrew like a lion protecting his mate.

"Charles Rieman, this is Andrew Stewart," Kate said quickly. "Andrew is the lucky man who has just become engaged to Lauren."

"Glad to meet you." Charles spoke through clenched teeth.

"There you are, Andrew," called Lauren, coming into the lobby and rushing forward to grasp Andrew's arm possessively.

If Kate hadn't been so upset, she would have laughed. This whole scene was so ludicrous—Charles standing ready to defend her honor while Lauren pried her fiancé away from the harlot.

"Congratulations. I hope the two of you will be very happy," said Charles dryly, his jaw rigid.

"Why, thank you, Charles," drawled Lauren, while Andrew merely smiled. "Now, if you'll all excuse us, my daddy's waiting to take us to lunch."

As the elevator closed on them, Kate found Charles's dark eyes regarding her closely. She knew he wanted to ask, wanted to know what had really happened between her and Andrew. But he wouldn't. She'd made it clear to him the night they'd reconciled. The subject of Andrew Stewart was off limits.

"You all right?" he asked, his brows knitted together.

"Of course."

He seemed to hesitate for a moment. "Then I'll be going. Will I see you tonight?"

"Call me here. I'll be working late."

After he had left, Kate walked to the window and stared vacantly out at the scenery below. In spite of his denial, she still believed Andrew had used her. But what good did it do to regret her actions? She had been so angry at Charles. And Andrew certainly hadn't forced her. No matter how much she now wished it hadn't happened, it had.

Kate almost felt sorry for Lauren because of the way Andrew's eyes had undressed her a few minutes ago. That was one man who would always stray. Even Lauren and all her money wouldn't be enough to keep him faithful.

At the same time, she had hoped he'd go the way of all Lauren's past boyfriends, and there had certainly been scores of those. At least then she and Lauren would have had a chance to salvage what was left of their friendship. Now Kate sincerely doubted that was possible.

Mary escorted Victoria D'Arcy Mandeville and her brother, Theo, into Kate's office and directed them to the client chairs while Kate came around to perch on the edge of her desk.

"We've come to talk to you about Sandra," said Victoria, immediately taking charge.

Waiting for Victoria to continue, Kate took in her thin, pinched face. Theo looked tired, his face haggard and drawn.

"First," advised Victoria, "we'd like your word that what we say here is confidential."

"I can't promise that. Sandra is my client," explained Kate. "Not either one of you."

Victoria moved her shoulders in such a way that Kate knew she wasn't pleased, while Theo looked clearly uncomfortable.

The woman went on in her overbearing manner. "We feel it would be best if Sandra pleaded guilty."

Trying to hide her surprise, Kate asked. "Best for whom?"

"For everyone. A long, drawn-out trial will only smear the D'Arcy name. Besides, that unemployed actor . . ." She gestured. "What's his name?"

"Tommy Bartholomew."

"Yes. Well, he's already admitted he killed James. It doesn't take a genius to figure out he didn't get the idea by himself."

When would the D'Arcy family stop trying to manipulate things? Kate wondered as she forced her voice to be friendly. "I'll relay your concerns to my client. But it's up to her."

"What about my nephew? Think of what this publicity is doing to him."

"It's not good," agreed Kate. "But he'd benefit the most from his mother's acquittal."

"Not likely." Victoria shook her head. "You should reconsider. There are advantages to be gained from doing as we ask . . ."

Kate heard what sounded like a warning in her voice. She leaned forward. "I'm afraid I've said all I can on the subject."

The woman's thin lips curled into a sardonic smile. "One

word from my mother and your career could be over like that." She snapped her fingers.

"Victoria, for God's sake," broke in Theo. He turned to Kate, his face flushed with embarrassment. "Please forgive my sister. She's overwrought. We all are."

Kate nodded, relieved to hear that Theo didn't approve of Victoria's behavior. How dare the woman threaten her.

His sister sallied on, unperturbed. "Mother related to us your nasty accusations against my brother James. You deeply offended her."

"I'm sorry," said Kate, "but I had an obligation on behalf of my client to ask."

"James was never abusive," insisted Victoria. "It's a vicious lie."

"I've someone who says it's true."

"Who?"

"I'm afraid I can't say at the moment."

"They're lying." Victoria's eyes glittered with anger.

Kate turned to Theo. "Mr. D'Arcy, do you have anything to add? Did you know of any abuse?"

He looked down as if unable to meet her gaze, playing instead with the watchband on his wrist.

Victoria answered for him. "Of course not." She pointed her finger at Kate. "If one word about James being a wife beater gets out, we'll sue you for slander."

Sliding off the desk, Kate walked around to her chair. With one hand on its back, she said firmly, "I don't believe we have anything further to discuss."

"You'll regret this." Victoria stood up. "Let's go, Theo."

As he looked at his sister, then back to Kate, she saw the indecision on his face.

"I'm sorry." He held out his hand to Kate.

"Are you coming?" shouted Victoria from the door.

"Tell Sandra I send my best," said Theo hoarsely.

"And . . ." He hesitated, then his words tumbled out. "Do whatever you think is right for her."

"Thank you." She reached out and shook his hand.

He gave her a brief smile before he followed his sister out the door.

* * *

"Some brother you are," fumed Victoria on the way home.

"You had no right to threaten Kate," he protested. "She's only doing her job. You said we were merely going to discuss the possibility of Sandra's pleading guilty. I wouldn't have come if I'd known you were going to threaten her lawyer."

"That bitch only cares about the notoriety she's getting. Every day her name is in the paper. While our good name is being dragged through the mud."

"She can't help that." He found himself defending Kate. "It goes with the job."

"She doesn't have to give out those damn press releases, or even speak to the media, as far as I'm concerned. Now, are you coming to see the deputy D.A. with me?"

"Absolutely not. I couldn't stand to watch a replay of what just occurred."

Victoria peered at her brother with apparent scorn. "You always let me do the dirty work," she said nastily, "while you sit on the sidelines and shake your head."

As Theo glared back at her, a frightening thought struck him. My God, she was beginning to act more and more like James every day. And James had become just like his father. He sighed as he thought of the years he'd spent trying to please his family. For some reason Theo had never been able to understand, he'd never measured up. Not even his fashionable art gallery and his growing reputation in the art world mattered to any of them.

When Sandra came on the scene, he'd found himself rather liking her. Maybe it was because she looked up to him. Other than Sandra, it seemed only Dickson understood how Theo felt—most likely because Dickson couldn't seem to merit his father's approval either. It was something they had in common.

* * *

After Theo and Victoria left, Kate thought about their visit. Did the D'Arcys really believe Sandra was guilty, and was that why they didn't want a trial? Or was it more insidious than that? Were they afraid of something? Or did they want her out of the way because of the child? It was obvious the family didn't feel Sandra was good enough to be the mother of the heir to their kingdom.

Victoria was calculating and ruthless, like Abigail and possibly James, on whom the jury was still out. Kate had seen two different sides of James the night before he died; she still didn't know which was closer to the real man. Theo was the family member she found most interesting. Sandra had said he was the only one in the family who'd ever been nice to her. Kate had seen something in his eyes today, but she wasn't sure what.

She drummed the top of the desk with her fingers as she remembered the argument she'd heard between James and Theo the night before the murder. Apparently, the animosity between the brothers was no secret. Even Charles had told her James and Theo didn't get along. But why did Theo think his brother had changed his will? So many things didn't make sense, and her intuition told her Theo was hiding something.

Grabbing a folder off the pile, she began to look for the police report that had been handed over by the prosecution. Her eyes scanned the list of names. There it was: *Theodore D'Arcy, brother of the murder victim. Mr. D'Arcy states he was home alone that night. There is no one to vouch for his story.*

38

"**T**hanks for coming," said Theo as he opened the door for Dickson.

"You sounded quite upset."

After they were settled in the living room, Theo began to pace the room. "I . . ." He hesitated, as if searching for the words.

Dickson tried to put his friend at ease. "Whatever's bothering you, you can tell me."

Theo cleared his throat. "I need some advice."

"That's why I'm here."

"Look, let me start at the beginning." Theo took a deep breath, exhaling loudly. "Kate Alexander's claiming James abused Sandra."

Dickson's eyes widened in surprise. "Really?"

"Yes," mumbled Theo. "But this isn't for anyone's ears but your own."

"Of course."

"Thanks," sighed Theo. "As you can imagine, my mother's quite upset."

"Ah yes." Dickson chuckled. "Poor Abigail. But where on earth did Kate get such an outlandish idea?"

"Well . . ." Theo peered at Dickson. "Kate insists it wasn't Sandra who told her and Mother tends to agree. She says Sandra wouldn't dare make up such an outrageous lie."

"Do you have any idea who would?"

"No."

Dickson crossed his leg. "So you want me to find out?"

"Not exactly."

"What then?"

"What if . . ." Theo's voice cracked. "What if . . . hypothetically, I knew it was true?"

Dickson leaned toward him. "True that James abused Sandra?"

"Right."

"Do you know such a thing?"

Theo's voice was very low. "Let's keep it hypothetical."

"O.K. So, hypothetically of course, what's the question?"

"Just this," said Theo, looking nervous. "If Sandra's attorney asked me if I had any knowledge that James abused Sandra and I denied it . . . am I breaking any law?"

Dickson sat back, trying to understand what was going on. "No. Not unless she asks you the question under oath. In that case, if you lied and they could prove it, it's perjury."

"I see."

"I'm afraid I don't," said Dickson. "What is it you really want to know, Theo?"

"Do I have a duty to tell what I know . . . to anyone—hypothetically, that is?"

"Only if it's pertinent."

"And how do I know that?"

"Let's say," Dickson explained, "hypothetically of course, that James did abuse Sandra. What of it?"

"Well . . . wouldn't that be a defense to his murder?"

Dickson laughed. "There was no sign of a struggle, and someone has already confessed to pulling the trigger. Remember Tommy?"

"Yes, but if—"

"Look, if James was mistreating Sandra she should have gone to the police. You can't hire someone to kill for you, no matter how good the reason."

"But what if she was too afraid to go to the police?"

Dickson crossed his other leg and patted the crease into place. "If you truly want my opinion . . ."

"I do. But Dickson, you have no idea what a real bastard James could be."

"I think I do, Theo. But that's beside the point." He tugged on the cuff of his shirt, measuring his words carefully. "My advice to you is to say nothing. Don't volunteer one word."

"And if I'm asked the question on the stand?"

"We'll cross that bridge if we ever get to it."

"Thank you for seeing me," said Victoria.

"No problem," responded Madeline. "We like to keep the victim's family up to date on the proceedings. So let me tell you what you can expect to hear at Sandra's upcoming preliminary hearing—"

Victoria cut her off. "I didn't come to discuss that. I need a favor."

Madeline's face grew somber as she evaluated James D'Arcy's sister. "A favor?"

"Well"—Victoria smiled—"why don't I explain my family's position on all that's been happening?"

"Go ahead," urged Madeline, suddenly wary.

"Our first and primary concern is my nephew. My mother and I believe the longer this murder trial goes on, the harder it will be for him—if not now, then in the future."

"I'm sure that's true, but—"

"Let me finish," snapped Victoria. Then, as if realizing she'd been offensive, she immediately apologized. "Please forgive me." She put her hand to her heart. "It's just that I'm so upset."

"Of course."

Victoria took a deep breath. "This is all such a strain on us," she said, her voice breaking.

"I can imagine." Madeline handed the woman a tissue.

"Let me ask you something." Victoria wiped her eyes. "You do believe Sandra is guilty . . . don't you, Ms. Gould?"

"Yes, of course. That's why I'm prosecuting her."

"Well my family"—Victoria dabbed at her nose—"wants you to know there's no doubt in any of our minds that . . . that Sandra is guilty."

"Let's hope the jury feels that way too."

"That's just it. We don't want a jury to decide this."

384

Madeline clucked sympathetically. "I'm afraid that's not up to me. The right to a jury belongs to the accused."

"I mean, we don't want it to go to a trial."

"I don't understand." Madeline's brow knitted.

"We want Sandra to plead guilty."

"Again," explained Madeline, "that's not up to me."

James's sister was suddenly animated. "You could make it attractive enough so that Sandra couldn't refuse."

"I—"

Victoria hurried on, waving the tissue at Madeline. "Offer Sandra whatever you have to, as long as she pleads guilty. We want her to spend at least ten years in jail."

"I can't—"

"Of course you can."

Madeline was becoming perturbed. Every time she opened her mouth to speak, Victoria cut her off.

"I've been told you want to run for D.A. next year?" A faint smile of amusement appeared at the corners of Victoria's thin lips.

"I've thought about it."

"My family could be of tremendous help."

Jesus! thought Madeline, shocked. This woman was offering her a bribe! Maybe Victoria was too distraught to realize what she was saying.

"I'm sure you didn't mean that to sound the way it did. Let me explain how this works. Legally, I mean. After the police bring us their evidence, our office decides whether or not to press charges. And if so, what the charges are to be. We also make all decisions about a plea bargain. We discuss it with the family of the victim as a courtesy. And although we like to take your feelings into consideration, if possible"—her voice was confident—"this office makes the final decision."

"Of course," agreed Victoria.

Madeline stood up to indicate the meeting was over. "I hope I've answered your questions."

"One more thing," said Victoria, also standing. "We don't want Sandra out on bail."

"I've opposed bail and I'm expecting Sandra's lawyer to

bring a motion any day, which I'll also oppose. But the final decision is not up to me but a judge.''

"Well, thank you so much for seeing me and for listening to my family's concerns,'' said Victoria sweetly.

As Madeline walked her to the door, she was baffled. Had Victoria offered her a bribe, or had Madeline imagined it?

Kate rushed into Charles's office. "Frank called. He's got a lead on Maria, the maid who worked for Sandra.''

He glanced up from the papers he was working on. "Where is Frank?''

"In San Diego. He followed Maria there but she'd already left for Mexico. He thinks he can catch up with her across the border.''

Charles frowned. "Mexico can be more trouble than it's worth.''

"I know,'' agreed Kate. "But Frank can handle himself and he speaks the language well enough to get by.''

"The Mexican police don't like it if certain procedures are not followed.''

"This isn't a police matter,'' she insisted. "It's just a missing witness.''

His handsome face was thoughtful for a moment. Then he brightened. "If you issued a subpoena for her, Frank could probably get some cooperation down there.''

"No, Charles. I don't want to do that. I don't want to scare Maria away. I believe she was in the country illegally and was terrified by the police, afraid they'd turn her into immigration.''

"She couldn't have been illegal. James wouldn't have hired her.''

"I think Sandra hid the truth from him because she felt comfortable with Maria.''

"I still—''

"Charles, I know what I'm doing. I came in here to see if you would initial the release of funds so I can wire them to Frank.'' She waved a piece of paper at him. "Rita said I needed a partner's O.K. on this.''

His brow furrowed. "Franklin instituted some emergency measures around here for the next few weeks—in order for me to get things squared away on the D'Arcy estate. He put that ass Dickson in charge of initialing expenses."

"Damn!" Kate's green eyes flashed with impatience. "Charles, I can't be expected to do my job without access to funds. My department can't work that way."

"Listen, let me see what I can do. How much do you think Frank needs?"

She held out her fingers. "Well, there's motels, a rented car . . ."

"Bribes," he added.

She grimaced. "You said it, I didn't. I guess about three thousand to begin."

"Fill out the necessary forms and I'll try to sneak it through."

"Thanks, Charles," she said, relieved. "You're a life-saver." She threw him a quick kiss and rushed out.

Kate was preparing a motion to suppress certain evidence in Sandra's upcoming preliminary hearing, when Dickson strutted into her office. He waved a piece of paper in her face. "You must think we're made of nothing but money."

She tried to hide her annoyance at the interruption. "I'm afraid I don't follow you."

"This." He hit the paper with his hand. "You just requested three thousand dollars for our private investigator to go to Mexico."

Her heart sank. It was obvious Charles's attempt to by-pass Dickson had not worked. "It's of the utmost importance," she insisted.

"*That* is a matter of opinion."

Kate had a sickening feeling he wanted to see her squirm. Well, if that's what it took, she'd oblige him; Frank was waiting. "Why don't you have a seat and let's talk about this sensibly." She gestured to a chair. "I need the testimony of the Hispanic woman who took care of Jimmy D'Arcy, for Sandra's upcoming trial."

"So . . . you don't need her for the preliminary hearing next week?"

"No. I don't expect to put on a defense. I'm just planning to cross-examine the state's witnesses and try to lock them into their testimony."

"Is that wise?"

"In my professional opinion, yes. It would be a mistake to tip my hand at the preliminary hearing as to any defense I may put on at the trial. I don't want the state lining up a million expert witnesses to contradict my witnesses."

"And what defense *are* you contemplating for the trial?"

Kate didn't want to discuss it with Dickson. She wasn't sure she could trust him. Especially in light of the visit paid to her by Victoria and Theo. At the same time, she couldn't afford to anger him.

"I'm waiting," he prompted irritably.

She studied his face for a moment longer before answering.

"Self-defense is one possibility. I think James abused Sandra."

"I don't care what you think. It never happened."

"I can appreciate your feelings, but I have to defend my client as I see fit. And I need the money."

"I think your requisition of funds is unnecessary. But if you insist, I'll bring it up at the next finance meeting."

She squinted at him suspiciously. "And when is that?"

"In a few weeks." He smiled as if enjoying himself.

"That's no good. Frank has a viable lead now. The woman may disappear in a few days, let alone weeks."

"Then that will just be too bad, won't it?" He started to leave.

Kate almost lost it. "You won't get away with this kind of interference, Dickson. I'll go to your father."

"And I'll say you're lying. Then I'll personally see that you are thrown out of this firm on your ass." He calmly walked to the door, where he turned and waved the piece of paper. "Do you still want me to put this on the agenda for the meeting?"

"Absolutely," she said, through clenched teeth.

After he left, she had to wait for her shaking to stop. She was so angry she couldn't see straight. Grabbing the phone, she started to dial Charles's extension. Then she put it down. He had enough on his mind. She'd tell him about it later, when he had a free moment. Why was Dickson doing this to her? To get back at Charles? Or was it the other matter?

Thinking quickly, she called her secretary into her office. "Mary, I want you to arrange to wire Frank three thousand dollars on my personal credit card. He's in San Diego at this address." She handed her card to the young woman with a slip of paper.

"Sure," said Mary, taking the things.

"And Mary . . ." Kate hesitated.

Her secretary appeared curious. "Yes?"

"Don't tell anyone, and I mean *anyone*, not even the senior partner, about this, O.K.?"

Mary smiled. "You can trust me, boss. Mum's the word."

39

"**H**ow are you?" asked Kate when Sandra came into the attorney's room at the jail.

Sandra shrugged. "O.K., I guess."

Kate looked at her client's pinched face. She was beginning to show the strain. Her eyes were puffy, as if she'd been crying, and there were deep circles under them. She looked ten years older than the night Kate had first met her. Thinner too. "I want to spend time today getting you up to speed for the preliminary hearing. What to expect. What happens. What it all means. That sort of thing."

"I only care about getting out of here."

"Let's do this my way, O.K.?"

Sandra slouched down in the chair. "Shoot."

"First off, I want you to wear something simple. Not sexy."

Sandra frowned. "I thought this wasn't in front of a jury."

"It's not, but even a judge can be biased sometimes. I want to make sure you have everything going for you."

"Whatever." Sandra gnawed on her nail.

"I'll go over to your place and pick out the clothes I think appropriate," said Kate. "You need anything while I'm there?"

Sandra seemed surprised. "You're going?"

"Victoria was going to do it, but after yesterday . . ." The moment the words were out, Kate could have bitten off her tongue.

"What happened?"

Kate explained the visit she'd received from Victoria and Theo and the things they had asked of her.

"That bitch!" cried Sandra. "And Theo too?"

"Yes. But he got quite upset with Victoria."

"A hell of a lot of good that does me." Sandra's voice was bitter. "I can't believe she'd do that to me."

Kate didn't mention the threat Victoria had made about her own career being in jeopardy. Sandra had enough to contend with. "I'd like to believe they were thinking of Jimmy." Her voice fell flat, even though she tried to make it sound like the truth.

Sandra was too smart to be fooled. "Those bastards think I'm guilty, don't they?"

"Could be." Kate's eyes solemnly met Sandra's. "By the way, did Tommy and Theo ever meet?"

Sandra shook her head. "Why?"

"Nothing. Just wondered." She drummed her fingers. "You called Theo the night of James's death, didn't you?"

"Yeah. But he didn't answer. I left word on his machine."

"And was that before or after you called Charles?"

"After. Hey, what's the matter?"

"Just trying to get a few things straight." Kate took out a pad of paper. "Let's get you ready for the hearing. If you're bound over for trial, we'll discuss the D'Arcy family in more detail. O.K.?"

"I can't wait! How long's the damn hearing anyway?"

"Anywhere from a few days to weeks, depending on how many witnesses the state calls," explained Kate. "Now as for what goes on in the hearing itself, the prosecutor, Madeline Gould, puts on the state's case by calling witnesses who'll testify to facts or inferences she wants to put into evidence. A court reporter takes down every word. After she finishes with each witness, I cross-examine and try to weaken or damage the effect of their testimony. In some instances, I may choose not to cross-examine a witness, reserving it for the trial."

"Why?"

"I may not want to tip my hand before the trial."

"When do I get to say I didn't do it?"

"Not at this hearing."

A dark cloud came over Sandra's features. "But I want to."

"I know. But if I put you on the stand, the prosecutor gets a chance to cross-examine you. That's dangerous. She'll want to show you lied, like about meeting Tommy in the parking lot."

Sandra angrily slumped back in her chair.

"Anyway, the purpose of a preliminary hearing is to determine if there's sufficient evidence for the judge to bind you over to trial."

"What's bind mean?"

"Hold you over for trial, as opposed to dismissing the charges. My job is to pick apart the testimony of the state's witnesses, poking as many holes in it as I can. Once in a while, the defense gets lucky and the judge finds there's not enough evidence to warrant a trial. But that rarely happens, so don't count on it."

Sandra's expression remained sullen.

"Next," said Kate, "I want you to be prepared for what

will be said about you. It'll look bad, and it won't be fun. The state only calls people who'll tell the story they want the judge to hear. They won't call witnesses with favorable information.''

"That stinks. Why can't I tell my side?''

Kate took a deep breath. "I don't believe in presenting a defense at a prelim. Now if you had an alibi . . .'' She gestured with her hand. "Say, you could prove you didn't know Tommy at all before he was arrested. That's an affirmative defense and I'd put on evidence as to that fact at the hearing.''

"I have an alibi,'' protested Sandra, her eyes alive for the first time. "I was in the house when he was shot.''

Kate shook her head. "You weren't accused of pulling the trigger. The charges against you are conspiracy and murder. You could have been with the President, it wouldn't matter.''

"But if people only hear the bad things, they'll think I'm guilty.''

"It's hard, I know. But I want you to understand the difference between a preliminary hearing and a trial. At the prelim, the state's only got to show there's a strong probability you committed the crime. At trial, the state's got to convince a jury of your guilt beyond a reasonable doubt. That's much more difficult.''

"I want to tell them I didn't do it!'' insisted Sandra stubbornly.

"The more often you testify, the more chance there is you'll contradict yourself. The prosecutor can use that against you. Best to save your testimony for the trial.''

Sandra's eyes smoldered. "What's the fucking use? No one believes me anyhow.''

Kate hesitated. She needed to choose her next words carefully. "Sandra,'' she said quietly, a serious expression on her face, "you've got to level with me. If James abused you, I need to know *now* so—''

Sandra jumped up. "I'm sick of you not believing me. I'm fucking innocent.''

"I didn't say—''

"I'm sick of it!" yelled Sandra, her face red with anger. "Do you hear me? Sick, sick, *sick* of it!!"

"Why don't you tell the truth, damn it!!" Kate's voice rose too as she slammed the table with her fist. "Maybe I can get you acquitted. Or at least get a reduced charge." She forced herself to speak more calmly. "I need to know—so I can prepare a burning bed defense."

"There's no burning bed," shouted Sandra, "whatever the hell *that* means!!"

Kate gestured again. "It was a case about a woman who was so terrified, so powerless, so helpless that she set the bed her husband was sleeping in on fire, in order to escape his terrible beatings."

"You're kidding?"

"No," said Kate gently.

"What happened to her?"

"She got off."

Sandra chewed on her lower lip as she looked down. Finally, she said, "I didn't kill him."

Although Sandra kept protesting her innocence, Kate wasn't sure. "O.K.," she said, hoping that soon her client would trust her enough to tell her the truth. "It's your life."

"What's left of it," scoffed Sandra.

Madeline stuck her head into Philip's office. "Hi, got a minute?"

He looked up and motioned for her to come in. "Sure."

She couldn't help but notice that instead of giving her his usual warm smile, he was noticeably subdued. She gazed at his face, remembering how handsome and youthful he'd looked at her house that night. Was he still upset with her?

"What's up?"

"Victoria D'Arcy Mandeville just left here." Madeline proceeded to tell him what had happened.

When she'd finished, Philip said, "Sounds like a bribe."

"It did to me, too," she admitted. "But given the circumstances. I mean . . . she kept apologizing and saying how awful this whole thing was for her and the rest of the D'Arcy family. And that they were all under a lot of stress."

She watched his attractive, boyish face as he sucked on his unlighted pipe. "How did you handle it?"

Madeline filled him in.

"Did she bring the election thing up again?"

"No. She just mentioned it that one time."

He peered at her, his voice quiet but firm. "What would you like to do about this?"

She hesitated. "I think I'd like to forget it."

"Why is that?"

"I want to give the woman the benefit of the doubt. I mean with her . . . with James D'Arcy's being murdered . . . and Sandra and her boyfriend on trial . . ." She stumbled for a second, searching for the right words. "The publicity for the family must be terrible."

"Would you like to sleep on it?"

"Yes." Her eyes brightened. "Yes, I would."

"Good. Why don't you do that. Then we'll talk about it tomorrow." He started to fiddle with the papers on his desk. "Now if you'd excuse me?"

She felt her cheeks burn. "Of course. I'm sorry." Madeline rushed out his door, feeling oddly embarrassed. Philip had never been short with her before. Whatever had happened between them the other night, she prayed it hadn't ruined their easy and open working relationship. She adored the man. In fact, she admitted to herself with a stab of remorse, he was her best friend. What on earth would life be like without that friendship?

Kate and Sandra were still preparing for the preliminary hearing, when Kate stood up to stretch. "Now for the difficult part," she explained as she held her hands up over her head. "Tommy's testimony against you."

"He's lying, you know!"

"Why do you think Tommy would lie?"

"They must have scared him, forced him to say he did it."

"Sandra . . ."

"Tommy didn't do it," she protested angrily. "He couldn't have."

"What if he did it because he cared about you?"

Sandra's chin jutted out stubbornly, but she said nothing.

"You've got to be prepared. Tommy's going to repeat all the things he's already admitted the two of you talked about. Like wishing James were dead. I've brought you a transcript and I want you to study it."

"It's not a crime to wish somebody dead."

Kate took a deep breath. "It's time you told me about Tommy and you."

"I met him. I slept with him. That's it!"

It was Kate's turn to pace the room. "I can't defend you if you won't talk to me. Something you think's not important may be. I've got to be the judge of that, not you." She came to stand in front of Sandra. "We can take it one step at a time and we'll be here all night. Or you can start talking."

Sandra pulled a cigarette out of her pocket and Kate gave her the matches. "I met him at exercise class. He looked like a movie actor, with sexy eyes and that blond hair. We started to talk."

"What did he tell you about himself?"

"He's from Kansas. He's got a mother and a sister, older than him. His father's dead. Tommy fucked around a lot and almost didn't graduate high school. At eighteen, he joined the army."

"Go on."

"He always wanted to be an actor. So after the army, he came to Hollywood. He rented a studio apartment in Northridge, signed up for acting, dance, and exercise classes, and got a job with a construction company. He worked mornings, so by three o'clock he was through and could go to class."

"What did you like about him?"

"He listened to me," she said wistfully. "I never had a

real boyfriend. My father wouldn't let me date.'' There was a tinge of bitterness to her voice. "He didn't want me to give the boys any of what he was getting."

Kate cringed at the thought of a father keeping his daughter for himself. No wonder Sandra had fallen for James, an older man to take care of her. To be the father she never had. "What else?"

Sandra's voice faltered. "At first . . . Tommy and me, we'd grab a cup of coffee after class, or a yogurt, and just talk about movies and TV. Nothing much. It kind of made up for not having boyfriends when I was younger. I was only eighteen when James and I got married . . .''

Kate leaned forward, prompting her to continue.

"James . . . was so . . .'' She stopped; her fingers fiddled with the fabric of her garment. "Other than Jimmy, Tommy was the only good thing in my life.''

"Was it that bad living with James?"

She nodded. "Everything had to be perfect. I had to dress a certain way. My hair just right. I used to feel like a doll, all dressed up. But then I was just supposed to be there, looking good, keeping quiet. He and his friends didn't give a damn about me—what I had to say, what I liked or didn't like. They didn't think I had opinions about anything.''

"And Tommy was different?"

"Yeah." She shifted in the chair. "We talked a lot. Hours, every day. We became kind of like . . . well, like best friends. I told him things I never told anyone before.''

"Did you tell him about the incest?"

Sandra looked down. "Yeah.''

"How'd he take that?"

"He thought that a guy who did that to his daughter was scum and didn't deserve to walk the streets.''

"Did he blame you in any way?"

"Oh, no!" Her chin jutted out proudly. "He believed me.''

"And when did your relationship become more?"

Sandra shrugged and coughed.

Kate wanted to tell her not to smoke, but held her tongue. "Please continue, Sandra. You're doing just fine.''

"We started going to the park. We'd lie there talking. One day he kissed me . . ." Her voice cracked.

"And?"

"It was nice."

"Then what happened?"

"We . . . started to get heavy. You know . . ." She fidgeted. "It just kept getting more and more."

"Where did you first sleep with him?"

"In the back of his car. We were lying on the grass when all of a sudden it started to rain. We were laughing so hard I almost peed in my pants. We barely made it to the car. Our clothes were wet . . ." She didn't finish.

"Go on," urged Kate.

"Well, you know, one thing just led to another."

"And after that first time?"

"We started to go to his place."

"And that's what you did for the next four months?"

"No. Sometimes we went to a movie or to get a hamburger."

"Do you think James suspected you were having an affair?"

"He would have killed me!" The words were out before Sandra realized what she had said. "I mean . . ."

"It's O.K. You don't have to pretend."

"I only meant—he would have wanted to kill me."

"I see." Kate judged her client shrewdly. Not wanting to stop the story, she didn't press her about her slip of the tongue. "Did you feel guilty about having an affair?"

Sandra shrugged. "I knew it was wrong to sleep with another man, when you're married and all that. But with Tommy it seemed O.K. I wasn't taking anything away from James. I never refused him sex, you know . . . or anything."

Kate thought that was a strange way to refer to making love with your husband. "Did you and James have a good sexual relationship?"

Sandra ignored her. Kate tried another route. "Did you and Tommy talk about love?"

"He said he loved me."

"Did you love him?"

"I guess so."

"Ever talk about marriage?"

Sandra became wary again. "A little. He wanted to marry me. I told him James wouldn't give me Jimmy *and* a divorce."

"How did you know that? Had you ever asked him?"

"Yeah. Once, after a bad fight. I don't even remember what it was about now. I told him I hated him and wanted a divorce."

"What did he say to that?"

Sandra paled. "He laughed. Told me to go right ahead. He wouldn't stop me." Suddenly, she burst into tears.

Kate handed her some tissues and waited.

Finally, she continued. "The bastard said he'd give me money—more than my prenuptial agreement said he had to give me—if I'd get the hell out of his life." Her voice dropped. "Just as long as I left my baby with him."

Oh God, thought Kate, shocked. That sounded like the cruel side she had seen in James the night of the party. The hateful things he had said to Theo came rushing back into her mind. "Did that scare you?"

"Yeah." Sandra wiped her eyes. "He told me how he'd gotten all the judges elected and there wasn't one judge in Los Angeles who would give me my child." She sniffled.

"That's not true," said Kate quietly.

Sandra seemed startled. "It's not?"

"No. He was just trying to frighten you."

"Bastard!"

"Did you tell Tommy?"

"I told him there was nothing we could do."

Except murder him, thought Kate. But she didn't say it. "You know, Sandra, there are those who say that when a man threatens to take a child away from his mother, it's just another form of abuse. Verbal abuse. Sometimes it can be as bad as the other kind. Often they go hand in hand."

Sandra said nothing, just coughed.

Kate despaired of ever getting the truth out of her. "I told you about Dr. Kelsey. She's coming to see you tomorrow. I want you to tell her the things you've just told me. Sandra, I want you to tell her everything. O.K?''

"Yeah, O.K.," said Sandra in a softer voice, sounding almost like a child.

Kate stood up to leave. "We'll continue tomorrow."

Back at Manning & Anderson, there was a phone call from Frank with no message and no phone number. Kate was upset. Then she remembered her instructions to Mary: Tell Frank not to say he's calling from Mexico. Maybe no number was a good sign. She prayed he found Maria before it was too late.

40

Mary brought the psychiatrist into Kate's office and Kate stood up to greet her. "I appreciate your coming here today, Dr. Kelsey. We have quite a job ahead of us."

The doctor responded with a smile. "I'm glad to help."

She looks like a kindly, gray-haired grandmother, perfect for the witness stand if need be, thought Kate as she came around her desk and gestured toward the couch. "Please, let's sit down over here."

Before she left, Mary asked, "May I get you something, Doctor?"

"Why, yes, thank you. A plain cup of tea, if it's not too much trouble."

"And you, boss? The usual?"

"The usual will be fine, Mary," said Kate.

While they waited, Kate asked the doctor a few general

questions. After her secretary brought the tea and Kate's coffee, Kate got down to business. "I'd like to tape our conversation so I can go over it if I have to."

"Go ahead."

Kate turned on her machine. "Can you tell me, Dr. Kelsey, what you thought of Sandra in general?"

"Please call me Brenda."

"And I'm Kate."

"Good. Now to Sandra. She's an extremely defensive person," said the doctor. "Basically very much a hurt child; one who, unfortunately, learned at an early age that the world did not get any better as she got older. And that hurt has colored her entire personality."

"I had that sense of her too," confessed Kate.

"I can understand why you found Sandra so difficult to work with," continued the doctor. "She has a hard outer shell and it's nearly impossible to break through it, even for me, and I've had years of experience with that type of patient. It's going to take more time for me to get through to her, but with your permission, I'd like to try."

"Absolutely." Kate leaned toward her. "As I told you on the telephone, everyone I've talked to, from Sandra's parents to her schoolteachers to her foster mother—they've all indicated that Sandra told lies." She took a sip of her coffee. "Needless to say, that makes it very difficult for me to defend her. Unfortunately, the police and the D.A. have caught her in some lies—stupid lies. And they're hoping that because of those lies, a jury will find her not credible and convict her."

"Sadly," said Brenda Kelsey, "lying is one of the ways Sandra learned to deal with the incongruity of her life. After all, the rules handed down at the dinner table were broken in the darkness of her bedroom or in the bathroom. Added to that is the knowledge that her mother knew and did nothing to help her. Certainly that exacerbated the situation. In fact, in most cases of incest, the girls end up hating their mothers even more than their fathers."

"I see," said Kate, noting that the doctor had just confirmed what she herself had gleaned from her reading on the subject of incest. "Perhaps it would be best if you tell me what new information, if any, you found out about Sandra's past. Then we can talk about whether the past has any bearing on the present, and how I might use it in Sandra's defense."

"Good idea." The doctor nodded. "One of the things I discovered is that Sandra seems to have specific phobias which are consistent with my belief that she suffered emotional, physical, and sexual abuse as a child. For instance, Sandra is terrified to this day of being in the shower."

Brenda Kelsey stirred her tea. "Her fear is so bad that she has to force herself to shower. As we talked, I began to suspect that she was often bent over the toilet or in the shower when her father penetrated her."

Kate felt the bitter bile of her anger rising in her throat as the doctor went on.

"Another area that's significant is that Sandra remains afraid to be alone in the dark. There were many other things she also backed away from: She has difficulty making friends, although it's hard to distinguish whether this stems from her childhood abuse or something that came later. She had difficulty having an orgasm. I believe that changed with Tommy—who, by the way, appears to be the only one Sandra has even remotely allowed to pierce her defenses. But she remains very closed off. I don't have to tell you how hard it is to get her to talk."

"Like pulling teeth."

"Anger control is another aspect. Sandra appears to be chronically angry."

"I can certainly attest to that," Kate agreed with a rueful smile. "Most of the time, I feel I'm going to lose it with her."

Brenda Kelsey gave Kate a sympathetic nod. "That's very understandable. She's a trying person to be with. And Sandra's ambivalent about you too. At first, she said she didn't like you because James's mother shoved you down her throat. Sandra hates the woman and possibly with good reason."

"Definitely with good reason."

"I want you to know, however," added the doctor, "that Sandra has come to respect you greatly." She put her cup to her lips, then set it down. "For one thing, you've never lied to her. That's very important. She's beginning to trust you."

"I'm glad to hear that, even though I'm afraid my patience often wears thin."

Brenda Kelsey's eyes reflected her empathy. "That's because someone like Sandra goes about getting what she wants the wrong way. The more she wants love, the more she tends to push people away. It's the same thing with understanding, et cetera."

"I've done little to help her then."

"Don't blame yourself. There was no way for you to know. And besides, that's not your job."

Kate glanced at the doctor with gratitude. Then she drummed her fingers on her legal pad. "You know, Brenda, as horrible as Sandra's past was, I'm not sure I'll be able to enter any of it into evidence unless it's relevant. For instance, if Sandra's husband abused her and if we could show that the trauma she experienced as a child left her emotionally damaged . . ." Her words hung in the air. "What I'm getting at is this. Say, for argument's sake, that when James started to physically abuse Sandra, all of her old anger at her father erupted violently against James. Does that scenario strike you as plausible?"

Brenda Kelsey folded her hands. "I haven't been able to find out whether or not there was any physical abuse by Sandra's husband, although I'm certain he was abusive in many other ways. From what she said—and didn't say—I gathered her sexual relationship with her husband was less than pleasant for her. She merely submitted. That's usually a sign. Also, she was in mortal fear that he was going to take her child away from her if she did anything to anger him. The combination of those things is very damaging to a woman who was already severely damaged coming into the marriage relationship. However, if he did in fact abuse her, I'd say your hypothetical is very possible."

"O.K.," said Kate, jotting down a few notes.

"What bothers me," asserted the doctor, "are the highly complex coping mechanisms that Sandra, like so many victims of incest, developed in order to distance herself emotionally from what was going on in her daily life."

"Can you explain that to me in lay terms?"

"I'll try. Sandra tries to numb herself out by not being present in her own body. She also has trouble feeling reality—in other words, being able to tell what is truly real, and what people actually mean."

"That opens up a whole set of new possibilities," said Kate, her mind working quickly.

"Why don't I finish what I'm saying and then you can ask questions?"

"Please."

"Sandra admits that she and Tommy discussed how to eliminate her husband." Dr. Kelsey paused. "But I must tell you that just talking about it for Sandra might have been sufficient to release a lot of her pent-up anger at both her father and her husband. It's very possible that she cannot even distinguish between what she wanted to have happen and what actually happened."

Kate underlined some words on her legal pad.

"That is to say, Sandra might have just been blowing off steam in telling Tommy she wanted him to kill her husband. And Tommy believed her and went ahead and did it without Sandra realizing he was actually going to do it."

Kate stood up and began to pace. "You're talking about a complicated defense. I'd have to show the judge and jury that Sandra didn't plan the murder of her husband in cold blood, because she wasn't attached to reality enough to understand the implications. Thus, without intent, the charge moves down to manslaughter." Kate shook her head. "I'm not sure it would fly. Especially if we have no other evidence that James abused her." She peered at the doctor. "Do you have any reason to doubt that Sandra knows the difference between right and wrong?"

"No. In a legal sense, she knows the difference."

Kate sat back down. "Brenda, do you have any idea why

Sandra might not want to tell the truth about being abused? I mean, after all, James D'Arcy is dead.''

"I believe she's still frightened."

"Of what? He can't hurt her anymore."

"I sense it's his family. I have the feeling they've intimidated Sandra in some way not to tell what really happened."

"Of course," muttered Kate. "I should have guessed."

"I wouldn't be so hard on myself," the doctor rushed to assure her. "Sandra's a tough little cookie."

"True," agreed Kate. "But I've also had a hard time dealing with Abigail." She shook her head sadly for a moment. "Well, what's done is done. Is there any way we can help Sandra overcome her fears now and get her to tell us the truth?"

"I'll need to work with her a little longer before I can answer that."

"We're right up against it, Doctor, timewise." Kate sighed. "But I guess we have no choice." She chewed on her lip. "Let me ask you a few more questions. Did Sandra tell you why she bought the gun?"

"Yes. She wanted it for protection after the burglary."

"Was she able to explain why she waited until six months after the burglary to purchase it?"

"Not really. She just said she didn't get around to it."

"I see. Do you think it's possible Sandra bought the gun without ever thinking of using it against James?"

"Absolutely."

"And do you also think it's possible she innocently showed the gun to Tommy?"

"Yes."

"I'll tell you what I'm faced with. Tommy says he killed James—so we accept that as fact even though Sandra insists it's not true. So here are the possible scenarios." Kate shifted in the chair to find a more comfortable position before continuing. "Either the whole murder was Sandra's idea and she bought the gun and paid Tommy to do it; or she bought the gun, discussed murdering her husband with Tommy, then forgot about it or changed her mind, and he did it anyway. Or, she bought the gun the way she said, and although she and Tommy discussed getting rid of James, she had no idea he'd take her seriously and actually kill her husband."

Brenda Kelsey smiled. "I can see now what you're up against. Obviously, a lot depends on what Sandra says she did, and—"

"And she's a liar. So how do I prove anything?"

"Not easily."

"We're talking about a tenuous defense at best, even without a client that lies, but I may have no choice. Unless . . ." Kate hesitated. "Unless I can convince the prosecution to reduce the charges based on your examination of the defendant."

"Is that possible?"

"Anything is possible. But is it likely? No." Kate was silent for a minute. "The preliminary hearing is due to start tomorrow. Sandra has forbidden me to ask for a continuance. I'm afraid we'll have to go forward. Maybe you'll be able to break through to her and get her to tell us the truth. Then we'll use self-defense at the trial."

"I'll help in any way I can," promised Brenda Kelsey.

Kate glanced at her watch. She had so much to do before tomorrow. But something was nagging at the back of her mind. "One more question, Doctor, because it's getting late for both of us. Did Sandra's childhood experiences predispose her toward picking an older man for a husband, one possibly similar to her father?"

"Ah, Kate," Dr. Kelsey said, "that is a lot more than one more question. Let's leave that for further exploration. However, I will say that abused children often find themselves in abusive situations when they get older. Sandra's father, by sexually abusing her, in fact betrayed her. It's likely she very well may have been looking for another father."

Kate held up her fingers. "One more tiny question. Is a betrayal also considered abandonment?"

"Very often."

"I see," said Kate quietly, turning off her recorder. "This has been very illuminating. With your help, we just may be able to find out what really went on in that mansion in Bel Air.''

"I'll do my best,'' promised the doctor.

And I will too, Kate promised herself as she saw Brenda Kelsey to the door.

After the doctor had gone, Kate sat on the couch, absorbed in her own thoughts. Could she use what she had learned today to help her client? Most of what Dr. Kelsey had told her wasn't relevant to the preliminary hearing, which was something they had to get through to find out if Sandra would be facing a trial. On the other hand, if the doctor found evidence of abuse by James, maybe Madeline could be convinced to reduce the charges. Of course, the prosecutor would argue that Sandra didn't kill James herself, so the abuse only indirectly affected Sandra's motivation.

But if Sandra didn't have the necessary intent . . . maybe she could make a deal.

As the shadows deepened in her office, Kate didn't rise. Something the doctor had said disturbed her. Had the death of Kate's father when she was only eight affected her in a similar way to what had happened to Sandra? Death was abandonment. Did I also turn to an older man in a search for my father? She shook her head. Sandra was twenty-five years younger than James. I'm only thirteen years younger than Charles. That makes quite a difference. Or does it?

Inside the Criminal Courts Building, Kate took the crowded elevator up to the fifth floor and, passing the people gathered in the hallway, entered the division where Sandra's hearing was being held. She recognized the bailiff standing at the door in his smartly pressed khaki and tan uniform. "That's quite a mob out there," she joked.

"Yeah," he agreed. "You should have seen the line of folks waiting outside the building when I got here this morning. It was something else." He looked at the clock on the wall. "Soon I'll be counting off the lucky ones who get to come in."

"I hadn't expected so many spectators for a preliminary hearing."

He chuckled. "When they're rich and famous like the D'Arcy family, the public's dying to hear all the messy details. Better than going to the movies."

"And cheaper too," she noted. "See you," she called to the bailiff as she went through the courtroom to where they were holding Sandra, stopping only long enough to brush a speck of lint off her navy-blue suit.

"How you feeling?" she asked her client, who was wearing a black wool skirt and light gray sweater, her blond hair falling softly around her colorless face.

Sandra's voice was testy. "Like the fucking queen of England!"

Kate realized Sandra was probably scared but wouldn't admit it, even to herself. "Everyone's nervous at first," she said, reaching over to squeeze her hand in encouragement.

Sandra pulled back from Kate's touch. It was a curt reminder for Kate that even though things had improved between them, they were still not good. After meeting with Dr. Kelsey, however, Kate was sure she understood her client better. At least she'd promised herself to try harder. "After a few days, you'll get used to the routine," she said.

"I'll never get used to it." Sandra's bloodshot eyes showed clearly she'd been crying as well as not sleeping.

Kate also noted that Sandra had a cough and a runny nose. She knew that the body's defenses often broke down under stress. After all, it was Sandra's life that hung in the balance. Looking at her watch, Kate ushered her client into the courtroom, showing her where to sit at the defense table.

"Excuse me. I'll be right back." Kate felt bad leaving

her there, but since she was still in custody, Sandra wasn't allowed to go beyond the courtroom or even to the public rest room unless escorted by a bailiff.

In the hallway, Kate saw the television newscasters setting up. The media circus was about to begin. She made a quick call to the office. Coming back into the courtroom, she saw that Madeline had arrived and was busily organizing her paperwork.

Madeline's glance shifted from her papers to the defendant. The press was having a field day with her. You could always count on sex, blood, and money to sell. In her wool skirt and sweater, Sandra hardly looked like a femme fatale today. But Madeline wasn't fooled by appearances. As if reading the D.A.'s thoughts, Sandra glanced up. Then her blue eyes darted away. She can't look me in the eye, thought Madeline.

Sitting next to the defendant was Kate. Although her future as well as Kate's could be riding on the outcome of this case, Madeline had to admit that she greatly admired Kate for her poise in the courtroom. She'd seen many a witness collapse under Kate's skillful barrage of questioning.

A distinguished-looking man walked in to take the seat directly behind Kate and Sandra. Madeline recognized him as Charles Rieman, one of the top partners at Manning & Anderson and the man who would testify as to the provisions of James D'Arcy's will. He had also apparently been good friends with D'Arcy. How did Rieman feel about the defendant? Madeline wondered.

"All rise, the Honorable Judge Henry Jackson presiding."

Everyone in the courtroom stood as Judge Jackson entered and took the bench. He was a tall, heavyset man with dark skin and an intelligent face. Madeline had been glad to get him, as he was a no-nonsense, tough judge. The large room hummed with anticipation, the onlookers anxiously awaiting the beginning of the preliminary hearing as if the curtain were about to rise on a Tony-winning drama.

As *The People v. D'Arcy* commenced, she silently wondered if the cold-blooded murder of James D'Arcy would be avenged. Certainly, she would do her best to make it happen.

"The people call Dr. Neil Bernard," said Madeline, and in a firm voice began to direct her questions to one of the county pathologists, a slender, small-boned man with a florid complexion. His speech was clipped, as if he knew exactly what to say, nothing more or less than was required.

Madeline, who had called the doctor out of order to accommodate his busy schedule, led him through a lengthy, routine set of questions to establish his qualifications. She expected Kate to rise at any moment and stipulate that the defense would accept Dr. Bernard as an expert in pathology and forensic medicine, but for some unknown reason she chose not to.

Finally, Kate stood up. "Your Honor, I think we can stipulate to the doctor's expertise."

Madeline shot her a look that conveyed, What in the hell took you so long?

The judge directed that the record reflect their agreement, and Madeline went on. After establishing that Dr. Bernard had performed the autopsy on James D'Arcy and that he had personally supervised all of the necessary organ and tissue studies, she asked him for his findings as to the cause of death.

"I concluded that James D'Arcy died from a gunshot wound to the head," said Dr. Bernard.

He also testified that he had fixed the approximate time of death as between 5:45 and 6:30 on the evening of February 25 and that he had made this determination based on the contents of the victim's stomach, the degree of rigor mortis, and the degree of lividity from pooled stagnant blood in the parts of his body on which he had fallen.

To Madeline's next inquiry, he explained how he had removed a bullet from the dead man's brain and turned it over to the crime lab to run ballistic tests.

Kate's cross-examination of the doctor lasted less than two minutes.

Next up was the patrol officer who had received the help call from his dispatcher at 6:20 on the evening in question. He testified that he arrived at the scene a few minutes before the paramedics and that a neighbor was there to greet him, but Sandra was not. He also testified that he felt for a pulse, determined James D'Arcy was dead, and called for homicide. Then he went up to the house to see Sandra D'Arcy.

When the officer finished, Madeline called on each of the police officers who had collected and preserved blood samples and other crime-scene evidence, clearly establishing the chain of evidence.

When it was her turn, Kate did her best to poke holes, trying to show sloppy police work wherever possible, but without much success. It looked like the police had preserved a clean chain this time.

Kate noticed how Madeline seemed to be hitting her stride as she waited for the next witness on the stand to answer her question. He was Jeffrey Kimbell, owner of Kimbell's Sporting Goods. After establishing that he owned the store and was familiar with all types of guns, most particularly weapons like the one that had probably killed James D'Arcy, Madeline went on.

"Have you ever seen the defendant, Sandra D'Arcy, prior to today?"

The store owner nodded.

"Mr. Kimbell," said Judge Jackson, "please answer yes or no. The court reporter cannot acknowledge a shake of the head."

"Sorry," said the man, clearly embarrassed and uncomfortable.

Madeline repeated the question.

"Yes, I have," he answered.

"And where was that, Mr. Kimbell?"

"She came into my store to buy a gun."

"You're positive that it was the defendant who bought a gun from you?"

He pointed. "Yes, that's her sitting right over there."

Madeline faced the judge. "I'd like the record to reflect

that Mr. Kimbell has identified the defendant as the same woman who came into his store.''

"The record will so reflect," said Judge Jackson.

Madeline turned back to the witness. "Can you please tell us when you first saw the defendant?"

"During the first week of January of this year."

"Did you help her?"

"Yes, I did."

"Did the defendant ask for anything in particular?"

"She asked for a gun she could keep by her bed at night."

"Did she in fact buy a gun from you, Mr. Kimbell?"

"Yes."

"And would you tell us what kind of a gun that was?"

"A .22 Ruger semiautomatic."

"Did you sell the defendant any ammunition for the gun she purchased?"

"Yeah. A box of .22 rounds."

As Madeline continued with the witness, Kate took copious notes which would be vital when her turn came for cross-examination.

"Did the defendant say anything else to you at that time?" asked Madeline.

"Yes, she did."

"Would you please tell us what she said?"

"She asked me to demonstrate how to load and unload the gun, and how to use the safety."

"And did you do that, Mr. Kimbell?"

"Yes."

"Would you please tell us in your own words what happened next?"

"I remember the store was real quiet that day. I left my assistant, Bob Clay, in charge and I took Mrs. D'Arcy over to the area where I usually like to demonstrate. I showed her several times how to put the ammunition in and cock the gun."

"Was this live ammunition you were demonstrating?" Madeline asked.

"Oh, no. Although I sold her live ammunition, I always demonstrate with blanks."

"I see." She strode back to her table and picked up a pad of yellow paper as if checking on something. When she turned back toward the witness, she asked him to identify the registration slip Sandra had filled out when she purchased the gun and which he had given to the police.

"Did Mrs. D'Arcy come back to claim her weapon after the registration period was over?"

"Yes."

"And when was that?"

"Exactly two weeks later, at which time I personally gave her the gun and cartridges."

"Thank you," said Madeline; then, looking over at Kate: "I have no further questions of this witness, Your Honor."

Kate stood up to begin her cross-examination. After going over several points, Kate asked Mr. Kimbell, "Did Mrs. D'Arcy tell you for what purpose she needed a gun?"

"Yeah. Her home had been burglarized and she wanted a gun for protection."

"Did she tell you anything else about that burglary?"

He rubbed his chin for a moment. "Not that I can think of."

"Mr. Kimbell, is it not a fact that the defendant told you that after the burglary, her husband insisted that she buy a gun?"

The store owner looked puzzled for a moment, then responded, not as definitely as he had earlier: "I'm not sure."

Smiling at him in the hopes of instilling confidence, Kate asked softly, "Mr. Kimbell, this is very important . . . and I ask that you search your memory again to the best of your ability. Isn't it true that the defendant identified herself as the wife of James D'Arcy?"

As if suddenly remembering, he sat up. "Yes, I think she did."

"Did Sandra D'Arcy inform you that her husband had purchased guns and ammunition from you previously?"

"Yes, I believe she did," he said, looking unhappy.

Kate had accomplished what she set out to do, by establishing an element of doubt as to Sandra's purpose in buying the gun. "No further questions," she said as she sat down.

Next on the stand was the criminalist, a short black man with a graying beard.

Sandra squirmed in her seat next to Kate as he testified that the footprint found by the police in the mud near James's body matched the footprint made from the boot found in Tommy's room. He also testified that the soil sample taken from the bottom of Tommy's boot matched the one taken from the ground near the body.

"Why are they putting on all the stuff about Tommy if he says he did it?" whispered Sandra to Kate during a fifteen-minute recess.

"The prosecution has to prove each element of the crime so we have a chance to cross-examine the people that testify against you. It's a fundamental right that belongs to you as a defendant, and Tommy's actions don't waive it for you," explained Kate.

Sandra frowned and bit her fingernail.

With court back in session, Madeline continued to question the criminalist. In answer to one of her questions, he said, "The bullet taken from the body was fired from a .22 Ruger semiautomatic. And the bullet was consistent with a .22 Ruger semiautomatic as listed on the sales receipt and gun registration for the gun Mrs. D'Arcy bought."

"In your opinion, could the gun Sandra D'Arcy bought have been the murder weapon?" asked Madeline.

"Yes."

"That's all I have for this witness."

Kate's cross-examination was brief. "Mr. Smith, were you given any weapon to test-fire?"

"No."

"So then you wouldn't be able to say for sure that the bullet came from that particular gun purchased by the defendant, Sandra D'Arcy?"

He squirmed in the chair. "No, I can't."

"Thank you." She turned to the judge. "I have no further questions of this witness."

"You may step down," said Judge Jackson.

As Kate turned to go back to her seat, her eyes scanned

the room. Theo D'Arcy was there. He sat looking forward. He seemed dejected, almost sad. Next to him, glaring at her with unmasked disdain, was Victoria D'Arcy Mandeville.

I bet you're going straight over to your mother's house to report every word that is uttered here today, thought Kate, staring back. I'll probably get a call from dear old Abigail tonight, telling me again how she wants me to throw the fight, won't I, Victoria?

42

Driving downtown the next morning, Kate listened to the newscaster on the radio. He told his listeners that the coroner, ballistics expert, and gun shop owner had all offered testimony that implicated the defendant, Sandra D'Arcy, in the murder of her husband. God, it was amazing how they could make it sound like a perfect package, neatly wrapped and tied with a bow.

Preliminary hearings frustrated Kate. She could only hope to make small inroads into the testimony of the prosecution's witnesses, forced to wait until the trial to put on a plausible defense for Sandra. But just what was that defense going to be? Was it going to be self-defense or not? Damn, why didn't Frank call? Why was it taking so long to find Maria?

The courthouse seemed even more crowded than the previous day. Bodies were jammed one against the other and overflowing every bench in the hallway. Kate wondered if Sandra's parents would show up today. She had called to tell them the place and time, but had yet to see them.

When Kate strode into the courtroom, she spotted Madeline joking with several police officers who were waiting to testify. The prosecutor's face was glowing. It's all going her way at the moment, thought Kate. No wonder she looks so happy.

Kate went to greet her client. Sandra's face looked flushed and her cough was worse as she waited, huddled in the holding cell. Today she was wearing a simple beige wool skirt and white sweater, her blond hair caught back in a barrette.

The first witness that morning was the neighbor who saw the white, late-model car leaving the scene the night James was killed. He told how he had seen the body and the blood and rushed up the hill to the D'Arcy house, bringing Sandra back down with him. When she saw her husband, she became hysterical, he said. He testified further that he did not know if James was dead or not, but was too afraid to touch him, for fear of causing him more harm. He said he told Sandra to call the police from the cellular phone in James's car, which she did. Afterward, she raced back up to the house and he waited by the car for the police.

"Did the defendant look to see if her husband was alive or dead?" asked Madeline.

"No."

"Thank you," said Madeline.

After several preliminary questions, Kate approached the witness. "Mr. Winter, you've testified that it was very dark that night. Is that correct?"

"Yes."

"You're positive, sir, you saw a male driving a white car away from the scene that night?"

"Yes."

"Are you also positive, sir, that the male you saw driving away that night was Caucasian?"

"Yes."

"You've also testified that there was only one person in the car that night, correct?"

"Yes."

"Mr. Winter, would you please tell us if you need glasses to assist you in any way?"

"Well, uh, yes. Sometimes."

"What do you wear glasses for, Mr. Winter?"

"Usually driving."

"Isn't it true that you have a restricted license, Mr. Winter?"

"Yes."

"Were you wearing your glasses during your walk the night in question?"

He suddenly seemed confused. "I'm afraid I don't remember."

"You don't remember whether or not you were wearing your glasses that night?"

Mr. Winter thought for a moment. "I must have been wearing them because I saw the partial license plate."

"But you're not sure?"

"I must have been."

"Mr. Winter, can you state unequivocally that you were wearing your glasses when you saw the car fleeing the scene the night in question, yes or no?"

"Ah, I must have—"

"Your Honor, please instruct the witness to answer with a yes or no."

The judge leaned over and instructed the witness.

"Now, Mr. Winter, I ask you that question again and I remind you that you are testifying under oath. Did you have your glasses on while out walking your dog on the night of February twenty-fifth?"

"I don't remember."

"Thank you. Mr. Winter, had you ever heard gunfire before the night in question?"

"No."

"Now, you've testified that you ran up, got the defendant, and brought her down to the street. How did the defendant react when she first saw her husband lying there?"

"She put her hand to her mouth. Her eyes were opened wide, like she couldn't believe it, and then she looked at me. I thought maybe she was in shock. So I told her to go around to the other side of the car, reach in, and call nine-one-one."

"And did she do as you instructed?"

"Yes."

"You told this court that after the defendant made the call, she ran back up to the house?"

"Right."

"Did she say anything to you before she did that?"

"Yes. Something about being afraid her son might wake up."

"Have you ever seen someone panic at the scene of an accident?"

"Not that I can remember. But it's very possible she could have been in shock."

Madeline moved to strike the last part of his answer as nonresponsive and the judge sustained her objection.

"Mr. Winter, based on your own personal experience, can you state one way or the other whether the defendant panicked the night in question after seeing her husband?"

"Objection," said Madeline. "Lack of foundation. Calling for an opinion he's not qualified to make."

"Your Honor, I'm merely asking for his own personal observations," said Kate.

"I'll allow it."

Mr. Winter fidgeted in his chair. "No. I don't know whether Mrs. D'Arcy panicked or not."

"I have no further questions." As Kate sat down, she felt good about the points she had made, even though Tommy was going to testify it was he in the car that night. She didn't like to give the prosecution one free piece of evidence. She had also shed a different light on Sandra's actions.

Madeline next called Detective Bower to testify. Wearing his best suit, he took the stand. She took him quickly through his arrival at the crime scene and what he had found.

"The body was facedown," he said, "and there was blood splattered on the driveway."

Madeline asked him some specific questions about the crime scene, and the detective took out a copy of his report and consulted it before answering. When she asked him about the condition of the ground where the footprint had been found, he testified that it was muddy. He also reiterated that the gardener had given them a statement to the effect that he had watered the grounds that same afternoon.

She deftly elicited from Bower details of the anonymous phone call he had received disclosing that Tommy Bartholomew was the killer and that Tommy was having an affair with Sandra D'Arcy. He explained that he ran a D.M.V. check on Bartholomew and found that his license plate matched the partial tag number the neighbor had given them. He then related how he and Donaldson went to question the defendant and, after seeing Sandra, went to see Tommy Bartholomew.

Bower next described his questioning of Tommy and Tommy's signing of the consent waiver to the search of his apartment. He also described the talk in which Tommy admitted to seeing Sandra at least four or five times a week for the last four months, and admitted the intimate nature of their relationship. Madeline next asked him about the note found at Tommy's apartment.

"Detective, did Tommy Bartholomew tell you that the defendant loaned him money and that it accompanied the note you're holding?"

"Yes. He told me Sandra D'Arcy loaned him two thousand dollars for his rent. And that she put it in an envelope with this note and left it with his manager."

"In a subsequent interview with the defendant, did you ask her about the same loan?"

"Yes," said Bower. "I asked her if she'd given Tommy Bartholomew any money with the note."

"What was defendant's answer?"

"She said she'd loaned him five hundred dollars."

Kate, watching Madeline, could not suppress an ex-prosecutor's respect for her approach. Her questions were smooth and short, presented in a way that got the information across clearly and developed a rhythm that led up to the important points. Breaking that rhythm was Kate's job. However, with Bower, it would not be easy. He was a seasoned officer, used to taking the stand.

Madeline continued: "Did you also ask the defendant when she'd last seen Tommy Bartholomew?"

Bower's head nodded as he said, "Yes."

"What did the defendant respond?"

"Last time she saw him was five days before her husband's death."

"Did you have reason to disbelieve her statement?"

"Yes. I had photos taken by an undercover officer showing that the defendant met with Tommy Bartholomew in a market parking lot a few days after D'Arcy's death."

"Did Tommy Bartholomew admit this meeting to you?"

"Yes."

Sandra's lies are going to bury her, thought Kate.

Madeline continued:

"Did he tell you what the purpose of the meeting was?"

"Yes," responded Bower.

"And what was that?"

"He said they'd met for her to give him one thousand dollars."

"Was anything else discussed, according to Bartholomew?"

"Yes. The defendant told Bartholomew she couldn't see him for the time being."

"That's not what happened," whispered Sandra angrily into Kate's ear.

Kate jotted down a note on her legal pad and focused her attention on Bower again.

Madeline showed the witness the telephone records she had previously marked as an exhibit. "Detective Bower, did you obtain a search warrant for the defendant's telephone records?"

"Yes."

"And pursuant to that search warrant, did you obtain the telephone records for the defendant's residence for the five days prior to the death of her husband?"

He shifted in the seat. "Yes. I did."

"Could you tell us, please, what they showed?"

"There were phone calls made from the defendant's place in Bel Air to Bartholomew in Northridge."

There was a loud murmur in the courtroom.

"Detective, did you also examine these same records for the night of James D'Arcy's death?"

"Yes."

"Can you tell us, please, what those records showed?"

"There was a call placed from the defendant's home in Bel Air at six twenty-two on the evening of February twenty-fifth to the Northridge apartment of Tommy Bartholomew."

Madeline had a smug smile on her face. "And after that?"

"Several calls placed to Tommy Bartholomew's residence that night."

"I also called Charles," Sandra whispered to Kate.

"Local calls are not recorded," explained Kate.

Madeline asked Bower what time he arrived at Sandra D'Arcy's and what time he left, and with Bower's help, she was able to establish that Sandra had called Tommy Bartholomew's residence repeatedly between the time the police were called and the time the police left that evening.

As Bower continued to testify to the things Tommy told him, both at that first visit and after his arrest, Kate watched her client's demeanor. Whenever there was a gasp in the courtroom, Sandra slouched farther down in her seat.

Kate, however, was sure that if the case went to trial, she would be able to establish an element of doubt as to the reason for the calls. Just as Madeline was hoping Sandra's calls to Tommy were evidence of her guilt, Kate planned to argue that they showed that Sandra couldn't possibly have thought Tommy had killed her husband. She wouldn't have expected him to be racing away from the scene and to be home at the same time. The inference would be that Sandra had merely wanted to seek comfort from Tommy because of her husband's death.

Kate turned her attention back to Bower's testimony.

"And," said Bower, responding to another one of Madeline's questions, "Bartholomew told us in his recorded statement that Mrs. D'Arcy said, 'I'd give anything to get rid of James,' and then she showed Tommy her gun."

"That's a lie," muttered Sandra, who then proceeded to have a coughing spasm.

It may be a lie, thought Kate, but a jury isn't going to like it.

The judge called a fifteen-minute recess.

When court resumed, Madeline continued her questioning of Bower. He testified that a child's trike had been found in the driveway blocking the gates to the D'Arcy mansion the night of the murder and the victim's car was idling and stopped short of the trike. He also testified that a bottle of champagne had been found on the front seat of the car, and that he later discovered many bottles of the same champagne—Dom Perignon—same year, in the deceased's wine cellar.

Kate stood up, recalling ironically how as a prosecutor, she had always had the cops as witnesses. Now that she was a defense lawyer, the cops were on the other side.

She established that Bower had found a receipt for the bottle of champagne lying on the front seat of James's car the night of his death, and showed him the receipt, which he identified.

"Did you visit the liquor store where the champagne was purchased?"

"Yes."

"Did you find out who sold that particular bottle?"

"Yes."

"Who was that?"

"The owner of the store."

"Did you question the owner about the person who made the purchase?"

"Yes."

"Did you subsequently show the owner a photo lineup that included Bartholomew's picture?"

"Yes."

"Was the owner able to identify anyone in that photo

lineup as being the person who purchased the champagne on the night of February twenty-fifth?''

Bower squirmed in his seat. "No. He couldn't."

It was Kate's turn to smile slightly as she walked back and forth. "Isn't it true, Detective, that no weapon has been found in this case?"

Bower blinked slightly as he admitted, "Yes."

"Did you obtain a search warrant for the defendant's home?''

"Yes."

"Could you please tell us what was the result of that search?''

"We didn't find any weapons or other evidence of the crime."

"That's all, Detective. Thank you," concluded Kate. The judge adjourned for lunch.

Kate and Charles emerged from the courtroom into the glare of a corridor bombarded by television lights.

"Are you planning to put your client on the stand at this hearing?" asked a newscaster, holding the microphone toward her.

"At the moment, no. We're taking the position that the state doesn't have sufficient evidence to try Sandra D'Arcy for the murder of her husband."

"And at the trial, will she take the stand?"

"We don't know yet. We believe the state doesn't have sufficient evidence to support a verdict of guilty. My client maintains she's innocent. If there's a trial, we want to be able to vindicate her." She smiled. "That's it for now. Thank you."

"Ms. Alexander."

"Ms. Alexander, did Sandra D'Arcy . . ."

As Kate walked away, she heard Madeline being asked to say a few words.

"We expect the evidence to show that this was a cold-blooded murder, and the defendant to be bound over for trial at the conclusion of the preliminary hearing. At trial, we will ask the jury to find the defendant guilty of first degree murder and conspiracy to commit murder," said Madeline.

During the lunch recess, while Charles picked apart everyone's testimony, Kate quickly made notes. She was too keyed up to eat. Finally, she put down her pencil and looked at him. "There are so many things only Sandra can explain," she said. "Like running away from the scene after she made that nine-one-one call. It sounded bad today, but if Sandra stated that she didn't remember doing any of it, the harm to her would be significantly reduced. But the thought of putting her on the stand gives me chills."

He frowned as he munched on his chicken salad sandwich. "Afraid she's a loose cannon, huh?"

She shook her head. "The least little thing sets her off. We'll just have to see. A lot will depend on Tommy's testimony," said Kate. "He's obviously the key to their case."

"Yes. I think you're right."

"Are you ready for your testimony?" she asked.

"Absolutely."

Back in the courtroom, Madeline called Charles Rieman as her next witness.

Charles identified himself as James D'Arcy's lawyer and friend, and after he satisfied the court that he was in possession of James's original will, which had been filed with the probate court, the two attorneys, Kate and Madeline, stipulated to allow a certified copy of the will to be entered into evidence.

Madeline then asked Charles what Sandra stood to gain by James's death.

"James D'Arcy's will left his wife five million dollars in trust," Charles explained.

"Do you personally know of any other will made after the date of the will you have filed with the probate court on behalf of James D'Arcy?"

"No, I do not."

"However, as a matter of public record, there is a challenge to the will you have filed with the probate court, isn't there?''

"Yes, there is."

"Would you tell us the basis for that challenge?"

"Affidavits have been filed by Theodore D'Arcy and his attorney, Dickson Manning, to the effect that a new will was made by James D'Arcy and witnessed by two people. But apparently, that the document has been lost," replied Charles.

"Does the challenge set forth any provisions of the alleged lost will?''

"Yes."

"Could you tell us, please, in what areas this alleged will differs from the will that has been filed with the probate court?''

Charles explained the differences and then went on to say that as to the provisions pertaining to Sandra, nothing was purported to have been changed in the alleged new will.

Madeline asked about the provisions made in both wills for James and Sandra's minor child.

Charles explained that the bulk of James D'Arcy's estate had been left in trust to his minor son. On further questioning, he admitted that Sandra could ask for a family allowance from her son's trust to pay for the support, maintenance, health, and education of her son. He clarified for Madeline that these funds could be used by Sandra to cover all sorts of things, from the house she lived in with her son and all of its amenities, including staff and cars, to the schools her son would go to, vacations she would take with him, and so on.

Madeline smiled at him. "Considering the size of the estate left to James D'Arcy, Junior, is it fair to say that the sums available to the minor child for the things we have just discussed would be considerable?''

"The word 'considerable' has many different meanings,'' he hedged.

Kate realized that Madeline was now forced to backtrack, and watched as the prosecutor went to check her notes. In the meantime, she thought about Charles's testimony. Although he wore his usual confident smile, his smooth delivery was a trifle off. She guessed it was because he was trying too hard to shape his answers so as not to show Sandra as greedy. She silently chastised him. He should know better than that—the truth was always the best answer. In her experience, however, the more intelligent the person testifying, the more often his or her intellect got in the way. Lawyers were the biggest offenders, always trying to outwit the questioner.

Madeline brought her notepad back with her and stood in front of Charles. "Mr. Rieman, Mr. D'Arcy left an estate valued in the neighborhood of one billion dollars, isn't that correct?"

"Yes."

"Isn't it up to the trustee to decide what are necessary expenses for the minor child?"

"Yes."

"You are that trustee, are you not?"

"I am designated the trustee in the will, but I am not the trustee at the moment."

Madeline asked him to explain what he meant.

"I think I can explain better by saying that James D'Arcy's will appointed me to act as executor of his estate during the probate of his will, and thereafter as trustee of the estate. The objections filed with the probate court by Theodore D'Arcy have kept the will from being admitted to probate. Therefore, I have been appointed by the probate court to act as special administrator until the will challenge can be decided."

"I see," said Madeline. "As special administrator, do you have the same authority to act for the minor child?"

"Yes."

"Now, Mr. Rieman," Madeline went on, "under the terms of the new will Theodore D'Arcy claims his brother made, would the provision regarding the minor child change in any way?"

"Only as to the trustee."

"What would that change be?"

"Under the alleged new will, the trustee would be Theodore D'Arcy instead of me."

"Would the change in trustee have any practical significance in your opinion?"

Kate objected, but Madeline argued that Charles was in a position to give an opinion. The judge allowed it.

"In my opinion, as to the minor child and what I would consider a proper expense as opposed to what Mr. D'Arcy would consider a proper expense, I would have to say the answer is no."

"Thank you, Mr. Rieman." Madeline smiled. "I've no further questions."

Kate felt a momentary twinge of nervousness as she stood to question Charles. She knew she had to defuse the motive issue. For although it wasn't a necessary element to be proved at a trial, as a practical matter it was always helpful for the prosecutor to show a motive. Especially in front of a jury. And Madeline had done a skillful job of showing that money was a motive to be considered.

Kate started by asking Charles several general questions. After a few minutes, she walked over to the table, glanced at her legal pad, and turned to face him. "Now, Mr. Rieman, what provision did James D'Arcy's will make in the event he and the defendant, his wife, divorced?"

"She was to get the same five million dollars, in trust," he responded with calm assurance.

"As to the will alleged by Theodore D'Arcy, were there any changes in the provisions for the defendant in the event of a divorce?"

"No."

She gestured with her hand. "If the defendant had divorced James D'Arcy, in addition to the five million dollars she was entitled to, would she, in your professional opinion, have been entitled to ask for child support payments?"

"Absolutely. The five million dollars was only meant to be for the defendant in lieu of specific property or spousal support. It had nothing to do with the minor child."

"In your professional opinion, Mr. Rieman, did the defendant have anything more to gain from her husband's death than from a divorce?''

"Objection," said Madeline.

"I'm only asking for his professional opinion. As James D'Arcy's lawyer and as the man who drafted the will and the prenuptial agreement for James D'Arcy, this witness, as you yourself have argued, Ms. Gould," said Kate, addressing Madeline directly, "is qualified to give his opinion."

"I will allow it," ruled Judge Jackson.

Kate asked the question again, hoping Charles would give the answer she expected.

"No," said Charles, smiling slightly. "In my opinion, the defendant had nothing more to gain from her husband's death than from a divorce."

"Thank you." With a smile of satisfaction on her face, Kate ended her cross-examination. "I have no further questions."

Madeline called Theo D'Arcy to the stand. His testimony shed no light on the will question beyond what Charles had already stated.

"Mr. D'Arcy, as the decedent's brother, in your opinion, did the defendant have anything more to gain from her husband's death than from a divorce?"

"Objection," Kate said. "Mr. D'Arcy is not a lawyer and does not have the professional standing on which to base such an opinion."

"Objection sustained," said Judge Jackson.

"No further questions." Madeline sat down.

Theo was one witness Kate didn't need to question until the trial. Then she'd use the animosity between the brothers, Theo's reasons to have wanted his brother dead, as well as his desire to be the trustee of his brother's estate, to plant the idea of reasonable doubt in the minds of the jurors as to Sandra.

Later that evening Kate answered the private line in her office. "Frank!" she almost shouted. "I was getting so worried."

There was static on the line as Frank answered, "I'm

sorry. But I'm in Mexico. I was trying to call at a time when you might answer, because Mary said no one is to know where I am.''

"Unfortunately, that's true, but don't ask.'' She laughed grimly. "I ran into a stone wall named Dickson Manning. He wouldn't O.K. the expenses for you to go to Mexico.''

"So how . . . Where's it coming from?''

"I'm footing the bill.''

"That's crazy.''

"I'll get it back, don't worry. Any luck?'' she asked, unable to hide the hope in her voice.

"I found a place where Maria was two days ago.'' He sounded discouraged.

"Frank, we've got to find her.''

"I'm doing my best.''

"I know, I didn't mean . . .''

"That's O.K. Listen, I'm going to need more bucks. Is that a problem?''

"No, I'll have Mary wire funds to you. Where are you going next?''

"Guadalajara.''

"O.K. Pick up the funds at the Banco de México there in the morning.''

"I will. How's the preliminary hearing going?''

"It's going. But I'm sure the judge is going to bind her over for trial.''

"Did Sandra admit James pushed her around yet?''

"Nope.'' She sighed. "I sometimes feel like she's beginning to trust me. And just when I'm sure she does, what happens? Wham, right between the eyes—she pulls back. I'm beside myself.''

"Shit!''

"But the shrink has met with Sandra and she also thinks we're right in believing James roughed her up. I'm hoping she'll be able to get through to her. The doctor also has some interesting psychological theories we can possibly use in our defense.''

"Great.''

"I'll fill you in when you get home. Just find Maria and

hurry back," she implored. "Besides needing Maria's testimony, I need your shoulder to cry on."

"Thanks, Kate, that's the nicest thing you ever said to me."

"I'll send you the money in the morning."

"Good."

"And good luck."

"I'll find her, even if I die trying." Frank chuckled.

43

Sandra looked haggard and wan when Kate saw her the next morning in the holding cell. "Do you have a temperature?" Kate asked.

"I'm O.K.," insisted Sandra irritably.

"You look terrible." Without thinking, Kate put her hand on Sandra's forehead. The young woman backed away, but not before Kate could feel she was burning up. "You've got a fever. I'm going to tell the D.A."

Sandra stopped her. "No, damn it. It's just a bad cold. The sooner this is over, the sooner I get to go home." She stuck her chin out defiantly. "You said you'd ask for bail again at the end of this hearing."

"I'm planning to, yes."

"Then I don't want anything to get in the way," snapped Sandra.

"I still—"

"What am I paying you for if you don't listen to me?"

"For heaven's sake, one day won't matter," said Kate in exasperation.

"Tommy could be on the stand today."

Kate nodded. "It's possible. But you should be both physically and emotionally up to that. It'll be very hard on you to just sit and listen."

"I'm fine," insisted Sandra. "Let's go."

When Kate escorted her client into the courtroom, she heard her exhale loudly as if gearing herself up for the crowded courtroom and what she perceived was a hostile atmosphere.

As soon as Judge Jackson was seated, Madeline stood up and said the words everyone in the courtroom had been waiting days to hear: "The people call Tommy Bartholomew."

Next to her, Kate felt Sandra tense. This would be the first time she had even seen her boyfriend since their secret meeting in the parking lot after James's death.

While Tommy was led into the courtroom, Kate gauged Sandra's reaction out of the corner of her eye. She appeared to be trembling and holding her breath, almost as if by sheer force of will she could make Tommy look at her. But he kept his eyes down.

Tommy was dressed in a blue blazer, gray slacks, and a red-and-blue-striped tie. He seemed heavier and pastier than when Kate had seen him at his last court appearance. She knew Andrew had to be in the courtroom, but she refused to turn around and check. Nevertheless, she sensed his eyes burning into her from behind.

"How old are you, Mr. Bartholomew?" asked Madeline.

"Twenty-four."

"And where are you presently residing?"

"L.A. County Jail."

"Mr. Bartholomew, were you first charged with first degree murder with special circumstance in the death of James D'Arcy?"

"Yes."

"Did I offer you a plea bargain in that matter?"

"Yes."

"According to the terms of that plea bargain, did you agree to plead guilty to murder with a life sentence and a possibility of parole, in exchange for your truthful testimony against your accomplice, Sandra D'Arcy?''

"Yes."

The courtroom continued to buzz as Madeline asked her next question.

"Did you want to testify against Sandra D'Arcy?"

"No."

"Do you want to see the defendant convicted?"

Tommy gazed over at Sandra for the first time and Kate thought she saw sorrow in his eyes before he quickly looked away.

"No," he responded quietly.

Madeline took Tommy through a brief history of how he had met Sandra D'Arcy, and his relationship with her.

Mostly, Tommy answered in short sentences. Madeline had to keep prodding him. It was clear to Kate that he was not at all happy about testifying. She listened as he told the court that Sandra had not been friendly to him at first.

"I thought she was kind of stuck-up and a snob," he said. "But little by little, when we talked at breaks during class, I saw she was really shy, and we became friends."

"Did you know the defendant was married?"

"Yes." His brown eyes were somber as he added, "She told me right away."

"Just answer the question," admonished Madeline, clearly perturbed.

Kate smiled inwardly. Madeline didn't want Tommy embellishing his answers, especially if the added statements helped make Sandra look good.

"Did you ever meet James D'Arcy?"

"No."

"Did the defendant tell you anything about her marriage?"

"Yes."

"Did she say it was a happy marriage?" Madeline turned to face the spectators as she waited for his answer.

"She said it wasn't."

The courtroom buzzed.

"I'll have order in this courtroom," warned Judge Jackson as he slammed down his gavel.

"What exactly did the defendant tell you about her marriage?"

"That her husband was a lot older than her. Rich and important. But not very nice to her."

"I see." Madeline went to stand in front of him. "Mr. Bartholomew, did you and the defendant ever talk about killing James D'Arcy?"

The tension in the room was audible and Kate heard Sandra's sharp intake of breath.

Finally, Tommy answered in a low tone.

"Yes," he said, his voice cracking.

"Did you discuss this subject on more than one occasion?"

"Yes."

"How many times did you discuss killing James D'Arcy?"

"Five or six times." His face was solemn. "I'm not sure."

"That's not true," whispered Sandra. "We talked about being *free* of him, not killing him."

Kate pointed to the yellow pad on the table in front of Sandra and motioned to her to write. Then she scribbled some notes to herself. When Sandra tried to protest further, Kate put her finger to her lips.

Madeline continued. "Did the defendant ever tell you how happy the two of you could be if James D'Arcy was dead?"

Tommy brushed back the hair that had fallen into his eye and gazed at Sandra. "Yes."

"Could you tell us, please, what she said?"

"She said if he was dead, she and me and little Jimmy could live happily ever after."

Kate felt her client squirm in her chair.

"Did the defendant tell you anything else in the last two weeks before her husband's death?"

"Just how unhappy she was. And how she couldn't divorce him because she'd lose everything."

"Did the defendant tell you what she was willing to do to get rid of her husband?"

"Yes."

Madeline walked back and forth in front of Tommy. "And what was that?"

He took a deep breath. "Anything. She said she'd do anything to be rid of him."

"I didn't mean that," insisted Sandra as chattering could be heard around her. She coughed loudly several times.

"Order!" The judge pounded his gavel and glared at the crowd.

Clearing her throat, Madeline asked, "Did the defendant ever show you her gun?"

"Yes."

"And what kind of a gun was it?"

"A .22 Ruger semiautomatic."

Next to Kate, Sandra was digging her nails into her own arms so hard she had drawn blood.

"After the defendant kept asking you to help her, did there come a time when you finally agreed to help her get rid of her husband?"

Tommy swallowed hard. "Yes."

"Did the defendant give you some more money at this time?"

"Yes," he said, then added, "but I thought some of it was a loan."

"Just answer the question, please," said Madeline, frowning.

Kate smiled to herself as she made a note to ask Tommy some questions about that "loan."

"Did she ask you to repay any of the money?" asked Madeline, obviously trying to regain the ground she had just lost.

"No. She never asked for any of it back."

There was nervous laughter in the room.

"Did you plan to marry the defendant when her husband was out of the picture?"

"I wanted to, yes."

433

Sandra wrote in big block letters and shoved her pad under Kate's nose. *I never said I would marry him!*

The prosecutor walked over to the evidence table and picked something up. "Mr. Bartholomew, I show you a pair of boots that have been placed in evidence. Are these your boots?"

He blinked and swallowed hard. "Yes."

"Were you wearing these boots the night James D'Arcy was killed?"

"I don't remember."

There were whispers as Kate wrote herself a note and underlined it in red. She knew Madeline had no choice but to backtrack now.

"Did you sign a consent waiver allowing the police officers that came to your house to search your apartment?"

"Yes."

Kate thought Madeline looked annoyed as she continued, "And did the police find these boots of yours in your apartment?"

"Yes."

"Were these boots covered with mud?"

Tommy put his head down. "Yes," he answered, in a voice so low Kate wasn't sure Madeline had heard him. She hadn't.

"Was that a yes?"

"Yes."

Madeline went over to the table, picked up a piece of paper and brought it over to Tommy. "I show you this note which has been marked as an exhibit and entered into evidence. Have you ever seen this note before?"

"Yes."

"Could you tell us when that was?"

"Sandra left it for me with the manager of my apartment. It was in the envelope with two thousand dollars cash."

"What was that money for?"

"My rent and things."

"How much was your rent at that time?"

"Five hundred."

Sandra scribbled a note to Kate. *It was a loan.*

Madeline clasped her hands together. "I'd now like to take you to a point in time after the death of Mr. D'Arcy. Do you remember meeting the defendant in the parking lot of the Bel Air Hills Market in Bel Air on February twenty-eighth of this year?"

"Yes, I do."

"Mr. Bartholomew, can you tell us why you met the defendant at a market parking lot?"

"I kept calling, wanting to see her. Finally she said O.K. But it had to be away from her house and my place. She told me to meet her at the market and to get in her car when she pulled in."

"Can you tell us what happened at that meeting between you and the defendant?"

"She said we couldn't see each other for a while because people were getting suspicious. Especially the police. She said she thought her phone was bugged, and I shouldn't call."

"I never said that about the police," Sandra whispered to Kate and Kate shook her head.

Madeline went on. "Did anything else happen at that meeting?"

He looked down at his hands. "Sandra gave me another thousand dollars."

Kate didn't like the way his answer sounded and made a note to try to explain it away as another loan.

Madeline glanced across the courtroom before continuing. "Did the defendant ever tell you she wanted to divorce her husband?"

"Yes."

"Did she ever tell you she had *asked* her husband for a divorce?"

"Yes."

"What did the defendant tell you her husband said to her request for a divorce?"

"That she could have the divorce, but not her kid."

There was shocked murmuring in the courtroom, and reporters could be heard scratching furiously in their notebooks. As the judge pounded his gavel for silence, Kate wondered how Theo and Victoria felt about what Tommy had just said.

Approaching the witness, Madeline asked, "Did you believe her?"

"Yes."

As Madeline turned away, Tommy blurted out, "I believed her because when she told me, she had a black eye."

Sandra went rigid. Then she started to cough.

The courtroom broke into pandemonium as Kate's heart leapt almost out of her chest.

"Order!" shouted Judge Jackson, beating his gavel on his bench. "There will be *order*."

Kate couldn't believe her ears. She had been racking her brain wondering how she was ever going to get Sandra to tell her the truth, and here was Tommy blurting it out in open court. Did that mean the question of abuse would now be an issue?

She was also aware that Madeline had no choice but to ask the next obvious question. If she didn't, everyone would think she wanted to keep the truth from coming out.

"Did the defendant tell you her husband had given her the black eye?"

"Not exactly."

"What did the defendant say?"

"I don't recall. But I knew it was him."

"Please just answer my questions," said Madeline as Kate scrawled another note to herself. "What was your response to the defendant's black eye?"

"I swore. Then I begged her to leave him. I told her I loved her and would take care of her."

"What did the defendant respond to that?"

"She couldn't leave him."

"Did you ask her why?"

"Yes."

"And what was her answer?"

"He'd threatened to take her kid away if she left him."

"And what did you say to that?"

"That . . ." He hesitated, then finished. "That I'd kill the fucking bastard!"

It was quiet in the courtroom as all eyes focused on Tommy and the back of Sandra's head while she continued to cough.

Unless I can tear apart Tommy's testimony, realized Kate, there's no question now—Sandra is going to be tried for the murder of her husband.

When Sandra couldn't stop coughing, the judge finally asked Kate if her client needed a recess.

"Please, Your Honor," she responded gratefully.

Kate escorted Sandra to the holding cell, where she asked the bailiff to bring some water. Sandra couldn't seem to catch her breath. As she tried to calm her down, Kate's mind was reeling. Even though Madeline wasn't required by law to show that Sandra had a motive for James's murder, it always helped a jury to decide guilt or innocence if they knew the reason why the defendant might have done what he or she was accused of.

Sandra tried to say something, but the coughing got worse.

"Don't talk. Wait for the spasm to subside," advised Kate.

The bailiff came back with the water.

Kate handed it to Sandra. "Here, drink this."

Sandra sipped from the cup, then slumped down in the chair, her face in her hands.

"It's crazy to continue," insisted Kate. "You're obviously very ill."

"I don't want a continuing, or whatever it's called," Sandra struggled to say between racking coughs. "I want this damn thing to be over so I can get out on bail."

"I'm only talking about a day or two. You look like you're about to faint."

Sandra started to cough again.

"I can't get a continuance without your permission," explained Kate, "because as a defendant, you have a right to a continuous preliminary hearing. I can't waive that right for you. But surely you can see that you're not up to this?"

"Do whatever the fuck you want!" cried Sandra, her voice cracking. "You always do anyway."

"I need you to agree."

"All right! If it will shut you up!"

Kate opened the door and asked the bailiff to get the clerk. Both the clerk and Madeline rushed over.

"My client's too sick to proceed. We need to request a continuance."

The clerk hurried to tell the judge while Sandra and Kate went back to the defense table.

After he was seated, Judge Jackson looked at Sandra. "As a defendant, you have a right to a continuous preliminary hearing. Do you understand?"

"Yes."

"Do you now wish to waive this right and ask for a continuance?"

"Yes." Her voice was barely audible as the court reporter took down every word.

Judge Jackson appeared to be checking his calendar. "Since it's already Wednesday and the courtroom is black on Friday, is Monday at eight-thirty A.M. good for counsel?"

"Yes, Your Honor," said Kate.

Madeline agreed also.

"Very well, this hearing is continued until eight-thirty A.M. in this division, on April fifteenth."

Kate took her client to the holding cell. The bailiff assured her that Sandra would be taken to the infirmary at Sybil Brand, where a doctor would examine her.

Kate waved goodbye. "I'll come to see you tomorrow and I'll call later. Then we can discuss Tommy's testimony."

"I can hardly wait," croaked Sandra.

Outside in the courtroom, both Kate and Madeline got ready to leave. "I'm going back to the office to catch up on everything I haven't had time for," said Madeline, stuffing some papers in her briefcase.

"Me too," said Kate, clearing off the table. "See you Monday."

* * *

Madeline wasn't particularly thrilled to have the hearing continued. It would only back up her entire calendar. But Sandra did look rather sick.

What did that black eye mean? she wondered as she headed upstairs. The more she thought about it, the less it seemed to mean. One black eye hardly constituted a basis to kill someone in self-defense. Nor did it prove that Sandra was in fear for her life. Besides, according to Tommy, she hadn't even said her husband gave it to her.

When court resumed Madeline intended to move on to another line of questioning with Tommy. It was suicide to ask any more questions to which she didn't know the answers.

Philip was waiting for her when she got back to the nearly empty office. "Hi," she said, glad to see him. "Boy, am I bushed." She threw her briefcase onto the extra chair and sank down on the one behind her messy desk.

He was in his shirtsleeves. "So how did it go?"

"The defendant got sick and my star witness dropped a bombshell. Other than that, it went well."

"What happened?"

She told him about the black eye.

"What do you think it means?"

"If it actually happened?" She smiled wryly.

"You think it's a ploy?"

"Who knows. But if it did happen, I don't believe it was anything more than an isolated incident." She shook her chestnut hair. "Up until Bartholomew blurted that out, I thought the evidence was piling up nicely against Sandra. I only wish Kate would put her on the stand. I'd love to shake her up."

"I doubt there's much chance of that."

"Unfortunately"—she smiled—"I agree. Kate would have to have rocks in her head to let me get my teeth into Sandra now."

Philip started to pace the room, then turned to her, seeming uncomfortable. "I think you're doing a fine job on a difficult case."

Her soft brown eyes came alive. "Thank you, Philip."

There was an awkward silence. Madeline bent over, took off one shoe, and wriggled her toes. "When I'm presenting my case, my feet always hurt."

"It takes a few days until your mind and body adjust to the pace."

"Every part of me is tired." She waved her high-heeled pump at him good-naturedly. "This is one handicap you don't face."

"You've got me there," he admitted, a slight blush creeping up his neck. "So. Do you still expect Kate not to put on any defense at this hearing?"

She laughed. "What defense?"

"Don't count one out yet. Kate's too good a lawyer to go down without a fight."

"The only defenses I can think of necessitate Sandra taking the stand. For instance, she could testify that she didn't know Tommy was going to kill her husband. Or that it was Tommy's idea and she thought he was kidding. Something like that."

"It's a tough call for an attorney to make. I wouldn't want to be in Kate's shoes on this one."

"Or mine," she kidded, shaking her shoe at him.

He smiled, then seemed preoccupied as he stroked his chin. "With the bombshell Tommy dropped today, do you think it's possible Kate's going to claim self-defense at the trial?"

"Philip, besides the danger of putting Sandra on the stand, if a man gives a woman a black eye, does that mean she can go out and hire a killer to blow him away? Let's be reasonable. She didn't point the gun at James herself in the middle of being terrified for her life."

"True . . ."

Seeing him smiling at her again, she prayed he had forgiven her for whatever it was she'd done. On impulse, she decided to ask him to have a drink. She glanced up hopefully. "Philip, would you like to go for a—"

He seemed to anticipate her words as he backed up toward the door. "No thanks. I've got to go. See you tomorrow." He waved goodbye.

Since that evening was one of the rare occasions when Sam actually had the kids, Madeline thought about running after Philip. But she didn't. With a sigh, she decided she had better work for a while. She was falling too far behind.

An hour later, immersed in her files, Madeline was jarred by the ringing of the telephone. Answering, she heard a familiar, deep voice. It was Gary.

"I hoped you were coming over."

She caught her breath. "I've lots to do."

"I heard you got a continuance until Monday. This is only Wednesday. You have plenty of time."

She hesitated, unsure. "I don't think so."

"Please," he asked softly.

That got to her. "All right."

"Then come on already."

"I'll be there soon." She hoped her voice didn't betray her nervousness. "Do you want me to stop for anything?"

"Nope, I've got it all. Just bring that gorgeous body of yours."

"I'll see you in a little bit."

"Hurry." His tone was a cross between an invitation and an order.

She forced herself to work. She had about thirty minutes more. The harder she tried to concentrate, the more impossible it became. The same anticipation she had experienced the last time she had been with him was starting to build inside her. It was a breathless sensation. Her chest felt constricted and it was as if the bottom had dropped out of her stomach.

"Hell." She threw down her pencil. Then, as if suddenly making up her mind, she put her shoes on, stuffing papers and documents into her large briefcase, grabbed her purse, and left.

She drove quickly, anxious to get there and be with him again. In spite of the physical attraction that had been there from the start, she wondered where her relationship with Gary was going. He had still made no effort to spend any time with her and the boys. The last time she'd been with Gary, she had chided herself for sleeping with him before working out any of their problems. Yet she couldn't seem to help herself; it was as if she had no guardrail for protection against him. This must be how it felt to be dependent on drugs or alcohol. All one could think about was the need to be satisfied.

At the same time, Philip's obvious dislike of Gary bothered her more than she cared to admit. Could it be jealousy? Or was there something Philip knew and didn't want to share with her? As chief deputy, he had access to all of their personnel files. Maybe she should ask him. She quickly rejected the thought. The truth was, she didn't want to know.

The wind blew against her face and she sensed an element of risk pulling at her, daring her to do something the more rational side of her was against. Giving another being such power over her made her feel vulnerable, exposed. But at this juncture, she was willing to gamble, just so she could feel that special way. One more time.

44

Dickson strutted around the conference room, thanking three of his partners, Arnold Mindell, Nathan Ornstein, and Harrison Emery, for coming to his hastily called meeting. Than he introduced the tall man with dark, thinning hair standing next to him. "This is Paul Kenter, from Livingstone & Kenter. He wanted to meet with those of us who'll make up the management committee when our two firms merge. Of course, this won't happen until after my father retires and I become senior partner. But it may well be sooner than we think."

He went on. "I'm also sorry it's so late, but I wanted to make sure everyone else at Manning & Anderson was gone. As my friend Paul knows, a few of our partners view a merger as an end to our firm rather than the beginning of a prosperous future." Dickson smiled. "So let's get started," he suggested, taking the seat at the head of the table.

"You'll see in front of each of you a draft of the proposed merger agreement. In particular I want you to take a look at paragraph four . . ."

Kate opened the door to the conference room and walked in. She was surprised to see Dickson and three of Manning & Anderson's partners sitting around the table, with another man whom she couldn't place. "I didn't realize the room was in use," she apologized hastily.

Her curiosity over what Dickson was doing at such a late hour propelled her forward. "I was going to use the table to do some sorting."

She waited for Dickson to introduce her to the fourth man. Then, realizing he had no intention of doing so, she walked up to the stranger and offered her hand. "Hello, I'm Kate Alexander."

The man stood up. "How do you do. Paul Kenter."

Kate recognized his name immediately. He was with the New York firm reportedly interested in a merger with Manning & Anderson. "Nice meeting you. Please excuse the intrusion." As she beat a hasty retreat, she sneaked a look at one of the documents on the table. She couldn't believe her eyes.

She was halfway down the hall to her office when Dickson overtook her.

"You had better not mention what you saw to anyone."

Even in the dim light of the hallway, she saw the fear in his eyes. "And I'd like you to stop threatening me," she said as forcefully as she could.

"This is very serious business," he warned. "It goes far beyond what someone who's slept her way to the top could possibly understand."

She sucked in her breath. "You're way out of line."

He grinned. "Perhaps. But the odds are against you, Kate. This firm was founded by my father. If he had to make a choice, it wouldn't be you."

"I don't have to listen to this." She started to walk away but his arm shot out and grabbed her. Because her other hand was holding a batch of documents, she was caught off balance.

"Even my father's misguided fondness for Charles won't help you. You should reconsider leaving. I can make it worth your while."

As she yanked herself free, she lost her balance entirely and her papers scattered on the floor around her. Her eyes blazed at him. "Threaten me one more time and I'll charge you with harassment." With as much dignity as she could muster, she picked up her things and walked away.

"Remember what I said," he called after her.

"Go fuck yourself," she said through clenched teeth.

Sandra, on her cot in the infirmary at Sybil Brand, had never felt so sick in her life. Her throat was raw and she was hot and chilled at the same time. She pulled the covers up around her neck, shivering under the mound of blankets. "I'm so cold," she whispered to the nurse who came to check on her.

"You have a high fever and that makes you feel cold. But that shot I gave you contains antibiotics. By morning you'll feel a little better."

"What do I have?"

"A bad case of bronchitis. The doctor says if you're not careful, it could end up in pneumonia. So why don't you drink some more of this?"

The nurse held some water up to her mouth. But Sandra shook her head. "No, it hurts to swallow."

"You've got to force yourself," insisted the nurse.

As the pain seared her throat, Sandra silently cried, How did this nightmare happen? Why did you say those things today on the stand, Tommy? And why were you afraid to look at me?

Across town, Kate was frantic as she got into her car. The document she'd seen in the conference room was a merger agreement for the two law firms. Knowing that Franklin and Charles both vehemently opposed such a merger, she didn't know what to do. If she told Charles, could he protect her from Dickson's wrath? Of course, she had something else on Dickson—something he wanted to keep secret. But could she betray a client confidence? She doubted it. And Dickson's threat, unfortunately, was probably true. If it came to a showdown, it wouldn't be Dickson who would suffer but she. Yet she owed it to Charles to tell him what she'd seen.

She hated calling Charles at home. But this was an emergency. She dialed her cellular phone.

"Hello."

Shoot, muttered Kate under her breath, recognizing Ann's voice. "Mrs. Rieman, this is Kate Alexander."

"What do you want?" came the cold reply.

"I'm so sorry to bother you, but I must speak to Charles."

"*My* husband?"

"Yes, please. It's important."

"I'll see if he can talk to you."

Charles sounded worried when he picked up the phone. "What's wrong?"

Kate heard a click and realized Ann had picked up the extension. Her mind raced furiously. "Can you meet me at Sybil Brand? Sandra's taken a turn for the worse."

"We're . . ." He hesitated. "We have guests."

"Charles, I need help."

"All right. I'm leaving. Are you at the jail?"

"No. I'm in my car. I just left the office."

"Tell me where you are and I'll pick you up."

"Wilshire and Santa Monica."

"I'll be there in ten minutes."

She waited until enough time had passed and then called him in his car. "Meet me in front of the office, in the bank parking lot. Leave your lights off. I'll explain."

When he pulled up, she jumped out of her car and hurried to him.

In his car, Kate related what she'd seen. Even in the darkness, she saw the incredulity on his face.

"Those fucking bastards."

When she got to the part about Dickson accosting her in the hallway, he became enraged.

"If that bastard hurt you, I'll kill him."

"I'm O.K."

His mouth was set in a grim line. "If I go up there now, Dickson will know you told me. But I've got to get my hands on the evidence."

"Can't you just tell Franklin?"

"I intend to. But I need the document. With the proof in my hands, we shouldn't have anything to worry about." He clenched his jaw and stared out the car window. Then he turned to her. "You're too upset to realize it, but this could be good for us. I can't believe Dickson would be so stupid."

"Charles, I know Franklin and you think the same way about the firm's future, but don't forget that Dickson is still Franklin's son. That counts for a lot."

He nodded. "Don't worry. Franklin will see this meeting behind his back as a betrayal. I'm sure of it. Trust me, Kate. I promise not to let Dickson hurt you."

Kate shivered as she thought of what Dickson might do to her. "He already knows I saw him," she sighed. "If you feel you have to confront him, go ahead."

"Thanks, darling." He pulled her close and kissed her. "I love you, Ms. Alexander."

"I love you, Mr. Rieman," she said. Then she frowned worriedly. "Good luck."

When Charles opened the door to the conference room, he saw that Paul Kenter and one of the partners had already left.

Dickson looked shocked to see him. "This is a closed meeting." His voice was brittle. "And this room is signed out to me. So please leave."

Ignoring Dickson, Charles walked over to the table in two strides and grabbed one of the documents. "I don't give a damn who it's signed out to," he said as he waved the merger agreement in the air toward the remaining partners. "I didn't know you men had taken to slumming with my *esteemed*"—his mouth twisted downward at the last word— "brother-in-law. I'm sure Franklin will be most interested to hear about this meeting."

Harrison stood, his hands held out in front of him. "Now listen here, Charles, we have a right to meet privately . . ."

"A right to meet privately," scoffed Charles. "Is that supposed to negate the fact that you're breaching your fiduciary duty to your other partners?"

The man's face paled considerably. "I must go," he said hurriedly to Dickson as he ran out of the room.

Charles smiled grimly. "Looks like one of your rats just deserted the sinking ship."

It was Mindell's turn to stand. "I think I'll leave the two of you to work this out. I'll talk to you tomorrow, Dickson." He made a hasty exit, mumbling a good night to Charles.

"You have no right to break up my meeting!" Dickson's right eye began to twitch.

"I have every right! This merger would kill your father."

"He'll adjust. Especially when he sees how impressed our old clients are and the barrage of new clients who'll immediately flock to us. We'll be the second or third largest law firm in the country."

"That will certainly inflate your ego and bank account." Charles's eyes narrowed to two slits. "But as for clients, you couldn't care less about any of them, old or new."

"And since when did *you* consider anyone but yourself? You certainly weren't averse to taking my sister's money."

Charles advanced upon Dickson. "How would you like me to wipe that shit-eating grin off your face?"

Dickson's smirk faded as he backed away. "Don't touch me."

"There's no one here to rescue you." Charles laughed.

"You're going to be finished after I show this to Franklin." He waved the agreement in the air.

Dickson's face turned red. "I'll tell him about you and Kate. Then you'll be out. Out!"

"I'll deny it. And after this"—Charles smacked the document—"he won't believe anything you say. This agreement is treachery. It's like destroying his life's work, his dreams."

"I'll see that Ann divorces you and leaves you penniless."

"And I'll break every bone in your scrawny little body." Charles headed for the door.

"Bring back that document!" demanded Dickson.

"Not a chance," said Charles, walking out.

When Gary opened the door of his apartment for Madeline, there was a brooding look on his ruggedly handsome face. "What took you so long?"

"I had to pack up my briefcase and—" She heard herself making excuses and stopped.

"I don't like waiting for you," he complained. "It makes me feel like I'm not important."

Madeline's eyebrow rose. "And I thought you'd be happy to see me. After all, you pressured me to come over here."

When he answered her, his voice was cold. "I never *pressure* anyone."

"Hey!" She held up her hand. "This evening's getting off to a bad start. Either we start over—or I'm going home. I've had enough trauma for one day."

Suddenly, he smiled. "You're absolutely right. I'm sorry, baby." Wrapping his arms around her, he kissed her cheek and nibbled on her ear.

Although she was stiff at first, the urgency of his strong arms and his warm breath on her neck caused her to surrender to his embrace. Her head went back as his lips traveled down to the area between her breasts.

"Forgive me," he murmured. "I got upset because I saw Philip waiting for you when I left the office."

448

She hugged him. "Oh, Gary, Philip merely wanted a debriefing on court today. We've always done that on cases with lots of media attention." Rushing on, she explained. "You should have seen the reporters and the hordes of spectators. It was a zoo."

"You don't have to rub it in," he said sulkily. "We all know you've got the biggest case of the year."

She pulled away from him abruptly.

Immediately he brightened again and his eyes grew soft. "Don't mind me, I get cranky waiting for my girl. Why don't you make yourself comfortable? Use my silk robe. I'll get our pasta started and bring you a glass of wine."

A sigh escaped her lips. "I'd like that."

"Come here." He drew her into his arms and they kissed, a long, deep kiss that left her breathless, heart pounding.

He rubbed her back suggestively, then ran his hands over her breasts. Her reaction was immediate as her nipples hardened.

"Want to have dinner later?" he murmured.

"Yes." Her lips found his again.

As he kissed her, he pushed her gently back against the island in the center of his kitchen until she felt the wood grain of the cabinet at her back. His body, hardened with arousal, pressed against her.

He threw the jacket she was still clutching over the back of a chair. Then he pulled her sweater dress up over her head, slipping her stockings down with one deft hand, while the other slid up her bare thigh. His fingers pushed beyond her bikini underpants and she shivered as she felt him touch her moistness. When he took her taut nipple into his mouth, she cried out.

Now his hands were everywhere as he literally ripped off her pants, flinging them away. His mouth pressed hungrily to hers, he quickly undid his jeans and slipped out of them. Madeline could feel that he was naked underneath and her excitement grew. She rushed to pull his T-shirt over his head, not happy until she finally felt his bare flesh pressed against hers.

"Gary," she whispered urgently, "you need some protection."

"I've only been with you, baby, I swear."

Before she could say anything more, he lifted her up, balancing her between the island and himself as he thrust into her.

"Oh!" she moaned. Her legs wrapped around him as his hands clutched her buttocks. Feeling him thrusting himself into her again and again, she cried out, "Fuck me, Gary. Fuck me. I can't stand it. It feels so good."

Unexpectedly, he lifted her up and, still pulsating deep inside her, carried her to the living room. Before she knew what was happening, he put her over the couch and shoved himself at her behind, trying to enter her.

"Don't, Gary!" she cried. "It hurts."

"Shhh," he soothed. "Just relax. I won't hurt you, I promise."

She tried to wriggle away.

"Please. Please, babe," he whispered. "I want to do this so badly."

"Gary, I—"

"Just relax. I won't move until you get used to it."

"No. Please, I don't want to . . ."

"But I do!" He suddenly lost all patience as he shoved himself fully into her.

The more she cried out for him to stop, the faster and deeper he went. She tried to get away but he held her down, his grip like a steel vise. Pinned against the couch, she couldn't move. She felt as if she were suffocating while being ripped apart.

"Jesus . . . Jesus!" he groaned, slamming into her so hard she thought her head would come off.

When he finally pulled out, the sticky wetness oozed out of her. She crumpled against the sofa, angry and in pain. Worst of all, she felt humiliated. She didn't want to cry. But the tears came anyway.

He came back with a towel and tried to clean her up.

"No!" she screamed. "Get away. Don't touch me."

"Come on, Madeline. Grow up."

"How dare you?" She yanked the towel away and tried to cover herself up, more for the shame she felt than for her nakedness. "You had no right to do that."

"What the hell are you talking about?"

"I told you it was hurting me and to stop."

"Funny," he scoffed. "I could have sworn I heard you yelling 'Fuck me, fuck me.' "

Through her tears her eyes glittered furiously. "That was different, you bastard."

"You know you loved it," he taunted.

"You shit! You raped me."

"I believe I made love to you." His voice was cold.

"Love? You don't know the meaning of the word." She ran to pick up her clothes. "You want to control me, not love me," she yelled, then locked herself in his bathroom. She was so upset she was shaking.

How often had victims told her about being sodomized against their will. Oh God, she sobbed, I never expected this from Gary. From anyone.

As she washed herself, her mind raced with revenge fantasies. Just because she'd cried out for him to fuck her didn't give the bastard the right to do whatever else he wanted.

Gary knocked on the door. "Don't be like this, baby. If I hurt you, I'm sorry." His voice became silky. "Come out. I'll make love to you the way you like."

She felt revolted. Gazing at her tear-streaked face in the mirror, her makeup smeared across her face, she realized she would never let him touch her again. Never. She also knew she'd better get tested. She couldn't believe anything he'd ever told her.

He pounded on the door. "Come on out!"

A chill of fear traveled up her spine. Gary's mood swings were more than mere temper tantrums. His behavior was erratic. Something was drastically wrong with him.

His voice was growing ugly. A man who would do what he'd done to her was capable of anything, she realized. She shivered as she searched the tiny room and saw the window. Could she get out that way? She was certainly going to try.

45

Charles arranged to meet Franklin Manning for breakfast at the Holmby Hills Country Club. After he filled Franklin in on the preliminary hearing testimony and Sandra's illness, he inquired as to his father-in-law's health.

"I feel old," sighed Franklin. "I hope you never know what it's like to feel this vulnerable."

"You're not old by any means," argued Charles. "As the distinguished U.S. senator from California, people look up to you, still seek your advice."

"Ex-senator," reminded Franklin.

"It was your choice to retire."

"I felt I had to get back to the private sector in order to get my practice going again. I didn't want to go back to Wolfe, Scott & Green. I wanted a place I could call my own."

Charles knew what Franklin really meant. He had founded Manning & Anderson so Dickson would have a secure future. "It was good for me," Charles pointed out, "because you brought me into the firm."

"That was because I was impressed with you, not because you married my daughter." Franklin peered at the younger man from behind his spectacles.

Charles smiled and nodded.

Franklin cleared his throat. "I may be old and sick, but I'm not blind. I've been noticing how you and Dickson bristle like porcupines in each other's presence. Is it due to the senior partnership?"

"I won't deny we both want it, but . . ." Charles stopped.

"Go on."

"I don't know how to say this except straight out." Exhaling loudly, Charles hurried on. "Dickson's been meeting secretly with one of the partners from Livingstone & Kenter."

Franklin put his hand to his heart.

"Are you all right?" Charles gazed at him worriedly.

"Yes. It's just such a shock. I can't believe my own son would go behind my back."

"That's why I debated whether or not to tell you. Ann will never forgive me for upsetting you." Charles poured him a glass of water and watched as Franklin swallowed one of his pills, then dabbed at his mouth. "I shouldn't have told you."

"You had no choice. I needed to know." Franklin seemed dejected. "Why would my son want to destroy the firm I've spent all these years building?"

Charles shrugged and signaled the waiter for more Pellegrino.

"Tell me all of it," demanded Franklin.

"O.K. But first I want your promise to protect the person who warned me . . . because, well, Dickson threatened her."

"Her? For God's sake, Charles, tell me."

"Very well. Last night Kate thought she was alone; the rest of the office was dark. She went into the conference room and there was Dickson meeting with Paul Kenter, Arnold Mindell, Nathan Ornstein, and Harrison Emery. She apologized and left, but not before she saw a merger agreement sitting on the table."

Franklin turned white. "How dare they meet under our very noses! Manning & Anderson is my firm. I built it. I *refuse* to let it become another large firm prostituting itself for fees!"

"After Kate called, I went up there to confront Dickson. When I told him I was going to tell you, he threatened to make up all sorts of vicious lies to discredit me."

The senior partner slumped back in his chair.

"I've got a copy of the proposed merger." Charles opened his briefcase, took the document out, and handed it to Franklin. "However you choose to handle this, please don't let Dickson hurt Kate. She's a good lawyer with a promising future.''

"I know how valuable she is. You don't have to worry. I'll take care of this with a view toward damage control.''

"Thank you, Franklin. And I'm sorry.''

The older man was silent for a few minutes. Finally, he spoke. "Perhaps it's my fault. I shouldn't have insisted Dickson become a lawyer.''

"Don't blame yourself.''

Franklin gave him a halfhearted smile as he excused himself. When he came back to the table, Charles noted that he seemed to have regained his color and his control.

"Charles, I know what I have to do and I'll do it.'' He signaled to the waiter to refill his water glass. "Tell me, how are you doing on finding personnel to run the D'Arcy empire?''

"I've hired two top people.''

"Good. And what's happening with Theo?''

"I've done as you and Abigail asked. In fact, I've already met with Theo twice. He seems to have a genuine love for the Foundation. However, with Dickson insisting on going forward with the lawsuit over the will . . . it confuses things, not to mention it's keeping the will from being admitted to probate.''

Franklin's cheeks sagged. "I don't like that. I've insisted Dickson drop that suit immediately. My son, unfortunately, doesn't listen very well.'' He removed his glasses and rubbed his eyes. "How long do you figure Sandra's trial will last?''

Charles was surprised at the change in subject. "The trial itself could take a month or more. I'd say it depends on what kind of a defense Kate decides to put on.''

"Do you think Sandra did it?''

"Who knows? Sandra foolishly discussed some things she shouldn't have with Tommy, like telling him she wanted James dead. But actually asking Tommy to kill James?'' He shook his head. "I think the boy might have gone farther with the whole thing than Sandra ever intended.''

"Those are my sentiments too. I hope it's true. For the

sake of the child at least." Franklin sipped his water, then pressed his napkin to his mouth. "I heard about the black eye. I can't believe James would do something like that. And he's not here to defend himself."

"He did have a vicious temper," Charles pointed out.

"But hit a woman? I was friends with William D'Arcy for a lot of years. A fine man. James did a good job of carrying on his traditions." He seemed pensive for a moment. "Charles, as soon as the trial's over, I'm going forward with my retirement."

Charles's nerve endings tingled in anticipation.

"However, I must do certain things for the sake of propriety," said Franklin. "Therefore, I won't announce my support for either one of you."

His mind racing with possibilities, Charles waited to see if Franklin would say anything else.

"But I *will* lobby behind the scenes for you. And you have my word," continued Franklin, "that if you don't become senior partner on the first vote and there's a tie, I'll be on your side."

"You won't be sorry," Charles assured him as he tried to contain his excitement. Dickson had sabotaged his own chances to become senior partner by arrogantly holding that meeting on Manning & Anderson's premises. What a lucky break.

"In the meantime," cautioned Franklin, "please don't say anything, not even to Ann. I want to make the transition as painless as possible for Dickson."

"Of course."

Franklin sighed. "It won't be easy for him." He looked out the window for a moment. Sadness appeared to be etched into his face. "You'll treat Dickson well afterwards, Charles, won't you?"

Charles nodded. "You know you can count on me."

When Kate came into the infirmary and saw how ill Sandra was, a feeling of sympathy welled over her. Jail was a rotten place to be sick and alone. She put a golden stuffed bear on the bed. "Thought I'd bring you some company," she said lightly.

Sandra nodded, apparently too weak even to sit up.

"The nurse says you have bronchitis, but your fever has gone down."

"Uh huh." Sandra's voice was so faint Kate had to lean forward to hear her.

"Is there anything you need?"

"Yes," croaked Sandra, "to get out of this fucking place."

"If you're swearing, you must be feeling better." Kate smiled warmly at her client. Then she walked around to the other side of the bed. "Want some water?"

Sandra shook her head, her blue eyes solemn.

"Do you have any questions about what happened in court yesterday?"

The young woman sat up a little ways, straining to talk. "Is Tommy in trouble for what he said?"

"About James giving you a black eye?"

"Uh huh."

"No. It didn't make the prosecutor very happy. But he's not in trouble."

Sandra sank back against the pillows, looking relieved.

Kate marveled at her client's concern for Tommy. This was a side to her she hadn't seen before. "I take it you're not too angry at Tommy for testifying against you?"

"I'm mad." Sandra's voice was raspy. "But he must have been scared."

"Lying here going over it all," said Kate softly, "do you believe it's possible Tommy killed James thinking he'd be helping you?"

Sandra coughed, then turned toward the wall, the stuffed animal clutched against her heart. After a few minutes, she responded, "Maybe."

"You didn't give him the gun, did you, Sandra?"

Kate could see Sandra shaking her head.

"But Tommy knew where you kept it, didn't he?"

Sandra nodded and seemed to curl up even smaller.

Kate felt ambivalent as she sat in the chair at the side of

the bed. As a lawyer, she needed to push her client, especially now when she was down, to get at the truth. That was the only way she was going to be able to help her.

But as a woman, she felt her heart silently break for the sick young girl. Sandra had been abused her whole life—first by her father, then by James. It wasn't hard to understand why she had such a chip on her shoulder.

And finally, thought Kate, a young man broke through the defenses Sandra had built up for her own protection. It was amazing that she had trusted Tommy enough to tell him about the incest with her father. And Tommy had known instinctively it wasn't Sandra's fault. That a father who did something like that was the scum of the earth.

Who could honestly say Tommy hadn't tried to help the woman he loved the only way he knew how? Kate was angry at Andrew. He should have dug deeper into this case. He should have made a better deal for Tommy. It was obvious Tommy had only wanted to keep James from hurting Sandra or taking her child away from her. Murder was never right. But when a man like James had all the power on his side, what chance did a poor kid like Tommy have?

Kate felt bad for Sandra's son, Jimmy. How frightened he must be all alone in that terrible house with Abigail. She had to get Sandra off. That child also had suffered enough. He needed to be with his mother. For, whatever else Sandra might be, and she could certainly be impossible, it was clear she loved her son.

Kate knew what it meant to be a child alone, scared, powerless, and helpless, at the mercy of another person who had all the power on his side. From the time she was eight and her own father died, she too had felt that fear. She sighed. Life really did boil down to a question of power.

She listened to the deep, raspy breaths coming from the bundle on the bed. Should she wait for Sandra to wake up? Standing, Kate walked to the head of the bed. Sandra was sleeping soundly, her mouth slightly open. She put her hand on Sandra's head. It felt hot. Asleep, Sandra didn't pull away. Kate smoothed the silky blond hair back from her client's face, lost in thought. Suddenly, she made a decision. "I'll see you later," she whispered to the sleeping form.

Madeline surveyed her bruised and scratched body in the mirror. The previous night she'd crawled out Gary's bathroom window, tearing her clothes and scraping her arms and legs in the process. Sneaking to her car, terrified he'd come out and grab her before she could get away, she'd driven home, crying all the way and grateful the kids wouldn't be there to see her.

In the morning she'd called in sick—something she didn't ever do. Thank God Sandra D'Arcy had taken ill yesterday and the hearing had been postponed. Madeline didn't know how she would have managed a hearing this morning.

She remembered how she'd cried for hours before finally falling into a fitful, disturbing sleep. When she woke up, her entire body had hurt. Taking the phone off the hook, she'd gone back to sleep.

She never wanted to see Gary again. But how could she be positive he'd stay away from her? How did I ever get myself in such a mess? she asked her reflection in the bathroom mirror.

Madeline took another hot shower, scrubbing herself from head to toe. She felt used, dirty, all the things she had heard rape victims express. Had she been raped? Was a person raped when she consented to intercourse? Hell, she not only consented, she had begged him to fuck her. The memory of her passion shamed her.

No! she thought, the moment I said "no," he should have stopped. At that instant it had gone from something she had lovingly participated in to an act of control and violence.

The thought of bringing rape charges against Gary made her feel better. But she'd have to face everyone at the office. They'd all know. And Philip. His kind face flashed across her mind. She couldn't bear for him to know. Besides, there was the other reality of the situation. As a prosecutor, she knew hers wasn't a case she'd ever issue a complaint on.

Kate gave her name to the guard and waited for him to call up to the house. He was frowning as he came back to the car. "Mrs. D'Arcy said she was not expecting you."

The exchange that followed was even worse than Kate had anticipated; she had to threaten to get a court order before Abigail finally agreed to allow her inside the compound to visit Jimmy. Although Kate hated to face that intimidating woman, she had to do it for the child. He was probably wondering right now where his mother was. Kate was afraid of what Abigail might have told him. Or worse yet, she might have said nothing, leaving the child to think that he had been abandoned.

As she made her way up the driveway to the house, the memory that had flashed into Kate's mind as she sat by Sandra's bed was still with her. After her parents had separated, it seemed forever to her as she waited week after week, month after month for her father to visit her. When she was eight years old, she had written a letter to him at his last known address begging him to come. One day a letter arrived addressed to "Miss Kate Alexander." Written on flowery stationery permeated by the pungent smell of sandalwood, it was from a woman who explained that her father had died, and how much he'd loved his little girl.

The letter was postmarked from a small town on the southern coast of Italy. To Kate's dismay, there was no return address. In later years, Kate wished she'd known the woman's last name. She wanted to meet her, to try at least to find out more about her father. But it was impossible.

Tears welled up as she recalled the yearning, the regret. With renewed resolve, she pulled into the motor court, parked, and rang the bell.

Inside, she followed the butler up the grand staircase to the landing. At the door to Abigail's suite, she braced herself before walking in. "Hello, Mrs. D'Arcy," she said as pleasantly as she could manage.

"What exactly is the meaning of this?" demanded Abigail.

"I have a gift and a message for Jimmy from his mother. She's sick and I gave my word I'd deliver it personally."

"Sick?"

"She became quite ill in court yesterday. Bronchitis. But the doctor's afraid of pneumonia because she has a high fever and has been listless and not eating."

"Do not expect my sympathy. She took my son away from me."

"In all fairness, Mrs. D'Arcy, Sandra may not have known what Tommy was going to do."

Abigail smirked. "I doubt that."

Kate held her tongue for Sandra's sake. "May I please see Jimmy?"

"This is not at all to my liking, Ms. Alexander. I do not approve of your showing up here without advance notice."

"I apologize for any inconvenience. Now, may I see Jimmy?"

Abigail must have seen the determined look on Kate's face, because she rang for the butler. "Take Ms. Alexander to the nursery. Five minutes is all she is allowed. Understood?"

"Yes, ma'am."

"Thank you," Kate mumbled.

The butler knocked and opened the door into a cheerful sitting room with a bedroom beyond, filled with toys and books. Kate felt a momentary wave of gratitude. At least the old witch hadn't forced the poor child to live in adult surroundings.

The governess came into the room, holding Jimmy by the hand. Kate was taken aback. This wasn't the friendly little boy she'd met such a short time ago. This was a frightened, clinging child.

Kate got down on her haunches. "Hi, I'm Kate. I met you at your mother's house. Remember me?"

The boy nodded. His blond hair fell forward and covered one eyebrow and Kate could readily see the resemblance to Sandra.

"I've brought you presents." She held out the stuffed animal and the wrapped toy. "Want to open it?"

He nodded again, but didn't make an effort to come any closer.

Kate realized what the problem was and introduced herself to the governess. "Is it O.K. if he sees what his mother sent him?"

"Of course. Go ahead, James."

He came over and grabbed the bear. "I'm too big for stuffed animals." His little chin jutted out in a proud way that made Kate think of Sandra.

"Your mother wanted you to have him," explained Kate.

"What's his name?"

"What would you like it to be?"

"Mr. Bear."

"Then Mr. Bear it shall be. Your mother sent him to you because she didn't want you to be lonely."

"Did you see my mommy?"

"Yes. I just came from her."

"Where is she?"

Kate looked into the child's solemn blue eyes. "In a place called Sybil Brand. She wanted me to tell you she loves you and as soon as she can, she'll come and see you. I'm supposed to give you a big hug and kiss and get one back. O.K.?"

He smiled a beautiful smile. Kate was moved nearly to tears as he came into her arms. She hugged him and planted a kiss on his soft cheek. "There, that's from your mother. Can I give you one from me too?"

He put his face out and she kissed him again. "O.K. Now you give me one for your mother."

The child squeezed Kate and kissed her—a big, wet, sloppy kiss. "Thank you," she said.

"What's in there?" He pointed to the large wrapped package.

"Go ahead and open it."

He tore apart the paper and ribbon and his face broke into a smile when he saw the shiny yellow truck.

The buzzer in the room sounded. Kate watched as the woman answered. When she hung up, her eyes were full of sympathy. "Mrs. D'Arcy says your five minutes are up."

Kate stood up. "I'll come see you again, Jimmy. I promise. Is there anything you want me to tell your mother?"

"Come and get me."

"I'll tell her, Jimmy. I promise."

Kate walked out the door feeling that life wasn't very fair. Why was it the children were always the ones who suffered the most?

Kate threw her evening gown on the bed and started taking off her clothes. There was nothing she felt less like doing than going to a fundraiser, especially after the draining day she'd had. Between her visit with Sandra, the confrontation with Abigail, and then the visit with Jimmy, she was beat.

Yet she pushed herself to get ready. As soon as Sandra's preliminary hearing and trial were over, Kate had a political career to salvage, and tonight could be an important step in that direction. It was the first big Democratic party gathering since James D'Arcy's death, and it was being held on the grounds of the grand estate of another bigwig in the party.

An hour later Kate found herself standing in a lavishly decorated tent surrounded by a group of well-dressed people. Pretending to pay attention to what was being said, she thought back to the party at the D'Arcy mansion the night before James's death. What a night that had been! Her future had seemed so reachable, so possible.

Now it all seemed so far away—as if years had passed instead of months. Kate was getting to hate going to the office. The tension between Dickson and Charles was palpable, and after her altercation with Dickson last night, it was bound to get worse.

Sometimes Kate wished the choice for the next senior partner were over, either way. The worst that could happen would be for Dickson to win. She knew if that happened, Charles would want to leave Manning & Anderson. Any number of the best law firms in the country would jump at the chance to get him. Much more so than Dickson.

Then, of course, Charles could also start his own firm. Bright, talented lawyers would flock to join him; he had a fabulous reputation. The way many firms were breaking up today, there was no longer any real stigma attached to leaving a firm or starting over. What difference did it make anyway? At least then Charles could divorce Ann.

Kate realized the person next to her was asking her a question. My God, she had stopped listening entirely. That wasn't like her. "I'm sorry." She smiled, playing for time. As soon as she could, she excused herself.

As she made her way through the crowd, her glance was continually pulled as if by a magnet toward a corner where Charles and Ann stood talking with a group that included Governor Brandon and his wife. Why did Charles have to look like he was having such a good time? And why did Ann have to be so blond, so pretty? Her ice-blue gown was elegant, showing off her petite figure to full advantage.

Heading for the bar to get a glass of ice water, Kate suddenly stopped. Standing a few feet from her were Lauren and Andrew. She didn't feel like talking to them. She'd go to the powder room instead. As she started in that direction, she saw that the group with Charles and Ann were now blocking the entrance to the house. Damn!

Quickly Kate turned and exited the tent. Striding along a used-brick path, she found herself on the side of the house. The night was beautiful and the wet grass shimmered in the moonlight. Across the rolling lawns, beyond the pool, there was a small structure. Pool house or guesthouse? she wondered as she headed for it. Maybe there was a powder room in there?

At the door, Kate heard soft music coming from inside.

She turned the handle and found it locked. She peeked around the small patio. Perhaps there was another entrance? Drapes from the French windows billowed in the soft breeze, indicating an open door, and she made her way to it.

Inside, it was cool and very dark. As she groped for a light, she heard voices.

"I don't think we should be doing this here."

The man's voice sounded familiar but she couldn't place it.

"No one's around." Another male voice.

"I'm too nervous."

"Come on. I want to feel your mouth on me, just for a second."

It sounded just like . . . No. Don't be silly, she told herself. She decided she'd better get out of there before she embarrassed someone. As she made her way toward the door, she bumped into something. Her heart thudded at the loud crash that followed.

"What was that?" a voice said.

"Who's there?" someone called out.

"I was just looking for the powder room," she said softly into the darkness, realizing she was shaking.

A blinding light made her jump. Standing in the hallway facing her was Theo D'Arcy. He looked very handsome in a casual, loose-fitting suit. His face flushed as the door behind him slammed shut.

"I'm so sorry," she blurted out, disconcerted. She didn't know what to say or do.

"No problem." He smiled. "I had the same idea, but someone beat us to it. Why don't I show you where there's another one." He took her arm and led her through the French doors and across the patio and grass back to the house.

As she walked, Kate's heart was still pounding. So many things now seemed to make sense.

"Are you here alone?" he asked suddenly.

"Well, yes." She paused. "I am."

"Then perhaps you'd like to accompany me in to dinner."

She wondered if maybe he didn't realize she'd heard that exchange in the guesthouse. "I'd like that," she found herself saying.

After she returned from the powder room, Theo took Kate's arm and led her to the huge buffet tables set up in the magnificently decorated marquee. "I hate going to these things alone," he said.

"Me too."

When their plates were heaped with food that Kate knew she would never eat, she and Theo made their way toward one of the many tables nearby.

"Anyone in particular you want to break bread with?" Theo asked.

Kate shook her head. She was dying to ask him all sorts of personal questions, but obviously couldn't. Besides, she didn't want to hurt him; Theo seemed to be the one decent person she had met since this whole D'Arcy nightmare began.

"I suppose you don't want to be too close to Charles and Ann?"

Kate's heart skipped a beat. Theo knew? Who else knew? Was she the laughingstock of the whole world?

He seemed to realize his faux pas and a redness mottled his skin. "Forgive me."

"I'm feeling rather warm," she said shakily, wishing she were anywhere but here.

"Want to eat by the tennis courts?"

She sighed with relief. "Sounds perfect."

"Follow me. I play here sometimes." His arm on hers, they made their way out of the tent and into the refreshing night air. By the court, he held out a chair for her. It was far enough away so that the sounds of the band were not deafening and the strains of music wafted pleasantly toward them.

For a few minutes Theo ate slowly, while Kate nibbled and mostly pushed her food around on her plate with a fork.

"Look. I'm sorry for what I said back there. I didn't mean to upset you." Theo's voice sounded remorseful.

There was a brief, awkward silence. "That's all

right. . . . I was just surprised . . ." Kate stammered, not sure what to say.

"We're a lot alike, you and I." Theo settled back more comfortably in the patio chair as his brown eyes scrutinized her.

"In what way?"

"We both feel we have to hide our feelings, pretend to the world we're happy when we're not."

Kate was unnerved by his remark. She tried to think of some appropriate response, but none came. Then, suddenly, she realized there was only one person who could have told him about her and Charles. "Theo, if I ask you something off the record, would you answer me truthfully?"

"If I can."

"You told the police you were home alone the night of the murder."

He gazed down. "Yes."

"Sandra said she called you and when there was no answer, she left a garbled message on your machine."

"I was taking a nap."

"Then how did you manage to get hold of Dickson and end up at her house a few minutes after Charles and me?"

"I heard the message come in. I was lucky enough to reach Dickson in his car and he came for me . . ."

"Theo, you weren't really alone, were you?"

He played with his fork, giving her a long, thoughtful look. "No," he finally said. "When did you guess?"

"Actually, back at the pool house. Up until then there were many pieces that didn't fit, didn't make sense."

"I see."

"I suppose you know that Dickson and I don't much like each other?"

"Dickson's a difficult man to get along with. No one knows that better than me."

"Do you love him?"

Theo took a few sips of his wine. "I used to think so," he said quietly, "but lately, most particularly since my brother's death . . ." He hesitated as if deciding how much to divulge. "I'm not sure."

"Why are you being so open with me?" she asked, voicing her thoughts. "I could blow your world apart."

"Not mine. I've only kept my life private for Mother's sake." He fingered his chin. "And frankly, I doubt you'd do anything to Dickson, either."

"What makes you so sure?"

"If you had wanted to, you would have done it already."

"What do you mean?"

"You bailed him out of jail that night."

"You knew about that?"

"Of course. I was there."

"Then Dickson hadn't wandered into that gay bar by mistake?"

"No. I'd already left because Dickson was drinking too much and becoming abusive."

"That must have been when he picked the fight."

"Probably. At any rate, I really respected you because you never breathed a word."

"I appreciate your faith in me, but the truth is, I had no choice. I couldn't very well breach my client's confidentiality."

"Kate, I've been around attorneys all my life. They breach whatever they damn well please." He dabbed at his mouth with his napkin. When he spoke again, there was a puzzled expression on his face. "I understand you went to see my nephew today?"

Briefly she told him about the letter she'd received after her father's death and how it had made her want to reassure Jimmy of his mother's love.

Theo reached out and touched her hand. "Thanks for thinking of him," he said quietly.

"Jimmy seemed so lonely in that big house."

"I can well imagine."

She heard the sadness in his voice. "Tell me what it was like being a D'Arcy child."

He gave her a rueful smile. "It was not easy, I can tell you that. So much was expected of us from a very early age. And my father . . ." He paused. "He was a very demanding and exacting man." There was a look of sorrow mixed with anger in his eyes. "I spent a lonely childhood with a brother and sister who delighted in taunting me and a father who was hard and cruel."

"How terrible."

"You know, I was dreadfully frightened of my father."

Kate sensed the torment he had suffered, as more pieces of this grotesque puzzle fell into place for her. "Your father . . . he . . . he physically abused you, didn't he?" Her voice was quiet, her words more of a statement than a question.

Theo stared at her as if deciding whether to confirm or deny her words. Finally, in a voice so low she had to bend forward to hear it, he whispered a hoarse, "Yes."

"I'm sorry," she said, wondering how much more he might tell her. Aware that at any second he could clam up, she hurriedly pressed on. "So James was mistreated also?"

He released a tense breath. "Yes. But not for long. Very quickly James became bigger than my father; then they would try to hurt each other."

"And Victoria?"

"For a time. But then James protected her. James and Victoria were very close."

She swallowed hard. "Your mother, too?"

He looked at his long, tapered fingers. "Yes. The proud, indomitable Abigail was also tormented by my father until James learned to protect her, too."

"My God," said Kate, finding it difficult to imagine a woman as formidable as Abigail ever being afraid of anyone.

"When my father died," Theo continued, "my mother became a tyrant just like he had been."

Her mind raced. After all he'd just disclosed, would he also be willing to divulge something that could help Sandra? "Violence passes from one generation to the next. Did you ever see James physically abuse Sandra?"

He was silent.

She leaned toward him. "Please, Theo. If you saw anything"—her voice was urgent—"anything at all, tell me now."

"And be forced to testify?"

"Would that be so terrible? Your testimony would show the judge and the world how brutality can exist even in the best of homes."

Fear washed over his face. "No . . . I couldn't. The media would have a field day."

Kate reached out and squeezed his hand. "If you saw James violent toward Sandra, I might be able to get her acquitted."

He peered down at her hand. "James was a bastard. But what you're asking of me . . . goes beyond what I feel I can do."

"Did you know that Sandra was sexually and physically abused by her father?"

He paled. "That poor kid. She's really had a lousy life." There were several seconds of silence before he continued. "You know, I hated James too. When my father died, James shut me out of the D'Arcy Foundation. It was the only thing I cared about in my entire life because it has a real commitment to the arts." His eyes were full of misery. "The more James knew I wanted something, the more he delighted in taking it away from me. When I'd fail at something, he'd laugh."

He paused. "I wished my brother dead on many occasions," he said finally, his words filled with bitterness.

Kate's heart was pounding. Was Theo about to tell her he was somehow involved in his brother's death?

Looking at her intently, he seemed to read her thoughts as his jaw became rigid.

"If you're thinking I had anything to do with his death," he said solemnly, "you're wrong."

Kate inhaled deeply. She couldn't help but wonder if that was really true.

47

The next morning Kate hurried to see Sandra in the infirmary. She was relieved to find her sitting up in bed, sipping what looked like soup. "You look much better today."

"I feel awful."

"I've got some news to cheer you up. I saw Jimmy yesterday after I left here."

"How is he?" Sandra's pale face was pathetically open and vulnerable.

"Fine."

"No. Tell me how he really is."

"Quieter than the last time I saw him, but thrilled to get your present."

"A present from me?"

"Yes." Kate told her what she had done.

Sandra's face crumpled. "I . . . don't know what to say."

Kate rushed on to cover her own embarrassment. "I was relieved to find his rooms filled with toys and books. I don't know what I was expecting."

"It was nice?"

"Yes."

Her chin lifted as she spoke. "What did he say?"

As Kate repeated the details of her visit, Sandra fiddled with the spoon in her soup, her eyes unable to meet Kate's.

"What made you go?"

"I was waiting for you to wake up, and remembering how lost and lonely I felt when my father went away. I couldn't stop thinking how Jimmy must have felt, given the way you left so suddenly, with no warning. I wanted to reassure him you're still here."

"Was the wicked witch there?"

"Yes."

"What did she say?"

Kate explained how she'd had to threaten Abigail with a court order.

For the first time, Sandra smiled. "I would've given anything to see her face."

"Yeah," admitted Kate with a rueful grin, "it felt pretty good to use muscle and have it work. Anyway, she was her usual arrogant self. But I held my tongue."

"Tell me." Sandra tried to sit up farther as she pushed the tray out of the way.

Beginning with her appearance at the gate, Kate related the entire visit to Sandra. When she got to the end, she repeated what she'd said to Abigail. "So I told her that you may not have known what Tommy was going to do, but she refused to believe me."

Sandra was silently fiddling with the bedcovers. "It figures. But is that what you really think happened? That Tommy killed James thinking it was what I wanted?"

"You keep saying you're innocent. Isn't that what you want me to believe?"

"I want you to believe we're both innocent."

"Sandra," said Kate gently, "I want to, honestly I do. But I can't comprehend why Tommy would confess to something if he didn't do it. I know his lawyer and although I don't necessarily think he's done the best job in the world, I can't see him letting his client cop a plea to a crime he didn't commit."

"Not even to avoid the gas chamber?"

"No, not even to avoid the gas chamber."

"It just doesn't feel right." Sandra looked at the ceiling. "Tommy was so nice. Shooting James in the back of the head, well . . . it doesn't seem like Tommy. Did you see the way he tried not to badmouth me yesterday?"

Walking around to the other side of the bed, Kate nodded. "I noticed."

"I don't know . . ."

Kate cut in. "The entire room also heard Tommy admit you had a black eye. Why don't you tell me about it?"

Sandra's fingers gripped the covers. "I can't."

"I'm going to find out anyway." Kate looked at Sandra's face for a reaction. "I spoke to Theo. He told me the truth about the history of abuse in the D'Arcy family."

"He did?" Sandra seemed shocked.

"Yes, he did. I know you're afraid. I know you think James's family will do something if you say anything. But I promise I'll do my best to keep them from hurting you. O.K.?"

Sandra appeared too overcome to speak. When she did, her voice was weak. "Abigail made like no one would believe me. She threatened not to pay you if I said one word about James touching me." Tears ran down her face. "She said they'd take Jimmy away . . . I was afraid." Her eyes seemed to be pleading with Kate for understanding. "I had no choice. . . ."

"I understand. Now will you tell me what happened?"

Exhaling loudly, Sandra tried to stop crying. "Tommy only saw the black eye the one time. He didn't know the rest of what James did to me." Her words faltered. "I mean, he knew James was mean to me, and all that. But I was . . ." Her voice dropped. "I was too ashamed to tell him the truth. That James was beating up on me all the time."

It was finally out. "I'm so sorry," Kate said. "It must have been terrible."

Sandra's eyes filled with tears again. "You have no idea."

"Can you tell me?"

"Well . . . at first he used to push me around, yank my hair. Things like that. Then one day he knocked me down, kicking me and beating on me with his fists. But he was careful to stay away from my face. That is, until the night of the big party, when for some reason he lost it altogether and socked me in the face."

Kate was again aware that when Sandra spoke about terrible things that had happened to her, she did so in a dull, almost monotone voice. As if it had happened to someone else. Kate was sickened at the picture of the gracious and charming James D'Arcy beating up on a woman half his age and half his size.

She wished James were still alive so she could have the satisfaction of seeing him humiliated before the whole world as he'd humiliated his wife. Oh, what she wouldn't give to see James spend some time in jail.

As Sandra told story after horrible story, each incident worse than the one before, Kate's rage built. She had to do something to calm herself down. Something productive. "I think you'll be with Jimmy sooner than you realize," she said. "Once the judge and jury hear this, I don't see how they can find you guilty of murder."

"But I didn't kill him."

For the first time, Kate began to really believe her. "Then what do you think actually happened?"

"I don't know. I did tell Tommy how I hated James and wished he was dead. He could see how miserable I was. And we did talk about getting rid of James. But it was a game. A make-believe game." Her eyes begged for understanding again as she pulled the blanket up under her chin. "I don't expect you to believe me, but after I talked with Tommy about killing James, I felt better."

Brenda Kelsey's words hit Kate between the eyes. "According to the doctor, sometimes talking is enough."

"Dr. Kelsey said that?" There was a glimmer of hope in Sandra's blue eyes.

"Yes."

"Then I'm not crazy?"

"No. But Sandra, somewhere along the line, Tommy stopped thinking it was a joke. He came to believe it. And," she said matter-of-factly, "he did something about it."

This time Sandra cried openly. "Poor Tommy. I didn't want him to get hurt. I didn't mean for him to kill James."

Kate waited patiently for her sobbing to stop. Did she believe Sandra? Yes, she thought she did. But if she herself had all this doubt, how was she going to get a jury to believe her client? Could Sandra ever come across to a jury as sympathetic? Or would her belligerent attitude work against her too much? When the jury heard about all the money, the magnificent home, the jewels, the trips, et cetera, wouldn't they see her as a spoiled woman who made up stories so that her boyfriend would help her to get rid of her husband?

Something didn't add up. If Tommy hadn't known about all the beatings, why was he angry enough to kill James? What if Sandra was using a few isolated instances to cash in on the abuse theory now that she knew it might save her life?

Kate's mind reeled. She had to find Maria. That woman was the key. Only she had lived full-time in the house with James and Sandra. All the other help came in for the day. "Sandra," she asked gently, "did Maria see any of these things?"

"She must have."

Oh God, I certainly hope so, thought Kate. "Do you have any idea where she might be?"

Sandra shook her head.

Madeline walked into the Criminal Courts Building, praying she wouldn't see Gary. Was this how she was going to feel from now on? Ashamed of what happened and fearful to face him? Didn't she have an obligation to other women who might go through something like this, to see that he was stopped?

She walked down the hall to her office. Suddenly, he was there. Leering at her.

"Hi, beautiful. What happened to you yesterday?"

"I've nothing to say to you, Mr. Sutter, not now, not ever. Stop bothering me or I'll see your ass in jail." She glared at him and rushed off, relieved he didn't follow her. Taking a deep breath, she went into Philip's office.

His smile was warmer than it had been in a while but it changed to worry, as if he could read her thoughts. "Is something the matter?"

"Yes."

"Am I supposed to guess?"

"No." She hesitated.

"Madeline, this isn't like you. What is it?"

To her supreme humiliation, she burst into tears.

Philip came over to her. "My God, Madeline, what's happened?"

"I don't know if I can talk about it."

"Try." He guided her gently toward his sofa. "Here, sit down. Let me get you a cup of tea."

"No. I don't want anything. But could you lock the door?"

He peered at her in astonishment. "Certainly." He flicked the lock, then came back to sit on the edge of the sofa.

After she had regained her composure, she asked, "Philip, when you left my house so suddenly that night, was it because I said I didn't know if I was seeing Gary anymore?"

He stood up and began to pace. Finally, he stopped in front of her. His face was solemn. "Yes."

Gary had been right about one thing, Madeline realized. Philip had cared for her. She could tell by the look on his face. Oh, what a fool she had been.

Philip jumped in as if uncomfortable with his admission. "You know, I made a few discreet inquiries with the office where Gary last worked."

She held her breath. "And?"

"I was told he was erratic, moody, responsible for stirring up trouble. In general, a very unsettling and unstable person to deal with."

"Philip, I'm not going to see him anymore. But I don't know how he'll take it. There's something frightening about him. He scares me. If I request a transfer, will you help me?"

His brown eyes bored into her until she felt they seared her soul. Then slowly he nodded. "I'd rather he left. But I'll do whatever you ask."

"I've been such an idiot."

"Gary's a very manipulative person. Don't be so hard on yourself." Unexpectedly, his arms were around her.

"But I should know better. I really should," she said,

tears welling up in her eyes as she rested her head on his shoulder.

"Hindsight is wonderful."

His arms felt so good around her. She looked up at him. All the time she'd been enthralled with Gary, this kind and gentle man had cared about her. And she had thrown it away. "I could really use a good friend these days. Do you think you could ever forgive me for being such a fool?"

"Nothing to forgive. You had no idea I was . . . in love with you. I didn't tell you. It's my fault too."

A warmth spread through her at his words. "You think maybe someday . . . when I feel better . . . we could . . . start over?"

He smiled at her. "I don't see why not."

After Sandra finished telling Kate about her marriage, she was exhausted. The nurse insisted she was not yet well and needed to rest. So Kate raced back to Century City. Once there, she called Mary into her office and closed the door. "Have you heard from Frank?"

"Yep. I told him you were at Sybil Brand. He said he'd call back."

"Please think of all the places he's already been. Get on my phone in here, because I don't want anyone hearing you, and start calling Mexico. We have to find him."

"O.K., boss."

As Mary started to make the calls, Kate paced back and forth in front of her window. She had the most difficult case of her career and no one seemed to want to help. Dickson was obviously determined to keep the truth about James from coming out. Why else had he refused her request for funds so Frank could find Maria? And although Theo hadn't said a definite no about testifying on Sandra's behalf, she cautioned herself not to count on him. In fact, the chances were that Theo's concern for the D'Arcy family name, as well as for the welfare of his mother and sister, would probably keep him from admitting anything had ever happened. Even Charles didn't want to believe James was capable of hurting Sandra.

Kate shivered as she thought about how difficult things would be once Abigail got wind of the defense she planned for Sandra. Abigail might even try to remove her from the case. Kate knew the court wouldn't allow it as long as Sandra wanted her. Things would probably also get worse at the firm. But in her heart Kate knew she had to do what was best for Sandra. Even though she might lose everything.

She wondered what Charles was doing about Dickson's clandestine partnership meeting the other night. And what would Charles and she do if Dickson told Franklin about them?

Stop panicking, she admonished herself. One thing at a time. First find Maria. If there was to be a trial, she was a vital witness. Even if Theo had seen violence between James and Sandra and by some miracle agreed to testify, it probably wouldn't be enough by itself to get Sandra acquitted. Kate needed a witness who had seen the continuous abuse firsthand.

Mary's voice broke through Kate's reverie. "Boss! I've found him."

Kate moved quickly over to the desk.

"He's going to call back. I found the hotel where he's staying. The rooms don't have phones. The clerk agreed to get Frank to call you from the lobby."

"Thank God. What would I have done if you didn't speak Spanish?" Kate gave Mary a grateful smile.

"You would have managed. You always do." Mary stood up and headed for the door. "I left your private number, so you can answer."

"Thanks for all your help."

"My pleasure. Anything else I can do?"

"If anyone wants me, tell them I'm taking a nap. I don't want anyone interfering with my call."

"You got it."

"Good. I'm going to lock my door."

"Have fun."

Kate quickly locked up and headed toward her desk as her private line started to ring.

"Yes?"

"Kate. It's me. Frank."

"You don't know how glad I am to hear your voice."

Mary looked up and saw Charles coming down the hall. She intercepted him as he was about to open Kate's door. "My boss is taking a nap."

He looked surprised. "I've never known Kate to sleep in the daytime. Is she sick?"

"No. Just exhausted. She spent the day at Sybil Brand with Sandra. She came back looking upset and told me she needed to rest and didn't want to be disturbed."

"That doesn't sound at all like Kate."

Mary wavered. She'd been Kate's secretary the entire three years she had been at Manning & Anderson and although they did their best to hide it, she knew her boss was in love with Charles. Would Kate be angry at her for keeping him out? No. Kate had said *everyone*. She shrugged. "There's always a first time for everything."

"O.K. Buzz me the moment she's up. It's very important."

"Sure thing," she promised.

48

"**R**epeat that again, Frank," said Kate because of the bad connection.

"Maria said James used to knock Sandra around quite a bit. It was getting worse, and she was worried for Sandra."

"That bastard. Now at least we have our witness." Kate felt justified for her relentless pursuit of Maria. "I had to be sure and Maria's the corroboration I've been looking for."

"I know."

"What else did Maria say?"

"Sometimes James got so angry he chased after Maria, too."

"Why on earth did Maria stay?"

"I asked her the same question. She obviously loved the little boy. But it was something else, too. She felt genuinely sorry for Sandra. Apparently, Sandra was one of the few people who was ever nice to Maria."

"Finally, someone who saw a different side to Sandra. I hope Maria agreed to come back and testify for us?"

"That's a big problem." He sighed. "She's terrified."

"Of what?"

"Immigration."

"Why is she worried about immigration now that she's back in Mexico?"

"She was in the process of getting into the U.S. legally. She's afraid they'll find out she was there illegally and it will be used against her."

"Does she realize Sandra may be found guilty of murdering her husband without her testimony?"

"Yes. I've made that point to her over and over again."

"Did Maria seem to be worried that Sandra might be guilty?"

"Nope. She didn't think Sandra had anything to do with the killing. The police, of course, kept coming to the house to ask questions, but she thought it was because of the robbery before the murder."

"So what spooked her? The actual arrest?"

"When she saw Sandra taken away," Frank explained, "Maria felt she was the only one left to take care of Jimmy. But later Charles showed up and told her in broken Spanish that he had to take the child to Abigail's. Knowing how much Sandra hated Abigail, she tried to stop him. But Charles wouldn't listen. After Charles left, she packed up and took off."

"Did Charles say anything that scared her?"

"I don't know."

"Is she still at your hotel?"

"Yes. She and her cousin are both upstairs in my room."

"Can you ask her if Charles said anything to her the night he picked up the child?"

"Do you want to hold on?"

"Yes. I'm afraid if not, we won't get through again."

"O.K."

Kate took notes and worked on her trial brief as she waited. Finally after five minutes, which seemed like five hours, Frank was back on the line.

"He didn't say any more to her than what I've already told you," said Frank. "But I could swear she got a scared look on her face and clammed up. I figured I'd better get back to the phone before you thought I'd disappeared."

"Thanks." She swiveled around in her chair. "Frank, you've got to get Maria to tell you what Charles said to her. Maybe he said she'd have to testify at the trial and she's afraid she'll be forced to tell something bad. Maybe she saw Sandra show the gun to Tommy. Whatever it is, we have to find out. Tell her Sandra's life hangs in the balance."

"I'll try," he promised. "But don't get your hopes up."

Kate was silent. "I've got an idea. Frank, go back upstairs and tell Maria that Sandra is *very, very* ill. Tell her, in fact, that she might die. Ask her if she could live with her conscience if Sandra died with everyone thinking she's guilty of murdering her husband."

"Kate, don't you think—"

"Damn it, Frank, I have to save my client's life."

"O.K. O.K. I'll be back. Hang on."

She waited nervously. Her mind raced with unbidden thoughts as she doodled on her pad. Just when she thought she couldn't stand waiting another minute, he was back.

"I'm not sure what to make of what she told me."

"Tell me."

"Maria says a few weeks before James died, Charles showed up real late one night after she'd already gone to bed. But she couldn't sleep and decided to go make some warm milk. As she was returning from the kitchen, she heard James and Charles arguing. She heard the word 'will' over and over again. Suddenly, the study door opened and

Charles rushed out, madder than hell, with James running after him, shouting. Maria cowered under the stairwell until Charles left and James went back to his study and slammed the door. Then she sneaked back up to her room.''

That's strange, Kate thought. Charles never said a word about arguing with James. She'd have to ask him.

"Kate, are you still there?"

"I was thinking. What's that got to do with what Charles told her when he picked up Jimmy?"

"I'm sorry. I left part of it out. Maria said Charles asked her if she'd heard James and him arguing that night."

"What did she say?"

"That she went to bed early because Jimmy gets up at dawn. But she wasn't sure he believed her."

"And what else?"

"That's it. That's all she said."

"I'm afraid I still don't understand."

"Well, then we're both in the same boat."

"Frank, you've got to convince her to come back with you. I don't care what it takes, or what it costs. Only she can save Sandra. We'll protect her from immigration and find a safe place for her to live. And tell her we'll get permission for her to stay in the country legally when this is all over."

"Kate, you can't promise that."

"Tell her we'll try," she said. "I will try. I promise."

"I'll see what I can do."

Kate sat in her office a long time after the call, wondering what the maid knew, wondering what else Maria might have witnessed that could hang Sandra rather than help her. Maybe I'm doing the wrong thing by trying to bring Maria back, she thought.

Dickson was fuming at the arbitrary way his father had summoned him, as he drove to his home. Once there, he strode into his father's study, where he saw the old man reclining on his leather couch in front of the fireplace, a plaid wool blanket over his legs. "Hello, Father, you wanted to see me?" He kept his voice on an even keel.

"Yes, Dickson. Sit down."

Franklin Manning's face looked grim and Dickson couldn't read anything in the eyes behind the glasses. He sat toward the edge of his seat, feeling somewhat uneasy. "What's so important I had to come out this late?"

His father seemed to be choosing his words. "Dickson, you've done something I find unforgivable."

"Unforgivable?" Dickson's eyes narrowed warily. "Don't you think that's a little melodramatic?"

"Let's not play games," said Franklin firmly. "You've met secretly with representatives from the New York law firm of Livingstone & Kenter—"

Before he could finish, Dickson jumped up. "That fucking asshole! Charles told you, didn't he?"

"Sit down," his father commanded, throwing the blanket to the floor as he swung his legs into a sitting position. "How dare you use language like that in my presence."

"Oh, come off it. Charles tattled to you and now you're going to rip my balls apart over it."

"He only brought me the confirmation I've been waiting for. I discovered your treachery from an old college chum of mine."

Dickson was caught off guard. "Who?"

"I'm sure you've heard me mention Osgood Thornwaller. He's of counsel with Livingstone & Kenter now. He called to congratulate me several weeks ago on the opening of negotiations for the merger of our two firms. I've been waiting for you to tell me about it ever since."

"I don't believe you. Charles told you and I don't intend to let that bastard get away with it." Dickson's eye began to twitch. "Want to hear the truth about your most precious son-in-law? Charles is fucking around with your bright little associate, Kate Alexander." There was a smirk of triumph on his face. "Now how do you like your dear Charles?"

Franklin turned white and Dickson could see he was thinking.

Then his father strode over to the desk and picked up a document. "I don't believe *you*, Dickson." He shook the paper. "You're trying to take my focus away from the real issue here."

Dickson was stunned by his father's blindness about Charles. But it looked like his father had the agreement Charles had taken. The best thing to do right now was to defuse the situation. "It was only a preliminary session," he explained.

His father pointed his finger at him. "You went behind my back and met with those vultures. I told you I didn't want to merge with that firm and I meant it. Since you obviously don't respect me or my opinions in this matter, you leave me no choice." Franklin's eyes glittered with anger. "I'm not going to support you for senior partner."

"You'd rather support that whoring motherfucker Charles to run your precious firm than your own flesh and blood?"

"That despicable language will get you nowhere with me, Dickson. As to the senior partnership, I'm afraid there's nothing more I can do for you."

"Let me tell you the sad facts of life, my dear father. I may have enough votes to become senior partner without your help. You're an old man whose days are numbered. So why don't you just resign and get the fuck out of my life and out of Manning & Anderson's hair."

"How dare you!" Franklin roared at his son. "I'll remind you that Manning & Anderson is my firm, not yours. As long as I'm alive, I control the majority of shares. Say one more filthy word to me and I'll boot you out on your behind, son or no—" Suddenly, Franklin clutched at his heart.

"Father," cried Dickson, seeing the older man stagger to the couch and fall sideways.

"Get me some water," croaked Franklin, still clutching his chest.

Dickson stood there, unable to decide if he should help his father or not. What would happen if he did nothing and the old man just died? But he didn't know whether his father's will still designated him as the heir to the partnership shares in the firm. What if he had transferred it to someone else? Like Charles?

Franklin had managed to open his pillbox and stick one of his pills under his tongue. His color was starting to come back.

Knowing he'd better move quickly to help his father or he would never be forgiven, Dickson rushed to pour a glass of water. "Here." He handed it to his father, then helped him to sit up.

After a few sips Franklin coughed and gasped for air. The pill must finally have begun to take effect. "Get your mother," he whispered hoarsely, his voice cracking.

Dickson, wondering if Franklin had guessed what he'd been thinking, ran to do his father's bidding.

When Irene Manning came rushing into the room, she took one look at her husband and reached for the phone. Dialing 911, she told the operator her husband might be having a heart attack. After giving the address, she went to check on him. "Did you take a pill?"

He nodded, unable to talk.

"Then the best thing to do is stay calm until they get here. Lie back." She sat down, taking both his hands, rubbing them between her own. "You're going to be fine, Franklin. You're going to be fine," she kept murmuring.

The sound of a siren could be heard wailing in the distance.

When Irene looked up at Dickson as if for reassurance, he could not bring himself to meet his mother's worried gaze.

49

Kate buzzed Charles to tell him she had to see him. When she opened the door to his office, he was sitting at his desk, his legs up and a drink in his hand.

"Kate." His feet hit the floor as he rose to greet her. "I was so worried. It's not like you to take a nap."

"I went to see Sandra. It was an exhausting session."

"Want to tell me about it?"

"Not now, if you don't mind."

He put his arms around her, but she gently pulled away. "Let's sit down." She motioned toward the sitting area.

"Sure. Want a drink?"

"No, thank you."

His forehead creased into a frown as he took a seat opposite her.

"This is about Ann again, isn't it? You're angry because I didn't act unhappy enough at the party last night. For God's sake, Kate, what would you have me do? We're this close"—he held up his fingers—"to getting everything we want. Can't you be patient a little longer?"

"It's not about that," she said quietly. "It's about the truth." Her expression was serious. "If you can't tell me, say so. But don't lie."

"O.K."

"Why didn't you mention you had an argument with James over his will two weeks before he died?"

"How do you know I did?"

"I said no games. Either level with me or I go to the D.A."

"Surely you're kidding."

"Try me."

He stood up to fill his glass with scotch, plunking another ice cube into it. When he spoke, his voice was low. "It didn't change anything."

"Shouldn't I be the judge of that?"

"When did you become judge and jury?"

"I'm defending a woman for murder." She gave him a sharp look, her indignation rising. "I've a right to know anything that may be relevant and certainly from a member of my firm."

"So now you know," he said curtly. "We fought over some proposed will changes to put Theo in charge of everything. Then James changed his mind. Can't a man fight with his best friend?"

"Yes. But when you hide the evidence of the fight, especially with a will contest going on, that worries me.''

"Kate, be reasonable. My best friend's brutally murdered. My life's thrown into turmoil. I've got to run the D'Arcy Company and Foundation, deal with his will and the probate court, fight that ass Dickson and his puppet Theo over changes James didn't make.'' He swirled his drink. "I'm trying to win control of the law firm because Dickson wants to sell us down the river to some New York City sharks and Franklin's counting on me to stop his son without hurting his damn feelings.'' He shook his head. "Don't you think I've got a few things on my mind?''

Kate leaned forward, her attitude more conciliatory. "I've made excuses for you because of all that. And I've put my own personal feelings on the sidelines while we solve some of the problems. But not divulging that James discussed changing his will wasn't right.''

"What does my fighting with James over some proposed changes have to do with anything?''

"For one thing, it makes you a suspect in James's murder.''

His glance hardened. "So now I'm a murderer?''

"No.'' She backed off. "But certainly a suspect the police didn't know about.''

"Because we had an argument?'' he said with disbelief.

"Yes.'' She nodded. "You withheld vital information.''

"Then I fucking apologize!'' He stormed over to his phone and lifted the receiver. "Here, call Detective Bower, call Madeline Gould, call whomever you damn please and tell them.''

"Calm down.'' She gestured with her hand. "I'm trying to have a rational conversation and you're overreacting.''

He scowled at her. "It's rational to tell someone they're a suspect in the death of their best friend?''

"You aren't a suspect now. Tommy's confessed.''

"Is that supposed to make me feel better?'' He replaced the phone and came to sit next to her on the couch, running his finger slowly up her arm. "Kate, this is crazy.''

Even though she felt little goose bumps from his touch,

she pulled away. "Please, I want to keep this conversation on a strictly business level."

"O.K. Have it your way, Counselor." He went back to the couch across from her. "In the interests of full disclosure, James also mentioned changing his prenuptial that night. He said he wanted to give Sandra more money because she'd given him a son. It didn't sound like James. Anyway, I advised him not to do anything until I could check a few things out."

"Why?"

"I'd heard a rumor she was having an affair."

She couldn't conceal her surprise. "And you told James?"

"I mentioned it."

"How could you tell your best friend something like that?"

"No one could hurt James. The man had thick skin." His expression was not discernible as he twirled his glass.

Kate thought of what she'd learned from Sandra and Theo. James had indeed been a cruel man. "After what Sandra told me, I'm inclined to agree."

"What did she say?"

"That James beat the shit out of her, choked and strangled her, threw her around. Even forced her to have sex with him at knifepoint."

He looked at her, clearly shocked. "I knew he had a violent temper, but I didn't figure him for being a complete bastard. You're sure she's telling the truth?"

She nodded. "We've found Maria."

"Where?"

"In Mexico."

"Frank went to Mexico after Dickson refused to pay for it?"

"You didn't think I'd let a few thousand dollars keep me from finding out the truth, did you?"

A smile formed around his lips. "That's my gal."

"So what did James say when he heard about Sandra?"

"He told me to hire a private eye and have her watched."

"Did you?"

"Yes."

"Who?"

"Remember Marty?"

"You said he took an out-of-town assignment."

"This was before he left."

"Did he actually tail her?"

"You know, in all the excitement, I'm not sure."

"I'd like his number, I want to call him."

He peered at her. "Sure."

"Now, please."

He went to his desk and brought it back to her.

Kate drummed her fingers on the pillow, her mind working. "What kind of a man was James really?"

He pointed the glass at her. "A man of extremes. One minute he was jovial and the life of the party. Warm, generous, the best friend a man could have. The next minute he was cruel, vicious, cutting. The total opposite."

"Must have been hard on you."

"I was used to it. It wasn't easy, but we'd long ago learned to live with each other's idiosyncrasies and achieve an amicable method of dealing with each other."

"And what was that?"

"I did all the work and if he didn't like something and yelled about it, I could tell him to go fuck himself."

She laughed in spite of herself, and he smiled back.

"So you see," he said, "our fighting was certainly not news. Why, I probably fought more with James in the years we knew each other than anyone could imagine. But that was James. Surely if you've investigated his death and questioned witnesses, this can't be news to you?"

His criticism stung her. He was right. She did know James had been volatile. She'd seen it with her own eyes. "Why did you fight about the will?"

"The whole thing really started because Dickson was pressuring Theo. He wanted Theo to have more say in the Foundation and other D'Arcy family matters. As part of their whole plan, they wanted the will changed. Theo, of course, always did what Dickson asked of him, so he was badgering James."

"Why did you care?"

He leaned back against the sofa. "It's complicated."

"Try me."

"You might not like some of what you hear." His smile this time was self-deprecating.

"I'm not a child. I know you're far from perfect."

"Do you really, Kate?" He eyed her critically. "Don't you look up to me because of my 'connections' and the strings I pull politically?"

"That's not fair."

"It's true, isn't it?"

She stood her ground. "Why didn't you want Theo?"

He exhaled. "I didn't want to share the power. I'd gotten used to doing things in the D'Arcy Company and Foundation my way. James always expected me to handle everything. I used to think it was because he realized how smart I was, and that he could trust me." He laughed, revealing even, white teeth.

"But the more work I did and the more dependent I thought James was becoming on me, the more he enjoyed himself at my expense. It took me a lot of years to understand he was playing the old carrot-and-stick game with me. He let me run with the carrot until the power became important to me, then he threatened to take it away if I didn't do something his way."

She shook her head. "It looked to me like there was a lot of mutual respect between the two of you."

"If I wanted him to treat me like that in public, I had to allow him to rant and rave and sometimes even humiliate me in private. That was the price he exacted."

"And you paid it?"

"Yes."

"I see," she said quietly. "Had Theo had any say in the Foundation up until that time?"

"No."

"Why was that?"

As Charles told her how James had always tried to block anything Theo wanted, she felt relieved, realizing his story was the same as Theo's. "Why did William let one son have that much control over the other?"

"Ah." His eyes lighted up. "Old William was a masterful manipulator. He didn't want to let James have all that control. But one day James simply took the power away. Theo never had a chance against either of them."

She sat silently for a few minutes. "How could Theo possibly hurt you?" Her tone rose slightly in spite of her efforts to remain calm.

"Money," he said simply.

"I don't understand."

He hesitated as if deciding whether or not to proceed. "Kate, the bulk of my money is Ann's."

"But you make at least a million dollars a year as a lawyer."

"I make a salary of over a million dollars a year," he corrected. "By the time I pay taxes and our living expenses—remember, I have two kids in Ivy League colleges—there's almost nothing left. My home's worth eight million, but the money to buy it came from Ann's separate property. The vacation homes, the stocks, the boat, the lavish entertaining—it's all basically paid for with a lot of her money. The Manning money is old money. Ann had trust funds of millions when I married her. It's still her separate property. I've managed them and increased them to staggering proportions, but I'm only entitled to a portion of it all upon a divorce."

"If money's so important, how could you even think of leaving her?"

He smiled. "Because I love you. Surely you know that. I've just had to make certain arrangements for our future."

"I make a nice salary too," she pointed out testily.

"I've become accustomed to great wealth," he said, grinning. "I don't want to work this hard all my life. I want you and me to be able to take trips. To have a beautiful home and a couple of vacation places. A boat, a plane. Cars. Then, of course, there's the other love in my life: politics. To play in the big leagues takes large sums of money plus influence and power. As the head of the D'Arcy Company and Foundation, I have them both.''

"We could live in my condominium," she said, as if she hadn't heard him.

"We could. But if you're asking me if I'd be happy"—he shook his head, his dark eyes somber—"the answer's no."

"I had no idea you felt this way."

"That's because I've been taking care of it myself."

"How?"

"By borrowing D'Arcy Foundation funds to put into some surefire deals I knew about."

She drew in a sharp breath.

"The money will all be put back," he assured her. "I just didn't need Theo snooping around and discovering it."

"Are you saying you *stole* from the Foundation?"

"I prefer to use the word 'borrow.' "

"How can you be so cavalier about something so wrong?"

His eyes narrowed. "Because I don't feel it's wrong. Let me tell you a little story. When James was going crazy a few years back after the bottom fell out of the real estate market here in Southern California, he desperately searched for a solution. I listened to James throw around figures, looking for a worthwhile sales scheme, and I began to think.

"So one day I asked if he'd give two percent of the stock to anyone who came up with an idea to boost sales. He looked me straight in the eye and said, 'Absolutely.' And I said, 'Even if that person is me?' James knew how badly I wanted to be independently wealthy of Ann. He said, 'Sure.' "

Kate's eyes were riveted on him as he continued.

"I went all over the country. It took me two months where I didn't pay attention to my law business, but I talked to everybody I could find. I came up with an idea for financing buyers into their first homes. It was a way for the D'Arcy Company to invest in the future by investing with these people."

Kate was impressed. She'd never realized the brilliant

marketing strategy of the D'Arcy Company had been Charles's idea. "So what happened?"

"James loved it. Told me to implement it. I asked about the stock and he told me to draft up those papers, too." His dark eyes became even darker as a scowl marred his handsome face. "But somehow, James never got around to signing those papers. When I demanded he sign, he laughed."

Her stomach was in a knot. "Did James ever find out what you were doing?"

"No. He had no idea."

She felt relieved. "So how did you stall him on Theo?"

"By pointing out the truth. That Theo would bring Dickson with him and James would regret the day Dickson got involved in his family's affairs. And he agreed. But only after we argued and fought and accused each other of terrible things." He chuckled. "We could really go at it sometimes. And I admit that night was a real winner. But the next day he told me he wasn't sure again. He asked me to think about ways Theo could be useful and I promised to try. And that's how we left it."

"You still haven't explained why you kept quiet."

Her last comment seemed to make him angry. "Kate, what did you want me to do after James was dead? He didn't change any documents. The fact that he thought about it makes no difference legally. All I would have succeeded in doing was humiliating myself. And besides, James could've been playing one of his cruel games. The way he changed his mind the next day is proof of that. Who have I hurt by keeping quiet?"

"That wasn't your decision to make, Charles," she insisted quietly.

"If I was wrong, *mea culpa*. I'm sorry." He leapt up and went to the bar.

"Don't you think you've had enough?"

"That's wonderful!" he shouted. "The woman I love is tearing my fucking guts out. Now she wants to take away my scotch. Well, here!" He flung his drink against the bar.

The sound of glass shattering startled Kate. "Charles, calm down."

He came over and slumped down next to her, putting his head back on the pillows. "I'm tired, Kate. Tired of being the strong guy everyone leans on. Tired of being the invincible Charlie Rieman."

She patted his arm. "Even if I understood what you've done, and I'm not at all sure I do, you should have told the truth on the stand."

"What do you mean?" he asked crossly.

"You said you knew of no other will."

"That's the damn truth," he protested. "No one fucking asked me if James ever contemplated a new will."

She jumped up. "Charles, this is crazy. Lying is lying."

"You're wrong, Kate. No one asked me if James ever mentioned changing his will, only if he had changed his will. I did not lie," he insisted stubbornly. He reached for her hand and drew her down next to him. "Don't do this to *us*. What I've told you has no relevance to James's death. Tommy killed James. Don't ruin us, our life, because of a lousy argument."

She got up and walked over to the bar, where she bent and started picking up the pieces of shattered glass.

"Stop that," he ordered, "you'll cut yourself."

"Don't talk to me like a child," she snapped.

He brought over a trash container. Down on one knee, he took her hands in his. "You asked for the truth. I gave it to you. Don't punish me now."

She gazed into the eyes she loved so much. Inside, she was in turmoil. Part of her wanted to throw herself into his arms and tell him she understood. James had treated him badly too. He also might be right that legally he had no obligation to disclose mere talks about changing a will.

"I don't know what to do," she said truthfully, standing up. "But I've had all the trauma I can take for one day. I'm shell-shocked. I need to think."

"Can I at least give you a hug?"

Kate nodded and he grabbed her and held her close. She hugged him back quickly, then pulled away. "I'll talk to you later," she said, leaving his office.

After Charles left to go to his club, Kate sat at her desk working on her notes for the resumption of the preliminary hearing. Try as she might, however, she couldn't stop thinking about their conversation. Was Charles right? Was she being unreasonable? Wanting to go over his testimony, she searched the top of her desk for the hearing transcripts. "Damn," she mumbled out loud. "Where are they?"

Maybe Charles had wanted to read them over. As she went down the hall to his office, she noted that the firm was deserted. Not even the word processing department is working this late on a Friday night, she mused. Everybody's gone home to families or loved ones. Or out on dates. Everybody, that is, but me.

When she reached Charles's door, she flipped on the lights and hurried across the beautiful Oriental carpet toward his desk. Her glance was drawn involuntarily to the area around his bar. She was grateful to see that the cleaning crew had already been there and that the remaining pieces of glass were gone from the floor. What on earth had possessed Charles to throw his glass? In the three years Kate had known him and their one year of intimacy, she'd never seen Charles act violent before.

She started to sort through the stacks of papers and files on his desk, anxious to find the transcripts yet careful to put things back into place; Charles was a stickler for order. Kate knew she wouldn't feel comfortable until she had reread his testimony and satisfied herself that he had been truthful.

Gazing around his office, she found her attention drawn to the wall of pictures of Charles with all those important world leaders. Had he been right? Was that what had attracted her to him? She knew it was impossible to separate Charles from the aura of power that surrounded him. Yet she liked to think she was more sincere than he had made her sound.

The shrill ringing of the phone startled her. Without thinking, she lifted the receiver, holding it to her ear while she continued to sift through the documents.

"Don't hang up on me again, Charles," said a nasty voice. "I want that hundred thousand. If I don't get it in twenty-four hours the D'Arcy case blows up in your face." The man hung up.

Kate, shocked, realized she had picked up Charles's private line. That voice sounded so familiar. Who did it belong to? She racked her brain for plausible answers. It sounded like the caller was blackmailing Charles. Who would do that? Suddenly, Kate's memory clicked on. The voice—it was Marty, the private investigator who used to do work for them. How strange that she and Charles had just discussed him earlier this evening. If it was Marty, what could he have meant?

Feeling weak, Kate sat down in Charles's chair. What was Marty saying? Charles claimed that James was only thinking of changing the will. That he hadn't done so. On the other hand, Dickson had sworn in court documents that he had seen a new will. Her mind raced with possibilities. Was there in fact a new will? Had Charles hidden it or destroyed it after James's death? She went over her conversation with Charles. He kept saying there was no harm done. James had not done anything more than talk about some proposed changes. But now she also knew that Charles was capable of lying. . . .

If Charles had been in possession of a new will, he would have destroyed it, wouldn't he? But if not, where would it be? Kate knew Charles kept her love letters in a safe in his desk, and started to search for it. In the second-to-bottom drawer, she located a piece of wood that was loose. Upon closer inspection, she saw that it pulled out. Behind it was a button. When she pushed the button, the bottom of the drawer slid away revealing a safe. It had a combination lock. She tried it. It was locked.

Quickly, making sure not to disturb anything, Kate opened and sorted through each drawer on the other side of the massive desk, noticing how organized it all was. At the bottom of the third drawer was a book. Lifting it out, she was surprised to see it was the Bible. What on earth was Charles doing with the Bible? In all the time Kate had known him, he had never gone to church, except for the requisite funerals and weddings, or made any reference to a religious belief of any kind. Could this be something new, something he had turned to for comfort since James's death?

He was obviously taking the loss of his friend a lot harder than she had realized. She flipped the pages. At the back of the book, he had written a small list in his neat handwriting: *Chapter 18, Exodus. The Twenty-Third Psalm. The Five Books of Moses.* She searched for the designated readings, wondering why he had singled them out. When she was unable to find one of them, an idea suddenly entered her mind. She turned the combination right to 18, back to the left to 23, then back the other way, passing 0, to 5. It clicked. With a light jerk forward, the door to the safe came open.

Charles looked around the dining room of the Wellington Club. He'd had a nice dinner with two other lawyers who had just left. Because he had more to drink than he usually did, he was wondering if he should go home or sleep it off here at the club. He decided to walk into the lobby and see what was going on; he really didn't want to go home to Ann. There had been no happiness in that house for years. He saw the faces of his daughter and son in his mind's eye. Good kids. But they were on their way to their own futures.

Kate's beautiful face swam before him. He was luckier than most. He was getting a second chance. Kate was wonderful. Gorgeous, brilliant, dynamic. Every day she was becoming more and more politically savvy. He had no use for a woman who wasn't intelligent. Ann was clever, but in a devious way. He had learned a great deal from his wife. But Kate's perceptive intelligence excited him. Thinking about Kate, he felt the familiar rush to his loins. He looked at his watch. Could she still be at the office? It wasn't that far, and since he had had too much to drink, he decided to walk; the fresh air would do him good. He quickened his pace as he thought of her long, full-breasted body pressed naked against his.

Kate quickly but carefully riffled through the contents of the safe. In the front were several long white envelopes, the kind used in law firms for testamentary documents. One was marked "Last Will and Testament of Charles Rieman" and the other "Last Will and Testament of Ann Rieman." There were a few more documents, some gold coins, and a jewelry box, which was empty. Toward the back there was another large white envelope. Reaching for it, she saw that it was marked "Codicil to Last Will and Testament of James D'Arcy."

She took it out of the envelope, her mind whirling. A codicil wasn't a will but an amendment of sorts. The probate court had the original will. She racked her brain trying to remember if there had been any mention of codicils to the will. Perhaps this was just a copy. She opened it, startled to see that it was an original handwritten document. The date leapt out at her. My God, this document was dated two weeks before James died!

Below where the envelope had been lay a cassette tape. She reached for it, wondering what was on it. Suddenly, the fear of being caught shuffling through the private papers in Charles's safe made Kate feel claustrophobic. She had to get out of there. Keeping the codicil and the tape, she closed the safe and put back the Bible. Then she hurriedly tried to straighten up any mess she might have made.

All thoughts of the transcripts she had been looking for flew from her mind as she rushed to get out of his office. What the hell did all of this mean? She heard a noise. She stopped. At the sound of the door opening, she froze. Pressing the documents against her chest, she frantically looked around for a place to hide. But it was too late. She was trapped.

"Oh, Miss Alexander, I'm sorry. I didn't know anyone was still here."

Kate's heart pounded wildly. It was one of the firm's law clerks. "You're working late tonight, Dave," she croaked. Her voice sounded like sandpaper.

"Yeah. Mr. Rieman gave me a research project that's due at the beginning of the week. I've been having a hard time with it. I thought I'd come in tonight when it was quiet." He peered at her closely. "Are you O.K., Miss Alexander?"

"I'm fine." She tried to smile. "You just startled me." She made a feeble attempt to laugh. "I thought I was the only one crazy enough to work late on a Friday night."

Dave laughed heartily, as if Kate had just said something terribly witty.

Poor guy, she thought, he looks as scared as I feel. "I've been looking for the D'Arcy preliminary hearing transcripts," she said by way of explanation. "But I can't find them. If you see them anywhere, would you bring them to my office?"

"Sure thing."

"Great. Well, I'll leave you to your research." She gave a little wave and rushed past him, her stomach knotted in fear.

Kate practically ran down the hall to her own office. Once inside, she locked the door and pressed her back against it. Her hand to her chest, she tried to catch her breath. Beads of perspiration formed on her upper lip. She needed to get out of there. But first she had to find something.

Hastily Kate rummaged through her papers looking for the copy of James's will that she had used at Sandra's hearing and the attendant documents. She was sure there was no mention of any codicil. She wanted to compare the documents, but was afraid to take the time. Was a handwritten codicil to a typed will valid, as a matter of law? She couldn't remember. The handwritten document in her hand was not witnessed. Kate recalled vaguely that a holographic will did not need to be witnessed.

Oh my God, she muttered to herself. This codicil changes the very provisions Dickson and Theo have been claiming were changed in a new will. What did it mean?

This wasn't a will, it was a codicil. Technically, Charles had been correct when he said he knew of no other will. Neither she nor Madeline had used the words "testamentary document," which would have encompassed a codicil. How stupid of her.

She took the tape and put it into her player. After a lot of static she heard Charles's voice.

"Marty, you're acting crazy. Be sensible. Do you want to end up in jail?"

"You listen to me," said the voice she recognized again as the private investigator's. "I've done all the hard work, I've taken all the risks. For what? A lousy hundred thousand dollars. You get me the rest of that money or I'm going to blow this thing out of the water."

"I told you, I can't get the money right now."

"If you don't come up with that other hundred thousand, Charles, I'm going to the police."

"Now I know you're crazy—"

The tape stopped abruptly. Kate sat there for a moment, her mind filled with rage. He lied to me. Had everything he said been lies? His greed had blinded him. What was going on? She tried to come up with a logical explanation for the new evidence. The only thing she could think of was that after James made the codicil and was killed, Charles hid it, planning not to tell anyone. And then Marty somehow found out about it and was blackmailing Charles.

Kate decided to make a copy of the codicil and get the hell out of there. This was new evidence in the D'Arcy case. When she considered it together with the call she had answered, she was afraid she had a legal duty to turn it over to the police. It certainly sounded relevant.

She flipped through her address file until she found the number she needed. As she listened to it ring, she prayed she was doing the right thing. From this point on there would be no turning back.

"Hello."

"Madeline, it's Kate. I'm sorry to bother you so late, but I need to see you. As early tomorrow as possible."

"On the D'Arcy case?"

"Yes."

"Tomorrow is Saturday," Madeline complained. "Give me a break. Can't it wait until Monday?"

"No, it can't. It's important. I've got new evidence."

"What kind of evidence?"

"I'd rather not tell you over the phone. Madeline, I wouldn't ask if it wasn't important. I'll come to your house first thing in the morning."

"O.K. Remember where I live?"

"Of course." Kate thanked Madeline and hung up. She looked at her hands. She was shaking. Packing up her briefcase and her purse, she put them on the chair nearest the door. Then she took the codicil with her. One quick stop at the copy machine and she was out of there.

"Good evening, Mr. Rieman," said the security guard as Charles wrote his name into the logbook for nighttime visitors.

"Hi, Stan. How's the wife and kids?" His speech was slurred.

"Great. Yours?"

"Fine."

"You're working late tonight, aren't you?" the guard said, smiling as he escorted Charles to the elevator. Inside, Stan put his key into the panel and pushed the penthouse button.

"I need to get something I forgot. Anybody else upstairs?"

"That young law clerk, his name is Dave something, checked in a little while ago."

"That's the kind of student I like to see," said Charles, with a grin. "If they're willing to hustle now, they'll usually make good lawyers."

"If you say so." The guard smiled again.

"Did you see Kate Alexander leave yet?"

"Nope. From what I can tell, that pretty lady works harder than any two lawyers put together."

"That she does," agreed Charles.

The ringing of the telephone woke Philip.

"Are you sleeping?" asked Madeline.

He yawned and looked at the clock as he held the phone to his ear. "I must have dozed off. It's after eleven. What's doing?"

"I was in bed already," said Madeline. "But I can't sleep. I'm worried."

Philip rubbed his eyes. "Why?"

"Kate Alexander just called me. She said it was important and asked to see me first thing in the morning."

"She say why?"

"Something to do with new evidence in the D'Arcy case."

"What kind of new evidence?"

"She didn't say. I wish she had. Now I probably won't sleep all night wondering." She hesitated.

"What's wrong?" he asked, immediately sensing that something was really upsetting her.

"I don't know. Kate's voice sounded very strange. Almost scared."

"Scared?" He shook his head, trying to clear the cobwebs.

"Yeah."

"Where was she calling from?"

"I don't know. I called her back at home just to make sure she was all right, but there was no answer."

"Well, either she's gone to bed or maybe she's just leaving her office to go home. I wouldn't worry about it too much. Tomorrow will be here in a few hours and then you'll find out what's going on. Where are you meeting her?"

"She's coming to my house."

"Want me there?"

"No. I'm sure I'll be able to handle it." She sighed. "Well, I just wanted to say good night. And thank you, Philip, for our little talk today. It made me feel a lot better."

"You're welcome, Madeline. Sleep tight."

Across the street, Gary sat in his car and watched the lights go out in Madeline's house. "I wonder if the kids are there," he muttered into the silence.

He didn't appreciate the way Madeline had spoken to him today. Maybe he would check the windows in the back of the house. See if the kids were sleeping. If they were, he might take a chance. She had no right to talk to him like that. Who did she think she was?

51

Kate was making a copy of the codicil when the door opened behind her. Expecting to see Dave again, she turned around. Her hand flew to her mouth. "Charles," she stammered, "I . . . didn't expect to see you. What are you doing here?"

"Doesn't sound like you're too happy to see me," he mumbled, slurring his words.

"No . . . I'm just surprised, that's all." She made an attempt at a smile. "I thought maybe it was your law clerk. Dave's here, you know?"

"Not anymore." He grinned. "I just told him to go."

At the realization that she was alone with Charles in the office, she blanched. What if he saw what she was copying? How would she ever explain?

"What are you doing?"

She shrugged nonchalantly. "Making a few copies. I was just about to leave. I'm exhausted."

"Good. I'll leave with you." He came over and took her in his arms.

Kate smelled the liquor on his breath. She had never known him to drink as much as he had tonight. Obviously, he had continued after he left her. Panicked at the thought he would see what she was doing, she tried to edge him back toward the door.

He nuzzled her neck. "It's important to me that you understand how everything I've done is for our future."

She searched frantically for the right words, not wanting to antagonize him. The man who had confided in her about "borrowing" funds was not the man she thought she knew and loved. "You promised to give me a little time, remember?"

His lips curved downward in a sullen expression. "How much more do you need?"

"A day or two."

"What's the matter?" His eyes narrowed.

"Nothing." She realized the more skittish she acted, the more suspicious he would get. O.K., Kate, she told herself, this is your chance for an Oscar. You've got to get this man out of the office. "I know you've been planning for our future," she said brightly. "But what we both need now is to go home and get a good night's sleep." She headed for the door.

"Hey, you're forgetting your copies." He started over to the machine.

Her heart pounding, she ran back and grabbed her documents. God only knew what he might do if he saw what she was copying. She quickly picked up some blank paper to place on top of the codicil. "I've got 'em, let's go."

He gave her a funny look. "I was hoping we could get a good night's sleep—together."

"I'm too tired. . . ."

His forehead crinkled into a frown as his eyes clouded over. "You avoiding me?"

She forced herself to smile. "Of course not, darling. Tell you what," she said, jockeying for time. "Why don't you go to my place. You've got the key with you, don't you?"

"Yeah."

"Good. I've got to drop something off on the way home and I'll meet you there in nothing flat. And please take a taxi. If something happened, I'd never forgive myself."

He started to protest, but she put her hand over his lips. "After you're dropped off, fix yourself a drink, get comfortable." She smiled her most winning smile. "Before you know it, I'll be there."

"What do you have to drop off?"

"Jury instructions for my friend Rachel Shulman. You remember my telling you about her, don't you? She's got her first murder trial starting next week and she's scared to death."

"Can't you do it tomorrow?"

She glanced at her watch and shook her head. "I'm late and she's waiting up for me. Please, Charles, do it my way this once?"

"All right." He grabbed her and pulled her to him. Holding her in a tight grip, he pressed his lips against hers in a long kiss.

She forced herself to relax in his arms as she felt his mouth on hers, but a voice inside her cried out, Please, dear God, let there be some reasonable explanation. Only the truth could satisfy her now. And what the truth was, she was afraid to face.

Madeline heard the sound at her window and jumped up, startled, stifling a scream. What was it? It sounded like someone scratching against the glass. She got up quickly, reaching for her robe in the dark. This time she heard a soft knock, coming from the direction of the front door. Who could it be at this hour?

She turned on the light and made her way to the living room to look through the peephole. My God, it was Gary! What was he doing here?

"Madeline," he called softly, as if realizing she was

there. "It's Gary. Please let me in. I've come to apologize."

"Go away!" she said, in a clipped, angry voice.

"Please give me a chance to explain."

"No. Just leave."

"I'll sit out here all night. I don't know what to do to show you how sorry I am. But whatever it is you want, just tell me and I'll do it."

"I never want to see you again."

"If you don't give me a chance to redeem myself . . ." He let his voice trail off, "I won't feel like living."

"Don't talk foolish," she scolded, wrapping her robe tighter around her waist. "If I forgive you, will you go home?"

"Yes."

"Very well. I forgive you. Now leave."

"Open the door and tell me you forgive me to my face. Then I'll leave. I'm not going to pursue you if you don't want me anymore."

"O.K. But I am *not* inviting you in. Understood? You're to stay on the front porch, apologize, and then leave. Do I have your word?"

"I promise."

She undid the latch, turned the lock, and opened the door a tiny bit.

Gary stood on the front porch looking contrite, his hands stuffed into the pockets of his windbreaker. He made a puppy dog face. "I'm so sorry, Madeline." He shook his head, his green eyes sorrowful. "You were right to be mad. I just wanted to tell you how sorry I am for any pain I caused you."

"Fine. Now go home. And get yourself some help, Gary," she suggested, her tone even.

"Why do I need help?"

"Because you're sick."

His hand shot out so fast she didn't see it coming. "I'm not the one who's sick! You forget which one of us was yelling 'Fuck me, fuck me, fuck me!' " His words pierced the air like a knife as he slammed against her.

Madeline was terrified. This man was obviously mentally ill and now he was in her house. "I want you to leave now!" Her voice rose in spite of her best intentions to remain calm. She tried to back away from him.

With a menacing look in his eye, he reached out and grabbed her. "Come on, tell the truth. Didn't it excite you just a little bit the way I rammed my cock up your ass?"

"Leave me alone!" she screamed, losing control. "Get out!"

He ripped open her robe and jerked at her nightgown as she wrenched away; the flimsy fabric tore down the front. Her hands, which were shaking, came up to shield her nakedness.

"Madeline," a voice called from the front porch.

Kate stuck her head in the front door. "I'm sorry it's so late—" She stopped in midsentence. "What's going on?" she demanded. "Take your hands off her!"

Gary looked from one to the other. "Night, ladies." He turned to get past Kate and out the door.

Sounding on the verge of hysteria, Madeline blurted out, "He's crazy! This isn't the first time he's done this." She pulled at her robe trying to cover the torn gown.

"Go call the police," ordered Kate, stepping in front of Madeline's assailant.

"Out of my way, bitch!" Gary shoved against Kate so hard he almost knocked her down.

"Call the police," said someone behind Kate.

Kate whirled around. "My God, Philip," she breathed. "I didn't hear you come up behind me."

"It's no wonder, since this idiot was making so much noise." Philip came into the room, a gun pointed at Gary. "Don't move, you bastard, or I'll blast your damned head off."

Gary turned white. "This whole thing is just a stupid misunderstanding. I can explain." He slowly advanced on Philip.

"Don't take another step," said Philip, a cold, hard look in his eye. "You've gone too far, Sutter. We've got witnesses—your career is finished."

"Witnesses to what? My lawyer will have me out so fast—"

Before he could finish, Kate interrupted. "I saw him accost Madeline. He was hurting her."

"You lying cunt!" screamed Gary.

Madeline couldn't believe this was all happening. She heard the police siren wailing as it came toward the house. Within minutes, the backup Philip had called from his car had arrived.

Two officers entered the house; one of them recognized Philip and said hello. Philip pocketed the gun and put his hand on Madeline's shoulder. "You up to telling these guys what happened?"

Madeline inhaled deeply. "O.K. Yeah." She quickly explained to them what Gary had done and told them she wanted him arrested for assault and battery. Then they spoke to Kate. When she had finished her story, one of the cops took out his handcuffs and snapped them on Gary's wrists.

"You're making a big mistake!" Gary said angrily. "I told her we were through and she's getting back at me."

"Tell it to the judge," said the other cop, who then read Gary his rights.

As they led Gary out to the police car, he turned and gave both Madeline and Kate a look of pure hatred.

Madeline suddenly found that her knees were weak, and Philip, as if sensing her distress, took her into his arms. Sinking against his chest, Madeline thought how lucky she was to have Philip care for her. She had been too blind to realize how much she cared for him in return. Gently, he helped her down onto the couch, then sat beside her holding her hand.

"What were you both doing here, anyway?" asked Madeline, when she regained her composure.

"After I talked to you," explained Kate, "I realized I needed to bring the evidence over here right away. In fact, I was almost afraid not to get the stuff to you as soon as possible."

"And I came on a hunch," Philip said. "You sounded apprehensive on the phone and I remembered you saying you were afraid of Gary. So I decided to check things out."

Madeline sighed. "I don't know how to thank you both. If you hadn't helped me . . ." She couldn't finish the sentence. "I was terrified," she added finally.

"I could see," said Kate. She turned to Philip. "How come you carry a gun?"

"I've had some threats on my life from my days as a hotshot prosecutor."

"Things never change, do they?" Kate said.

"No." He smiled. "I'm afraid they don't."

Madeline motioned to Kate. "Well, since Philip and I are here, why don't you tell us about your new evidence?"

An hour later Madeline and Philip had heard Kate's entire story and the three of them had listened to the tape for the third time.

"I hate to say it, but I think Charles may be involved in this in some significant way," said Madeline. "But to what extent, I'm not sure."

Looking down at her hands, Kate told them both her relationship with Charles and that he was waiting for her at her condominium.

Madeline's eyes filled with sympathy as she watched Kate struggling to talk about her affair with a married man. No wonder Kate never talked about any special person. Madeline had wrongly assumed that Kate's ambitions left her no time to date.

"I can't believe this is happening. This is the man I wanted to spend my life with." Kate shook her head. "My whole world has turned upside down since James D'Arcy's death."

"It's not safe for you to go home tonight," said Philip.

"Charles wouldn't hurt me," she protested.

"No," said Madeline, "I agree with Philip. Kate, this is a side of Charles Rieman you've never seen. Now maybe there *is* a reasonable explanation. Maybe what he did is totally independent of Tommy and Sandra. The evidence we have against Tommy is certainly significant and the man has, after all, confessed." Madeline chewed on her lip. "Maybe it's just as you thought. Charles hid the codicil after Tommy killed James, and this investigator, Marty, somehow found out and is blackmailing him. At any rate, we have to find Marty." She turned to Philip. "I think we should get Bower in on this right away and let him decide how to proceed. In the meantime, Kate, you better plan on spending the night here."

After Bower arrived and was brought up to date, he agreed with Madeline and Philip.

"Kate, you're better off here tonight. Call Rieman, tell him you're too tired to drive home. Apologize, be nice, you know, the whole ball of wax." He hitched his pants up over his protruding belly. "Don't want him getting suspicious."

Philip nodded. "I agree."

Bower headed for Madeline's phone. "Gimme a chance to get some units into place."

Kate looked at Madeline. "I'm not sure how all of this affects my client's case," she said, feeling numb.

Madeline's eyes seemed noncommittal. "Look, let's give the police a chance to do their work. If they find Marty, he should be able to give us some answers. As for whether or not Charles has committed any crime, we'll just have to wait and see."

"I feel like an idiot."

Madeline smiled and gave Kate's hand a squeeze. "Me too. We sure know how to pick 'em. When the guys leave, you and I can make some hot chocolate and cry on each other's shoulders."

It was Kate's turn to smile. "Thanks. I could use that."

Bower came back to them. "We got your place covered. He'll be tailed. And I got units on their way here. Kate, you'll be under surveillance until this mess is cleared up. Also, I want this information to stay in this room until we find Marty and question him."

Kate jumped up. "I almost forgot. I've got a phone number for Marty." She ran to get her purse, scrounged around until she found the piece of paper, and handed it to Bower.

"Great. Should be a snap now. Lemme get someone working on it right away."

"It's time for you to call Charles." Madeline held the phone out to Kate.

Kate realized she was shaking as she dialed her condominium, let it ring once, and hung up. "Our code," she admitted, dialing again.

This time Charles answered on the first ring.

"Hi, it's me."

"Where are you?" His voice was gruff.

"I'm still at Rachel's. Listen, darling, I'm not feeling well. Foolishly, I had a glass of wine and it made me sleepy. I'm afraid I'm just too tired to drive home."

"Kate, I've now been waiting for you for almost two hours. I've been frantic thinking you had an accident. Just come home," he demanded, "and I'll take care of you."

"No, darling, I'm going to spend the night here."

"I'll come get you then."

"No. That's O.K. Please understand and I'll see you tomorrow." Not waiting for his response, she hung up.

"You're a good little actress," said Madeline.

"Yeah, one of my many talents." Kate's face crumpled. She suddenly felt so tired she couldn't move.

An hour later, after Bower and Philip had left and an unmarked car was parked on the street out of view, Kate and Madeline finally decided to call it a night.

"Mi casa es su casa." Madeline stood up. Quickly she returned with some sheets and blankets and a pillow. She stacked them all on the chair. She also brought Kate a nightgown, a robe, and some slippers. "Here, give me a hand." Together, they made up the sofa bed.

"I can't believe what a fool I've been." Kate sat down dejectedly on the chair to take off her clothes.

"Hey, want to see a complete ass, then look at me. For years I've been prosecuting men who commit acts of violence against women. Look at the jerk I fell for. I ignored *all* the warning signs. Tried not to think too much about the fact that Gary didn't like my children. Ignored the fact that he was moody and irritable. I was even stupid enough to open my door to him after he'd attacked me once. And I did all this because the man made my hormones rage? It makes me so mad at myself I could kill.''

Kate nodded.

''Let's get some sleep. Tomorrow we'll see if we can solve the world's problems. If you need anything, even if it's just to talk, come in and wake me, O.K.?''

''Thanks.''

''And help yourself to anything you want in the kitchen. There are some leftovers in the fridge.''

''I doubt I'll ever eat again.''

Madeline made a face. ''I know what you mean.'' She started to walk out of the room, then turned.

''Kate . . .'' She hesitated. ''I just want you to know that however this turns out, I'm really sorry for what's happening to you. It's a terrible blow when someone lets you down the way Charles has. And as for Sandra,'' she continued, ''you have my word I'll look at all the evidence carefully. I've no desire to convict an innocent woman. I hope you know that.''

''I do.''

''Good night then.''

''Good night,'' echoed Kate, ''and thanks again.''

''Thank *you*. You probably saved my life tonight.''

52

It was Saturday afternoon when Bower and Donaldson reached Lake Shasta, three hours north of Sacramento on the way to Oregon. Bower brought the car to a stop in front of what appeared to be a marine store. ''Looks like they sell bait and tackle here. If we're on a wild-goose chase, may not be a total loss.'' He smiled as he parked the car.

"Oh sure," scoffed Donaldson. "I can't remember the last time you took a day off."

In the store, Bower showed the picture of Marty to the man behind the counter.

"He's got a boat on the dock. Charters it for fishing." The man called a kid to show them the way.

The kid took the two detectives outside and down to the dock. Almost at the end, he stopped and pointed. "That's it."

Bower looked at the boat. It was about thirty-two feet long, with a cabin and a large fishing cockpit. It appeared to be somewhat run-down. "Know the man who owns it?" he asked.

The kid nodded. "Yeah. I seen him leave an hour ago."

"Know where he went?"

"Nope."

"What kinda car's he driving?"

"Green late-model Ford."

"Thanks. We'll be back."

Bower drove the car out of the lot and headed for the road to town. "We need to get us some local help."

Two hours later, armed with a search warrant signed by a judge unhappy to be disturbed on a Saturday, Bower and Donaldson headed back to the marina with a contingent of local police.

"Open up. Police." Bower knocked on the window of the boat. There was no answer. He climbed on board and tried the cabin door, but it was locked. As he walked around to the side, he noticed there was a window open. Cheap drapes flapped lazily in the breeze. He went back to the aft deck. "There's a window we can try."

"I'll do it," volunteered Donaldson. "You'd never fit." Within a few minutes, Donaldson had entered the cabin and opened the door for the rest of them. The four policemen started their search, two inside the cabin, two on the deck, while two others stayed on the dock.

Bower and Donaldson pulled apart the small master cabin. They looked under bedding, they rummaged in drawers; the musty smell of the boat wafted up at them from the dampness.

"You take the galley," said Bower. "I'll get the head."

As he searched a cabinet in the small head, Bower, wrinkling up his nose from the fishy smell, gave a yelp. "Over here! I think I've got something." Holding a gun carefully with two fingers so as not to mess up any fingerprints, he came into the main cabin, where he quickly put on a pair of gloves. After turning the gun over, he finally smiled. "Look at what we got here, fellas. A .22 Ruger semiautomatic."

"I got the serial number," said Donaldson, hurrying to the aft deck to retrieve the small notebook he'd left on the dock. Within a minute he was back.

The two men put their heads together.

"Hallelujah," Donaldson shouted, and went to tell the other officers that the gun matched. "It's Sandra D'Arcy's gun. I'll bet you anything it's the murder weapon."

One of the officers up by the store signaled that a green car had just arrived.

As they headed up the dock, Bower saw the kid come out of the marine store and say something to a man. The man turned, saw them, appeared to judge that the green car was too far away, and started to run in the opposite direction.

Luckily, Bower had asked several plainclothes officers to stay near the store. One of them quickly overtook the suspect.

In two minutes he was cuffed and being shoved down toward the boat where Bower was waiting. "Marty Vincent, you're under arrest for the murder of James D'Arcy."

"You're crazy," shouted Marty. "A kid down in L.A. has already confessed to that."

"You got a lot of explaining to do," said Bower. "This gun belonged to Sandra D'Arcy."

"I'm a private investigator. I've got a license to carry it. I bought it off of a man at a swap meet."

"We'll see." Bower walked around Marty for a minute, as if looking for something. Then he turned to one of the officers. "Take those handcuffs off a minute."

The officer did as he asked and Bower yanked Marty's

left hand toward him. With a quick jerk, he removed the watch Marty was wearing. "O.K. Hook 'im again."

Bower turned the shiny gold watch over in his hand. "Couldn't resist this, huh?" He laughed.

"What is it?" one of the officers asked.

"Probably the Rolex taken from D'Arcy the night of the murder. See those initials? J.D." Bower put it in an evidence bag. "O.K. Read him his rights."

As they headed back to the police station, Bower announced to Marty, "You're going to death row for this."

By the time they were back in Los Angeles, Marty was talking about a deal. Just like all the rest, thought Bower. When it comes right down to it, they all wanna save their own skins.

Charles Rieman awoke late that morning with a bad hangover. He hadn't had that much to drink since his college days. He recalled how he had waited for Kate at her condominium the night before for more than two hours. He'd taken off his clothes, had a shower and another drink. He must have been asleep when she called to tell him she wasn't coming home. He remembered hanging up and berating himself for telling her about the missing funds. Couldn't she see that he had no choice? If there had been another way for them to have a secure future together, he would have chosen it.

Finally, after several more drinks, he had dressed, taxied back to his car, and driven home. Then, ignoring Ann's questions, he had gone to bed.

Now, his head pounding, he showered and shaved and went downstairs. Ann tried to talk to him, but he buried his head in the newspaper while he had coffee, toast, and juice.

Damn, if Ann had had her way she would have totally emasculated him. She was so careful to hold on to the control of her funds. He could only be trusted to invest the interest from her capital. She had never once, in twenty years of marriage, transferred anything into his name. Even this house was in her name. And the Rolls Royce she had bought him for his birthday. Some present. She'd used separate property funds to buy it and put it in her name. He'd have to prove in court she meant to buy him a gift. Ann always managed to cleverly disguise her intentions behind innocuous documents. She thought she could hold on to him that way forever. But he had shown her. He was not for sale.

Charles took his tennis racket and headed out, ignoring Ann's queries about where he was going and when he'd be home.

In fifteen minutes, he was in Santa Monica. Was that car following him? No, he was probably imagining it. Kate's car was not in the garage. Where the hell was she? Telling himself there must be a message on her machine, he entered the condominium. He played the tape. Two girlfriends and Frank. He listened to Frank's message again.

"It's Frank. I'm finally home. I have Maria put up in a safe place. She'll testify. On the way here, she told me the real reason she was scared to come back. Call me as soon as you get in so we can plan our strategy."

Charles set the machine back so that when Kate came home, she wouldn't be able to tell he'd listened. He paced Kate's apartment, his hands shoved into his tennis shorts, his long, tanned legs taking purposeful strides. Finally, he made a decision. He peeked out through the shutters. *Was* he being followed? Better not take any chances. He called for a taxi to meet him one block away, sneaked out the back entrance, and walked quickly to the cab. Leaving the car on the street in front of Kate's place should throw off any tail, he thought.

"I can't stay here forever," insisted Kate. "I need to go to my place and at least get some clothes."

"We promised Bower we'd give him twenty-four hours."

The phone rang, startling them both. Madeline went to answer it. "When? . . . I see. What did he tell you?" She asked a few more questions, her face serious.

Kate's stomach lurched. What was Madeline hearing?

Madeline hung up. "Do you have a picture of Charles?"

"Of course. Why?"

"The police need to do a photo lineup."

"What's happened?"

"They've found Marty. He had Sandra's gun hidden on his boat. They're sure it will prove to be the murder weapon. And the stupid fool was wearing James's Rolex."

Kate sat down quickly, her heart hammering in her chest. Had Sandra somehow found out that Marty was tailing her and hired him to kill James? Or had Tommy discovered Marty and joined up with him? And how did Charles fit into it all? "Is he talking? What does he say?"

"He's ready to make a deal."

"What kind of a deal?"

Madeline didn't answer her. "Look, I've got to meet one of Bower's men. Do you have the picture?"

"I'll get it." Kate walked back toward the den. Every fiber in her body cried out, Please let the news not be bad for Charles or for Sandra. Coming back into the living room, she handed the picture to Madeline and watched as the D.A. gazed at his picture, then turned the photo over.

Kate knew what was written on the back. *To my darling Kate whom I love with all my heart.*

Kate had refused to be left behind. The last thing she wanted was to be alone with her thoughts. She couldn't stop thinking about the way Charles had manipulated her. Had it all been a lie, everything he had told her, everything he had promised her?

The car pulled up to the liquor store on Santa Monica Boulevard. Madeline and the police officer got out and Kate joined them on the sidewalk. Her stomach was tied up in knots and she prayed she wasn't going to get sick.

Inside, the owner reiterated what he remembered about the person who had bought the bottle of Dom Perignon found in James D'Arcy's car the night of his death. Under Madeline's intensive questioning, the man now recalled that the sale had actually been earlier in the day.

The policeman took out his photos, and told the owner it was important he look at all of them carefully before he made any decisions. He then showed the owner two photo lineups with Charles's photo randomly placed in one and Marty's photo in the other.

The owner took off his glasses, looked, then put them back on and examined the pictures again. "That's him," he said, pointing.

"Are you sure?" asked the police officer.

"Absolutely."

Kate peered over the officer's shoulder, knowing which picture he was pointing to even before she saw it. "It's Charles," she mumbled.

Madeline came over and took Kate outside.

There were tears in Kate's eyes as she gazed at her friend. "How could I have been so blind?"

"He was a damn good liar, Kate. He fooled a lot of people."

When Bower arrived back in Los Angeles and found out they had lost Rieman, he was furious. At headquarters, he stomped around issuing orders. "Cover the airports. Check every airline. Notify all the airport police. International flights and domestic. Bus stations. Train terminals. He can't have gotten far—he's only been missing a couple of hours. We know he went to the office after Kate Alexander's, because he was spotted leaving there about two hours ago. His wife said he came home, packed a few things, and told her he had an emergency. She says his passport is gone. He's on the run."

On the way to the airport, Donaldson drove while Bower told Madeline all they had learned so far. Kate was following them in her car and every now and then Bower looked back as if checking to make sure she was still there. "Frank Jones took us to see Maria. She said Rieman had threatened her, told her that if she ever set foot in this country again, he'd see that she spent the rest of her life in jail."

Bower continued: "Maria overheard a terrible fight between Rieman and D'Arcy about two weeks before he was killed; Rieman musta been worried that she'd talk. He obviously wanted her outta the country and outta contact with anyone who might think to ask.''

"Did Marty tell you why Charles wanted James dead?" asked Madeline.

"D'Arcy double-crossed him. Rieman claimed it'd be the perfect murder." He laughed. "They all say that. But what happened is like this. Apparently, Marty followed Sandra just like Rieman told him to. He found out she was seeing Tommy and that the two lovers were shacking up at Tommy's place in Northridge."

Bower paused. "Marty said Rieman saw the affair as the perfect way to get rid of D'Arcy and blame it on someone else. According to Marty, it was only supposed to look like Tommy had done it. But Charles and Marty didn't count on Sandra doing all the stupid things she did that made us think she was in on it."

"Why didn't Tommy say he *didn't* do it?"

"That's the interesting part. Marty approaches this kid in a bar, buys him a few drinks, and tells the kid he's a talent agent. When the kid goes to the bathroom, he slips something into his drink. The kid gets dizzy. Marty offers to drive him home, where he puts him to bed. Then he takes Tommy's car and his boots and goes to Bel Air.

"Meanwhile, Rieman, who's got keys or something to the D'Arcy home, has already stolen Sandra's gun. It seems James told Charles about the gun and where it was kept. Then on the day they planned to kill D'Arcy, Rieman goes and buys the champagne. He gives it to Marty to put in the car so it looks like James stopped at a liquor store and from there was followed home and robbed.

"Marty also brings with him a kid's trike to put in front of the gates so D'Arcy has to stop and get out of his car."

"Another bike? Wouldn't that cause questions?"

"Marty said Rieman told him the kid had so many toys no one would ever know the difference." Bower coughed. "So far, Marty's story checks out."

"I still don't understand why Tommy didn't deny it was him."

"Seems the kid sleeps for two days," answered Bower.

"When he wakes up, he feels weird. His room's a mess, he sees he's been sick, but he's got no idea what's happened. My guess is, after Donaldson and I showed up and started questioning him, Tommy started to have doubts about where he'd been at the time of D'Arcy's death. When he found out about his footprint and the soil match, he began to think maybe he really did do it."

"And his lawyer didn't believe him," said Madeline. "He probably talked him into the confession. He should have searched harder for the truth."

"Listen. I didn't believe the kid was innocent either," said Bower.

"There was so much evidence pointing to Tommy," said Madeline. "We did the best we could."

As Kate followed the two policemen and Madeline, she felt she was going to be sick. It was as if the Charles she had known and loved didn't even exist. He lied to me, she thought, manipulated me, used me. He probably also lied about his feelings for me. Why didn't I see it? How stupid could I be not to know what was going on?

She drove by rote, weaving in and out of traffic, staying behind the other car. Images of Charles standing in Sandra's home listening to Bower tell him about his friend's death, and then later at the morgue, flitted through her mind. He had seemed devastated, a man who had just lost his best friend. What a damn good actor he had been! How could he look at his friend lying there dead knowing what he had done?

She had always prided herself on her ability to tell when someone was lying. Now she wasn't sure she'd ever trust herself again. As she went over things in her mind, she kept asking herself: What were the hints along the way? What should I have seen that I didn't?

Kate remembered Madeline's words: Charles had fooled a lot of other people, too. Yet that didn't make her feel any less stupid.

For a moment Kate thought about what had happened to Madeline with Gary. Here we are, two successful career

women, and what do we do? Pick men who turn out to be
rapists and killers. There must be some kind of prize for
that.

As Kate saw the airport looming in front of her, her heart
pounded and her stomach knotted in fear. She didn't really
want to hear what Charles had to say.

Once at the airport, Donaldson pulled into a restricted
parking place and showed his identification to the police
officer standing at the curb. Kate pulled up behind them.
Inside, Bower led the way. Donaldson followed. Madeline
held Kate's arm as they hurried to keep up with the long
strides of the two men.

Madeline studied Kate's ashen face. She felt terrible for
her. A few months ago, Kate's future was as bright as it
could be. Now it appeared shattered.

Madeline looked up to see they were headed for an international flight lounge. Charles had been discovered on a
flight out of the country. The plane was still at the gate and
police were boarding it to take him off.

With his badge, Bower gained access for them to the
upper area from which the international flights were leaving. Kate stood at the window looking out at the runway.
Workers had rolled out a stairway to a jumbo jet. At the
bottom of the stairs, she saw two men waiting, their hands
on their guns.

She had to pinch herself to make sure this was really
happening. Suddenly, she saw Charles standing at the open
door to the airplane. Her heart stopped. Then she noticed
there was a man behind him, obviously a police officer.

She watched him step out into the night, look around
warily, then start down the stairs. Quickly, the two men
below were at his side. In a second they had Charles hand-
cuffed and were leading him toward the building.

When Charles saw Kate by the door, his accusing gaze
pierced through her like a shard of glass. She held her chin
high. No one could see it was the worst moment of her life.

Inside the lounge that had been set aside for them, Bower gave Kate and Charles five minutes to talk.

Kate was grateful that Bower had allowed them to sit far enough away from the others so that while they were still in sight, they couldn't be heard. She searched Charles's face, her eyes filled alternately with anger and sorrow. Finally, she spoke. "They've got Marty."

He nodded.

"Just tell me why you threw it *all* away."

He looked down at the handcuffs and then his eyes met hers. "Why?" He paused and shook his head. "Don't you know? I did it for *us*. So that *we* could have a good life together."

"I never asked you for anything material, did I?"

"I wanted the things that were mine. James promised them to me. Then he took them away." His eyes smoldered with righteous indignation. "You didn't know him. You only saw him as a charming and gracious host, but that wasn't the real James D'Arcy. I told you, he was a vicious man."

"That was probably true, but you had no right to kill him. We could have gone anywhere, done anything." Her eyes filled with tears. "We could have made a good life."

He grimaced as though he hadn't even heard her. "You should have seen his face when he told me he was planning to make Theo the head of the D'Arcy Company and Foundation." He mimicked James's voice. " 'So, Charles, how do you think you'll like taking orders from my kid brother and his sidekick Dickson? That ought to be interesting!' "

His dark eyes blazed angrily as Charles related the story to her. "I begged him not to do it. I told him it would be a mistake. But he laughed. He said life was starting to get boring. Even his pretty young wife was getting to be a pain in the ass and he wanted to be rid of her."

Kate gazed at him, still not believing this was happening. It felt like a nightmare.

Charles went on. "James admitted that I was probably the best damn man there was to run everything, but he thought it would be fun to shake up the pot. He was so cruel. A toxic man."

For a minute he was silent; then his eyes met hers again. "Kate, be smart. We can still have our life. It's Marty's word against mine."

"The liquor store owner identified you. That corroborates Marty's story."

"You'll think of something. You can make a deal for me. I know you can."

His words hit her like physical blows. "How dare you ask that of me?" Her voice rose in anger.

"Please, Kate, with you on my side maybe I can beat this thing. Buying a bottle of champagne doesn't make a man guilty of murder. Marty did the killing—"

Kate stopped him, her fury mounting. "Don't, Charles, I can't represent you. You've lied to me, used me, manipulated me. You killed your best friend and you were willing to let innocent people die for your crime! You're disgusting!"

"But I love you," he said.

"Love—what do you know about love? You betrayed your best friend, your partners, your family." She paused to catch her breath. "I loved you so much, Charles, but you betrayed me, too." Her words were spoken harshly and she felt glad when she saw him flinch.

She stood up and with her hand signaled to Bower that she was through as she started to walk away.

"Kate . . ." Charles called out. She heard the plea, the anguish in his voice, but she didn't turn around.

53

Kate was busy working when she heard shouting in the corridor outside her office.

"I've got to see her, let me in."

She recognized Andrew Stewart's voice. Curious, she opened her door. Members of the firm were beginning to gather in the hallway as Andrew argued with Mary. "What's the matter?" Kate asked, trying to get his attention.

He turned around and shook his finger at her. His face was red with fury. "The D.A. just informed me that Tommy Bartholomew didn't kill D'Arcy. If you'd only been honest with me about the deal you were making for Sandra to plead guilty, everything would have worked out differently. It's *your* fault."

Kate was baffled. "I'm afraid I don't know what you're talking about."

"Come off it, Kate." His tone was sarcastic. "The charges are being dropped against Sandra, too. You could at least level with me now."

She stiffened as if she had been slapped. "*Mister* Stewart, I *am* being honest. I never had any meeting with the D.A. regarding a deal for my client."

It was Andrew's turn to be surprised. "You're telling me you never met with Madeline Gould to arrange for Sandra to testify against Tommy?"

She shook her head emphatically. "Absolutely not."

His face was incredulous.

"Andrew, what are you doing here?" Lauren had just arrived on the scene and clutched his arm in a proprietary manner.

"You told me Kate was making a deal with the D.A. for

Sandra to testify against Tommy.'' His eyes were questioning as he gazed at her.

Lauren glanced from Andrew to Kate and then at all the people gathered in the hallway. ''I suggest,'' she said in her best southern drawl, ''we go to my office to discuss this matter.''

''Is that true, Lauren?'' a strong voice demanded. Suddenly, the crowd parted to let Franklin Manning through. ''Did you give information to this man about one of *this* firm's clients?''

''Well . . . I . . .'' Lauren appeared at a loss for words.

Andrew shook her arm off and rushed over to Franklin. ''She certainly did.''

''Why don't the four of us go into Kate's office.'' Franklin gestured to the others. ''The rest of you can go back to work.''

Kate knew Franklin was under a doctor's care. She was worried about him as she listened in disbelief while Andrew related the things Lauren had said to him. When he finished, she was appalled. ''Why did you do that?'' she asked Lauren, trying to understand.

The other woman tossed her head. ''I had my reasons.''

''You're fired.'' Franklin straightened to his full height. ''Get your things and leave. I will not stand for a member of this firm breaching the attorney-client confidentiality rules and telling lies, dangerous lies, on top of that.''

Lauren cocked her head as if to say she didn't care. ''Let's go, Andrew. I only acted on information I thought was reliable.''

Kate spoke up. ''That doesn't change the fact that what you did was unethical.''

Her eyes blazing, Lauren turned angrily toward Kate. ''Don't tell me what's unethical, you bitch. You fucked my boyfriend.''

Unconsciously backing up from Lauren's attack, Kate was grateful when Franklin stepped between them.

''I want you *out* of Manning & Anderson and this building in fifteen minutes,'' he said, shaking his finger at Lauren. "I'm also reporting you to the State Bar for disciplinary action."

"I'm sure my daddy won't be very pleased about the way you're treating me."

"I'm sorry about that, Lauren," said Franklin, "but I'll explain to him that I can't have an unethical lawyer working for me."

"You'll lose all his business," she threatened.

"It's a chance I'll have to take."

Lauren turned and stomped out, and Franklin followed behind her.

"I had no idea she was lying," said Andrew. "I want you to know, Kate, I didn't solicit any information from Lauren. She offered it."

"It doesn't change the fact that discussing the case with her was wrong."

"You're being unfair." He tried to charm her with one of his intimate gazes. "I know you don't choose to believe me, but Lauren got me on the rebound."

There was an angry glint in Kate's eye. "I could have sworn you were seeing Lauren both *before* and *after* our regrettable little interlude."

To his credit, she noted, he blushed.

"Even though I may have seen her once or twice before you, I was ready to stop seeing her. I fell hard for you, Kate, and I believe . . ." He stopped as if searching for the right words. "We could have had something, you and I."

"Perhaps. But we'll never know, will we?" She strode to her door and opened it. "Mary," she called, "please show *Mister* Stewart out."

Later in the day, when Kate entered Franklin's ornate corner office, she was surprised to find Theo there. He didn't look too happy. And Franklin was deathly pale. What else has happened? she wondered.

"Tell Kate what you've just told me." Franklin's voice was hoarse.

Theo hesitated for a split second, then spoke. "I never saw a new will. James had told me on the telephone that he

had drafted something that would give me what I wanted."
He played with his watchband, then continued. "After he
died and Dickson and I couldn't find the new document,
Dickson said he'd have to claim some kind of legal fiction
to get us past the first hurdle. Apparently, he then told my
mother and a number of other people that he'd seen a witnessed will. He even put that in his affidavit."

"Theo, you should have come forward," said Kate, trying to hide her dismay.

"I know, but Dickson insisted he was the lawyer and
knew what he was doing."

"Surely your common sense must have—"

Theo flushed. "I'm afraid where Dickson was concerned,
I had none."

Kate knew immediately what he meant and glanced
quickly at Franklin. He showed no reaction; Theo's comment appeared not to have registered.

"What do you suggest we do?" Franklin asked Kate. His
tone sounded heavy with fatigue.

"I think Theo must tell the truth at once and withdraw his
suit over the will. The new codicil appears valid and it
changes everything anyway. I can't promise, but it's possible the D.A. won't file charges against Theo, since he was
being advised by counsel on whom he had a right to rely."

Theo exhaled loudly.

"And my son?" Franklin's face wrinkled with concern.

"In order to protect the firm, he should be asked to resign." She paused. "As for the rest . . . it sounds as if
Dickson has perjured himself."

Franklin seemed to shrivel before Kate's eyes as he too
let out a long breath. "I had already come to a similar
conclusion," he said softly.

Theo motioned with his hands. "Franklin, I'd like to ask
that Kate be the lawyer assigned to handle the D'Arcy family business."

Kate was surprised.

A weak smile crossed Franklin Manning's features. "I'm
grateful for the vote of confidence, but Kate has her own

agenda. Her area of expertise is criminal law. I'm afraid I'll have to leave the decision up to her."

The man who now controlled millions of dollars in potential fees turned to Kate. "What do you think?"

She clasped her hands together. "I'm honored," she said, "and flattered too." She started to pace, weighing her options very carefully. Her world had crumbled around her this last week. Would she ever pick up the pieces and start again?

Kate took a deep breath and came to stand in front of Theo. "I wish I could say yes. And I hope you too can understand," she said, addressing Franklin, "but that's just not the area of law I want to pursue." She smiled faintly. "I still dream of holding public office. Of course, right now, that's probably not in the cards, but as soon as the shock . . ." Her voice caught and it was a moment before she could go on. "As soon as the shock of everything wears off and I've had some time to think things through, I want to go forward again with my political career."

Her eyes asked for understanding. "I've wanted to be in politics since I was twelve years old. I still believe I can make a difference. Anyway, I've got to try."

Theo ran his hand through his hair. "I'll tell you what, Franklin. Because of the long-standing relationship between our two families, I'd like to give your firm another chance. Pick your best man or woman and we'll give it a shot."

Franklin stood, his gratitude apparent on his tired face as he shook Theo's hand. "You won't be sorry. As for you, Kate, I'm behind you all the way and I'm proud to tell you that you'll be this firm's newest partner."

It was a bittersweet moment for Kate. "Thank you, Franklin." She started to leave, but Theo stopped her, his eyes serious.

"I believe in you, Kate Alexander. Someone like you *can* make a difference and I'm going to take up where my brother left off. I'm going to support your candidacy for D.A. Maybe, together, we can regroup in time for the next election. If not"—he sighed—"there's always next time."

She could feel the tears pushing at the back of her eyes as

she willed herself not to cry. "Thank you, Theo. I won't let you down."

After Madeline moved to dismiss the charges against Sandra, Kate smiled wanly at her. Then Kate looked at Sandra, who was positively glowing as she stood in front of the judge. When the judge told Sandra she was free to go, the young woman turned around and grabbed her lawyer, burying her face in Kate's shoulder.

Locked forcefully in her client's embrace, Kate was almost knocked off balance. Sandra had been the most difficult challenge of her career, but Kate had learned the hard way that a tough exterior often hid a frightened child. She had learned a lot more from Sandra. How childhood trauma could cause scars that might never heal. Still, in her heart Kate knew that someday both she and Sandra would make better choices in finding the right person to love.

Madeline came over to wish Sandra well. Kate again smiled at her friend, relieved that Madeline had confided in her earlier that her first HIV test had come back negative. Now, Madeline and Philip could start their own life together with a good foundation of hope for the future.

Before they left the courtroom, Theo came over to congratulate Sandra. Kate noted that he was the only member of the D'Arcy family to show up for Sandra's big moment.

"I'll do whatever I can to help you rebuild your life," he promised Sandra solemnly. "I just hope you can forgive me, not only for doubting your innocence but for not coming forth with what I knew about my brother's cruelty."

Sandra clearly was wary. "Let's see how it goes, O.K.?"

Theo nodded.

Kate thought to herself that it was going to be a long time before Sandra trusted anyone, especially a member of the D'Arcy family. Yet it would certainly be good for Jimmy to have an uncle around as a father figure. Even if Sandra wanted to forget she was connected to the D'Arcy family, her son was the sole heir to his father's estate.

Theo's face showed warmth as he held his hand out to Kate. "I can't thank you enough for all you've done for Sandra."

"I only did what I was supposed to do," Kate said modestly.

He shook his head. "No way. You kept looking for answers. You went far beyond what another lawyer might have done. Is there anything I can do now to help?"

"We want to get Jimmy back from your mother without any more trauma, and I've been warned that she's trying to get a court order to stop us."

"Then let's go," said Theo, jerking his arm toward the door.

As the two limousines pulled up in front of the gates to Abigail's mansion, Kate's stomach tightened with anxiety. She watched Theo lean out of the window and calmly tell the guard to open the gate.

The guard pointed to the second limousine and shook his head. Kate was pleased when Theo opened the car door and physically removed the phone from the guard's hand, replacing it on the hook. "Open it *now*," she heard him say forcefully.

Inside the mansion, Kate, with Sandra beside her, climbed the massive stairway.

An angry Abigail sat in her wheelchair at the top of the landing, waving a walking stick at them. "Do not take another step. I will never forgive you for this, Theo, *never!*" she shouted, her voice shrill.

"Stuff it up your you know what," mumbled Sandra under her breath as she continued up the stairs.

"Calm down, Mother," said Theo. "You're making a spectacle of yourself."

"How dare you talk to me that way?" the old woman sputtered, her eyes filled with rage.

When Theo reached the top of the stairs, he took hold of his mother's wheelchair and rolled it toward her rooms.

"Stop it! I order you to stop this minute!"

"Now now, Mother," he said quietly, "it's time for your nap."

If Kate hadn't been so tense, she might have laughed at the spectacle of Abigail's impotent rage. There wasn't time, however—this had to be done quickly.

The door to the nursery was flung open and Jimmy came running out. "Mommy, Mommy!" the little boy cried.

"Oh my sweet baby, my Jimmy," sobbed Sandra as she grabbed her son and whirled him around.

"Can I go home with you?"

"You bet."

Kate felt the tears well up in her eyes. "Hurry," she urged, "we've got to get out of here. We'll get his things another time."

Sandra nodded. Clutching Jimmy in her arms, she raced alongside Kate down the stairs.

"What the hell's going on here?"

Kate looked up to see Victoria standing in the doorway, blocking their way, her thin face blotched and twisted by anger.

"We came to get Sandra's child," Kate explained, trying to shield her client from the woman. Kate could feel her heart pounding as sirens wailed in the distance. Were they coming to stop them? She didn't know and didn't want to find out. "Let us pass."

Victoria ignored Kate, pointing her bony finger at Sandra. "You little whore, just because the police released you, don't think you're home free! We all know you wanted my brother dead!"

Sandra handed Jimmy to Kate before planting herself squarely in front of Victoria. "You bitch! I may have wanted him dead, but I never would have killed him. You're the sick, twisted one. You, Abigail, and James. None of you let a day pass without being cruel to me. Maybe I wasn't born in a fancy house, but I'm more of a lady than you'll ever be."

"A lady. Ha, that's a laugh! You're nothing but a tramp! White trash!"

"You can't hurt me anymore!"

"Listen, you tramp, just keep your mouth shut. You dare to try to sully this family's name, you'll be sorry!"

Sandra straightened her spine and laughed mockingly. "You have no power over me anymore. My husband may have been a bastard, but he did love his son, *my* son. Someday Jimmy will inherit the entire D'Arcy estate."

"Never. I'll fight you until the day I die!"

"Then you'll have to fight me, too, and you'll lose," Theo said as he came down the stairs. When he reached the bottom, he took Sandra's arm. "Excuse us, Victoria, but Sandra and *my* nephew have somewhere else they'd rather be." His voice was hard as steel.

"You weak, spineless traitor!" Victoria shrieked.

"You better rethink that statement, Victoria," he said. "I'm in charge of the estate now!"

Victoria glared at her brother in speechless anger, her eyes filled with hatred.

"Move out of our way!" ordered Theo.

To Kate's surprise, Victoria grudgingly stepped aside.

The wailing sirens were getting louder as Kate followed Theo and Sandra to the waiting limousine, where she handed a now whimpering Jimmy to his mother. She was proud of her client and the poise and dignity with which she had faced Victoria.

Sandra hugged her child to her and turned to Theo. "Thanks," she said smiling. "Too bad your brother couldn't have been more like you."

"Better hurry," he responded. "Mother called the police and told them you were trespassing."

"Let's get off their property," cautioned Kate, nodding at Theo as she practically pushed Sandra into the back of the car.

The sirens were coming closer and Kate knew that neither she nor Sandra would feel safe until they were outside the gates. The limousine's wheels screeched as the driver careened down the driveway.

When the limo finally pulled out onto the street, Kate looked at Sandra and breathed a deep sigh.

Holding Jimmy close, Sandra smiled at Kate over her son's head. Her eyes were filled with gratitude.

Kate grinned. She felt good. Jimmy was finally back where he belonged. As for herself, well, it would take a while. At the moment it was enough to enjoy the happiness of others. Her time would come. Of that she was absolutely sure.

About the Author

MIMI LAVENDA LATT is a member of the California State Bar and brings with her an insider's-eye view of the world of law. This is her first novel. Latt lives in Los Angeles.